Special EDITION

Believe in love. Overcome obstacles. Find happiness.

A Surprise Second Chance
Anna J. Stewart

A Little Bit Of Love
Synithia Williams

MILLS & BOON

A SURPRISE SECOND CHANCE
© 2024 by Anna J. Stewart
Philippine Copyright 2024
Australian Copyright 2024
New Zealand Copyright 2024

First Published 2024
First Australian Paperback Edition 2024
ISBN 978 1 038 91045 5

A LITTLE BIT OF LOVE
© 2024 by Synithia R. Williams
Philippine Copyright 2024
Australian Copyright 2024
New Zealand Copyright 2024

First Published 2024
First Australian Paperback Edition 2024
ISBN 978 1 038 91045 5

MIX
Paper | Supporting
responsible forestry
FSC® C001695

Published by
Harlequin Mills & Boon
An imprint of Harlequin Enterprises (Australia) Pty Limited
(ABN 47 001 180 918), a subsidiary of HarperCollins
Publishers Australia Pty Limited
(ABN 36 009 913 517)
Level 19, 201 Elizabeth Street
SYDNEY NSW 2000 AUSTRALIA

Cover art used by arrangement with Harlequin Books S.A.. All rights reserved.

Printed and bound in Australia by McPherson's Printing Group

A Surprise Second Chance

Anna J. Stewart

MILLS & BOON

Bestselling author **Anna J. Stewart** honestly believes she was born with a book in her hand. After growing up devouring every story she could get her hands on, now she gets to make her living making up stories and fulfilling happily-ever-afters of her own. Her dreams have most definitely come true. Anna lives in Northern California (only a ninety-minute flight from Disneyland, her favourite place on earth) with two monstrous, devious, adorable cats named Sherlock and Rosie.

Dear Reader,

There's something so special about a second chance romance. I've written a few of them, and I think it's my favourite kind of story to tackle. There's so much to it: history, affection, loss and pain, but also that bloom of hope that springs to life when a broken pair find their way back to each other.

Daphne's had her heart broken by a lot of people, Griffin Townsend included. But she never stopped loving him. And Griff? Well, breaking up with Daphne was the biggest mistake of his life. It's also a regret he's been given the chance to erase. Bringing his two kids along wasn't part of the plan, but when the four of them finally arrived on the page, it felt like I was mending a real family. They need each other badly and fit like a perfect puzzle. Little Cammie and Noah stole my heart—and so did Taco the fish (don't worry—you'll understand soon).

Add in the chaos of Nalani's quirky characters and the summer paradise that is Hawai'i, and I hope everyone who reads this book feels transported to the islands for several breathtaking hours.

Happy reading,

Anna J

DEDICATION

For Suly & Jake

For the proposal and happily-ever-after inspiration.

Chapter One

"*Ua hala 'oe*, Remy." *You are missed.*

Daphne Mercer crouched at the ocean's edge and dropped the small ring of flowers she'd made while drinking her morning coffee on her front porch. The damp sand coated her thin-soled sneakers, the post-sunrise chill brushing over her bare legs with a familiarity that warmed her from the inside.

Waves lapped up and over the plumeria petals, which gave the faintest hint of the tropics, and she breathed it in. She pressed her hand into the sand, let the water coat her skin as the floral ring drifted out into the ocean. This was where, only a few months ago, Remy's friends and family had gathered to bid farewell and scatter his ashes among the waves he'd spent his entire life riding. He'd been one of the best friends she'd ever had. He'd helped her begin a new life here in Nalani, Hawai'i, when her old one had come crashing down.

Days like this, perfect days filled with so much promise, she could feel his presence, and the pain over losing him wasn't quite as acute as it once was. That was the magic of Nalani; here, the days that came before faded gently into the past and the future opened its arms wide for every possibility. It was a magic she would never take for granted.

The perfectly quaint small town boasted a luxurious yet

affordable resort, dozens of small stores and businesses, and a population that welcomed each and every visitor and newcomer with warmth and kindness. Not so long ago she'd been convinced it would be impossible to mend her broken heart, but Nalani, Remy and the people here, the new friends she'd made, proved that belief wrong.

"Some mornings are harder than others, aren't they?"

Still crouched low, Daphne turned and found Tehani Iokepa standing behind her, her suntanned arms crossed over a stomach that was gently rounded with the child she carried. Remy's child. "Aloha *kakahiaka*, Tehani." *Good morning.* Daphne pushed herself up, brushed her palms against the back of her shorts.

She made her way to her friend's side, but rather than leading the other woman away, Daphne wrapped both her arms around one of Tehani's and they watched Daphne's offering of flowers make its way out over the ocean waves.

"Haven't seen you up this early in a long time," Daphne finally said when she felt some of the tension in Tehani's body lessen.

"Morning sickness has officially loosened its grip." Tehani touched a finger to her throat where, until her pregnancy, she'd worn a solitary flower charm on a chain. "For the most part. The little man's moved from rejecting what I eat to wanting me to gobble up everything in sight."

"Aw, Remy Junior, shame on you." Daphne bent down and spoke to Tehani's rounded stomach. "Give your mom a break. She's taking good care of you."

Tehani laughed, a sound that had become familiar again since her initial grief over losing the love of her life began to lift. Her long black hair was as smooth and shiny as the obsidian created by an island lava flow and reached well past the base of her spine. The blousy thin-strapped tank tops she'd been wearing over her usual khaki shorts no longer hid her baby bump. Losing Remy shortly after discovering she was pregnant had been a particularly sharp wound Tehani had to endure, but she hadn't done it alone.

"I wasn't sure you'd be joining us this morning," Daphne said.

"And miss breakfast at the Hut-Hut?" Tehani looked a bit disbelieving. "I don't think so. This kid's wanting some Loco Moco and we need to brainstorm about those marketing ideas Marella's got cooking." She looked back up the beach. "Besides, we only have one tour scheduled later this morning. I can leave the office for a bit."

"And, since that would be my tour of the university botanical gardens—" Daphne tugged on Tehani's arm as they walked down the beach "—I absolutely can promise neither one of us will be late to gather up our charges."

July mornings in Nalani carried their own special magic. The warmth, the stillness, apart from the soft rush of the waves lapping at the shore, the bold sun rising in the sky. And the promise of heat, humidity and afternoon showers that would soon follow. Around them, joggers made their way up and down the beach while families, keen to get an early spot on the beach for the day, started to arrive.

Dogs leaped and raced in and out of the surf, playing catch with their humans. Beyond them, Jordan Adair, the latest addition to Ohana Odyssey's team of tour guides and water instructors, ran her early morning surfing exercises atop the waves, coasting as effortlessly across the water as a dolphin leaping in the tide. Training for a season of surfing competitions was not easy, especially given the 6:00 a.m. start times.

Greetings and waves were exchanged as they walked, then briefly stopped at a sight unique to Nalani.

"Kahlua's getting pretty good on that surfboard," Tehani said.

"Before I lived here," Daphne told her friend, "I could never have imagined a surfing pig. And yet, behold." She pointed to the very porky porcine wobbling back to shore on a unique, wide board that had been custom built by her owner and devoted master, Benji.

"Howzit, Benj?" Tehani called to the older man who stooped, and risked being blown possibly all the way to his one-story bungalow across town should the trade winds kick in.

Benji turned his sun-kissed, almost eighty-year-old face toward them, his smile of pride obvious.

"Tehani. Daphne." Benji clicked his tongue in a way that had Kahlua abandoning the board and trotting over in their direction. "There's a photographer coming by this week to take pictures of us." His eyes glistened with pride. "People all over the islands will hear about this story. I bet we get people coming out here to Nalani just to get a closer look at her."

"A closer look at both of you." Daphne crouched once more to get a handful of piggy face. "You are simply stunning this morning, Kahlua." Daphne heaped on praise and earned herself a number of enthusiastic oinks. "Love today's choice of shirt," she added. "Quite stylish, Benji."

Benji beamed, accentuating every single wrinkle of his weathered face.

While Kahlua was known for her aquatic antics and fine attempts at surfing immortality, the pair of them had earned their dual reputation for fashion forwardness by always wearing matching patterned shirts. Today's choice featured fluorescent jellyfish against a dark blue background, which made them both look like walking aquariums.

"Don't know if my girl will ever be as good as that one." Benji pointed back to the water where championship swimmer and now co-owner of Ohana Odysseys Tours Keane Harper arced and danced his way over the waves only yards away from his student, Jordan.

Even after years on the island, Daphne still marveled at the interplay of human and water, especially where Keane was concerned. It was as if the water simply waited to be told what to do when he was around. Even on an off day, he was better on a board than anyone else she'd ever watched. These days, more than a month after his surprise wedding to Marella Benoit—a woman most adverse to anything related to water—he seemed to have found an entirely different connection whenever he paddled out to catch a wave.

It was also—Daphne and Tehani glanced at each other and laughed when Keane caught sight of them and wiped out spectacularly—beyond entertaining when the tide literally turned.

"It is a wonder any of us get our work done around here," Tehani said. Together she and Daphne stepped back as Keane, board tucked firmly under one arm, made his sopping way over to them. He waited—as he often did— to give himself and his trademark long, dark blond hair a good shake, sprinkling everyone in sight with a good dose of perfect Hawaiian ocean.

"I thought Marella was going to start surfing with you in the mornings," Daphne teased. It was a running joke among the Ohana Odyssey family that Keane's new wife had actually requested surfing lessons as a wedding gift.

"Besides her work for Ohana, she has her hands full looking for the perfect house for us to live in." Keane plowed his board into the sand and swooped his hair away from his face in one elegant motion. "At least that's the excuse she's been using."

"You guys outgrowing the beach cottage already?" Tehani asked.

"Nah." Keane's smile was both genuine and affectionate. "If it were up to the two of us, we'd make Sydney an offer and buy it outright. No, we're having to deal with requests for comfort and convenience from Marella's family, which is fair enough. I don't think Pippy will be happy camping out on the couch when she comes back for a visit."

"Pippy could always stay with me," Benji offered with a wide-eyed stare. "Got plenty of space. She doesn't take up a lot of room."

Daphne bit the inside of her cheek and did her best not to laugh. The idea of Marella's eightysomething grandmother moving in with Nalani's one-man pig show was almost too much to stand.

"I'll run that idea by Pippy the next time we Zoom," Keane said almost a bit too seriously. "Just be prepared when you two have breakfast," he warned Daphne. "Marella is going to ask your opinion about the future house."

"And what should my opinion be?" Daphne asked with far too much innocence.

"In-law quarters would be nice. Not only for Pippy, but for Marella's folks. With Marella working remotely for Benoit & Associates, I anticipate her soon-to-retire father will be coming out for frequent visits and meetings. Meetings. Yeah, meeting space would be good."

"They can always use Ohana's offices," Tehani said. "Marella's got her own desk there now anyway since she's taking over our advertising and promotion."

"Offloading your responsibilities ahead of baby time, huh, T?" Daphne asked.

Something flashed across Tehani's face. Something Daphne couldn't quite identify.

"It's been good getting a new perspective on things," was all Tehani said. "You coming to breakfast?" she asked Keane.

"Gonna check in with Jordan then head home and take a shower. Have to give the roomies their breakfast before they cop an attitude with me."

"Noodles and his girlfriend, Zilla, are geckos, not roomies," Tehani reminded him.

Keane snorted. "Yeah, you try telling them that. I swear they end up eating every mango we buy. You guys have fun. Tell Marella I'll check in with her about lunch. Thanks." He grabbed his board and strode off the beach in the other direction.

"Did you ever think, did you ever imagine," Tehani said in a somewhat dazed tone, "that confirmed bachelor Keane Harper would be married, house-hunting and talking about his gecko roommates?"

Having gone to college with him, none of that would have ever crossed Daphne's mind. "One thing I've learned in my thirty-one years is that life is one big surprise after another." Surprises that often included heartbreak, disappointment and regret.

As she and Tehani approached the beachside restaurant and the half-filled patio of customers gobbling down platefuls of the Loco Moco and fresh fruit, she reminded herself to be grateful for the past. And the pain. Without either, she wouldn't be where she was today, where her heart had healed and she'd been able to trust again.

She had a different life now. A better one. A healed heart was far better than a broken, distrustful one.

Even if that heart felt incredibly lonely at times.

Griffin Townsend flipped open his leather-bound refillable pocket-size notebook, the one he'd been using since his early days as a photojournalist, and set it on the small square metal table.

His expectations of hearing the rattling of keys and the slamming of cell doors, as well as smelling the overwhelming odor of distress, regret and anger, went unfulfilled. This wasn't the cold, bare visitors' room of a maximum penitentiary. Nor was it the posh seating area of a country club pseudo-prison that offered coffee or tea while one waited to speak with one of the incarcerated.

No, the plain old regular federal jail located a few miles north of Portland, Oregon, was a sobering albeit surprisingly decent middle ground. The facility even boasted a large rehabilitation success rate, despite the number of inmates who would never again experience life on the other side of the fence.

Griff was already jotting down notes, tiny observations of the sunny visitors room, the long hall leading to a door that needed a paint job. It was here he'd meet with Richard Mercer, a man convicted a little more than three years ago on charges of fraud and embezzlement. He'd robbed thousands of people, most of them elderly, of their life savings.

Had justice been served? Were there answers to the still many unanswered questions the trial raised? A lot of people believed Richard Mercer's never seeing the light of day was more than deserved.

There were some involved who believed Mercer's claims of ignorance as to what his financial investment firm was doing with its clients' money. Everyone in the country it seemed had an opinion about Richard Mercer, a man who had refused all media requests for an interview since his arrest five years ago. Now, Mercer was the one making the request.

And for some unfathomable reason, Griff had gotten the call.

Interviewing Richard Mercer was a journalist's get of the decade, at least in Griffin's circles. Griff had made a name for himself after college as an internationally based reporter. He'd been bitten by the journalism bug while working at his college paper, where he'd exposed a slanted admissions policy giving preferential consideration not only to legacy applicants, but to parents willing to "buy" their kid a spot at the school. Illegal? Not necessarily. Unethical? Well, posing that question had earned Griff the opportunity to travel around the country. From there he went around the world as a freelancer for some of the biggest newspapers, putting his lifelong fascination for photography and the written word to good use. The fact that he was now back where he started as a freelancer for the *Portland Beat* definitely felt like a full-circle moment.

He was one of the lucky ones. He'd been able to walk away from the worst of the circus before he'd become too jaded or burnt out from witnessing the cruelty humans were capable of inflicting upon one another. The choice to leave had been his own. Mostly.

For the most part, obligation had brought him back. Obligation and the promise to take care of the parents who had always, *always* put him first. He just hadn't imagined the past two years being quite so…gut-wrenching.

His marriage breaking up, his father's rapid decline in health, gaining primary custody of his kids, eight-year-old Noah and six-year-old Cammie. Plus, juggling his ex-wife's frequent disregard of her visitation schedule after the divorce. All of that meant making major changes in his life and, fortunately for him, a return to the paper that had given him his start in the business.

He'd assumed his slide into journalistic oblivion would be just that. A slide into the unknown, where he'd be forgotten and his career would shift to one of predictability and safety.

Which made the message he'd received from Richard Mercer all the more confusing. Especially given their history.

Griff glanced up as the door across the room opened and Richard Mercer stepped through.

His prison garb wasn't the typical bright orange jumpsuit. He wore simple beige slacks and a shirt, and generic white sneakers one could purchase in any discount store. He was older than Griff remembered, but beneath the years he saw the man who had been responsible for Griff's first—and biggest—heartbreak.

The years he'd spent in prison had not been kind. Gone was the foreboding figure who stood tall and straight with an ever-present gleam of semi-superiority in his money-colored green eyes. The attitude had been tempered. The arrogance, as well. The taut, trimmed physique was quite a bit rounded now, as his circumstances had overtaken him.

Griff remained seated, watching as a man who once intimidated Griff to the point of speechlessness made his way around the other tables toward him.

Griff waited for the fear to descend. To feel his confidence slip and the teenager he'd been the last time he'd seen Richard Mercer in person emerge. But none of that happened. He didn't feel anything now beyond mild disgust. And pity.

"Good to see you, Griffin." Richard held out his hand. "I wasn't entirely sure you'd show up."

"Yes, you were." It was as if the last fourteen years hadn't happened. Not because Griffin still felt like the cowering kid who had been on the receiving end of a despicable ultimatum. No. It was because, Mercer's conviction and scandal aside, Griff saw absolutely no hint of regret in the other man's expression. No remorse or apology or even grief over his lack of freedom. *Contrite* probably didn't even register in the man's vocabulary. His self-importance still seemed very much in place.

"You're right, of course." Richard's tone lightened. "I knew you'd come. I've followed your work for years. It's clear you've never been able to resist a byline."

"And it's clear you still don't know the first thing about me." He'd never cared one iota about getting credit, only that the truth was exposed. "I'm not some teenager you can intimidate now. Your lawyer said you wanted to talk, so talk."

"Not talk so much as make you an offer." Richard claimed a chair, folded his hands on top of the table and acted as if he was back in the head seat at his investment firm. "I only wish I could do so in a more private arena."

Griff flipped his notebook closed, slipping it into his pocket. He'd known this was going to be a wasted effort. "The last time you asked to speak to me in private you threatened to call in a favor and have my father fired if I didn't stop seeing your daughter, so forgive me if I'm not anxious for a repeat of the past." It didn't take much to accentuate his words with ice.

"What about Daphne?" Richard's voice was as smooth as the cement floor beneath his sneakered feet. "I'm betting you still have some interest in her."

It took every ounce of control Griffin possessed not to react, but he wasn't going to give Mercer the satisfaction of seeing him lose his temper.

But inside himself? Oh, inside he could feel the past churning up like a hurricane in the Pacific. He'd spent a good portion of his adult life trying to forget Daphne Mercer, attempting to move past not only what he'd lost, but how things had ended between them.

She'd been Griff's first crush. His first love. There were days he'd argued she'd been his only love, which explained why his marriage to Lydia had faltered almost from the moment he'd said "I do." Griff had imagined a future with Daphne; at least whatever future a teenager could foresee. But her father had other plans for Daphne and none of them had included her marrying the son of a factory machinist and a schoolteacher.

"Is Daphne okay?" It was the only question Griff could think to ask that wouldn't open an additional floodgate of emotion.

"Couldn't really tell you." Richard sounded almost dismissive. "I haven't seen or heard from her in years. She left Oregon shortly after my conviction."

"That would be around the time her mother died." Griff had been in Afghanistan, covering the war. Richard's wife's death had made every paper in the US, which meant it was in just about every social media feed in existence. "Billionaire Fraudster's Wife Dies of Broken Heart." While the headlines had been tragic, in his mind Griff could still see those images of Daphne trying to get by the media to her mother's side before it was too late.

Griff had hated Richard Mercer well before that day, but after seeing that story? After reading about the fallout Daphne and her mother had been subjected to because of Mercer's criminal and self-serving actions? There wasn't a word strong enough to describe Griff's animosity. "Is that what this meeting between us is about? Walking down memory lane? It'll be a short walk. I haven't seen your daughter since the night I graduated high school."

"Yes, I know." Richard opened his hands, inclined his head. "You were a man of your word, even then. That brings me back to the deal I want to offer you, Griff."

"Your deals put people out of their homes. Your deals

left families destroyed. People died because of what you did to them." Griff stood up, shoved his chair back. The sound of the feet scraping against the floor echoed in the empty, windowless room. "I'm not interested."

"You sure about that?"

"Yes." There were very few things he was certain about these days. Making a deal with Richard Mercer? Yeah, he could walk away from that. Which is exactly what he did.

"What if I told you that I was willing to give you an exclusive interview," Mercer called to him when his hand clutched the knob of the door. "I'll give you my entire life story, all the way to today. The crimes, the trial, the sentencing. My time in here. Every single detail. You want a confession? You want to be the one to share it with the world? To bring all those people a modicum of understanding and closure? That's what I'll give you. Headlines galore."

Griff's hands fisted. He did not want to turn around. He did not want to give this man the satisfaction of knowing he was right about Griff. Not about the byline, but about the opportunity to expose the truth once and for all. He would not turn around. He would not...

He turned around.

"In exchange for what?" Griff asked. "You aren't capable of altruism or, heaven forbid, compassion. This offer isn't about closure for strangers. So, this must all be about you."

"Let me throw your words back at you. You don't know a single thing about me." Mercer's eyes sharpened. "I'm right, aren't I? You are interested."

"Depends. What's the price?"

"Daphne. I want to see my daughter."

"Good luck with that." If Daphne had disappeared, it

meant she wanted to stay that way, and Griff could not, would not ever, blame her for it.

"That is where you come in." Richard sat back and folded his arms across his chest. "I want you to convince Daphne to come and see me. I need to see her. To—"

"To what?"

Mercer's head dipped, but not before Griff caught what he could only describe as grief cross his face. But that wasn't possible, was it? "I need to see my little girl again, Griffin. And I think you asking her might be the gentlest way to bring her here."

Griff shook his head. "Even if I knew where to start looking—"

"I said I didn't know *how* she was. Where is another issue," Mercer said. "Besides, you've tracked bad guys and good guys in Afghanistan and Ukraine, for instance. I believe in you. I have no doubt you could find my daughter with minimum effort."

"Maybe." Griff returned to the table, but he didn't sit. It felt good, standing over this man, looking down on him. Something his younger self never ever would have thought possible. "But what I wouldn't do is bring her back for you to play games with her. If she wanted you in her life, you'd be there."

They'd both hurt Daphne enough for one lifetime. Griff wasn't going to re-inflict her father on her.

"You always had a connection with her that I never understood," Mercer said. "She listened to you. Trusted you in a way I could never interfere with."

"And yet you did interfere." *And broke both our hearts.* Otherwise it wouldn't have been fourteen years since Griff had seen or spoken to Daphne Mercer.

"How much is that nice care facility your parents are living in now, Griff?" Mercer asked. "That has to be costing you a pretty big chunk of change every month, especially with your recent pay cut and your father's condition. I can't imagine his pension covers all of it. And taking care of two children full-time can't be cheap. Have you started eating into their college fund yet? How's that mortgage treating you?"

Anger, slow and simmering, bubbled in Griff's belly. "If I didn't know better, I'd think you hadn't learned your lesson about bribing people." He planted his hands on the table and leaned in. "We both know your money's gone. There's nothing you have that can tempt me to take this deal."

"Really? National attention? A comeback? A spotlight on that ridiculous local paper you outgrew as a reporter almost as soon as you began working there?" Mercer mimicked him and leaned forward, the innocent expression on his face one that must have been responsible for the countless cons he'd run on unsuspecting and trusting clients. "You tell my story in your paper, you won't have to worry about covering your expenses. You'll be able to keep your parents where they are. You can keep living in that house your ex-wife couldn't live without and your kids can continue taking swim lessons and going on summer vacations. You won't have to spend another day worrying how you'll possibly scrape up enough cash to take care of all the people you need to." His brow arched even as his lips twitched. "Every paper in the country will be after you."

Griff gripped the table so hard his fingers went numb. Even locked away, Mercer had the means to dig up detailed information on him. "Some people aren't for sale."

"Everyone has a price," Mercer argued. "And even if you don't, peace of mind is a whole other transaction. Like I said, think of Cammie and Noah. Your little ones—"

Griff slammed a fist on the table. He glanced up as one

of the guards approached. "Sorry." He stood up, held up his hands and took a step back. "Won't happen again."

"I am offering you an exclusive interview that any other reporter out there would sell their soul to get," Mercer said, calmly looking up at him. "It's a story that could change everything for you. And all it will cost you is the price of a plane ticket and a conversation with my daughter. I know people, Griffin. More importantly, I know you. You're going to take this deal just like you took the last one I offered you. You're going to talk to Daphne and convince her to come see me and then you're going to bask in the rewards your story provides."

"What is it you want to talk to her about exactly?" The protective streak he'd always felt for Daphne reared up even stronger than it had previously.

"That's between me and my daughter," Mercer said with a wince, the first crack in an otherwise cool facade. "Find her. Convince her, Griffin. Do that and I will answer every question you pose to me honestly. You have my word."

Griff shook his head as temptation tingled. "You say that as if your word means something."

"All right, then. I swear on Daphne's life. You will have every answer you want." Griff could almost hear a silent "or" and braced himself. He wanted to believe there was a place somewhere in the man's heart that realized how lucky he was to have a daughter like Daphne. But Griff's faith in humanity had been stretched pretty thin as of late. Especially when it came to people like Richard Mercer.

"What's your plan B?" Griff asked.

"My plan—"

"What are you going to do if I say no?"

Mercer shrugged. "I don't have a plan B. Yet."

And that, at least in Griff's experience with the man, might just be the most worrying thing he'd said yet. It wasn't only temptation that slid through Griff, but concern. Was Richard Mercer the type to drop something that he really wanted? Even if Griff turned him down? This entire conversation was calculated thanks to Mercer's meticulously attentive mind.

The convicted felon understood what made people tick and he was a master at exposing people's weaknesses. Daphne was Griff's. As was the promise of financial and professional stability. Mercer must have heard that the *Portland Beat* was in trouble and, as usual, he was using what knowledge he possessed to take full advantage. "I'd just have to talk to her," Griff hedged. "Try to convince her—"

"Not try." Mercer's folded hands tightened to the point his knuckles went white. "I need to speak with her. Right here. In this place. You can do it, Griff. We both know it."

Griff could feel his resistance crumbling. He was struggling, more than he cared to admit. "It'll take me some time," he said slowly. "I've got arrangements to make and find out exactly—"

"Nalani, Hawai'i." Mercer's smile was slow. "I have enough contact with the outside world to keep track of her. Most of the time. She works as a nature guide for a tour company. An outfit called Ohana Odysseys. Guess she never outgrew her interest in plants."

What was that sound? Griff thought. Oh, right. The starting pistol of one of Richard Mercer's little games.

"So?" Mercer prodded as he held out his hand. "Do we have a deal?"

Griff looked down. His mind raced. The promises Mercer had made would be life-changing, not just for him but his family, too. It was tempting, so tempting. But Griff was focused on Daphne. One conversation between father and daughter… There was little else that could go wrong between them given the state of their relationship. And better the request come from a… Well, he could only hope he and Daphne were still friends.

Griff had to get on board and see where this would lead. "Yes." He slapped his hand into Mercer's. "We have a deal."

Chapter Two

"Daaaaaad!"

The familiar wail of a desperate six-year-old girl echoed through the house as Griff tucked his cell against his shoulder and carried the last load of clean laundry into the living room.

"Noah's pretending to turn Taco into sushi with his lightsaber!" Cammie yelled.

Considering Taco was a stuffed fish that had survived far more dangerous attacks than eight-year-old Noah wielding a plastic fluorescent tube, Griff knew what battles he could choose to ignore. "Yeah, I'll be gone two weeks," he assured his boss. "If this lead pans out, the story will be big."

"You aren't usually one to exaggerate," Colin, his onetime college roommate and now editor, mused. "You honestly can't give me anything more than that?"

"No, I can't." As hopeful as Griff was about an exclusive interview with Richard Mercer, he wasn't about to put all his faith in the man actually following through. Some faith, maybe. But definitely not all of it. "I know it's coming out of left field, especially after you've been throwing me a ton of freelance work." Enough he'd been able to shore up his emergency fund—the fund that was going to get him to Hawai'i. "You'll have to assign some-one else to the—"

"I've got plenty of reporters on deck," Colin said. "And like you said, you're freelancing. I can't exactly say no."

"Then what's the problem?" Griff asked.

"Between you and me?" Colin paused and Griff could imagine him sitting behind his desk, nibbling on the eraser end of a pencil. "I don't know if any of us will still have a job in two weeks."

Griff's stomach dropped all the way to his suddenly tingling toes. "I thought you talked the publisher out of selling *The Beat*."

"Yeah, well." Colin sighed. "The buyers upped their offer. Things are shifting faster than I can keep up with. This story of yours? It's big? Big enough to satisfy our publisher we're still viable?"

"Potentially," Griff tried to assure him. "When I can give you more, I will. But it's too new and too…unsettled right now."

"*The Beat* is on borrowed time, Griff," Colin said. "I don't say that lightly and I don't mean to stress you out—"

"Too late." His attempt at a joke fell flat for both of them. A new thread of panic was already winding through him. He'd come back to Portland not only because it was where his family was, but because he'd been assured of steady work. If the paper went down, his life and his fam-ily's would go down with it. He didn't have time for debate. It had been almost a week since Griff had met with Mer-cer and he still had a hundred things to do before getting on that plane to Hilo tomorrow afternoon.

"So what's the compromise?" Griff asked, knowing Colin was probably thinking two or even three steps ahead of everyone.

"I need you to touch base with me in a few days," Colin

said. "We'll see where we are then. I can't just tell the publisher you're taking off for two weeks without giving him more. If your story is as big as you say, it could help *The Beat* in the eyes of the publisher."

"Five days?"

"Or fewer," Colin suggested. "With actual details."

Griff dumped the laundry out on the sofa and began sorting the clothes into three piles. Everything hinged on his power of persuasion and when it came to Daphne Mercer, Griff couldn't be certain she'd talk, let alone listen to him. "I can't promise—"

"You can if you want to keep your job."

"Right." Griff sighed. "Okay. I'll talk to you in a few days. Gotta run." He hung up before Colin tried to lock him into anything tighter.

"Daaaaaad!" This time Cammie's wail was immediately followed by the heart-stopping sound of something significant tumbling down the stairs.

Griff spun in time to see Noah's wheelie suitcase come to a halt three steps short of the landing. He blew out a breath and touched a hand to his chest. Heart attack number 4,052 averted.

"Noah!" Griff called up and saw his towheaded son poke his head around the corner and grin.

"Sorry, Dad." Noah shrugged. "That happened sooner than I wanted."

Good thing Griff was headed to Hawai'i because boy oh boy did he need some downtime. Even with the arguing and the second suitcase—this one Cammie's—landing haphazardly on top of the first one, Griff couldn't stop thinking about the stress he'd heard in Colin's voice. As much as he was going to miss his kids while they were on summer vacation with their mother, he needed to focus on Daphne. And what he needed to convince her to do.

"Guys, enough, okay?" he called upstairs.

"Aw, Dad. I almost had it." Noah slumped onto the bottom step as his sister, two years younger, yet almost Noah's height, yanked the lightsaber out of his hand and conked him on the head with a soft thunk.

"I win! Taco is saved again!" Clad in her butt-sagging jeans and faded pink T-shirt, his pigtailed daughter did a little hip-swinging circle of a dance that would have made even the grouchiest of individuals smile.

The fact that, as she danced, she dragged Taco—a sixteen-inch stuffed orange grouper with bulging ping-pong-ball-sized eyes—behind her on his rainbow-colored "leash" only added to the pixie and sprinkles show that was Cammie Townsend. Every time he looked at her, at both of them, his heart swelled with love, pride and gratitude.

"You two get to carry those back upstairs so you can finish packing. Your mom's picking you up soon," Griff told them. "Grab your laundry, please."

"Aw, man." Noah's new favorite phrase had long ago stopped irritating Griff, but he shoved himself up and stalked over to the sofa to grab his pile of underwear, socks and T-shirts. "I miss Delores."

"I miss Delores, too," Cammie declared as she often did in support of her big brother, despite having conked him over the head.

"Yes, well, Delores retired to take care of her grandkids," Griff said of their former housekeeper and nanny. "And we don't need a housekeeper, remember? We can take good care of ourselves. Right?"

"I guess," Noah grumbled and nearly tripped when he dropped a sock. "I still hate folding laundry."

"You and me both," Griff muttered.

"Daddy?" Cammie tilted her head back and blinked her

big green eyes at him. "You're going to be here when we get back from vacation with Mama, right?"

"Of course." He rested a hand on the top of her head. "Why would you think—"

"We heard you on the phone. You're going to Hawayway and that sounds really far from here. I saw it on a map at school. You have to go over the ocean and everything. It'll take forever to come home!"

"Hawai'i," Griff corrected. It wouldn't be his first trip to the islands, but his purpose for going this time was definitely…different. "And I'm getting there by plane. It flies very fast, and I'll be home well before you are." He cupped her chin in his hand. "I promise. And you know what I always say about promises."

"A broken promise breaks a heart." Cammie rolled her eyes even as her dimple-deep smile exposed her slightly crooked teeth. Braces were definitely in both their futures.

"Exactly. And one thing we don't do in this house is break hearts." Not anymore, at least. Ironically, that had been his main lesson learned from his breakup with Daphne Mercer. Even at seventeen, she'd been completely straightforward with her reaction. Since that day, he'd never let himself forget the importance of a promise. Or the damage a broken one could do. He pointed to Cammie's clothes. "Laundry, please."

She huffed out a breath that had Griff holding back a smile and threw herself on top of her clean clothes before she scooped them against her chest. "Are you going to miss us?"

"Absolutely I will miss you," Griff said without hesitation. "But you're going to have a great time with your—" His cell rang and, after a glance at the screen, he held it up. "And that's your mom calling now. Go on. Remember, everything has to fit in your one suitcase!"

"Even Taco?"

"Taco's an exception," Griff said. Taco had been an exception since Cammie had found the stuffed animal in a clearance bin at the big-box store shortly after Griff had come home from his last assignment overseas. That fish had been dragged around lovingly on a leash ever after all around Portland. "I'll be up to help you finish when I get off the phone, okay?"

"'Kay." Cammie still didn't look particularly happy as she trudged up the stairs, with Taco bouncing, flipping and twisting behind her.

"Lydia." Griff gathered up his own laundry and dumped it back into the basket. "I was going to call you in a bit. Kids are packing now. They've made a list as long as my arm of all the things they want to do out in Florida with you and Raymond. This'll be a great vacation for all of you. What time does your flight get in from Seattle tomorrow? You can pick the kids up anytime."

"That's why I'm calling." The hesitation was just long enough to make him stop breathing. "I'm afraid the trip's off."

"What do you mean the trip's off?" Griff's stomach sank all the way to his toes. "Lydia." He heard Cammie gasp and spotted Noah walking slowly down the stairs to rest a hand on his sister's shoulder.

Griff lowered his voice to an urgent whisper. "Lydia, don't you dare do this to them." He tried his best to keep the anger out of his voice. "Not again." This was the third time she'd reneged on taking the kids for an extended stay. Even from a distance, he could see tears filling his daughter's eyes.

"I can't help it," Lydia said blithely. "Raymond has the opportunity to meet with the board on his company's yacht in the Mediterranean next week. I can't very well not go with him, can I?"

"Yes, actually, you can," Griff said sharply. "Because you promised your children—"

"Oh, they'll be fine." He could just imagine her waving her hand in the air casually, as if she were batting away a mosquito rather than her children's summer dreams. "They've got soccer and basketball and swimming or something this summer, don't they? They'll be busy. They won't miss me one bit."

"They've missed you every single day since you walked out on them," Griff reminded her and, because he couldn't bear to see the disappointment on his kids' faces, he turned away from them.

"As opposed to the years you spent away before then?" Lydia countered. "You had your time away, Griff. Now it's my turn."

Frustration overtook Griff. He'd known his marriage was in trouble almost from the second he and Lydia had said an impulsive "I do" in Vegas. He'd been trying to do the right thing considering she was pregnant with his child. They'd done their best to make it work, especially for Noah and then for Cammie, but it soon became clear Lydia had little interest in motherhood. He certainly didn't help the situation by always being on the road and he hadn't been surprised when she'd asked for a divorce; he'd been relieved. But learning she had no intention of asking for even partial custody of their kids…

"You don't get to pick and choose when to be a parent, Lydia." His emotions began to seep through.

"Said the man who spent most of their lives playing around the world."

"I wasn't playing, I was working, which meant you could buy this house you wanted and…" He stopped short.

He was not going to have this fight with her again. "None of this has been easy on them, Lyd. I came home. I changed everything for them."

"For them," Lydia said icily. "But not for me."

"Did you really want me to, Lydia?" He knew very well she didn't. She'd thought marrying a nationally recognized journalist would mean something completely different from what she'd ended up with. "You promised Noah and Cammie a month with you this summer. You promised them and the family court judge. They haven't seen you since Christmas." And even that had been a drive-by gift drop-off when she and her boyfriend-turned-husband had a layover on their way to Vancouver for the holidays. "They miss you, Lyd."

"I miss them, too." If that didn't sound completely rehearsed... "I'll call them next week and explain everything. It'll be fine, Griff. You'll see."

"No." Courage back in place, he faced his children as they slowly stood up. "No, I won't. You can't keep doing this to them. This is the last time."

"Oh, don't be so dramatic," she snapped. "They're big enough to understand life gets in the way sometimes. I'll make it up to them. I promise."

"Stop making promises you have no intention of keeping." Whatever regrets he had about marrying Lydia eight years ago—and he had a truckload of them—were immediately countered by the two little faces looking at him now with trembling chins, doing their best to pretend they didn't know what was going on.

He walked into the kitchen, stood at the double French doors that looked out into a garden he'd never tended to. The garden Lydia had insisted on having when they'd bought this house, which had become a financial anchor around his neck.

"Do you remember what the judge said the last time you pulled this on Noah's birthday?"

"Of course I remember." Lydia sighed as only she could.

"She told you if you did it again, you could kiss visitation goodbye." He took a long, steadying breath. He'd tried so hard for so long to keep things as amicable as he could. His job had been horrible for their marriage, and for his relationship with his children. But he'd made the pivot. He'd been too late to salvage anything with Lydia, but he was doing everything he could to make it up to his kids. "You do this, you cancel on them at the last minute, and I'm done, Lydia. I'll go to the judge and ask that your visitation be revoked." He couldn't—wouldn't—let his children continue to be disappointed.

"You wouldn't do that to me." Lydia's tone went instantly contrite. "You loved me once. You wouldn't hurt me like that."

"I'm not the one doing the hurting. Make a choice, Lydia. Are you coming tomorrow, yes or no?"

"I told you, I can't." Her desperate whine reminded him of Cammie when she didn't want to go to bed.

"Okay then. Thanks for calling. Have a good trip." He hung up and tossed his phone onto the counter that contained dishes from this morning's breakfast. When he turned around, he found Noah and Cammie standing there.

"We aren't going to Florida with Mom, are we?" Noah's lashes carried the hint of tears, but he'd wiped them away and kept an arm securely around Cammie, who was sobbing so hard her entire body shook. She hugged Taco to her chest and wiped her runny nose on him. "It's okay, Cammie. Dad did his best."

"I know." Cammie sniffled. "Did we do something bad, Daddy? Why doesn't she love us anymore?"

"Baby." Despite the anger rolling through him, he bent

down and lifted Cammie—Taco and all—into his arms. "She does love you. She's just—" He struggled for the right words. "Your mom is really busy right now." He looked to Noah. "We need to let her walk her own path, okay? I know you're disappointed."

Noah shrugged, but there was no mistaking the hurt in his son's eyes. Eyes that only minutes ago had been dancing with excitement at the prospect of a perfect summer vacation and, more importantly, time with his mother.

"It's okay to feel hurt and to be angry. I am." Griff kissed Cammie's damp cheek before she tucked her head under his chin. "But you know what?"

"What?" Cammie mumbled against his neck.

"You've still got me. You always will." He hugged her tight. "I'm not going anywhere."

"Yes, you are," Noah said.

"You're going to Ha-way-yay." Cammie's voice was thick with tears. "We're going to be all alone!"

"No, you won't." He took a hard mental detour and hoped he could adjust his reservations to work for three rather than one. "Because *we're all* going to Hawai'i."

"Really?" Noah didn't look completely convinced.

"It's not Florida," Cammie whispered brokenly. "They don't have—"

"No, they don't." Griff didn't want her dwelling on what she was losing out on, but on what she could count on. "Hawai'i has a whole lot of other fun stuff, like the beach and dolphins and all kinds of other things. You know what? I'll show you the website of the place we're going to be staying. It's a resort with an enormous pool and lots of activities to sign up for. We can go horseback riding if you want. Or swim in the ocean. I just need to make some calls first, all right?" He set Cammie on her feet. "Give me an hour and we'll get to planning, yeah?" He touched her cheek and waited for a nod. When she turned, she dropped Taco on the ground and dragged him behind her as she left the kitchen. "Noah?"

"It's okay, Dad." Noah shrugged again and heaved a heavy sigh no eight-year-old should ever have to heave. "Mom doesn't want to be a mom anymore, does she?"

"I don't know what your mother wants." It was, Griff thought later, the nicest response he could have come up with. "It's not your fault this happened, Noah. And it's not Cammie's. It's mine. I spent a lot of years away from you all and I shouldn't have." He hadn't seen what was important, until he'd almost lost it. "So, if you want to blame someone—"

"It's not your fault, either, Dad." Noah shook his head. "You know how I know?"

"How do you know?"

"You're here," his son said. "And she's not."

Chapter Three

Daphne pulled the multi-passenger minibus into the narrow driveway beside Ohana Odyssey's main office building and sat back with a relieved sigh. Every part of her ached, but in a good way. Her legs, shoes and clothes were spattered with mud thanks to the afternoon shower that had blown through during her outing. She was hot, sticky and sweaty, but as usual after finishing a half-day hike through the bamboo rainforest surrounding Nalani, she felt oddly exhilarated.

She pushed out of the cab and dropped to the ground, took a moment to press her hands against the small of her back and stretched. The promise of a day off tomorrow felt like heaven personified and she planned to make the most of it by doing absolutely nothing.

The late-afternoon sun beat down through the gently swaying palm trees with a summer feel that had her thinking about heading into town and grabbing a truckload of shave ice, topped with raspberry and mango syrup. Nothing was more refreshing on a day like this. She'd long since burned off the dried fruit and trail mix she'd munched on during the botanical hike to one of the area's premier waterfalls.

As she rounded the back of the bus, she caught sight of Ohana's owner and helicopter tour pilot, Sydney Calvert, stretched out on the stairs leading up to the office. She had her head back and her eyes closed and looked as perfectly at home as Daphne felt.

"Taking a break?" Daphne took a seat beside her.

"Needed one." Sydney didn't move. "I had three back-to-back helicopter tours before noon, one of which was a group of frat brothers who didn't think flying with mega hangovers would be an issue."

"Oh, no." Daphne wrapped her arms around her knees and winced in sympathy. "Did you have to hose out the chopper?"

"No, thank goodness." Sydney's mouth twisted. "But it was definitely touch and go for a while. I'm thinking we need to up the cleanup fee posted on the website. And add a warning that drinking alcohol and taking helicopter tours do not mix." She stretched out her legs. "How'd your hike go?"

"Pretty well. Saw some amazing bird of paradise blooms, which are a little late this year. And I think the path to Kaimukanaka Falls is getting easier to traverse. I'll need to explore a bit more before we add it to the full itinerary."

"I was actually more interested in our clients," Sydney teased with an understanding grin. "But I'll take that all to mean no injuries and everyone was returned safe and sound."

"I think at least three of them will need new tennis shoes." Daphne looked down at her well-worn hiking boots. "People really don't read instructions, do they?" Either that or people didn't understand what qualified as sturdy walking shoes. Who went on a hike in flip-flops?

"How much easier our lives would be if they did," Sydney said slowly. "You headed home?"

"Just going to double-check the schedule to make sure Tehani didn't sneak anything in on me for tomorrow."

"She didn't," Sydney assured her. "Oh, our Saturday dinner cruise booking canceled this morning."

"What happened?" Last Daphne had heard the large party had rented out the entire event.

"After spending the last two days in Hilo, they discovered more than half the family is prone to seasickness. They don't want to risk it."

"At least they let us know ahead of time," Daphne said.

"Yeah. Too bad Polunu and his wife have already done the shopping for the food."

"Want to put up a posting at the resort, see if we get any late takers?"

Sydney shook her head. "I have a better idea, although we could do that. I was wondering if we shouldn't enjoy the cruise ourselves. A reward for all the hard work everyone's been doing the past couple of months. Like a reward for the team."

"You won't hear me arguing with that idea," Daphne assured her. Since buying the *Nani Nalu*, a sixty-five-foot catamaran a few months back, Keane, along with handyman and jack-of-all-trades Wyatt Jenkins, had been gradually building Ohana's water excursion offerings. In addition to catered sunset dinner cruises, they'd added snorkeling and diving adventures to the roster along with sunrise fishing trips off the coast of Hilo, which was located about ten miles north. "Hey, T." Sydney arched her neck to look up as Tehani stepped onto the porch.

From the outside, the structure housing Ohana Odysseys looked like a bamboo-and-grass shack, something old-school that harkened back to the early days of Nalani. But the bamboo walls and grass roof were merely decorations hiding the sturdy structure beneath. Remy Calvert, Sydney's late brother, had done a lot of the rebuild himself with the intention of bringing the old in line with the new. The fact that every window provided a view either of the ocean or the road leading into downtown Nalani only spoke to Remy's dedication of showcasing the town he'd loved so much.

With thatched window ties, colorful posters and flyers depicting many of Nalani's offerings, and open-space floor plan, the vibe was laid-back and relaxed just like the rest of the islands. Here people worked to live, they didn't live to work. Play, relaxation and downtime were just as important as any job.

Of course, Daphne, along with her Ohana friends and coworkers, had the luxury of doing what they loved, which, in the end, really made her question whether it was work at all. Days like this, when their tours were over for the afternoon save for an evening dinner-boat event, made the time fly and preceded the best view of all—the island sunset—first and foremost in everyone's plans.

"Everything okay?" Daphne asked as Tehani leaned against the porch post.

"Fine." Tehani shifted her weight from one foot to the other. "Just wanted to get up and move a little." She touched a hand to her stomach. "I'm beginning to understand just how uncomfortable I'm going to get before this little guy decides to make his entrance into the world." She fanned herself with an activities brochure. "I've never had a problem with the heat before."

"You've never been baking a human before," Sydney assured her. "Say the word and we'll order some more fans from Luanda's."

"Noted and plan on it, thank you," Tehani said. "Mano called while you were out on your hike," she said to Daphne. "He asked if you could stop by and talk to him about a new project he's considering at the resort, related to landscaping."

"Oh. Sure, yeah, I can do that." There went her intention to head home and soak the night away in her hot tub. "Any idea what landscaping project he's considering specifically?"

"With my brother, you never know," Tehani said. "He's always full of surprises."

With more effort than expected, Daphne drew her legs back in and stood up. "I'll head over now before my body forgets how to work."

"Enjoy your day off tomorrow!" Sydney called after her as she headed down the hill into town.

"Call me if you need me."

"We won't," Tehani yelled back from the stairs. "Need you."

Daphne smiled as the sound of her friend's laughter echoed behind her. She did indeed stop for that shave ice at Seas & Breeze, the best place in Nalani to get anything cool and refreshing. How could she not treat herself when it was on the way to the resort? Frozen tropical treat in hand, she slurped along Pulelehua Road, the main thoroughfare of Nalani that stretched down to the dead end of the Hibiscus Bay Resort.

Growing up as the only child of wealthy parents had always put her front and center of the best of the best. The best nannies. The best schools. The best house. She'd attended the best parties and belonged to the best country club, but the truth was, she'd never once felt as if she truly belonged. How often had she wondered if she'd somehow been plucked out of obscurity and plopped into the Mercer nursery like a foundling gone astray? Too often.

Her parents had all but defined leaping the ladder of success through socializing, but Daphne always preferred solitude, and at the best times, spending her days in the expansive garden and greenhouse she'd learned to tend under the guiding hand of one of their longtime gardeners. Her mother had wanted the space as a showcase, but she'd inadvertently given Daphne not only a focus and escape, but a purpose in life.

Daphne never felt fully herself unless she was surrounded by the variant of greens and explosive colors nature launched every spring and summer. In the winter, she considered herself a kind of caretaker, keeping things safe and protected until the warmer months. That was the only place she'd fit, until she'd gotten to college.

Meeting Remy Calvert and his friends on her first day of a required biology class in college had been a kind of spiritual awakening. How he spoke about the islands, about the natural serenity of Nalani, the town he'd grown up in; he'd seeded something inside Daphne that had only sprouted to life on her darkest day. If Remy hadn't called her shortly after her mother's death, there was no telling where she might have ended up.

"Come to Nalani, Daphne," Remy had said when the headlines about her father's arrest first hit. "You liked it when you visited after college. I've got a place for you here. A job. Good people who don't care who your father is or what he's done. Give it three months and if I'm wrong, you leave."

She'd been so desperate to disappear she hadn't thought twice. Now she honestly couldn't fathom her life ever having gone in a different direction. She'd found where she belonged. She'd found her home. And the mainland offered her absolutely nothing but regret and heartache.

She tripped on a crack in the sidewalk. The nearly empty paper cone almost tipped out of her hand, but she caught her footing and her snack. That would have been a great way to bring the afternoon to a close: face-first on the pavement in front of Nalani's busy resort and hotel.

"Howzit, Daph?" Across the street, a young, dark-haired man wearing green board shorts and a clashing blue-flowered shirt waved from the front of Luanda's, the "we carry it all" convenience store that provided everything from house-made saimin and sushi to sunscreen and sundresses.

"Going good!" Daphne called back and dumped her empty cup into the trash can on the corner. The afternoon hustle and bustle in Nalani equated to nothing more than a steady stream of tourists and locals making their way in, around and about the dozens of small, independently owned businesses, stores and restaurants. Off to her left and closer to the shoreline sat the Blue Moon Bar and Grill, famous for their morning Loco Moco and evening mai tais. Personally Daphne preferred the Lava Flow, an amped-up strawberry daiquiri that provided a more subtle punch.

The outdoor seating area was filled with customers awaiting that coming sunset. In the air, she could smell the fresh scent of the beach and ocean intermingling with the spicy promise of Hula Chicken and their trademark roasted hens and traditional island sides.

There wasn't an inch of this town that hadn't twined its way around her heart. Remy had been right. This place—his offer—had saved her. Soothed her. Transformed her. Better still? The job offer to become a nature hike guide for his tour business meant putting Daphne's botany and horticulture studies to excellent use. She'd since earned a reputation as a go-to expert on the Big Island and had even taken up guest lecturing at Hilo University's science department. She loved teaching and getting people excited about the natural areas of the islands.

She flexed her frozen hand, shaking it out as she darted across the street to the front entrance of the Hibiscus Bay Resort. With its enormous spinning glass door and dark polished wood accents, the resort offered a peek into the past of Nalani as well as its future.

Mano Iokepa, Tehani's older brother, had taken over management of the resort shortly before Daphne had arrived in Nalani. Beginning when he was a teenager, the native-born Hawaiian had worked his way up from the lowest of positions until he'd become part owner. He'd made himself completely indispensable where both the resort and Nalani were concerned, and a lot of the improvements and advancements the resort had made had been done under his supervision if not his direction.

His attention to detail was impeccable; his devotion to the islands, unmatched. But it was the respect he'd earned from his employees and fellow Nalani residents that he considered a true badge of honor.

The building of the resort itself stood only five floors high. Back when it had been built in the 1970s, the idea was to keep it as unobtrusive against the natural setting as possible. Now, with the lush overgrowth of trees, plants and flowers all around, it had become part of that landscape. A true, lush paradise offering personalized stays for guests of all types. Families, honeymooners and solitary travelers alike found a home away from home on the other side of that spinning door. And they all learned within moments of setting foot in Nalani that once you did, you were considered *ohana*. Family.

"Aloha, Daphne!" Koa, one of the hotel's front desk receptionists, waved as she spun out of the hotel's glass door. Her dress was one of the trademark yellow-flower-patterned uniforms worn by the staff. "You here to see Mano?"

"Sure am."

"He's out by the south pool," Koa shouted over her shoulder as she headed straight for the entrance to the harbor.

"Thanks!" Daphne hurried inside, her hiking boots falling heavy on the tiled lobby floor. This time of day, when the sun was beginning to dip down and the winds were at their smoothest, a breeze blew through the open-styled lobby and set the potted trees and plants to swaying. Overhead, the speakers poured out the gentle strains of local musicians proficient in the ukulele and other traditional instruments. Guests milled about in the various seating areas, grabbing a late coffee at the cart stationed centrally, and browsing the various brochures of island events and happenings situated by the bell desk.

The scent of hibiscus permeated the air and sent thoughts of long forest walks and tumbling waterfalls through Daphne's mind as she strode past the registration desk, following the signs to Seven Seas. The restaurant was located by the enormous resort pool.

Her heart squeezed a bit at the sight of a man sorting through his wallet, one sleeping child—a girl—practically poured over his shoulder, a large stuffed orange fish dangling down his back like a recently caught dinner. Beside him, an older boy stood wide-eyed and agape as he tilted his head back to look at the intricate wood carvings in the crown molding outlining the ceiling. In his hand he held one of the resort maps.

"Wow, Dad, wow, this place is so cool!" The boy lost his balance and laughed as he tumbled to the floor. "They've got ukulele lessons and look! Cammie can make her own lei. And oh, wow! Look at the kids' pool!" Seemingly content on the floor, the boy curled his legs under him and continued to read. "It's got a water slide and everything! Can we go swimming today?"

"We'll see," the father said. "And see, I told you it would be great."

The boy's father responded in a tone that had Daphne's

mind and heart spinning back years. That voice. She froze. She knew that voice.

"I know it isn't Florida," he continued, "but—"

"Griff?" Daphne said the name before she thought it through. "Griffin Townsend?"

The man turned away from the counter and Daphne lost her breath. All these years, all this time and he was... How was it possible? He was *here*? She met his gaze and everything inside her warmed.

There was no missing the boy she'd loved in the face of the man he'd become. He was taller now, of course. Much taller than he'd been at seventeen when they'd first met, and he'd definitely lost that gangly, awkward physique he'd lamented on multiple occasions. No doubt carrying sleepy children in his arms had helped him bulk up. His once long, unkempt dark blond hair had been shorn short, to practical, easily manageable length, but it was those eyes. Those sparkling, stunning green eyes she never could have mistaken for anyone else's.

The stubble of a good day's growth of beard and his wrinkled jeans and polo shirt spoke of a stressful travel experience. Had she any doubt as to his identity, the camera bag resting at his feet locked in the truth. Those two years they'd had together came flooding back, every single wonderful yet ultimately heartbreaking moment.

"Daphne." There was surprise on his face, followed by uncertainty before finally, a smile of relief and friendliness that had her moving closer. "It is you, isn't it?"

"It is." No point in denying it now. And, of course, she looked a mess. Her hands flexed against the impulse to smooth a hand down her long braid and she wanted to knock some of the mud off her boots.

"We'll just need a minute to attempt to retrieve your reservation, Mr. Townsend," the older woman behind the desk told him as she accepted the credit card he handed over.

"Okay. Thanks. Wow. Daphne." He shook his head, keeping one arm solidly beneath the bottom of the little girl who slept on him. "You look...wow." His laugh had her smiling. He sounded just like his son.

He'd always been easily flummoxed. It was one of the things she'd liked about him. The nerves. The uncertainty. The authenticity few boys had ever displayed around her. Just being in his presence now was enough to knock aside the pain and regret of the past.

Giving in, she smoothed a hand down her hair and wished she'd stopped off at home to change clothes before coming over.

"Just wow?" She couldn't help but tease him, if only to keep him from falling back into the past. A past she hadn't allowed herself to dwell on over the years. "I'd have thought a world-renowned photojournalist like yourself would have improved your vocabulary."

"You've kept up with me, have you?" That once-upon-a-time twinkle in his eye appeared. "And here I thought I'd be your least favorite person in the world after my graduation night."

"Time heals most wounds." She'd been devastated when he'd broken up with her, out of the blue, when only a few days before he'd been hinting at a serious future. On their graduation day she'd been expecting a ring and instead she'd watched him walk away and disappear out of her life for good.

Until now. Happiness bloomed inside her.

"You've done really well for yourself, Griffin." Better than he probably would have with her tagging along. They'd been so young. So deliriously foolish. And yet she'd loved him without any hesitation or boundary. "I read that series of articles you wrote on the refugee crisis in Europe. Powerful observations." And even more powerful images. He had such a talent for capturing life-altering moments.

"Thanks." His smile was familiar and coy. "Not sure how much good it did—"

"It did plenty of good," she assured him, thinking on the donation she'd made to the charity he'd written so passionately about. One thing Griffin had always excelled at was taking on a cause. "What paper are you working for these days?"

"I'm back home, so the *Portland Beat*," he said. "Freelancing," he added. "Easier to keep up with these guys." He glanced down at his kids.

She shouldn't have been surprised. He'd always loved where they'd grown up. "So." She did her best not to let her gaze drop to his hand. "You're here with your family."

"Yes. Sorry. Noah." Griffin twisted and reached a hand back as his son shoved to his feet. "Noah, this is a friend of mine from high school. Daphne Mercer. Daphne, my son, Noah."

"Hello, Noah." Daphne held out her hand and she felt her smile widening at the easy way he took it.

"Hi." Noah's nervous smile matched his father's. "Do you work here?"

"Not here at the resort, no," Daphne said. "I work for a tour company called Ohana Odysseys that's just up the main road out there." She pointed to the door.

"I read about that right here." Noah held up the brochure and jabbed a finger into the paper. "Dad, they have helicopter tours and surf lessons! Can you fly?" Those hopeful eyes of his were so reminiscent of Griffin she had to take a beat.

"I'm afraid not," she said finally. "My friend Sydney's the pilot. And my other friend Keane gives the surfing lessons. I don't surf," she added. "At least, not very well. But I guide amazing wildflower and waterfall hikes."

"Cool," Noah said with a serious nod.

"And who's this?" Daphne couldn't help but lean over to get a peek at the little girl's face. Her hair was mussed and her mouth was open just a little as she let out a little girl snore that had Griffin rolling his eyes.

"Cammie." Griffin's other hand came up to touch the back of Cammie's head. "She was wiped out by the flight. We got out of Portland about five hours late and missed our connection from Honolulu. Trying to salvage my hotel reservation." His cringe made Daphne think he wasn't convinced that was possible.

"And your wife?" It was impulse that had her asking. Impulse, curiosity and more than a touch of envy.

"Mom's on a yacht with Raymond," Noah said.

"We aren't together anymore," Griffin explained quickly. "Long story. She was supposed to take the kids to Florida for the month. You know, the whole amusement park extravaganza, but plans changed."

"Mom's on a yacht," Noah repeated. "Dad got us."

"Well." Daphne couldn't wait to hear the longer version, especially given the sudden red tint to Griffin's cheeks. "I think your dad definitely got the better end of the deal." Out of the corner of her eye, she saw a familiar suited figure rounding the corner. "I'll be right back." She held up a finger and hurried toward Mano. "Sorry! I was coming to meet you and ran into someone I know from the mainland."

Mano Iokepa's tanned island skin and dark hair and eyes were accentuated by the stylish suit that fit his athletic build to a T. The heritage-inspired tattoos peeking out of the collar of his crisp white shirt were frequently on display outside the resort, especially when he grabbed a board and joined Keane on the waves.

Mano was the kind of man who made anyone feel safe and protected unless you were sitting across from him hammering out a business deal. In that instance, Daphne had heard, at least, he was ruthless and determined and rarely walked away without winning.

"No worries," Mano said easily. "I just got a call about something I need to take care of in the kitchen. You want to walk with me?"

"Um. Yeah. Sure." Daphne looked back to Griffin, who, unfortunately, had slumped a little while the receptionist continued clacking on the keyboard. "Can I ask you a favor?"

Surprise leaped into Mano's eyes. "Can't remember the last time you did, so yeah, go for it."

"That's Griffin Townsend." She pointed at Griff. "He and his—"

"The reporter?" Mano straightened and his brows rose. "There was an article he wrote like, five years ago, I think? He was part of exposing a corruption ring between East Asia and the islands. That really him?"

"It is. We went to high school together."

"Really?" Mano was rarely surprised. "That's a long time to go by to be able to recognize someone."

"Not really." Daphne wasn't about to get into details. She'd always kept her past under wraps, for a number of reasons. "Anyway, their flights were messed up and he got here late. The kids were supposed to be with their mom, but that went sideways. I think maybe his reservation got canceled?"

"Say no more." He touched a hand to her arm before heading to the desk. "Leilani."

"Mano." The woman looked more than relieved to see him. "It was one of our discounted rooms that was automatically canceled when he missed check-in." She tapped on the keys again. "I'm trying to find something—"

"Here." Mano touched a finger to the screen and murmured something quietly to his employee. "How long are you and your family staying, Mr. Townsend?"

"I'd planned on eight days, but if the rate's going to go up—"

Poor guy, Daphne thought as she watched the concern cross Griffin's face. It must have been a serious hassle to readjust flights and travel for him and the kids at the last minute. She could practically see him doing the rate addition in his head.

"Ten days it is," Mano said. "At the discounted price, please, Leilani."

"Yes, sir." Relief and surprise rose in her eyes before she gave a firm nod. "It'll just take me a few moments to make the adjustment, Mr. Townsend."

"Mano Iokepa." Mano came out from behind the desk and offered his hand, which Griff accepted after hoisting Cammie up higher on his shoulder. "I hear you're a friend of Daphne's, Mr. Townsend."

"Griff, please. Thanks for the assist. And yes." His smile was quick and carried with it the memories of after-curfew walks in the moonlight and stolen summer kisses. There weren't a lot of things she cared to remember before she moved to Nalani, but Griff definitely topped the list. "We went to high school together."

Daphne had to look away to stop him from seeing the sudden flush on her cheeks. Funny how in the space of a few seconds she was back to being that giddy, besotted schoolgirl who had fallen tail over teakettle for the school reporter and yearbook photographer.

"I look forward to hearing some stories about her from

back then." Mano chuckled. "I hope you enjoy your stay here at Hibiscus Bay. And you, young man. Welcome to Nalani."

"Thank you." Noah's eyes had gone saucer wide as he leaned back yet again, this time to look up at Mano's face. "I'm Noah."

"Good to meet you, Noah." Despite his size, Mano had a kind, charming way with people. He could put anyone at ease almost immediately. "Do you like to surf?"

Noah shook his head. "I don't know how."

"Well, we'll have to make sure you learn. Never enough surfers in the world if you ask me. Just be careful. You get bit by the surfer bug you'll never want to stop." Mano's smile was as warm as his arms were wide. "Daphne? Why don't you walk with me and I'll give you the details about that project I'm planning."

"Okay." Daphne nodded, nerves jumping to life in her belly when she faced Griff again. "I guess I'll see you around."

"How about dinner?" Griff glanced at his kids. "Tomorrow maybe? Or the next night? I'd love to reconnect, catch up. You know."

She hoped her smile didn't look as goofy as she felt. "I'd love to. Hula Chicken has a great menu for kids. Tomorrow night?" Every cell in her body seemed to be buzzing with anticipation. "I'll meet you here in the lobby, say about six?"

"Okay." That smile was back and it had just as much knee-weakening power as it always had. In that blink of a moment she wondered if simply seeing him again was enough to stoke those long-died-out embers of first love. "Yeah, sounds great. We'll see you then. Nice to meet you, Mano."

"You, too, Griff." He smiled and, after Daphne gave Griff and Noah a quick wave, she hurried to catch up.

"What?" she asked Mano when he looked at her with a brow raised.

"Nothing." But there was a laugh in his voice. "Just thinking about the fact that Daphne Mercer has a date. There's more to the two of you than just high school. What's the story?"

"It's not a long one," she said, trying to cut off his curiosity quickly. "We dated. It didn't work out." That wasn't what she wanted to dwell on just then. "He was a high point of my formative years. It's only a dinner," she added, as if trying to justify her actions not only to her friend but also to herself.

"Dinner with his kids," Mano added. "I'm just teasing, Daph." He nudged her with his shoulder. "You've never really given us much fodder for that in regards to your social life. I anticipate we'll be making up for lost time over the next few days."

Daphne wasn't entirely sure how to respond to that, so she remained silent.

Who would have thought it? Griffin Townsend, of all people, ending up in Nalani, Hawai'i. Her heart skipped multiple beats as her face flushed again. What were the odds he'd turn up out of the blue? And that he'd be single when he did? Was it possible... She took a long, cautious breath and tried to settle her nerves. Was it possible she and Griff were being given some kind of surprise second chance?

She glanced over her shoulder, found Griff still watching her as Noah tugged on the hem of his father's shirt. Daphne smiled to herself and turned the corner.

Maybe, just maybe, her romantic luck was about to change for the better.

Chapter Four

"Dad! Dad, wake up! It's almost nine and there are already a ton of people at the pool!"

For a moment, as he pulled himself out of one of the best night's sleep he'd had in months, Griff wondered if they were having an earthquake. Then he realized Noah had pounced onto the foot of his bed and was bouncing up and down. "Can we go down? Please? Dad, it looks so awesome from up here."

"Yeah, sure. Of course." Griff cleared his throat and shoved himself up against the bamboo woven headboard. He scrubbed a hand down his face and tried to shake himself awake. "What time did you say it was?"

"Almost nine!" Noah rotated in the air and dropped onto the mattress, then bounced a few more times before he landed on his feet again. "Should we order room service again? That was so cool last night."

"How about we check out that place near the pool for something to eat?" Room service had worked for dinner. All three of them had been exhausted and not feeling particularly adventurous. The fact that they were all in bed by eight, in Portland, would have been considered a minor miracle. "You're already dressed?" Griff blinked at his son's swimsuit shorts and flip-flops. Clearly Noah had adjusted to island life just fine. "Where's your sister?"

"Moping in the living room. She's watching reruns of *Proton Patrol*." Noah rolled his eyes, as if he himself hadn't been a fan of the show only a few years before. "Come on, Dad. We're hungry!"

"Yeah, yeah, I'm coming," he called after Noah's retreating back. But he didn't move. His mind, his dreams, had been filled with thoughts and images of an all-grown-up Daphne making her way down a mountain of island flowers. He took a deep breath, inhaled the subtle fragrance of hibiscus, then remembered it was the namesake flower of the resort and had nothing to do with the woman he'd come to see.

The woman who had effectively tied his tongue into knots the second he'd seen her in the lobby. Whom was he kidding? The woman had had him tied in knots from the moment they'd crossed paths in high school.

There was such a difference between the memory of who she was years ago and the idea of seeing her again. Frankly, doing so had every synapse in his brain short-circuiting at the mere sight of her.

That long red hair of hers, that beautifully island-tanned skin, the way her green eyes shone like the sun. The rays beamed in through the windows even now. She was a lightning bolt of awareness personified. Her smile had carried the hint of the closeness they'd shared, and a slight hesitation when she'd spoken his name, but he had seen true happiness on her face. Happiness he could only hope would remain once he told her why he was here.

He turned his head on the pillow and looked out over the ocean. His first impulse was to grab his camera and capture the image permanently. Instead, he made himself stay where he was and revel in the moment. It was a lesson he kept attempting to learn. That he could lie here and stare out at the water, hear the glorious waves tumbling over themselves, and know he was as close to paradise as he'd ever encountered. The sight almost made him forget why he was here.

Was it a mistake? Agreeing to Richard Mercer's terms? He scrubbed a hand down his face. Maybe. It certainly wouldn't be the first one he'd made in his life. If it was an error, he could only wish that it turned out as well as their room reservation debacle.

Upon first entering their third-floor room last evening—a two-bedroom suite that included a sitting room and small kitchen area—Griff had been convinced there was a mistake. But it had only taken one call to the front desk to discover that Mano Iokepa had indeed approved their lodgings and, shortly before dinner, had sent up a fresh fruit plate and an assortment of drinks as a welcome gift from the hotel.

The few times he'd been here, he'd always found the hospitality of the islands one of the biggest reasons to return. But so far, Nalani, and Hibiscus Bay in particular, had far surpassed any previous experiences he'd had.

With its soft green and baby blue theme decor, the room felt as if he and the kids had stepped into a beautiful dream. They'd eaten dinner—mini-burgers for the kids and an ahi tuna salad for Griff—out on the balcony where even a semi-cranky Cammie had seemed to enjoy herself.

Griff groaned loudly and shoved out of bed, made quick use of one of the two bathrooms and located the coffee maker. The almost instant aroma of the Big Island's Kona coffee was tantalizing enough to make up for the disastrous day and a half of travel they'd endured to get here.

"So, pool today?" Griff asked his kids.

"Yes, please," Noah said.

Cammie just shrugged. Still in her sleeper shirt, she hugged Taco against her chest.

"Cammie? Why don't you go put on your suit?" Griff suggested. She didn't respond, just kept her eyes glued to the television screen. "Cam?" He walked over and crouched in front of her. "I know you're disappointed about your trip with your mom, but we're going to make the best of things, remember?"

She buried her face in Taco and Griff reached out and clicked off the big-screen TV. It sat atop an open shelving unit decorated with various local artists' works, according to a card on the desk. The pretty items included an eye-catching yellow-, orange- and blue-swirled hand-turned bowl with sparkling shards of polished glass pushed into its smooth surface. It came from Inoa's Glass Shack, according to the sign.

A thick cotton quilt with an intricate floral design hung on the wall behind the two sofas situated to face one another, and on the coffee table sat a dark blue leather binder containing all the touristy information Noah had already committed to memory.

"Let's go down to the pool and see what we can grab for breakfast, okay?" Griff reached out and ran a finger down her cheek. "Once you see what all they have to do here, I think you'll start to feel better."

"Come on, Cam. I'll help you find your suit." Noah held out his hand. "There's a water slide at the pool. And there's this lazy river kind of thing that you can ride with an inflatable ring. It'll be fun. Come on."

Cammie sighed and unwrapped Taco's leash from her wrist, passed the stuffed fish to Griff and let Noah pull her back into their shared room.

"Taco, my man." Griff tucked the fish under his arm and went to retrieve his coffee. "I'm going to need a little bit of help with her. Please put on your thinking gills 'cause we've got work to do."

Beginning with what he was going to say to Daphne the next time he saw her.

Why was it, every time she had a few days off and her brilliant idea included nothing beyond sleeping in, Daphne found herself wide awake before the sun even came up?

She lay in bed, staring at the ceiling, her windows open to let the cross-breeze keep the house relatively cool. The humidity had barely ticked down overnight, but that wasn't the reason she couldn't sleep.

Seeing Griffin again after all these years, it brought so much back. But while she expected the pain of their breakup, rather the pain of his dumping her, to be foremost in her thoughts, it was all of the good times that rose to the top and made her smile.

Whatever had brought him back into her life, for however brief a moment, she would be eternally grateful for. If for no other reason than to remind herself that not everything that had happened before her moving to Nalani had been bad. Griff had been such a bright spot for a couple of years. A reason not to dread going to school or even dealing with her status-absorbed parents. She touched two fingers to her fast-beating heart. She couldn't wait to see him again. She shouldn't have to.

The ceiling fan whoop-whoop-whooped in its slow, steady rhythm, a rhythm that often easily helped to lull her to sleep, but not this morning. With a huff of excitement, she flung the sheet back and climbed out of bed, pausing only long enough to pick up her lightweight robe.

A while later, a hot cup of coffee beside her and her sketch pad and pencil in her hands, she sat curled up in the cushioned wicker chair on the back porch of her bun-

galow style home. This was her paradise that offered her
solitude and sanctuary. A house she'd decorated and fixed
up to her whims and desires, not at the behest of someone
else. The neighborhood was friendly, compact and offered
a helping hand if needed, with the gentle roar of the ocean
as background noise.

Here, surrounded by a burst of summer garden color,
she examined a printout of the photo she'd taken of the area
of the resort Mano had requested she put her attention on.

The idea was mostly the result of Jordan Adair's arrival
in Nalani last month. The vagabond surfer had shown up
with the hopes of getting Keane to train her for the upcoming surfing competition season. She'd convinced him,
of course. They'd all soon learned that Jordan definitely
had a persuasive way about her. Now that she'd found an
unexpected home here, she worked part-time for Ohana
Odysseys as Keane's assistant surf instructor and whatever else Sydney needed help with.

Originally, Jordan wanted to spend her time on the Big
Island traveling around in a rented van, or home on wheels,
but upon her arrival she'd discovered Nalani lacked one
thing she needed: a legal space to park. Commence an
amusing interplay between her and local law enforcement,
primarily Police Chief Alec Aheona Malloy. With the aid
of a number of residents, Daphne included, Jordan found
some entertaining solutions to her residential problem. Her
subsequent romance with Chief Malloy, which came as a
surprise to no one, resulted in her landing prime van-living
space in the chief's driveway only a few blocks from the
beach. But it was Jordan's experience with the zoning laws
and the issues her circumstances had raised that illustrated
how Nalani could improve itself even more.

Hence, Mano's notion to turn a significant previously
abandoned area of the resort property into dedicated

camper and van parking for those choosing to travel around the Big Island on their own. Motor home and van dwellers were an untapped customer base currently limited to day trips. As Mano rarely let an opportunity pass without giving it his full attention, he was in total solution mode. Even though his solutions rarely proved simple.

He didn't want a parking lot. He wanted island atmosphere that acted as an extension of the resort. He wanted paradise, nomad style.

Island atmosphere was where Daphne came in. Mano wanted color. He wanted a softening around the cement edges, and most importantly, he wanted a kind of meditative feel that would provide a place of quiet retreat for guests. He'd thrown all kinds of ideas at her as far as what he thought might work. Now, as Daphne's hand flew over the paper, she could envision just about everything he'd suggested as possible, including a dedicated shower and bath area that would service those without that equipment in their vehicles. He'd done his homework on the "van life ideal" and even consulted Jordan herself. If something was worth doing, Mano always did it the best way he could.

Sketching was second only to gardening when it came to Daphne pulling herself out of the circling thoughts of regret of the past. As the images took form, she could feel the tension that had been keeping her awake melt away. Her shoulders relaxed and the dull pounding in her head eased. The temperature dipped as the sun made its first appearance. Even as she shivered a bit in the transforming hours, she felt the promise of a new day—new possibilities—begin to take form.

There were no restrictions on her today. No obligations or appointments. She appreciated days like this, which Sydney had made certain to schedule for all Ohana

Odyssey employees at least once a month. Daphne's plans to recharge and reset today faded with each ticking second.

She added a cluster of snapdragons along the edge of a sketched collection of benches and tables situated at the edge of the property overlooking the ocean. Uki'uki, an island lily that produced bright purple berries, would be lovely, too. But even as she dotted in color with her pencils, she couldn't help but wonder what the day might bring for Griff and his children.

There was no stopping the smile that curved her lips at the thought of her onetime sweetheart. There had been moments, long ago, when she'd imagined the kind of man he'd become. The kind of father he'd be. The kind of life they might have together.

She couldn't be certain, of course, not after only a few minutes with him, but she'd venture to guess he'd lived up to her expectations, albeit in a completely different way than she'd dreamed. Whatever had made him choose to take his vacation in Nalani, he was here and it would be rude to refuse the universe's gift of a reunion. Wouldn't it?

She'd had enough surprises in her life. Too many, in fact. She tended to be leery of anything unexpected, but maybe Griff being here would cure her of that. Despite how things had ended between them, she rarely did anything other than smile whenever she thought of him.

By the time she swiped a purple pencil through a section of additional lilies she envisioned along the perimeter of the walkways, her coffee mug was empty and her feet were chilled. But she held out the tablet and tilted her head.

"I like it." She nodded, satisfied at this first attempt.

So many landscape designers used computer programs, clicking and pasting various elements onto a screen, but Daphne found she preferred the hands-on method, letting her imagination take flight, rather than reading suggestions initiated by technology. Of course, up until now all the plans she'd ever sketched out had been for her own property. She'd done something similar for Remy's front yard shortly after she'd arrived on the island, but she'd recognized that request for what it was: an offer to distract her from the life and problems she'd left behind on the mainland. But by completing the project, she'd dug out a new life for herself, with purpose and fulfillment. It was all she could have asked for.

Satisfied, she tore the sheet free and closed her notebook, gathered up her cup of pencils, her empty coffee mug and headed back inside.

Anxious as she was to get this initial rendering to Mano at the resort, she forced herself to slow down and tidy up the house. It amazed her how cluttered things could get when she was in full work mode.

The bamboo floors required a quick dusting. She did a load of laundry and fluffed and rearranged the pillows and blankets in the living room. Thankfully she wasn't a complete slob, so by the time she set the last dish in the sink to dry, she'd run out of chores.

She sent a quick text to Mano, checking to see when he'd be in his office. He answered almost immediately and said he had time for her after ten.

Yet again Daphne found herself wondering if the man ever stopped working. She knew the answer, but her friend's devotion to Hibiscus Bay hadn't come without a cost. His marriage had ended not too long after Daphne had settled in Nalani. At the time, Daphne had wondered if he'd realized the mistake he'd made, letting a woman like Emelia—who obviously loved him—go as easily as he had. But who was she to judge?

It didn't take long for her to shower and dress and tuck the folded-up sketch into a small, cross-body quilted purse she'd bought last summer at the Hawaiian Snuggler. The morning was officially in full swing.

She opted to ride her bike into town. She owned a car, but it gathered more pollen and dust than miles. She much preferred to walk or take her bike, which was painted a fun, cartoony turquoise blue and carried a bright pink-and-yellow woven basket between the handlebars as well as a pair of saddle baskets behind the seat. She could easily do her shopping or stop at one of the nurseries for seedlings or supplies and not have to lug them in her arms back up into the hills to her house.

The resulting breeze as she peddled through the hills into the heart of Nalani kept her in that bubble of peace she longed for. The closer she got to Pulelehua Road, the louder the ocean roared, and she found herself wondering if Griff and his kids had taken to exploring Nalani yet. There was so much to see and enjoy here and she hoped he saw everything that she did.

Today she would focus on the good and the beautiful, both of which were on full display in the greenery and flora in the front yards of the homes she rode past. Bikes leaned up against the sides of houses. Barrels of water collected the rain from their daily showers. A pair of cats—one orange and the other a sleek, shiny black, chased a butterfly through the grass before they rolled and splayed out in the warming sun.

Daphne eased on the brakes as she rode past the school where children still swarmed the playground even during their summer break. The spacious area teemed with kids ranging from five and six up to almost–high school age. Their shouts and cries and laughter were light enough to lift even the threat of dark clouds gathering. On days like this, she found herself giving silent thanks to whatever power—ahem, Remy Calvert—had brought her here.

Another two blocks had her easing around the corner onto the main drag. Before getting to the end of the road and the resort, she eased across the street and swooped to a stop in front of the semipermanent booth that had been built for one very special aunty.

"Morning, Maru." Daphne swung her bike to the side and left it beneath a palm tree with low-hanging limbs. Above the scent of the ocean, she could smell sugar and yeasty fried dough. "Howzit?"

"Daphne." Maru, a woman whose age rivaled that of Nalani itself, rocked in her wooden chair, her hand folded across the bulk of her stomach. Her smile, as always, carried the hint of curiosity and wisdom. "Aloha, *kakahiaka.*"

"Where's Lani? Or are you working all by yourself this morning?" Daphne teased and earned a chortle of amusement from the old woman.

"Here I am." Lani, Maru's granddaughter, popped up on the other side of the stall. "Just straightening things up. Had a good run this morning." She pointed at one of the many covered containers of breakfast goodness. "We've got the roasted pineapple *malasadas* you like. Freshly made this morning with lots and lots of love."

"I'll take three of those in a bag, please," Daphne told her. "And can I get a separate small box of four? Two regular coconut and two *lilikoi.*" Impulse, she thought, didn't have to be a bad thing. Sharing Manu's sweet treats with Griff and his kids might be a way to break whatever ice there was between them. She could just ask the bell clerk to take them to the room if she didn't encounter them on the resort or nearby.

She dug cash out of her purse and exchanged it for the sweet treats. Box and bag in hand, Daphne stopped in front of the rocking chair. "How've you been, Maru?"

"Maika'i," Maru said. *Okay.* She gripped the arms of

her chair as she rocked forward. "Heard you're designing a new area at the resort."

"Well, I put together a sketch for Mano," Daphne said. She shouldn't wonder how Maru had already heard about it. The woman heard everything that went on in Nalani. "I don't know if he's going to go with my ideas or not."

"It's good that he asked you," Maru said. "Laka has blessed you, gave you the touch with our lands and plantings. You understand what's important."

"Plants don't talk back," Daphne teased.

"Of course they do." Manu's expression sharpened. "They only speak in a different language. You help keep this place thriving and blooming. Whatever winds brought you to us, we are grateful."

Tears blurred her eyes. It took Daphne a bit off guard, hearing such gratitude from someone as well thought of as Maru. "I'm the one who's grateful." On impulse, she bent down and brushed a kiss on her cheek. "*Mahalo*, Maru."

"Aunty." Maru caught Daphne's arm and gave her a gentle squeeze. "You call me Aunty. Go on. Mano is waiting for you."

Daphne smiled. It was well known that Maru had a sense about everything going on in Nalani. Some said the wind didn't blow without her permission.

Daphne stashed the treats in the front basket on her bike and quickly steered down the street to the resort. Leaving the bike in the far corner by the outdoor bell desk, she waved at the employees as she headed inside. She reached into the bag and pulled out one of the still-warm doughnuts and strolled down the corridors to Mano's office.

"Morning, Alaua," she greeted Mano's assistant. "Did he tell you I was stopping by?"

"About five minutes ago." The affectionate frustration in the woman's voice was the result of years of loyal service. About the same age as Daphne, she wore her thick black hair in an intricate knot on the back of her head, her thin-rimmed glasses on the tip of her nose. "Go on in."

"Thanks." Daphne set one of the pineapple *malasadas* on a napkin on the desk. "Thought maybe you could use this."

"Mahalo."

Daphne knocked once on the double carved wood door before she pushed it open. "Morning." She poked her head in before stepping inside. Mano's office was a lot like the man: traditional yet unexpected and surprisingly open. The giant window on one side of the room overlooked the space the resort held available for special events like weddings and celebrations. "Just dropping off the sketch. And breakfast." The normally unflappable Mano looked more than a bit perturbed as she approached. "Something wrong?"

"Not really. Just an unexpected resignation." He flashed a smile and eyed the bag. "Maru?"

"Roasted pineapple *malasada*." She pulled out her own and bit in before she nudged the bag toward him. "Like you need the sugar rush."

"One thing I'll never say no to." But he left the bag where it was and accepted the sketch. "How'd you do?"

"You tell me." Until now she'd just been having a bit of fun with the plans, but now, as he unfolded the paper, nerves took root and sprouted to life inside her. "I based it on the budget you gave me. If you hate it, I won't be offended."

"Sure, you will," Mano said with a smile. "You're just too nice to say anything."

She pressed her lips together to hide her own grin. He really did know her well.

She stood there, munching on her doughnut, the seconds ticking away as he skimmed every inch of the paper.

"I like it." He nodded, slowly at first, then more enthusiastically. "I like it a lot. Especially this water feature here. Reminds me of Waiale Falls with how there's a larger and smaller flow. Yeah. I like it." He looked up at her. "You're hired."

"Hired to…" She didn't understand. "You want a more detailed schematic?"

"If you need it. I want you to do this. Oversee it. Hire the team to execute it, but I want your hands in the ground."

"Mano." Daphne had to set her food down. "I appreciate the offer, but I'm not a landscaper."

"All evidence to the contrary." He flipped her sketch around. "You understand the land, Daphne. More than that, you know what works and what doesn't and every plant you place in the ground you do so with respect. That's the kind of person I need overseeing the resort."

"The resort? You mean this project, right?" He wasn't offering her a job, was he? "Because my work at Ohana—"

"I don't expect you to leave Ohana Odysseys," Mano said. "Sydney would never forgive me for stealing you away, but this is something I can push off my plate onto someone who knows what they're doing and you can do it according to your own schedule. Mostly. I've got some other things in the pipeline that need my attention."

Daphne waited for more of an explanation, but when one wasn't forthcoming, she took a step back and sat down.

"The idea doesn't appeal?" he suggested at her silence.

"No, it does." More than appealed, actually. She loved her work as a tour guide and showing off the island, but being given the opportunity to create with what the island provided? "What does it pay?"

His lips quirked. "Straight to the point."

"No, I mean, yes." She tried not to blush. "I guess so, it's just…" She let out a long breath. "Sydney's asked me to buy into Ohana." She hesitated, uncertain of how much Mano knew.

"Remy's offer of partnership." Mano nodded. "The plan he was putting into play when he passed. Don't worry. Sydney and I have discussed it."

"Oh, good." She let out a breath. "That's a relief. So you got the email, too?"

"The one Remy didn't get a chance to send before he passed?" Mano's eyes darkened as if caught in shadows. "Yes. Sydney and I are working out the details of my investment. Keane's already bought in and Silas—"

"I lost touch with Silas a while back," Daphne admitted. "I don't know where—"

"He's still in San Francisco," Mano said. "With the SFPD. Although he took a desk job after he lost his wife. I reached out to him in a professional capacity a few months back about that company that attempted to buy Ohana Odysseys. He was able to get some information for me I thought we might need in the future."

"In the future?" Daphne asked. "I thought that whole buyout attempt was over and done. Sydney turned down the offer."

"Doesn't mean they aren't done trying. Golden Vistas doesn't surrender easily, if ever, so I thought it prudent to be cautious." Mano sighed. "Silas got the email about buying into Ohana. He didn't sound particularly anxious to talk about it, so I didn't push. I'm betting he feels guilty for losing touch with us even before Remy's death. The idea of buying into the business probably doesn't sit well at this point. He has a little girl to take care of and she's his priority. As she should be."

"It would be nice to see him." Daphne couldn't quite picture the Silas she knew in college as a part of the police, let alone a single dad. "Even if he just came out for a visit," Daphne said. "Maybe we can gang up on him and convince him to jump in."

"Maybe," Mano said slowly. "And you changed the subject."

"I did," Daphne laughed. The offer was beyond tempting. It was all she could do not to leap at the chance to try something new. "I need to talk to Sydney before accepting this. If my schedule can remain flexible—"

"As long as the project gets done, you can work any schedule you like," Mano said easily. "I'd like the landscaping completed by September so we can use it in our holiday advertising. That's when our new brochures go out and when the website will be updated. I'd like to include the new campground and amenities by then."

"Okay. I'll let you know by—"

"Tomorrow," Mano said. "If you say no it's going to take me time to find someone else."

"Because I'm your first choice?" she teased.

"No." Mano plucked the bag off the desk and peered inside. "Because right now you're my only choice."

Chapter Five

Aside from a few morning snacks, the poolside hut wasn't going to cut it for breakfast. Griff needed something more than fruit salad and orange juice to push him through the day. Noah's room service idea didn't seem quite so bad looking back. Not when the alternative was the main dining location that was far more formal than he was comfortable with at the moment.

"Dad, can't we just go swimming?" Noah whined as Griff led them back into the hotel, where he followed the signs to the Seven Seas, the only restaurant on resort property. It was higher end from what he'd read of the menu, but desperate times...

"Breakfast first, then play."

"I don't wanna go swimming." Cammie's pouting was heading for gold medal status. Nothing Griff had said or done pulled her out of her disappointed funk. Not that he was done trying.

"Then you can just sit with me in one of the cabanas," Griff told her. "Let's see." He planted his hands on his hips, debated between Seven Seas or exploring the town outside the resort. "I'm thinking we'll take a walk, yeah?" Noah sighed, Cammie glowered and Griff struggled to hold on to his patience. "Okay, guys, I think we all need an attitude adjustment. No, things haven't gone as we planned, but we adjust and find a way to have fun."

"I wanna see princesses," Cammie grumbled.

"I want to go swimming," Noah said.

And Griff wanted a do-over for the past few days. "Well, we'll just have to see what happens. Wait here, please." He walked over to the bell desk and the young man standing behind the counter. "Aloha."

"Aloha, Mr. Townsend." His badge displayed the name Oliwa and he smiled that now-familiar island smile of welcome Griff was becoming quite fond of. "What can I help you with this morning?"

"Breakfast. Nothing fancy," Griff added quickly and pointed to the Seven Seas.

"Can't beat the Hut-Hut." Oliwa set a printed copy of a town map on the counter and circled a place in bright pink. "Local food and also some familiar fare for little ones. If you need coffee and something quick, I suggest Vibe. Beats any large chain back on the mainland, in my opinion. And they're right across the street from the main beach walkway."

"It's never too early for the beach." Griff turned at the voice and found Daphne standing nearby, a small pink box in her hand.

He couldn't believe she'd sneaked up on him. She'd cleaned up to the point that she practically glowed. Her healthy, slightly tanned skin glistened and she'd left her luxurious red hair long and down her back. The thin-strapped blousy tank she wore, along with the snug black shorts, displayed fit arms and toned legs that, near as he could tell, went on forever. "Aloha, Daphne."

"Aloha." She hefted the box. "I thought maybe you and the kids might like an island treat this morning. *Mala-sadas*."

"Doughnuts?" Griff's stomach growled in anticipation. "I think we have a winner. Oliwa was telling me about Vibe. Can I buy you a cup of coffee?"

Oliwa chuckled, then shrugged at Daphne's arched brow. "Never known Daphne to say no to coffee," he said quickly.

"Nice save," Daphne said, smiling. "Come on." She angled her head toward the door. "We've missed the early morning rush, so it shouldn't take too long."

"Noah? Cammie?" Griff called his kids over. "Noah, you remember Ms. Mercer?"

"Daphne," Daphne corrected. "Good morning, Noah. And you must be Cammie." She crouched down to meet Cammie eye to eye. "You were asleep when I last saw you. How do you like your room?"

"It's awesome!" Noah announced. "Cammie and I have our own room and we had room service for dinner and the TV is like this big!" He held his arms out wide.

Cammie shrugged and hugged Taco tight against her chest.

"Who's this?" Daphne reached out to tug on Taco's fin, but Cammie twisted it out of her reach.

"Taco." Cammie eyed Daphne with suspicion. "He's my friend."

"Hello, Taco. I hope you're ready to have some fun here in Nalani. Do you like doughnuts, Cammie?" Daphne asked his daughter. "I thought maybe you'd like a treat. They're special in Hawai'i and someone here in Nalani makes the best ones I've ever had."

"I think they sound yummy," Noah said. "Don't you, Cammie?"

Another shrug, but there was at least interest in her doubtful eyes.

"Let's go find out, shall we?" Griff suggested, slinging his small camera bag higher on his shoulder. "I think there's some hot chocolate calling your names." Maybe an unhealthy dose of sugar would improve his daughter's mood. "Vibe has hot chocolate, don't they?"

"Oh, they most definitely do." Daphne stood up. "It's just a couple blocks into town."

"Great," Griff said. "Let's move."

Griff was hoping the walk would continue to ease his daughter's sour mood. Sullen, silent Cammie faded into the background as an engaged and intrigued one emerged, pointing and commenting and lamenting all the beautiful things displayed in the shop windows as they meandered alongside other morning visitors. The town seemed to vibrate with a positive energy all its own. Even if Cammie wasn't enamored of the offerings, from her conversation with Taco, her fish certainly was.

There was something about the air here on the islands that smelled and *felt* different from any other place he'd ever been. There was the warmth, certainly. And the humidity that kissed the gentle breeze with that hint of moisture. But inhaling that fragrance of the ocean, which was only steps away, seemed to clear out the lungs, defog his mind of all the emotion and mental baggage he'd brought with him. He still had no idea how to even broach the subject of Daphne's father, let alone convince her to visit him. Nor did he like the cloud of deception hanging over his head.

As they walked toward the corner and paused at the crosswalk, he found himself scrambling for a safe topic of conversation. "How did your meeting go?"

"My meeting?" Daphne appeared genuinely flummoxed by his question.

"With the hotel manager?"

"Oh, Mano, right." She smiled and nodded. "It went fine. Great, actually."

"Noah," Griff called out. "Please stay with your sister." He noticed his son about to protest but then quickly change his mind when Cammie pointed to a giant seashell in the next storefront window. "I sure hope they like traveling. We can go... Oh, sorry." Griff shook his head. "Please, continue."

"Don't apologize. It's nice to see how close you and your kids are. As for Mano, he's planning on turning a back lot of the resort into camper and van parking for people on the road. He asked if I'd put some design ideas together to keep the landscaping in line with the rest of Hibiscus Bay. I dropped off my initial sketches this morning. That's why I was at the resort."

Obviously, she didn't want him thinking she'd turned up because of him. And yet she'd brought them breakfast.

Griff's lips twitched. "I'm going to assume your sketches passed approval."

"Why would you say that?"

"Because when it comes to flowers and plants and pretty much everything that grows in the ground—" children included; he thought of her unflappable attitude in the face of Cammie's grumpy mood "—you've always had a bit of a magical touch."

She smiled. "That's very sweet of you to say."

"Sweet yet true," Griff said. "So, am I right? Did he like your plans?"

"He did." Her smile was quick and a bit embarrassed. "He asked me to oversee the entire project and act as landscape designer." She let out a laugh, shook her head. "Something new. I mean, I've helped friends with their yards, suggested certain ideas and even done some plantings, but never something on this scale. It's exciting to think about."

"And intimidating?" Griff asked, recognizing even after all these years that uncertainty and self-doubt she'd had a tendency to fall back on.

"A little, maybe. But I'd like to do it. I just need to make the time for it."

Griff wondered if she knew how her voice gentled whenever she talked about anything remotely related to gardening. "I remember all those plants and flowers you used to grow in the greenhouse back in Oregon," he said. "That gardener of yours—"

"Felix." There was no mistaking the fondness in her tone. "Felix Mercado. He had unending patience with all my questions. I still wonder if he gave me that little corner of his work area just to keep me quiet."

"More like he wanted to encourage your interest." Griff had never given much consideration to gardening or plants and flowers before he met Daphne. But once he'd seen her in her element, and it was very clearly where she belonged, in that expansive and meticulously groomed garden of hers, he'd never looked at nature in quite the same way.

Since then he didn't look at a flower without thinking about Daphne or her ability to make them bloom just by walking into their space it seemed.

"Do you keep in touch with him?" He cast a passing glance to the large market on the corner across from the resort. Luanda's boasted a one-stop shop for everything from quick meals to necessities like toothpaste and postcards. Did anyone still send postcards? he wondered.

"I do." Daphne crossed her arms across her chest. "Felix's wife, Calida, was our head housekeeper and one of my nannies when I was little." She shook her head, rolled her eyes. "That sounds so pretentious. But they were both great. After…" She caught herself, glanced down, then after a deep breath, lifted her chin again. "They've retired now, moved down south to be near their kids. They celebrated their fortieth wedding anniversary last summer. I get pictures every once in a while and lovely little notes at the holidays."

"You miss them."

"I do." She nodded. "They were always very lovely to me. Uh-oh." She pointed to Cammie, who had detoured into Luanda's. "Someone's gotten distracted by all the shiny things." Sure enough, Noah looked back at them with a pained look of exasperation.

"Daaaaaad," he whined. "I'm staaaarving."

"I'll get her." Griff ducked inside and made his way around a rack of clearance clothes and a shelf of discounted packaged snacks. "Cammie." It took him a second to find her and when he did she was standing beneath a selection of wind chimes and spinning glass suncatchers. Without looking down, he unzipped his camera bag and pulled out the Canon camera he'd had for the better part of ten years. Lifting the camera to his eye, he aimed, focused. Waited.

As the sun streamed through the front window, it caught and reflected sunbeams against the walls and surrounding merchandise.

Click.

"Aren't they pretty, Daddy?" Cammie pointed up at a blue glass circle displaying a sea turtle. It was maybe six inches around and beautifully handmade. Without even looking at the picture he'd taken, he stashed his camera once more.

"Those are *honu*." A young man wearing bright blue board shorts, flip-flops and a white tank that told everyone to "Hang Loose" joined them. "They're sacred animals of the islands."

"What does that mean?" Cammie asked Griff.

"It means they're very highly thought of," Griff said. "I've read you aren't supposed to touch them if you see any in the wild."

"True that," the young man said. "They represent wisdom and good luck. There's a sanctuary here on the Big Island, down south. The black sand beach there is filled with them."

"Sanctuary means it's where they're safe, Cammie," Griff told his daughter.

"Can we go see them, Daddy?" Cammie hugged Taco higher on her chest, a look of wonder on her face. "I won't touch them, I promise."

"We'll see," Griff said. "We only just got here yesterday," he told the young man. "We're still finding our island legs."

"Aloha. Nalani welcomes you both. I'm Koho. A gift." He held out a small *honu* charm necklace to Cammie. "Aloha, Cammie."

"Oooh, thank you."

"*Mahalo* means *thank you* in Hawaiian," he told her.

"*Mahalo,*" she whispered and held up the black cord. "Daddy, can I wear it now?"

"*Mahalo,*" Griffin told the young man. "But it isn't necessary—"

"My brother makes these charms," Koho said as he stood up. "And the suncatchers. Plenty more of them at home. Sometimes gifts choose the person. She lit up when she saw them. I could see it across the store." He slapped a hand on Griff's shoulder. "Signs are everywhere, brah. You just have to be on the lookout for them. Aloha."

"Aloha." Griff guided Cammie back out of the store, not an easy feat as she couldn't take her eyes off the necklace.

The second they stepped outside, she turned and handed it to Griff to put it on her.

Griff tried to unlatch the tiny hook, but his fingers fumbled.

"Let me?" Daphne offered. "If that's okay with you, Cammie?"

"I guess." She didn't look overly thrilled.

Daphne latched the necklace and Cammie covered it with her hand.

"What do you say, Cammie?" Griff prodded.

"Mahalo," Cammie said again but kept her chin down.

"If you have the chance, you should come to story time at the resort," Daphne said. "Many of our locals give classes and lectures on various sea and animal life in the area."

"Is that like school?" Cammie was clearly not impressed.

"Fun school," Daphne said without missing a beat. "And if you're really interested, I'd be happy to check the schedule at Ohana Odysseys, see what boat trips we have open during your stay. Unless you've already made plans for a tour or excursion?"

"We have absolutely no plans for anything," Griff assured her. "We are open to suggestions."

"Oh." She blinked and smiled. "Okay, then."

"It was very nice of that young man to give Cammie that necklace," Griff said. "Does that happen often?"

"Yes," Daphne confirmed.

"Giving things away," Griff observed. "How does anyone stay in business in Nalani?"

"Easily. Generosity is a way of life," Daphne assured him. "And what we give, we get back tenfold. It's one of the many reasons why I love it here so much. Everything's easy. Drama- and conflict-free. I'm so glad you're here, Griff." The happiness in her voice felt like a kick to his heart. "It's good to see you. Must be some powerful force in the universe sent you here for vacation."

"Yeah." Guilt nibbled at Griff's intentions. "Definitely a powerful force." He'd come here at the behest of her father, a man who was nothing but drama and conflict. Chances were pretty high she wouldn't appreciate the irony.

They made small talk as they continued down the block, past the homemade candle store, Inoa's Glass Shack, which fortunately Cammie missed because she was too busy admiring her new present, a pair of papered windows with a sign announcing a forthcoming cookie store. Next door to that was a quilt business called The Hawaiian Snuggler.

"Just up there a bit." Daphne pointed overhead to the wooden sign depicting a coffee cup chilling out on a lounge chair. "Be prepared. One cup of their Kona coffee and nothing on the mainland will ever suffice again."

"Consider me warned," Griff said.

A few minutes later, they emerged with Griff holding a cardboard tray of filled cups and carrying a paper bag filled with a selection of small, healthier breakfast options than doughnuts. He followed Daphne and the kids across the street to a collection of picnic tables lined up along the edge of the beach, lowered his camera case onto the table.

"Noah." Griff had to call his son over to the table as he unloaded their drinks, napkins and food. "You can check out the water after you eat something."

Cammie immediately took a seat next to Griff while Daphne popped open the box. "I stuck with the classics," she said as Noah joined them and sat beside her. "If you like these, there are about a dozen more flavors Manu makes fresh every morning for her stand." She pointed in the direction of the stand.

Griff removed the lids from the kids' hot chocolate and handed them each an English muffin sandwich.

"What's in it?" Cammie pried off the top and stared down at her breakfast.

"Spam," Griff told her. "It's a kind of ham. Try it. If you don't like it, you can take it off."

Cammie sighed and Griff found himself wondering yet again if the entire trip was going to go this way. She nibbled at the edges, took a bigger bite, then, after chewing a bit, nodded.

"It's okay."

"High praise," Griff teased as they ate. Noah was done first but only because, Griff realized, he wanted first crack at the *malasadas*. "Go ahead," he said when his son looked at him in expectant silence, then enjoyed the sight of Noah biting into his first real island delicacy.

"Mmmmm." He licked powdered sugar off his lips. "This is so good! Thanks, Daphne."

"You're very welcome. No, thanks." She declined Griff's offer of the box. "I already ate my quota for the day. So, you don't have any plans for your stay?"

"Not a one," Griff said and had to admit, she was right about the coffee. He was going to have to stock up before they headed home.

"I want to learn to surf!" Noah announced before he took another bite of the pillowy, filled fried dough. "Mr. Mano said there were lessons."

"There are," Daphne said. "You can make reservations at the bell desk if you want to give it a shot."

"Can I, Dad?" Noah's eyes were as wide as Griff had ever seen them. "I really want to try."

"Sure." Noah was notorious for his initial enthusiasm with different activities and hobbies—guitar, skateboarding, dirt biking and baseball, to name a few—but inevitably his interest slipped in a few short weeks. It had always driven Lydia around the bend, but Griff always saw it as

Noah exploring his interests and learning what worked and what didn't for him.

"Can we go down to the water now?" Noah asked when he'd finished his doughnut.

"I don't wanna." Cammie was still nibbling at her breakfast, but had made her way through enough of her sandwich that she'd earned at least part of one of the *malasadas*.

"Daaaaaad." Noah dropped his head back with a dramatic sigh. "She's so annoying."

"Am not," Cammie shot back.

"Are, too, and you're ruining our vacation," Noah accused.

"Noah, that's enough." Griff inclined his chin toward the water. "If you want to go down to the shore, go ahead. Just stay in sight, by that lifeguard there and only get your feet wet. Cammie can hang out with us while we talk."

"Awesome." The second Noah untangled himself from the bench, Cammie spun in her seat to follow, after which she unlatched her wristband and pushed Taco into Griff's arms. She jog-walked to catch up with her brother.

"Thought that might do it," Griff said, craning his head to make certain they remained visible. "She can't stand it when he does something without her."

When he looked back at Daphne, he found her watching him, her chin resting in her palm, a smile curving her perfect lips. "You love every second of it, don't you? Being a dad."

"I really do." He chuckled. "I wasn't always a good one. It took me a while to realize what was important."

"Are they why you stopped working on the road?"

"Yeah." Guilt twisted in his belly and he took a long drink of his coffee. "Yeah, I saw enough working those last few years in some awful circumstances to realize I was completely missing how good I had it. My kids were happy, healthy, well cared for and safe. Can't really say that for every part of the world."

"That's still a constant companion for you." She motioned to the camera bag at his elbow.

"Ever since I was ten." His now-late uncle, a wannabe photographer, had hoped to catch Griff's interest with his own. He'd never have imagined just how obsessive Griff had become over the years. Most people stressed if their cell phone wasn't in their hand. With Griff, it was all about the camera. "I've upgraded since high school." He pulled his camera out again and, with barely any effort, centered Noah and Cammie not far from them and caught their first steps into this part of the Pacific. "It's still magic."

He wondered if she remembered all the pictures he'd taken of her. Capturing her quiet moments in her garden, or when they'd been out with friends or even by themselves.

"I'm not quite so compulsive anymore," he added and put the camera down. "I've been trying to remember to live in the moment and not be so worried about capturing things for posterity. Especially since there are a lot of pictures I never even look at again."

Daphne glanced over her shoulder. "Some moments are worth it, though."

"Yeah," he agreed. "Some moments are." It was odd, feeling at peace with her, despite keeping the truth about his visit from her. In almost every way it was as if the years between them had vanished and his feelings, his almost overwhelming feelings about her, surged to the forefront once more.

"You did good work, with pictures and words." Daphne took another sip of her coffee and sat back a little. "I follow you on social media. You got into some pretty dangerous situations. Glad to know you got out of them all okay."

"Yeah?" He was glad he didn't know that before now.

He might have been a tad self-conscious if he'd known she was reading his posts. "I don't post a lot now that I'm staying put. I doubt most people would be interested in the trials and tribulations of a single dad. Not as much job security in ordinary life versus chaos, but I'm doing what I can to keep things going."

"I'm sure there's an audience out there for everything. What happened? With their mother?"

"Lydia?"

"If you'd rather not talk about it—"

"No, it's fine." He shrugged in a manner that was clear evidence of where Cammie got her attitude from. "Lydia liked the romantic notion of being married to an international journalist more than she enjoyed the reality of it. We met in New York a little over ten years ago. I'd just gotten back from spending six months in the Sudan and she was attentive and sparkly and exciting and so far removed from everything I'd been dealing with that I let myself get distracted." And he'd needed a distraction—any kind of distraction—from the suffering he'd witnessed.

"Then she got pregnant with Noah, so we got married," he continued. "She didn't anticipate me wanting to keep my home base in Oregon and, well…" He inclined his head and sighed. "She got bored very quickly. She wasn't particularly fond of motherhood and my parents weren't able to help as expected. Then Cammie came along and my reputation got bigger, so the stories drew me farther away and for longer periods of time." It was hard, admitting the truth. But he wasn't about to shy away from it. He'd stayed away because, in a sense, it was easier than all the arguing and bickering, neither of which was good for the kids. His thought at the time was that it was better to be absent than cause them damage. "It wasn't the life she'd anticipated and didn't want. She filed for divorce a little over two years ago and told me she was done. With all of it." He hesitated. "Me and the kids."

Daphne winced, glancing over at Noah and Cammie. "How are they doing with that?"

"With her being gone? Okay, for the most part." The disappointment in Lydia, and himself, surged. "It is what it is, right? She's gone on to live whatever life she is happy to live. New rich husband who thrives on social entertaining and being the center of attention. She just has a tendency to make promises she can't keep. That's the truly bad part."

"Like taking the kids to Florida." She dropped a hand over his and, for a moment, everything inside him quieted. "They must have been so upset."

"I don't know that there's a word for what they are. Cammie especially. It's a hard lesson to learn when you're six. That your mother doesn't want to be your mother anymore."

"It's a hard lesson to learn at any age," Daphne said.

He hadn't meant to walk down this particular road, at least not in this fashion. "I'm sorry. I didn't mean to bring—"

Daphne waved off his concern. "I hate to say it, but I probably understand Lydia better than you do. She sounds a lot like my mother. Expectations for the life she hoped to have with my father didn't exactly meet with reality and motherhood." She laughed a little. "I always felt like kind of, I don't know, an afterthought. Or a kind of doll they dressed up and put on display when the need arose."

He remembered her feeling like that all too well. There was a time it had been his all-consuming focus that she never ever felt anything other than completely herself when they were together. He'd wanted her to bloom, to flourish, not because of her parents, but more like in spite of them.

"Do you know," she said with a light laugh, "I haven't

worn a pair of heels since I moved to Nalani? The last ones I did wear were to my mother's funeral."

"I read about it when she died." He'd been in Taiwan when he'd heard about Veronica Mercer's death. He'd wanted to be there for Daphne. Reading those online headlines, seeing the pictures of her scrambling to get out from under the attention of the press camped outside the Mercer compound's front door. "I'm sorry you had to go through all that alone."

He'd come so close to getting on a plane and coming back but he hadn't. Because it would have meant facing the mistake he'd made years before when he'd been too young to understand the consequences of being unable to stand up for himself. Or for her.

"It's just as well you didn't." Her smile now was quick and bitter. "I know this is going to sound harsh, Griff, but it's probably best that she left when she did. Lydia," she added as if she needed to clarify. "If she'd stayed, she'd have only made everyone around her miserable and that isn't what you or your children deserve."

"Maybe." He lifted Taco and held him out to Daphne. "I hand-wash this thing at least once a week." He spun it around, looked into its googly ping-pong ball eyes. "And when I give it back to Cammie, it's like I'm giving her the world. Every time." He let his gaze wander to the shore where Noah and Cammie splashed in the water and chased each other in the damp sand. "As far as I'm concerned, being a dad's the best job in the world."

"Then it's definitely Lydia's loss," Daphne said. "But enough about her. How're your mom and dad doing?"

"Dad's had a series of strokes over the past couple of years. Another reason I came back to Oregon. Mom was trying to deal with everything herself." He didn't mention the fact that he hadn't heard about his father's health issues until months later. His mother hadn't wanted to "bother" him. The instant sympathy in Daphne's eyes had him flinching. "The last stroke left him in a bad state. He can't speak. I still talk to him over video or when I visit, of course, but…it's not the same anymore."

"I'm so sorry." Daphne squeezed his hand. "I know how close you are with him."

"I'm thankful they're living somewhere that Mom can be watched over, as well. She won't leave his side." He blew out a long breath. "They're in an assisted living facility now. Dad's retirement only covers a portion of his care. Mom's finally agreed to sell the house. I think part of her was clinging to the idea of moving back in at some point."

"But it's not possible?"

"I don't think so," he said and tried to ignore the gut punch of reality. "I've managed to stay on top of things so far, but I took a pretty big pay cut when I moved back home. I think the hardest thing is that my parents are in their early sixties." Disbelief was rarely far behind when he talked about this subject. "None of us expected anything like this for a good long time."

"Even when you do expect it, there's no taking the sting out of it," she said. "Your mom and dad were always very nice to me. Your mom especially."

"My mother has never forgiven me for breaking up with you," Griff confessed. "Seriously," he added when she laughed. "Especially after she met Lydia. 'Why couldn't you make things work with that lovely Daphne girl of yours, Griff? What did you do wrong?'" Oh, so many things he'd wanted to say.

"You didn't do anything wrong." Daphne's second hand joined her first in covering his. "We were kids, Griff. We didn't know anything about anything and I only had stars in my eyes when it came to you."

If only it were that simple.

"How about now?" he attempted to tease her. "Any stars left for me?"

"Maybe one or two," she admitted with a more serious gleam in her eye than expected. "There wasn't room for me in the future you wanted, Griff. You were right about that." There was a sadness now. On her face. In her voice. "It hurt when you told me that, but I eventually understood and accepted that you were right. Besides, it's just as well you didn't have to ride out my father's trial with me. That wouldn't have done your journalism career much good."

"I was stupid to walk away from you." And he hadn't been right. If anything, breaking up with her had been the biggest mistake of his life. But he couldn't wish things were different; if they were he wouldn't have two fabulous kids who filled his life with sunshine. Most of the time.

It wouldn't make any difference now, to tell her the truth about the source for their breaking up. To admit that he'd been caught between saving his father's job, his family's income, his college future and wanting a life with her was too much, would have been too much then. He liked where they were now, on the other side of something that had caused them both so much heartache. But he couldn't make the same mistake twice. He couldn't lie to her. Not again. Not if he had any hope… "Daphne, about your father—"

"Stop." Her command was gentle, yet firm. "I want to spend time with you while you're here, Griff. I want to get to know you again and get to know your kids and show you around the island. But…" Her thumb rubbed against the back of his knuckles. "I've got rules and my main one is I don't talk about my father. I've already broken that rule enough today, so that part of the conversation's done. I don't want him anywhere near this place. Not even to speak of. Okay?"

He nodded before he thought it through; before he reminded himself he'd be lying to her every moment of every day that followed and yet... "Yeah." He nodded again and offered a quick smile. "Yeah, I get it. We'll keep the past in the past."

"Thank you." Her relieved smile tugged at his heart.

"I should come clean about one thing, though."

Her brow arched. "What's that?"

"I didn't decide on Hawai'i on a lark, Daphne." His mind raced for a truth-adjacent lie. "I knew you were here. I wanted to see you again. Wanted to see if maybe..." Maybe there was still a spark. Still a chance. And now he did. What had been a spark years ago had, over the years, turned into a full-fledged inferno. It hadn't been his idea to come here, of course. But now that he was... "I came here to see you."

She blinked as quickly as a hummingbird beat its wings. "Well." She cleared her throat. "That's just about the most wonderful thing I've heard in a very long time."

He caught sight of Noah racing up the beach toward them.

"Dad!" Noah yelled and waved his arms. "Dad, come on! Come in the water with us!"

"I think you're being paged," Daphne teased. "Have a good day with your kids." She stood up, tugging him with her as he had yet to relinquish his hold on her hand. "I'll see you tonight for dinner."

They stepped clear of the table and he waited for her to turn and walk away. But she didn't. Instead, she moved close to him, reached one hand up to the side of his face and rose high on her toes. How she brushed her mouth against his felt like a butterfly's kiss. Soft, teasing and full of promise.

"Daphne." He wanted her to stay, to stay with him, with

them, for the day. He didn't want to take the chance of letting her go for fear he'd never be with her again.

"I'll see you tonight, in the lobby. At six." She rubbed her thumb across his lips and eased her hold on his hand. He stood there, watching, as she walked down the street back to the resort. And out of sight.

"Coming! I'm coming." Daphne darted out of the bathroom, still trying to thread her opal flower earring through the piercing in her ear. Her bare feet slapped on the hardwood floor as she hurried to the front door.

She pulled it open and smoothed a hand down the front of the sky blue wrap dress that had been hanging unworn in her closet for the past couple of months. This was the third outfit she'd tried on and she still wasn't sure it was right.

"Pua." Daphne poked her head out and looked past her neighbor to the house next door. "Is everything okay? Did Tux get out?" She hadn't seen the escape-prone cat since she'd arrived home. Then she caught sight of the parchment-wrapped package in Pua's hands. Daphne sniffed the air and felt her blood sugar spike. "You've been baking again."

Pua, who was somewhere north of sixty with the enthusiastic optimism of a toddler, had lived in Nalani all her life and filled her days with cooking and baking for Daphne and the rest of their neighbors on Ahua Road. With a sharp gray streak running through her still mostly black hair, Pua's round face and rather full-ish figure definitely made her the personification of an island aunty.

"New recipe," Pua boasted and pushed the package into Daphne's hands. "Banana and taro loaf. Makes for a good breakfast. Or to take hiking with you," Pua added, then looked Daphne up and down. "Pretty dress. Bare feet. Jewelry." She smiled slowly. "You have a date."

Definitely not the right dress.

Daphne touched a finger to the solitary black pearl at her throat. "A date?" She almost squeaked out the words. "No, not exactly. An old friend is here from the mainland and we're having dinner. With his children," she added as if that didn't make things sound even more interesting. The fact that she'd been arguing with herself most of the day over whether this evening's dinner plan was indeed a date wasn't something she planned to dwell on. "Come in, please. I have a few minutes before I need to leave." She also had the sudden urge to change. "Would you like some tea?"

Even before Pua responded, Daphne retreated to the small, open kitchen just off the living room and pulled open the fridge. She always kept a pitcher of her own concoction—orange pekoe tea with pineapple juice, a quick simple syrup and a handful of crushed mint leaves from the overspilling herb garden in her kitchen window—on hand.

Daphne grabbed two tall glasses out of her dark blue hand-painted cabinets. The screen door banged shut behind Pua as she stepped inside. The older woman stopped for a moment and took a deep breath. "Always feels like I'm walking into an oxygen tent when I step foot in here. In a good way."

Daphne grinned. "Yeah, I know. It's overkill with the plants."

In addition to her tours and classes at Hilo University, she'd inadvertently become a bit of a plant whisperer here in Nalani. Her home—a lovely two-bedroom bungalow with a huge screened-in front porch and enormous back and side yard—was considered a triage of sorts, where people from all over town brought their crisis-ridden plants to her in the hopes of bringing them to full bloom or, in dire situations, back to life.

She filled Pua's glass, then switched her glass for an insulated tumbler from the drying rack and, after filling it, stuck the pitcher in the fridge. "I'm going to save this for breakfast." She hefted the substantial loaf in one hand and placed it in front of the breadbox.

She'd spent most of her life living in showplaces. Homes that had been elegantly designed for appearances rather than comfort. When she'd moved to Nalani, she'd promised herself she'd fill her house with things that made her smile. The bright colors made her feel as if she lived inside a rainbow and the furniture was worn in and covered in soft fabrics. Her home never once made her feel anything but safe and happy. The countless plants hanging from the ceiling or perched on shelving units and a grouping of stands of different heights added that touch of nature that she'd strived to surround herself with back on the mainland.

"I haven't seen you since you got back from visiting your sister in Maui." Daphne leaned her arms on the counter and tried not to mentally go through her closet again. The welcome leis she'd picked up at Aloha Flowers—a small, off-white blossom one for Cammie and two kukui nut ones for Griff and Noah—sat on the edge of the counter so she wouldn't forget them.

Cammie's lei filled the entire room with that punchy floral scent that tickled Daphne's nose. She did not want to walk into this evening with anything other than the expectation of having dinner with a friend. Getting ahead of herself always got her into trouble. "Everything okay?"

Pua nodded, sipped and, after a smile of approval, reached across the butcher block countertop and patted Daphne's hand. "Everything is okay. The trip isn't as easy as it once was, but it was good to see my *ohana*. My nieces and nephews definitely command a lot of attention, but good attention."

Daphne could hear the trace of loneliness in her neighbor's voice. Pua's husband had died more than fifteen years before and they'd never been blessed with children, which was such a shame. Pua was a born nurturer and motherly type. Daphne should know. She'd been on the receiving end of Pua's attention from the moment she'd first walked through this house. Instead of children, Pua had an entire neighborhood of people who considered her their family. Aunty. Their *ohana*. Daphne included.

"Knock, knock."

Daphne stood up straight and Pua turned on her stool as Wyatt Jenkins rapped his knuckles on the door frame and toed off his sneakers before pulling open the screen door.

"Howzit, Aunty. Daph. Got your message about wanting something built for your backyard." With his teen-idol good looks, thick sun-kissed curly hair and a physique that was often the talk of many female gatherings, Wyatt was the kind of guy who would do anything for anyone. He lived life with an open heart and an open spirit that often just made everyone's day better. "Nice dress." He had that big-brother twinkle in his eye. "Who's the guy?"

"That's it." Daphne slapped a hand down on the counter. "I'm going to change." Again. "Entertain Pua, will you? Then I'll show you what I have in mind for the backyard."

"Sure thing."

"And there's tea in the fridge for you!" she called over her shoulder. Ten minutes later she'd returned the dress to her closet and opted for a comfortable pair of khaki shorts and a bright yellow strap tank. She left the necklace on and rather than tying her hair down in its usual braid left it loose down her back.

She could feel sixteen-year-old Daphne surging to the surface, with just as much excitement and nervousness as she'd felt once upon a time. She could still remember the butterflies she'd had when, after working together on a school science project, Griffin had clumsily asked her out to a movie. Insecurities at seventeen tended to be far more amusing than they were in adulthood. Even if she hadn't been hoping he'd ask, she'd have said yes just to put him out of his misery.

He'd been the first person to see her as an independent person, not the spoiled daughter of a wealthy businessman. With Griff, she could talk about all the things that never seemed to matter to anyone else, her parents included. Her dreams, her ambitions, her interests that were so far out of whack with everyone around her they isolated her even more. But with Griff...

Griff had always seen her for her. For a while, he'd been her biggest cheerleader and her protector. He'd stood between her and the affluent crowd she had no interest in being a part of. Dating Griff had given her the excuse she'd needed to step into her own life; a life that, before him, had seemed impossibly out of reach.

He'd been so kind, so encouraging. She'd seen that again, today, sitting across from him at the beach. Before Griff, she hadn't known what it was like to feel so... loved before. In his eyes, there hadn't been anything she couldn't do.

Before Griff she never would have had the courage to step out from behind her parents' expectations and map out plans for herself. Quiet, sullen, suffocated Daphne had been easily led, but happy, confident Daphne?

Happy, confident Daphne possessed the courage and temerity to reject her parents' control and step into her own life.

She had little doubt her father thought encouraging her to break up with Griff would have her scurrying back into that bubble of affluence and society she'd been brought up in, but once a butterfly was transformed, there was no going back into the cocoon. She'd grown beyond them and learned to stand up for herself.

As she looked in the mirror, for an instant, she could see trace hints of who she'd been before knowing, before loving, Griff. That insecure, intimidated girl who had been so worried about letting her parents down, of failing them, of disappointing them, was still inside.

She traced a finger over the black pearl at her throat. She'd done the work. She'd gotten herself to where she was now, but all she'd become might not have been possible had it not been for Griffin Townsend loving her all those years ago.

And for that, she definitely owed him her thanks. Dinner would be on her. Maybe an excursion, too? Neither seemed as valuable as what Griff had gifted her.

When she returned to the kitchen, she found Wyatt and Pua deep in conversation and Wyatt about a quarter of the way through her banana and taro bread. "Saving me from calories, I see," she teased as she leaned around him to reach for her tea.

"Always happy to help out a friend." Wyatt's grin was almost infectious. "It's delicious, Aunty."

He kissed Pua on the cheek. It was, Daphne thought, one of the things she loved most about life here on the islands. Friends, especially older friends, became family. Whatever she'd lost, she'd found something even more precious in Nalani.

"Makes me wish I lived within walking distance of your cottage," Wyatt added.

Pua got to her feet and set her empty glass in the sink.

"I might get up your way one of these days," she told him. "*Mahalo* for the tea, Daphne." She followed Daphne and Wyatt toward the door, and while Daphne pulled a pair of sandals out of the cubby by the stairs to wear into town, Aunty returned next door.

"You didn't answer my question," Wyatt said as he put his shoes back on. "Who's the guy?"

"Just someone I knew in high school." She leaned down to buckle the thin strappy sandals, then led her other guest down the stairs and around the side of the house. "I ran into him at the resort yesterday. He's here with his kids for a vacation. So, I was thinking—"

"I'm trying to remember the last time you went on a date. Have you?" Wyatt nipped at her heels. "Been on a date since you moved here?"

"You mean other than the time you asked me out to dinner?" she reminded him.

Wyatt shrugged. "You were new to town and looked lonely. And sad." There was real affection rather than teasing in his voice now. "And I wouldn't call that a date. We figured out in about two minutes there wasn't anything remotely close to a spark."

"Not of romance, no." But friendship was another matter.

They were now in the thick of her paradise of a backyard, a yard that surrounded her bungalow. It had been the land—more than two acres—and not the house itself that had sold her on the property. At the time, the back and side yards had been overgrown and out of control to the point of being wild. A challenge, she'd thought then. One she'd needed and embraced completely.

The landscaping had been an obstacle unto itself, but Daphne had been determined to reuse old items whenever possible. From old doors, window frames and boxes that she'd found at yard and community sales, to abandoned wooden pallets that now acted as means to display the multitude of plants, shrubs and trees she tended as carefully as she would children.

Wyatt was her go-to guy when it came to creating something new. She had great ideas, but was well aware of her personal construction-skill limitations. Thankfully she had access to one of the best all-around handymen in town.

Wyatt had won her over with his recycled window construction of the spacious greenhouse in the back corner of the property. It was where she stored all her gardening tools, supplies and equipment and also grew seedlings in the cooler months. The more humid environment was the perfect place for those wounded plants needing some extra TLC.

"I was thinking the new arbor could go here, in this back corner." She stood on one of the circular stepping stones buried in the narrow pebble path that allowed her to get in and around the more crowded areas of the yard.

There were still numerous areas that were for the most part empty, especially beyond where they stood now, but she had plans for that space, including a waterfall element that would trickle down through additional planting spots.

"I've got the final plans for the arbor in the house." She held her hands out to measure the space. "I'm thinking large square planters on either end, shelves in the middle, three, I think? And then the arbor connecting the two sides. With space for hanging things."

"Obviously." Wyatt was making notes on his phone and nodding. "I can put the word out about the planters. Might have someone in the area looking to offload ones they aren't using. The arbor I'll probably have to build. I'm thinking teak." He wandered into the corner, pulled out a measuring tape from his back pocket. "I wouldn't go beyond six feet for the hanging rods. Don't want you needing a ladder or anything to get to things. Yeah. I can see this working here. Maybe some inlay and contrasting paint colors on the containers and then just put a protective seal on the rest of the wood." He snapped the tape shut. "Time frame?"

"Whenever." She shrugged. "I just wanted to get on your to-do list. I know you're busier these days now that you're crewing the *Nani* with Keane."

"Always plenty of time for new projects. Speaking of projects." He hesitated a moment, as if second-guessing himself. "Does Tehani seem okay to you?"

"T?" Daphne blinked and frowned. "I suppose. A little stressed. And I think she's still coming to terms with Remy being gone." Did one ever get over the love of their life? She was beginning to feel confident in that answer. No, they didn't. "I can't imagine how hard it's been thinking about becoming a single parent. Why?"

"I don't know. Vibes." Now it was Wyatt who shrugged. "She just seems off. And yeah, I get she's still grieving Remy. I just worry about her, I guess."

"Well, you see more of her than I do. You do live next door to her, after all," Daphne teased. "All any of us can do is be there for her. And you have been. She's mentioned how much she enjoys your sunset chats on the porch."

"Yeah. I enjoy them, too." His smile was quick and he looked down at the ground. But not before she saw the hint of a smile on his lips. "Good way to end the day."

"She's going to need more help as time goes on," Daphne offered. "The baby will be born before we know it. A lot of things will need doing around her place and at the office." Daphne snapped her fingers. "That reminds me, I need to talk to Marella and Sydney about throwing her a baby shower." She frowned. "Is there something special we should be thinking about? I mean, traditionally, where the baby's concerned?"

"You know about the no closed leis or necklace thing, right?" Wyatt asked.

"I know about it." Daphne had been around a couple of pregnant women on the islands. "I don't really understand it, though."

"A closed lei, or a necklace or bracelet chain, is considered bad luck. Pregnant women wear leis open to symbolize an unknotted umbilical cord."

"Look at you with the pregnancy knowledge." Daphne smiled.

"You might consider having the shower down on the beach, at the ocean. Especially given Remy's connection with the waves. It's one of the customs that's supposed to bring an easy birth and at the same time you can have a blessing for the child. Oh, and you never cut a newborn's hair until their first birthday. And then there's a big party where everyone shows up."

"Like Leora's party earlier this year." It was impossible not to forget the bash Nalani had thrown for the little girl's celebration of turning one. That it had turned into a celebration of a different sort when Theo Fairfax had decided to take the island plunge and relocate here from San Francisco. That had made the event even more special, especially for a much-besotted Sydney. Daphne's boss had put on quite an interesting show as her relationship with Theo had developed.

"Might want to run things by Maru that have to do with traditions," Wyatt suggested. "She's not only a *malasada* genius, she's a wealth of information when it comes to that kind of stuff. And she's known Tehani since she was a baby."

"Good idea." Daphne made a mental note to have a chat

with their local *malasada* queen. Doing so would give her the perfect excuse to buy some of the older woman's renowned fried and filled doughnuts. "I'm sure T's okay. Just dealing with a lot." She tried to make him feel better, but now that she looked deeper, she could see the deep concern in his eyes. "You don't think it's anything with the baby, do you?"

"No." Wyatt shook his head. "It's something else. It's like she's keeping something from us. Maybe I'm imagining things. It's probably nothing."

"We'll just make sure to stay close and be aware. Trust me, that means more than anything else." Remy had been that for her, from college and beyond. Remy and Keane and their friend Silas. None of them had ever been more than a phone call away when she was dealing with the aftermath of her father's arrest, his trial and conviction, and then her mother's death.

It had meant so much that they hadn't turned their backs on her or deemed her guilty by association. They were her family. Her *ohana*. And there wasn't anything any of them wouldn't do for one another.

It was, Daphne thought as her stomach took a bit of a dive, the one thing that worried her about reconnecting with Griffin. After what had happened back when they were in school, she'd bet he hadn't been surprised about her father's arrest and conviction. But she also didn't want to think he'd hold her father's actions against her. She certainly hadn't gotten that impression this morning and he'd been more than understanding about her rule regarding any discussions about Richard Mercer.

Part of her wondered if he'd been pretending to be polite because his kids had been around. That was ridiculous. From what she could tell from his work and his reputation, both of which she'd been following even after all these years, she couldn't imagine Griff would ever deceive her like that. He had, after all, come this far to see her. He wouldn't risk that by lying.

"Earth to Daphne." Wyatt waved a hand in front of her face. "You okay?"

"Just thinking." When she felt her cheeks warm, she turned toward the house and began walking. "I'll go get those plans for you." She hurried inside, slipped off her shoes and left them by the door, then retrieved the information she'd compiled from a DIY website. Scooping the pages off her desk and looping the leis into the crook of her right arm, she grabbed the purse just large enough for her wallet and phone and headed into Nalani to meet Griff.

Chapter Six

"Just tell her first thing." Unable to sit still, Griff paced one of the seating areas in the lobby of the resort while Noah and a now very awake Cammie explored the children's activity center across from the registration desk. He'd needed a few minutes on his own, giving himself a good talking-to in preparation for what he was here for. "Just say, 'Daphne, it's not a coincidence I'm here. I have a message from your—'"

"Dad!" Noah raced across the lobby and plowed into him. "Dad, there's a spot tomorrow morning for surf lessons! I just met another kid named Braden and he's had three already and there are only a few more openings. Can I go, Dad? Can I?"

"Sure." His kid was practically a fish in the water. He'd proved that at the beach and then through the seemingly endless hours they'd spent in the resort's kids' pool. He imagined Noah and Cammie would be sleeping very well tonight given all the energy they'd burned off, while he'd spent an unusually lazy afternoon on a lounge chair. "I'll check with the front desk about making a reservation for you," he told his son.

"I can do it." Noah puffed up a good inch. "Can I do it myself?"

"Okay." Eight years old and ready to tackle the world.

"I'm pretty sure they'll need me to sign off on something, though. Let me know."

Noah beelined it to the concierge desk, where a young woman greeted him with a beautiful smile. After a quick glance at Griff, at which time Griff gave an approving nod, she made a good production of getting Noah on the list.

Pride burst through Griff as Noah answered questions and nodded and laughed. They'd been through a lot in the past two years, with Griff shifting his focus to where he wasn't traveling anymore and then all of them adjusting to what amounted to a new life once Lydia left.

Griff had the strong suspicion he was going to spend the rest of his days figuring out this whole single-dad thing. Taking care of his family was his priority now. He'd taken so much for granted for so long. He wasn't going to do that anymore.

That family, of course, also included his parents. His confession to Daphne this morning had been the first time he'd spoken any of that out loud, but it had been the truth. There were a lot of changes coming once they got back home. He only wished he'd been able to be as honest with her about his true reason for coming to the island. It should have been so simple, to tell her he was here upon her father's request, but her determined declaration that Richard Mercer was one subject that was completely off-limits presented a complication he wasn't quite certain how to tackle.

He'd figure it out. He had to. There was simply no other choice.

"And that's why you have to tell Daphne the truth," he muttered and circled back around to his pacing. "Be upfront. About everything."

"*Everything* sounds interesting."

"Daph." He turned at the sound of her wistful voice.

"Hey. Hi." The impulse to come clean swept right out of his head at the sight of her.

She smiled, those green eyes of hers sparkling with amusement. "Exactly what *everything* is it you need to be up-front about?"

"Nothing. It's…" He struggled against the truth. "Nothing. You changed your clothes. I love that color on you."

"Always the sweetheart. Aloha, Griff." She stepped forward, drawing a long circle of dark brown beaded nuts off her arm. He could smell the scent of flowers dancing off her skin as she stood in front of him and draped the lei over his head. She kissed both his cheeks. "Welcome to Nalani. I realized you probably didn't get a proper island welcome yesterday with all the chaos."

As if by instinct, Griff's hands came to rest on her hips. He bent his head forward until their foreheads nearly touched. He could feel the years and the lives they'd lived fade away. For an instant, there was nothing between them other than the mere breath of a summer breeze. How was it the bad and serious things between them disappeared when he stood in her arms?

"Dad, I'm in!" Noah's reappearance had Daphne stepping back and Griff's hands feeling oddly empty. "Hi, Daphne! You were right, Dad. There's a form you have to sign." Noah beamed up at Daphne. "I just signed up for my first surfing lesson."

"Well, that was fast," Daphne said. "Keane is an excellent teacher. He almost made the Olympic swimming team a while back. You couldn't be in better hands."

"The Olympics?" Noah gaped. "Way cool."

"Very cool," Daphne agreed. "You know what might make things easier for all of you? Head over to Ohana Odysseys and Tehani can fix you up with a schedule for your stay. We have tons of activities we can book you for. Keep things simpler than just grabbing at one thing at a time."

"We'll do that," Griff said. "Thanks."

"This is for you." She slipped another, smaller lei that matched Griff's off her arm and placed it over Noah's head. "It's a gesture of welcome to the islands. Aloha, Noah."

"Thanks." Noah looked a bit confused, but as the kid had practically said thank you the second he'd been born, remained utterly and completely polite. "What are these?" He picked the lei up to examine the shiny, threaded nuts.

"Kukui nuts," Daphne told him. "They symbolize peace and protection. The great Hawaiian chiefs wore them throughout history. It's a bit of a tradition to receive at least one lei while you're on the islands. And this one will last you forever."

"Awesome."

"I have a lei for Cammie, too." Daphne looked around.

"I'll go get her." Noah ran off before Griff could say anything.

"On his worst day, Noah has more energy than the sun," Griff said almost nervously and quickly headed over to sign the permission slip at the desk. Whatever script he'd been rehearsing to confess to Daphne was lost to him now. He'd take a few days, ease into talking about her father. "The kids shouldn't be long."

"Okay." Daphne's face softened, as if she were carefully pulling moments out of the past. "How did you all spend your day?"

"Waterlogged." Griff laughed. "I couldn't get them out of the pool once we got back here."

"Kids and pools tend to be a perfect combination," Daphne agreed.

"Found her!" Noah dragged a sour-looking Cammie

behind him. She had Taco under her arm and Taco's leash attached to her wrist. "Now we can go get dinner!"

"I heard you worked up quite the appetite at the resort pool," Daphne said.

"Uh-huh." Noah nodded enthusiastically. "It was awesome. I went down the slide like a million times."

"A million?" Griff challenged.

"Hmm, like twenty," Noah said sheepishly. "Can we go get dinner now?"

"I'm not hungry anymore," Cammie said. "And I was watching a video on dolphins. Do I have to go?"

"Yes." Griff left no room for argument. "If you don't want to eat, you don't have to."

"I brought you something, Cammie." Daphne held up a third lei. "It's different from your dad's and brother's." The lei was made out of small off-white flower buds that nestled into one another. With practiced ease, Griff pulled out his camera. "The flowers are called *pikake*. Can you smell them?"

Cammie nodded. "They smell good."

"May I put it over your head?"

Cammie glanced up at Griff, who left the decision up to her.

"I guess," Cammie said, finally.

"So it's said," Daphne told them as she slipped the lei over Cammie's head, "that it was Princess Ka'iulani who first made a lei out of these flowers. She named them *pikake*. After the peacock, which was her favorite bird."

"It's a princess lei?" Cammie's eyes went wide and her mouth dropped open. Click. Griff caught the moment before Cammie lifted her face directly into the light. "Daddy, it's a princess lei!"

"I heard." Griff couldn't help but laugh to himself. Leave it to Daphne to find the perfect way to connect with his daughter. "That's pretty special. What do you say, Cammie?"

"Thank you," Cammie whispered as she picked up the flowers and rubbed them against her cheek. "They're so soft."

"Can we please go eat now?" Noah pleaded as Daphne stood back up and Griff put his camera away.

"It's not far," Daphne said as Noah and Cammie went first through the spinning glass door. "Just a couple blocks into town." Squeezed together, they passed through the spinning door and stepped outdoors. Griff gently placed his hand against the base of her spine. He felt her jump, then relax before she cast an anxious smile at him. "I feel silly being so nervous around you."

"Enough nerves to go around," he agreed. "This town all but screams your name. You're surrounded by so much nature."

"I'm very lucky." Daphne beamed.

Griff smelled their destination before he saw it. The aroma of spit-roasted meat and spices powdered the smoky air as they stopped at the corner. Hula Chicken sat just on the other side, its patio seating larger than the building itself. Dozens of picnic tables were situated there, some clear of any cover while some sat beneath a white-and-red-striped awning.

"Should we get one under cover?" Griff asked when they crossed the street. "It's been raining."

"It rains every day," Daphne told him as she looked into the sky. "We're good for tonight." Her flash of a smile made him wonder what he was missing. "Grab whichever table you want," she told the kids. "Vivi, hey."

"Aloha, Daph!" A short, round young woman gave a chin tilt as she passed, her arms filled with a tray carrying various containers of steaming-hot food. "Howzit?"

"Going okay." She looked at Griff. "Are you drinking?"

"I wouldn't say no," Griff said.

"Four mai tais," she told Vivi. "Two regular, and two kids. It's just pineapple juice and coconut water," she added to Griff at his questioning look.

"You got it. Aloha," Vivi said to Griff as they passed.

"Daddy, sit here!" Cammie patted her hand on the empty space between her and Noah.

Daphne sat across from them, smiling up at Vivi as she brought over their drinks. "And here's a pitcher of water for you all, as well. Menu's over there." She pointed to the single laminated sheet sticking out from behind the condiment holder. "Daph, I'll let you give them the rundown on the condiments."

"Will do. Thanks, Vivi." Daphne reached over for the menu and handed it to Griff. "I recommend the hula chicken dinner plate with macaroni salad and purple sweet potatoes."

"Purple potatoes?" Noah scrambled onto his knees and peered over Griff's arm. "Are they good?"

"Oh, yes. I think so," Daphne said easily. "The shoyu chicken is a little less spicy than *huli huli*. You can't go wrong with rice, and the sweet bread rolls are always good. We can get a basket for the table."

"I'd like to try everything," Griff said. "Let's just get the family style for four and we can each sample what we want."

"Okay." Daphne smiled and sipped her drink, which had a small blue paper umbrella in it.

"One of the best things about my job was always trying the local food," Griff said. "Probably the biggest thing I miss about traveling. That and the people."

"You got to go to some pretty faraway places," Daphne said.

The strumming of ukuleles played against the dimmed

sounds of the ocean as strings of lights overhead blinked to life.

"Dad, can I go look at the chickens roasting?" Noah pointed across the restaurant to the pit area where dozens of chickens rotated on an open, flat spit. Smoke permeated the air, but not in that overly barbecued manner so many family gatherings suffered through.

"Go ahead. Cammie, do you want to go with him?"

"Okay." Cammie sighed. "I'm going to leave Taco here, though." She tore the Velcro strap off her wrist and wedged the stuffed fish under Griff's arm. "I don't want anyone to cook him by mistake."

"Perish the thought." Griff looked down at the pathetic-looking toy. "The glamorous life of parenthood. I'm the official fish sitter."

She laughed, reached over and tweaked Taco's over-stuffed mouth. "I think you look cute."

He'd take cute. "You back to work tomorrow?"

"I am. I have two botanical hikes, one in the morning, one in the afternoon. Any thoughts on what you'd like to do?"

"Noah has a surfing lesson in the morning. Seven a.m." He was already groaning thinking about it. "Why so early?"

"Softer and gentler waves," Daphne said as he set Taco on the bench beside him. "Especially for beginners. It's cooler, too, so trust me, you'll be grateful for the start time." Her smile widened. "Once you wake up."

Vivi returned to take their order, then quickly disappeared again.

"How did you end up here in Nalani?" Griff asked. He needed to find some way, any way, to slip in a comment or question or two about her father. Stepping into her past seemed the best way to do that.

"A friend." She sipped her drink, glanced over his shoulder to where the beach was lined with a long cavalcade of palm trees. "Remy Calvert. We met in college, became fast friends. He was born here, grew up here. Only came to the mainland for college and returned every chance he could. The year we graduated, the four of us came with him for the summer. He had plans to start a simple tour company."

"Ohana Odysseys?" Griff asked.

She nodded, but there was a sadness in her eyes that hadn't been there before. "He wanted to put Nalani on the map, make it the perfect getaway as one of the hidden gems of the islands."

"I'd say it's getting there." Griff looked around at the filled tables and crowds walking up and down the main road. The background roar of the ocean behind him only added to the perfection of the moment.

"When the trial began, Remy called me, reminded me I always had a place with him and the business. I said no, but it meant a lot that he'd called. I couldn't leave my mother, even though in almost every way that mattered she'd already left me."

Guilt nudged Griff, but he resisted temptation to apologize yet again for something he couldn't change. "The news accounts said she died of a broken heart."

Daphne nodded. "I suppose that's how best to describe it. She just faded away after my father's arrest. She was there, every day of the trial, but other than that, she stopped living any kind of life. She knew from the start he wasn't going to come home. It was only a matter of time before she gave up completely. She'd tied her life so tightly to his, she didn't know how to be without him."

"And you stayed with her, despite everything?"

"She was my mother." Daphne's gaze was sympathetic. "I was all she had left. And, to be honest, she was all I had. Or at least, I thought so at the time. There's this, I don't know, stifling blanket that drops over everything when someone close is considered a monster by all those around you. I don't know how else to describe him, probably because it's how most people still think of my father. I can't exactly argue the point. The callous, careless way he behaved with people who trusted him. He didn't care one iota about what would happen once the bottom fell out of his schemes. If people who'd invested in his firm lost their life savings, their homes, so be it. And he knew the bottom would fall out. He knew it and he didn't stop, and what's worse? He knew the pain that would be inflicted on everyone around him once the truth came out." Her brow furrowed. "I still don't understand how anyone is capable of that much cruelty. I mean, he wasn't the best father, not by a long shot. He wasn't a dad, like you are to Noah and Cammie. He would never have hand-washed my stuffed fish. But even knowing that…" She shook her head, pulled her hands back and shoved them under her knees. "Look at me, breaking my own rule and talking about him like he matters."

"He's your father," Griff said quietly around the guilt pressing in on him. "He's always going to matter. No matter what."

"I really hope that isn't true." She looked at the customers next to them, tucking into their meal. "It's funny. Well, sort of funny. Remy helped me realize that loving someone and liking them are two entirely different things. I don't understand how I do, how I can, but I do love him. I'll never forgive him or understand him. But he's still my father, you know? Remy made me see that."

"Remy sounds like a really good guy." Griff couldn't quite rationalize the jealousy he felt at the mention of her college friend. The fact that Remy—and others apparently—had been there when she'd needed them felt like a particular twisting of the knife. But he'd made his decision when he'd agreed to Richard Mercer's ultimatum. He hadn't earned any right to slide back into her life simply because circumstances had changed. "I'm looking forward to meeting him."

"Yeah, I'm afraid that won't happen." He could hear the tears in her voice as she reached up to tuck her hair behind her ear. "Remy died earlier this year. Very sudden and unexpected."

"I'm so sorry." He wasn't often at a loss for words, but it was clear Remy's death had left a resounding void in her life.

"His sister, Sydney, has taken over the business. Before he died, Remy had this plan in place to make all of us—me, Keane and Silas—partners in Ohana Odysseys. Mano, too. Sydney's honoring that plan and his offer of partnership."

"Are you going to take her up on it?"

"Absolutely," she said without hesitation and just like that, the grief faded from her eyes. "Not only because Remy's offer was a good one, but because this is where I belong. It took me most of my life to find a home, someplace that I fit in and that I love. I'm not about to walk away from it."

No, Griff thought. She wouldn't. Why would she when there was nothing but pain waiting for her back on the mainland. "I take it you don't have any plans to return to Oregon."

"None." The finality in her voice placed another obstacle in his path. "There isn't any reason I would ever go back. There's nothing left for me there, if there ever was anything in the first place."

He wanted to take offense, to scream to the world that he was there for her, but he'd lost that chance when he'd let her father bully him into leaving Daphne behind. "Tell me something?"

"Sure."

"You kept your name," he observed. "You could have changed it before you got here."

"I considered it." She grew silent, as if the memory caused her to pause. "I talked to Remy about it, in fact. He's the one who talked me out of it."

"How? Or why?"

"Because I'm still Daphne Mercer. What's listed on my ID doesn't change that. For the most part, once I arrived in Nalani, no one cared about my last name. I'm Daphne from Ohana. That's all I ever want to be."

"Dad, you should see these chickens!" Noah dived at the table, Cammie nipping at his heels. "They look so good! Are we going to eat soon?"

Griff caught sight of Vivi, her arms loaded with a large, circular silver tray. "I think you're here just in time. Come on." He pointed to the space next to Daphne and reached for the bottle of hand sanitizer in the napkin and utensil holder. "Something tells me this is going to be a messy affair."

And he wasn't necessarily talking about dinner.

"Can we walk you home?"

Griff's offer had Daphne's cheeks warming as they walked side by side along the shore. He still had Taco tucked under one arm. His children raced circles around them and the cool water lapped gently up and over her bare feet. Sandals dangling from her hand, she shook her head.

"It's a ways off." They were already so far out they'd lost sight of Hibiscus Bay behind them. "And eventually these two are going to crash." Dinner had been exceptionally entertaining and she'd been impressed with both kids' adventurous attitudes toward their meal. The purple potatoes in particular had been a big hit.

Cammie yelped and squealed as Noah threw handfuls of ocean at her. They raced away and out of earshot.

"Would it be presumptuous of me to say I hope to see more of you while we're here?" Griff asked.

"Yes," Daphne teased. "But that doesn't mean I'm going to say no." She reached down and slid her fingers through his. "I'd like to see more of you, too." There was little she loved more than the sensation of her feet caught up in the evening tide, but holding Griff's hand definitely rated high, as well. "I've got a few busy days of work coming up, especially this weekend, but we live on island time around here. Let's play it by ear and see where things land."

"I've got your cell number." That warm, tempting smile of Griff's appeared once more on his lips. "I'll text you?"

"You'd better." She checked how far away Noah and Cammie were and, determining they were far enough away, Daphne rose up on her toes and kissed him. "Don't," she whispered when he tried to pull her closer. "They've been through enough the last few days. Seeing you with another woman might not play very well."

"I have no doubt they've seen me looking at you with googly eyes all evening." She leaned into him, and he slipped his arms around her waist. "I would hope me kissing you wouldn't come as a complete surprise."

"Googly eyes?"

"My vocabulary has been sanitized for everyone's protection," he teased. "I'd like to see you tomorrow?"

"I told you." She laid her palm on his chest, felt his heart's steady beat. "We'll play it by ear." She kissed him again and quickly extricated herself from his embrace. "Text me."

"Bet on it."

She waited, tried not to give in, but eventually, she looked back at him. There was no surprise on her part to find him standing with his camera aimed directly at her. She smiled, tucked her flyaway hair behind her ear and turned to walk away. "Good night, Noah. Good night, Cammie," she called as she passed them.

They both stopped, and Noah waved and gave her a smile so much like his father's that Daphne almost ached. "Night, Daphne!"

Cammie simply stood there, watching with those big eyes of hers, as if she had yet to determine whether Daphne fell into the camp of friend or foe. The sun had just about slipped beneath the horizon. The last of its rays streamed across the water as she continued her walk down the beach, past the outcropping of rocks and around the corner. She could feel Griff's eyes on her and the mere thought of that kept her warm as the cool evening breeze kicked up.

She continued on, reveling in the silence and gentle whooshing of the tide. The water tickled her feet as it tumbled over her bare skin. Another half mile, looping around to the private residential area that waited at the end of the shore, where the beach cottage owned by Ohana Odysseys sat.

She heard Keane and Marella before she saw them. Or rather she heard Marella's distinctive and joyous laughter as the two playfully wrestled halfway into the water.

Daphne couldn't stop the smile that formed, watching and listening to her longtime friend experiencing his unexpected happily-ever-after with the New York businesswoman turned island transplant.

Marella's appearance on the island had coincided with her sister Crystal's June wedding. In fact, Crystal and her groom's wedding had gone so well that Marella and Keane had unexpectedly also tied the knot. The surprise wedding had indeed surprised everyone, including Keane and Marella.

Clearly, judging by her friend's current activities, he was more than happy with the outcome.

"Daphne!" Marella's voice carried on the breeze as she waved in welcome, only to find herself tugged into the water by a determined and quite wet Keane.

Daphne reached them as they tangled around one another in an attempt to surface.

"Are these the surfing lessons you asked for at your wedding?" Daphne teased as Marella tried to shake off her exuberant husband.

"As a matter of fact, yes." Marella laughed as she dragged herself out of the water. The dark one-piece swimsuit matched her slicked-back, wet hair. She had a lush, curvy figure and a smile that, as near as Daphne had seen, had yet to fade since her arrival in Nalani. Her wedding band glinted against the final light of the day. "What brings you by?"

"Just walking home," Daphne said. "Thought I'd take the long way back."

"How was your date?" Keane asked as he jogged up to join them.

"Date?" Marella's brown eyes widened. "Oooh, do tell."

"The island grapevine strikes again." Daphne rolled her eyes. "It wasn't a date, exactly," she warned Keane with a look. "His kids were there."

"A family affair?" Marella bent down and grabbed a towel, tossed it to Keane. "Even better."

"We're about to have dinner," Keane said.

"Oh." Daphne held up her hands. "I don't want to intrude."

"Don't be silly." Marella grabbed her arm and held on tight as they strolled up the beach to the bungalow cottage

Keane had been calling home since his return to Nalani. "Who's the guy? Where did you meet him? Are you seeing him again?"

"Don't mind me," Keane called from where they left him in the sand. "I'll just trudge back on my own."

"It's your turn to feed the geckos," Marella tossed over her shoulder. "So? Who is he?"

"An old friend from high school," Daphne admitted. "His name is Griffin Townsend. He's here with his kids for vacation and..." She didn't entirely know how to say this without giving Marella matchmaking ideas. "He might have come out to Nalani because he heard I was here."

Marella gave a little squeal that shot Daphne straight back to high school. "That is so romantic." She sighed and they stepped onto the side porch.

Marella led Daphne to the round metal table and matching chairs situated in the far corner of the covered porch. The location was the best spot to observe the ocean and watch for the perfect wave, something Keane was always on the lookout for.

"You hungry, Daph?" Keane asked as he headed into the bungalow.

"No, thanks. We ate at Hula," she explained as Marella took a seat beside her.

"You definitely never leave that place hungry," Marella agreed. "So. Rekindling a romance with this Griff..." Marella trailed off, her brow furrowing. Her hair sprung into curls as it dried in the warm breeze. "Hang on. Do you mean Griffin Townsend the reporter?"

"Yeah." Daphne flashed a smile. "We dated in high school for a couple of years."

"Oooh." Marella leaned her chin in her hand, then sat back as Keane brought out two glasses and a bottle of chilled white wine.

He poured one for Marella, held up the bottle as if asking Daphne if she wanted one. "Just a little." She nudged the glass forward. Wine and a sunset went hand in hand and the mai tai had been hours ago. "Thanks."

"Don't tell me this is the high school guy who broke your heart." A bottle of beer in his hand, Keane leaned back against the railing.

"What?" Marella gasped. "Oh, no."

"We were kids," Daphne reminded Keane, who shrugged as if that didn't matter in the least. "But yes. He is—was the one who... None of that matters now," she added. What there was to forgive, she'd done so long ago. Forget, on the other hand...

"It sure mattered back then," Keane reminded her. "You walked around campus like a deflated volleyball."

"He was my first real love," Daphne explained to Marella. "Those are hard to get over." In Daphne's case, however, Griff hadn't only been her first love. He'd been her only one. She'd never been particularly trusting before dating Griff. After? Well, she'd just locked that part of her heart away and focused on everything but finding an emotional partner to go through life with.

"Not always," Marella said with an almost fairy-tale princess faraway look in her eyes. "I married my first love."

Keane leaned over and clinked his bottle to her glass. "That's my girl."

"Although, don't forget, if it hadn't been for my ex's fooling around with my sister's bridesmaid, we might never have met."

"Sure we would have," Keane insisted. "But you wouldn't have had an excuse to kiss me on the beach. In front of everyone."

"Ah. True." Marella's smile was full of affection.

Daphne grinned and then cleared her throat. "Sorry, Daph. So, this Griffin guy, I remember reading his reporting back when I lived in New York. He got around. Went to some dangerous areas around the world. Risked his life a few times."

"He did. He's back for good now, raising his kids after his divorce." It dawned on her that while she knew the basics of why he'd come back, he hadn't been overly forthcoming with information. "His ex was supposed to have the kids for the summer, but she backed out at the last minute, so he brought them with him."

"Oh." Marella frowned. "Well, I'm sure they'll have a great time while they're here."

"His son, Noah, just signed up for surfing lessons," Daphne told Keane. "So you'll probably meet them tomorrow or the next day."

"Excellent. Sydney will be happy to hear that. Sold-out classes are a boon for advertising. Now I'm going to make myself scarce so you two can talk freely. If you see Noodles or Zilla, send them in for food."

"Don't be disappointed if they stand you up," Marella said of their gecko roomies. "They prefer breakfast to dinner." She waited until the screen door banged shut behind him. "They're probably in there searching the fruit containers. I swear they know how to open the fridge. So." Marella leaned her arms on the table. "Griff. Spill. What are your plans?"

"My plans for what?"

"For a summer romance?" Marella explained. "How long is he here for?"

"Eight, well, seven days now." Days she anticipated would fly by. And then he'd be gone again. Was it possible that she already knew she'd miss him?

"Counting the days, are we?" Marella joked.

"There's nothing that's going to come of this," Daphne said not only to caution Marella, but also to remind herself of the reality of the situation. An island romance might have worked out for Marella and Keane, but there were a lot more variables involved for her and Griff. "He has a life back on the mainland. A job. Parents to take care of. His kids have lives." And she had her life, here, in Nalani.

"Lives change," Marella said. "Mine did. A whole lot. Speaking of which, Keane and I finally found a house."

"You did? Where is it?"

"It's on the corner of Alaina and Pahua." Marella's smile grew as Daphne's eyes widened. "The Topeni house. We got in early to see it before they put it on the market."

"But that's only a block away from me!"

"That was one of the selling points." Marella toasted Daphne with her glass. "It has tons of acreage and a workshop where Keane can keep his surf boards, which are pretty much all in storage right now. There's also enough space for us to build a separate guesthouse. For Pippy and my parents." She paused, examined her drink far too closely. "Word is you're branching out into the landscaping business."

"I'm—what?"

"Keane had lunch with Mano today. He said you agreed to head up the RV area he's adding to the resort. You came up with plans apparently?"

"I haven't said yes yet," Daphne said almost sourly. Honestly, she hadn't given it much thought. Probably because she'd already decided to say yes. "Why?"

"You've seen the Topeni property," Marella said. "It needs some serious TLC. The owners—"

"The yards got away from them years ago," Daphne said. "It's been a chore just for them to mow back the grass."

"I want an oasis," Marella said with enthusiasm. "Some-place Crystal can shoot videos for ButtercupDoll, you know, her online fashion brand, but also just be a show-place for every native species we can grow. And also for entertaining. In a couple of years, we could even start add-ing garden tours to Ohana's offerings. What do you think?"

"Oh." A new seedling of excitement sprouted to life in-side her. "Garden tours. What a wonderful idea." Another way to showcase Ohana Odysseys and Nalani to tourists. She'd have to put more thought into that.

"It's something I've been working on for a few weeks," Marella said with more than a bit of pride. "You up for the challenge?"

"I am." Mano's job offer had put her on track to make a down payment on her partnership in the tour company. Marella's bit of genius could help seal the deal. "Let me know next time you're heading over there and I'll tag along to take some pictures. It's never too soon to start playing with some ideas."

"Sounds like a plan." Marella drew her feet up onto the edge of her chair. "Something's in the air tonight. Look who's here. Hey, Theo. Keane!" she yelled. "Theo's here!"

"Aloha." Theo Fairfax, clad in long, bright blue board shorts and a matching button-down shirt with seahorses, flip-flopped up the stairs. He still had some distance to go before giving up on his uptight ways. But the differ-ence in him since moving to Nalani, and getting serious about Sydney and the island lifestyle, was nothing short of astounding.

Gone was the stuffy, office dweller, replaced by a more relaxed, go-with-the-flow kind of guy. Except for the worry in his eyes. That was new.

"Where's your other half?" Daphne asked.

"She and Tehani had work to do at the office. Hey,

Keane." Theo sank back onto the railing as Keane banged out of the cottage. "Hope I'm not—"

"I'm going to have to put up a sign." Marella sighed. "No one intrudes here. We're *ohana*, remember? Open doors always."

"She's really taking that idea to heart," Keane explained. "What's going on, brah?"

"I need your help. All of your help, I think." Theo reached into his pocket and pulled out a small, square box, held it in his palm.

Marella and Daphne let out identical squeals of excitement that had them both laughing.

"You're going to propose to Sydney?" Daphne asked. "Let's see the ring. Oh." She sighed and sat back, tears blurring her vision at the delicate arrangement of stones. "Oh, Theo, it's beautiful."

"I had it made. Took forever," Theo admitted. "I just couldn't decide on anything then one day Sydney was going through her parents' things and came across her mother's engagement ring and wedding band."

"I thought that teardrop stone looked familiar," Keane said. He'd known Sydney and her family—Remy, in particular—since childhood. "Wonderful sentiment, using it as the center of your ring."

Theo's face turned bright red. "I hope she's okay with it. She's had them locked away for years now."

"Trust me," Keane assured his friend. "You'll be greatly admired and rewarded with your attention to detail and sentimentality."

"Sky and Earth did a really good job," Theo said and pulled out another smaller box from his other pocket, opened it to show the contents. "They made matching wedding bands for us, too."

"That's a big investment before you even ask her," Keane teased. "You feeling that confident?"

"Well, I was," Theo said. "Which is why I need your help. I'm afraid my plans have gotten a bit out of control." He put the ring boxes back into his pockets.

Daphne glanced at Marella, who looked appropriately sympathetic.

"We're going to need more information," Marella suggested.

"You see, I had this whole thing organized. I was going to propose Sunday morning, at sunrise. Up at Wailele Point. You know, at the waterfall? There's a bench there that we go to sometimes. It's just…perfect. And it's one of her favorite places on the island."

"Sounds excellent so far." Keane prodded, "What's the problem?"

"I hired a photographer to hide and take pictures of the whole thing. Flower petals lining the path on the way up. This whole romantic setup waiting for us and…" He sighed heavily. "The photographer just canceled on me. He got another job back in Honolulu and leaves on Friday."

"So get another photographer," Daphne suggested.

"Easier said than done." Theo held his hands up as if surrendering. "There are at least a half a dozen weddings between Kona and Hilo. Everyone's booked. I was hoping a few of you could lurk in the area with your cell phones. I really wanted something professional and special, but that's not looking poss—"

"So we'll get professional and special," Daphne said easily. "Would a former world-class photojournalist work okay?"

Marella turned surprised eyes on her. "You want to ask Griffin?"

"Sure." Daphne shrugged. "I mean, proposals might be

new for him, but I bet he'd be happy to help. Who's doing the decoration for the area?"

"Ah, decoration?" Theo said hesitantly. "I thought maybe I'd have a blanket and a bottle of champagne waiting?"

"Or," Marella said, "you could leave those details to us. You just worry about getting Sydney up there. You really want to do sunrise?"

"Yeah," Theo said. "It's her favorite time of the day."

"Then sunrise it is," Keane said. "Don't worry," he added at Theo's slight look of horror. "I'll leave the details to them. In the meantime, here's to another happily-ever-after." He straightened as a timer dinged in the house. "Let me get dinner out of the oven. I'll be right back. We've got all kinds of things to talk about."

Chapter Seven

"**W**ay to go, Noah!" Griff cheered his son on from where he and Cammie sat farther up on the beach. While Noah, on his second morning of lessons, had wiped out on his first three attempts at getting his feet planted on his board, the fourth time proved the charm as he stayed up for a good ten seconds before the board went right out from under his feet and he hit the waves butt first. "Did you see that, Cammie?"

"Uh-huh." Cammie sat cross-legged on her beach towel, Taco hugged against her chest. She'd eased up on her grumpy mood enough to allow Griff to French braid her hair and slather her with sunblock this morning, but that was where her beach enthusiasm ended.

She'd been on the cusp of emerging from her shell of sadness until last night when Lydia had called to video chat. Everything his ex-wife said, no doubt inadvertently, was a stark reminder that she'd chosen her new life over them. Cammie, perched on Griff's knee for the entirety of the five-minute call, had tried to ask when they'd see her again, but instead of listening to their adventures in Hawai'i, Lydia had become distracted by whatever was happening in her world.

After the call ended, Griff had done his best to distract the kids with anything he could think of for the rest of the evening. But even the hotel's ukulele and hula performance out on the pool patio hadn't cheered them up.

Noah had bounced back with the sunrise, but Cammie?

Griff didn't know what to do about his little girl's broken heart.

"Are you sure you don't want to go in the water?" Griff asked. She'd been so excited about her new goldfish-patterned swimsuit when they'd bought it before leaving the mainland, but this morning she'd had to be talked into putting it on.

"I'm sure." She sighed. "How much longer do we have to stay here? I'm tired."

Griff grappled for patience and understanding. He was out of ideas and it was far past time for appeasing her or trying to draw her out of the cocoon of sadness she'd wrapped herself in. She'd even left her princess lei looped over the handle of the bathroom door. At least she hadn't taken off the honu charm necklace she'd been given at Luanda's. That was a win. Of sorts.

Personally, Griff was anxious to hit the waves. His time in the water so far had been limited to the pool. Watching Noah every day had become bittersweet. It was only because of Daphne that he felt the possibility they'd make it over this bump in the road.

Whatever disappointment and anxiety he'd been dealing with had been mitigated by becoming caught between his past and present. Back in high school, he and Daphne had stayed up until all hours texting back and forth. He could all but hear her girlish giggles implied in her messages when they'd bared their teenage souls to one another.

Now, here, in another life, once again texting with her had become one of the best parts of his day. He'd checked in with her during the day, found out she was working, but at night, once she was home, he could just imagine her sitting on her sofa curled up, smiling as they conversed back and forth. More than once he thought about calling her, but that might remove more of the filter he was trying so hard to keep in place.

He had to remind himself that Daphne had to work, was busy with so much, and that it had been his decision to come here during her busy season. His decision to…

No. He rubbed a hand against his heart. No, that wasn't true. It hadn't been his idea. And that was part of the problem. He was lying to her. Every single moment they spent together, on- or offline.

"Dad! Dad, did you see?" Noah yelled from the shore, then spun around when his instructor, Keane Harper, called him over to give him follow-up advice.

"Sure looks like Noah's having a good time," Griff said. "Cammie—"

"Had a feeling I'd find you guys out here this morning."

Griff jumped to his feet at the sound of Daphne's voice. He kicked up enough sand that he got a glare of annoyance from his daughter before she brushed off her towel. "Good morning," Griff said, relieved to see the relaxed, pleasant expression on her face. He was afraid he'd put her off last night when he'd tried to get her to open up about her father. But looking at her now, it seemed most, if not all, was forgiven. "I thought you had an early morning tour today."

"I did." She held up a large plastic bag filled with cookies. "It's almost ten and I've got a break until after lunch. I made cookies last night."

"What kind of cookies?" Griff asked as if it mattered. His kids were sugar hounds and would eat just about anything sweet. But when he looked at Cammie, she kept her eyes on the water and her mouth scrunched up tight.

"White chocolate and macadamia nut." Daphne didn't seem offended. Given she'd reminded him on more than one occasion that this wasn't something he could relate to, he let her take the lead. "They're my favorite."

"I don't think we've ever had one of those," Griff said. "You want to try one, Cammie?"

Cammie shrugged.

Griff sighed and planted his hands on his hips. "Cam—"

"Dad! Come watch!" Noah yelled. "I'm going to go again! Hi, Daphne!" Noah waved at her and jumped up and down.

"Hi!" Daphne waved back. "Griff, go on. I'll keep Cammie company."

"Yeah?" Griff wasn't entirely sure that was a great idea, especially given the narrowing of his child's eyes, but he'd already let his daughter's attitude hold them hostage from having fun for too long. He got to his feet, discarded his shirt and kicked off his sand-filled sneakers. "Okay, I'll be back in a few minutes. Don't eat my share," he ordered Cammie as he ran over to Noah. "All right, Noah. Let's see what you've got!"

The second Griff's feet hit the wet sand he felt the unease inside him settle. The tide lapped up over his ankles, the sensation soothing and tempting him to step farther into the water. He could completely understand how his son had become a bit of a fish since his first lesson.

"He's doing great." Keane Harper walked over to stand beside him as Noah and the other two students—a girl and a boy about Noah's age—waded out into the water. Other than an initial introduction, the two hadn't spoken much given Griff's need to stay closer to Cammie than his son. "He's a natural," Keane continued. "He's got an instinctual feel for the waves. Maybe more than any other young student I've taught to date."

"Really? He hasn't spent a lot of time in the water,"

Griff said. "Indoor pools at the most. Oregon isn't the best surfing area."

"Tides can be brutal in that area," Keane agreed. "Hope for your sake he doesn't get too bitten by the bug or it'll make going home a bit rough."

"Definite truth there." Griff glanced over his shoulder to where Daphne had taken a seat beside Cammie. "I'll let him get his fill while we're here."

"Daphne mentioned you'd be here about another week," Keane said in a way that had Griff looking back at him.

"Sounds right. Is there a problem?"

"I don't know." Keane folded his arms across his chest. Like his students, who were wearing knee-length surf suits, Keane left no doubt he was in peak physical condition. His tanned skin and sun-highlighted hair spoke of countless hours in the water, but it was his current unreadable expression that had Griff's attention. "Other than when she comes down to place a tribute into the ocean, Daphne rarely visits the beach." Keane angled a look at him. "Must be something new to attract her."

"Keep a close eye on what attracts Daphne, do you?" Griff saw the other man's wedding band flash against the sun.

"She's a friend," Keane said easily. "A good friend, and I know how much you breaking up with her in high school hurt her."

"You went to college together," Griff observed. "With Remy Calvert."

"Yeah." Keane's smile was quick, but his eyes flashed with pain. "As irritating as Daphne would find it, I feel a kind of responsibility toward her. Especially now that Remy's gone."

"I feel one, too." It was one of the reasons he had yet to broach the subject of her father. He was going to have to, obviously. But he hadn't found the right moment yet, or the perfect words to use. But he needed to and quickly. "Things ended badly back then and I take full responsibility for what happened." Griff shoved his hands into the pockets of his own board shorts. "Breaking up with her is the biggest regret of my life."

"Is that why you're here? To make up for the past?"

"That's definitely part of it." He didn't see how he could admit the truth without getting slugged.

"Daphne's *ohana*. She's family." Keane's lips twitched. "I just wanted to make sure you know about the dragons at the gate."

"How many dragons are we talking about, exactly?" Griff played along.

"Well, there's me," Keane said. "And Mano Iokepa."

Okay, that could prove dangerous.

"Uh-huh." Keane's grin was back when he caught Griff's dubious expression. "And then there's Sydney and Tehani and, well, just about everyone in Nalani. Daphne has a good heart," he went on. "Everyone loves her and no one wants to see her hurt. But you know that already, don't you?"

"I do." Daphne had the kindest heart of anyone he'd ever known. "I don't want to mess with her heart, Keane." But he was going to. There was no way around it. But so far he had been able to delay it.

"Good to hear." Keane surprised him by slapping him on the back. "Okay, your boy's about to take another run. I told him to get a little farther up on the board. His back foot's been too close to the edge. If he plants a bit more firm—yes! There he goes." Noah practically leaped out of the water and landed on the board without taking an extra hop.

Pride surged through Griff as Noah, arms out to his

sides, coasted effortlessly in on the lapping tide. When he jumped off this time, it was by choice, and when he surfaced, his face was brighter than the Hawaiian sun.

"Oh, man, have you got a problem." Keane laughed. "He's got the feel for it now. He's hooked."

"You think?" Griff had seen that look before on his son's face. But he'd also seen it fade faster than a light was switched off.

"I know. I see it every time I look in the mirror. He's a lifer for sure." Keane ran forward to greet his students, then pulled them on shore for another lesson.

"Would you like one?" Daphne ripped open the baggie and offered the cookies to Cammie.

The little girl peered inside, looked tempted for a moment, then shook her head, choosing instead to hug her stuffed fish tighter against her chest. "No, thank you," she whispered.

Daphne had to admit, Griff had very polite children.

"They'll be here if you change your mind." Daphne closed the bag up and set it aside on the blanket she'd sat on. She kicked off her shoes and plunged her feet into the warming sand. "Do you like the water?"

Cammie shrugged.

"You want to know a secret? It makes me really nervous," Daphne said. "I mean it's beautiful to look at, but it's just so intimidating and big and, I don't know. Different. I bet you feel that way about Hawai'i right now, don't you? Because it's not where you want to be."

Cammie pursed her lips.

"I'm sorry your mom changed her mind about taking you to Florida."

Cammie looked up at her.

"Your dad told me," Daphne said easily. "And Noah

mentioned it, too." A half dozen times. The little boy might put on a brave face, but it was evident, to Daphne at least, that Noah was as hurt by his mother's actions as Cammie. "It really isn't fair that she changed her mind, is it?"

Cammie shook her head and looked down at Taco, played with one of his flippers.

"Broken promises are the worst. They hurt." She touched a hand to her chest. "They hurt your heart."

"That's what Daddy says," Cammie said. "He says you never break a promise because it breaks a heart."

Daphne gasped, her throat tightening with sudden tears. "Y-your daddy says that?"

"Uh-huh." Cammie nodded. "All the time. But he never breaks a promise."

"Then you're very lucky," Daphne told her. She couldn't remember her parents ever making her a promise let alone if they'd ever kept one. "It's sad when you think someone you love doesn't love you as much as you love them. It makes you feel all alone."

"It's scary," Cammie whispered. "I don't know how to fix it."

Daphne couldn't remember her heart aching for anyone more than it did for Cammie at this moment.

The bright-eyed little girl looked up at her, her eyes filled with tears. "How do I make Mama love us again?"

"I—" Daphne's mind raced as she searched for Griff at the shore. There were so many things she could say to at least ease Cammie's fears, but Daphne knew, from experience, that would only keep Cammie lost longer. "I don't know that there is a way, Cammie."

"Oh." Disappointment erased some of the pain in her eyes. "So maybe I should stop trying?"

"Maybe." She didn't like saying it, but she liked lying even less. "Maybe it's as simple as accepting who she is and what she's capable of." She couldn't help but think she was speaking beyond what she was capable of comprehending. How could a six-year-old understand the concept when Daphne, a woman in her thirties, couldn't.

"Did your mama love you?"

Daphne swallowed hard against the truth. "I don't know." She smiled a little at Cammie's wide-eyed stare. "Sometimes I think she did. But she's gone now so I'll never know for sure." She reached out and touched the back of Cammie's head. "You're very lucky, Cammie. Your daddy loves you so much. So much. You know that, right?"

"Uh-huh." This nod nearly tipped her over. "He tells me all the time."

"That's a really good thing." Somewhere deep inside, the little girl Daphne had been cried a little, in envy and relief. "He's the kind of daddy who gets sad when you're sad and he wants to make everything better, but some things just are. It's not fair, I know. But you are loved, Cammie. And you always will be. By your dad and your brother for sure."

"Should I still love Mama?" Confusion clouded her eyes. "Even though she broke my heart?"

Oh, baby. Daphne wanted nothing more than to cuddle this little girl into her arms and hug away her pain. "It's never a bad thing to love anyone," she managed finally.

"Do you think Daddy's mad at me because I've been sad?"

"Your father's worried about you," Daphne said. "But no, I don't think he's mad."

"Maybe I should stop being sad, then."

"You'll have a lot more fun if you aren't," Daphne told her. "But that doesn't mean you shouldn't feel your feelings."

Cammie's smile seemed genuine this time. "Daddy says that, too. Can I ask you something?"

"Of course."

"Would you watch Taco for me so I can go tell Daddy I'm not sad anymore?"

"I would be honored to watch Taco." Daphne accepted the stuffed fish with a bow of her head as Cammie ripped the Velcro leash off her wrist. "And when you get back maybe you can have a cookie?"

"Okay!" Cammie nodded and raced off, her feet kicking up sand as she catapulted across the beach to her father.

Daphne watched, tears in her eyes once more as Griff bent down to swing a giggling Cammie into his arms and hugged her tight. Over the little girl's shoulder, their eyes met. He smiled, his eyes brightening as he mouthed a silent thank-you.

"I have a favor to ask you," Daphne said to Griff when he collapsed on the towel beside her and splayed onto his back. She'd spent the past hour watching the three of them in the water, his son whipping around on his borrowed surfboard and Cammie and Griff splashing and playing together. She couldn't, no matter how hard she tried, recall a more beautiful sight. Noah's surfing lesson had ended long ago, but as he was still diving into those waves, Daphne had little doubt Keane had let the boy keep the board for the rest of his stay.

"Right now you can ask me for the world and I won't say no." His hair damp around his face, Griff offered a smile that, for the first time since he'd arrived in the islands, seemed genuine and relaxed. "You are a genius with my daughter. Look at that smile." He rolled onto his side and pointed at the shore. "I can see it all the way from here. What did you say to her?"

The truth. "I just told her how lucky she was to have a father who loves her without reservation and that sometimes we have to accept people for who they are. Not who we wish they were."

"That sounds like a very healthy view," Griff said. "Is that how you look at things with your father?"

An icy chill raced down her spine. "I suppose." How had that conversation detour happened without her seeing it coming? "I don't—"

"Don't you ever wonder what his reasons were? Or if there's anything salvageable for the two of you?"

"No, not really." Daphne frowned. "I don't. There's no acceptable reason for what he did, Griff. I'd think you of all people would see that."

"I'm not necessarily talking about his crimes." Griff seemed to be looking anywhere other than at her. "I mean about the two of you. Your relationship. There must be something behind how he—"

"How he what?" Daphne challenged. "How he raised me? He didn't. How he ignored me, except when it was to his advantage?" She attempted to understand why he'd ask her such a thing but failed. "Do you know what he said to me when the FBI came into our home and arrested him? He didn't tell me not to worry. He didn't say don't be scared or that it was a mistake or that he'd fix it." She ducked down to catch his gaze so he would see the pain she found impossible to hide. "He told me to call the lawyers and that if I said anything to anyone about anything he'd know. He's incapable of feeling, other than a responsibility to himself, Griff. And I can't believe…" She stopped, took a centering breath. "This is why I don't talk about him. Ever. With anyone. He's not worth the energy." Or the heartache.

"You said it yourself the other day, though, Daph. You

still love him. He's still your father. Wouldn't talking to him help?"

"Help with what?" She honestly couldn't figure out where this was coming from or, worse, where it was going. "He's not going anywhere and neither am I."

"Maybe he's sorry for some of the things he's done," Griff suggested. "Maybe if you gave him a chance, it could be different between you."

Daphne balked. "Where is this coming from, Griff? What does any of this matter to you?"

He winced, looked back to where his kids continued to play. "It doesn't matter to me. Maybe I'm just thinking about what happens down the road for Noah and Cammie. When they're really old enough to understand and process all the stuff that comes with having Lydia as their mother. I want them to be able to take charge of their lives and heal somehow, because otherwise it's a wound they're going to carry around with them. Maybe I just want that for you, too."

"Well, I don't." She was perfectly happy carrying around her anger and resentment to the extent that she did. Honestly, before Griff had arrived she hadn't given her father more than a passing thought in years. "I appreciate the sentiment." She supposed. "But as I told you the first time you brought him up, I don't want to talk about him."

"What if he wanted to talk to you?"

"I'd tell him it's too little too late. He broke my heart before I was old enough to understand what one was. It's not something that can be fixed with a conversation." She reached behind her for the baggie.

"But—"

Daphne shoved a cookie into his mouth.

"End of discussion," she told him in what she hoped

was a firm and decisive tone. "Now, after you're finished, I have that favor to ask of you."

"Wt knd f frvr?" he mumbled with his mouth full.

She laughed, grateful to feel the threatening sadness abating. "This kind." She grabbed his camera case and set it on the towel between them. "But it requires you getting up very early on Sunday."

Griff heaved a sigh as he swallowed his cookie. "The one day I don't have to get up for Noah's surf lessons. Of course." Heaving a dramatic sigh, he looked at her. "Let's have it."

"Sydney's boyfriend is planning on proposing to her on Sunday at sunrise. Up by one of the waterfalls." She pointed behind them into the mountains backing Nalani. "He's been looking for a photographer to capture the moment and it is not the season to find an easily available one."

"Oh." Griff sat up. "Well, sure, yeah. That's a simple enough request. I take it this is a surprise proposal?"

"Hmm, I bet Sydney's been expecting it for a while, so I don't imagine it'll be a complete surprise but—"

"I would be happy to help." He pulled out the camera he'd been carrying around with him every day, hefted it in one hand before he aimed the lens at her and took a picture. "Just practicing." He grinned as her cheeks warmed.

"What happened here?" She reached out a finger to trace the divot and scratches along the side of the camera.

"Hazards of the job." He ducked his head, but not before she saw him wince.

"Griff?" She curled her legs in, faced him. Put all her attention on him. The background noise of the growing beach crowd, the squeals of his children, the cresting waves growing along with the intensity of the sun.

"Just a close call on one of my last assignments." He

ran his own finger across the scratch. "A wake-up call, one might say."

She leaned closer, saw a more defined impression and felt the blood drain from her face. "Is that from... Is that from a bullet?"

He shrugged, but there was nothing casual about the gesture. "Cameras provide little protection in war zones."

"Griff." She shifted closer, pushed the camera down and caught his chin in her hand. "Were you hurt?"

"Not really." The flash of a smile didn't come close to meeting his eyes. "Not as badly as others around me. It's not something..." He let out a whoosh of a breath. "Okay, I'm getting your attitude about your father in a completely different way now. This isn't something I like to talk about."

"You can't compare my convicted criminal of a father to surviving a war zone."

"I didn't survive it, Daphne. I wasn't fighting. I was there to document and while I firmly believe in getting the truth out to the rest of the world, what I did doesn't come close to what the people fighting to survive are going through. So that's that, yeah?" He tucked the camera away. "Let me know the details about the proposal and we'll take it from there, okay?"

"Okay," she whispered and sat back before they were set upon by two very wet, very giggly and wiggly children. Cammie landed between them with a bit of a grunt, splattering them with what seemed like half the ocean. "I bet you guys worked up an appetite."

"Yes!" Cammie announced on a squeal as Griff tickled her stomach.

"That's what happens when you don't eat breakfast. You want to join us for lunch?" Griff asked.

"No, thanks. I need to get back and prepare for my afternoon hike."

"What kind of hike?" Noah asked.

"It's a nature hike. We look for certain plants and flowers and follow a winding route up to one of the waterfalls where we have a snack. Then we come back. It's only a moderate sort of trek today. Not one of our ankle killers." She didn't think they'd get the joke they used at Ohana to determine activity difficulty.

Noah's nose crinkled. "Sounds boring."

"I think it sounds fun!" Cammie announced, shocking the three of them into silence. "I like pretty flowers. Can we go, Daddy?"

"Well, I—"

"But I want to keep surfing," Noah complained.

"You've spent the entire morning surfing," Griff said.

"Cammie can come with me," Daphne offered. "If she wants to. Drop her off at the Ohana office after lunch and I'll get her back to you when we're done." She looked at her watch. "It would be around three or three thirty."

"Are you sure?" Griff didn't look convinced. "She gets bored pretty easily."

"Do not," Cammie protested.

"Do so," Noah grumbled.

"As long as she knows that if she does she's stuck with me," Daphne told them both. "It's a lot of walking, Cammie."

"Okay."

Daphne wasn't entirely convinced but it was one of the first times she'd seemed excited about something and, to be honest, she found the little girl simply adorable. "Great, I'm willing to risk it if you are," she said. "I've got a fun bingo game I give to the kids to play along the way. And it's a small group, so no chance of her getting lost."

"Please, Daddy?" Cammie scrambled onto her knees and pressed her hands together. "I'll be good, I promise."

"You'll mind Daphne? And no whining. No matter how bored you get?"

"Uh-huh." Cammie nodded so hard she almost fell over. "Promise."

"Okay, then. I guess you're a go." Griff still didn't look entirely convinced it was a good idea. "Let's get you back to change."

"Does she have sturdy shoes? Good walking shoes?" Daphne said.

"She has her travel sneakers," Griff said. "Will those work?"

"Not if she ever wants to wear them again. What's her size?"

Griff threw out a number and Daphne made a mental note. "I'll get what she needs. And some socks, too. The bus leaves at one sharp."

"Okay." Griff shook his head at Daphne, as if she didn't know what she was getting into. "We'll see you then."

Chapter Eight

Griff still wasn't entirely convinced Daphne would survive her outing unscathed. It wasn't that he wasn't happy to see Cammie excited about something, or that he wasn't looking forward to some one-on-one time with his son, but Cammie was like Noah in a lot of ways, including her instant lack of interest in something new at times.

"Can Taco really see from back there?" Cammie tried to look over her shoulder at the new child's backpack she was carrying that Griff had picked up at Luanda's after lunch. Cammie had naturally expected Taco to come with her on this new adventure with Daphne but the idea of her dragging the poor stuffed fish through the rainforest left Griff dreading everybody's return.

"Taco can see just fine." Griff tweaked the stuffed fish's tail and readjusted him so his ping-pong eyes stuck out of the top of the rainbow-colored bag. "Don't forget to ask Daphne to help you with your sunscreen after a little while."

"I know. You've told me a bajillion times." She had taken meticulous care with her outfit for her outing and chosen a bright pink T-shirt to go with her shorts. He had no doubt upon her return they'd be seeking out the resort's laundry facilities.

Their walk down Pulelehua ramped up the hill, curving around one way, then the other on their journey to the Ohana Odysseys office. Cammie was practically flying along but Noah trudged behind.

"The faster you walk, the faster we'll get back to the beach," Griff told his son.

"But, Dad—"

"Hey." Griff stopped and caught Noah's shoulder. "I get it. You want to do what you want to do. But this vacation is about all of us, not just one person. I'm happy to let you get as much surfing time in as you'd like, but we share in this family, and that includes time. Okay?"

"She's been a pain all week," Noah whined. "Now it's like she's getting a big reward for it."

"You're the one who didn't want to go on the hike," Griff reminded him. "Are you changing your mind?"

"No." But Noah's frown said otherwise. "Not really. I want to surf some more. Keane said I could get really good if I worked at it."

"Then we'll work at it as long as we can," Griff said. "But not at the expense of something that makes your sister happy. Unless you'd rather she go back to her crankypants status."

That seemed to get through to him. "Okay." He sighed. "I think it still sounds boring, though."

"You want to know something?" Griff said as they resumed walking. "I'm thinking I'd like to give surfing a shot myself."

"Yeah?" Noah brightened at that thought.

"Do you think maybe Keane has another board?"

"Really?"

"Really," Griff confirmed. "Think you could give your old man some pointers?"

"Sure! Oh, this'll be cool!" He scooted ahead, almost caught up to his sister, then abruptly stopped. "Hey, Dad?"

"Yes?"

"Mom really isn't coming back, is she?"

The change of subject gave Griff emotional whiplash. "No, she's not."

"Is Daphne going to be our new mom?"

"What? Cammie, hold up!" Griff called to his daughter. She turned, thumbs looped through the straps of her backpack, and stomped her foot in frustration. "Just a minute, okay?" Griff shifted to stand in front of Noah. "Is that what you think this trip is about?"

Noah shrugged. "I dunno. She's just around a lot and you seem happy when she is. I was just thinking…"

Griff crouched in front of his son, making it a point to meet him eye to eye. "I like Daphne a lot, Noah. I'm not going to deny that. I liked her a lot when we went to school together and I still like her." Maybe even more than he did back in the day. "But we live in Oregon and she lives here. And your mom is your mom. She always will be, even if she isn't around. I'm not looking to replace her. But I would like to enjoy the time I do have with Daphne. We were really good friends once."

"Oh." Was it Griff's imagination, or did his son look disappointed. "Okay. I guess I just thought, I dunno. She's fun, Dad."

"I agree. But vacation fun isn't necessarily reality fun." He'd be lying if he didn't admit he'd found himself wondering, more than once, how great it would be to live here, but that would be a very different life. Nowhere close to the one he was currently living. "Day-to-day stuff is a lot different than what we've got here in Nalani. I'm glad you like her, though."

"Dad?" Noah grabbed Griff's arm and tugged him back down. "It'd be okay with me if you wanted to be happy. With Daphne."

Griff could see how important the sentiment appeared to be to Noah. He had his serious, brow-furrowing expression firmly on his round, young face. "I appreciate that, Noah." But he stopped short of telling Noah any more hard truths. Daphne didn't belong on the mainland. She belonged here, in Nalani, where she'd thrived and found a life he'd spend the rest of his life being envious of. "We'd better get walking again before your sister stomps her way through the asphalt."

"Man, she's such a brat," Noah whispered more to himself than to Griff as they quickly caught up with Cammie, who'd been scowling and waving her arms the whole time.

They reached the Ohana Odysseys office, and it was almost time for the tour to leave. He spotted Daphne, a tablet tucked under her arm, standing among a group of adults and several children lined up to climb onto the small passenger bus.

"There you all are." Daphne's welcoming smile upon seeing them had Griff's heart skipping a beat. He'd bet every penny in his bank account she didn't have any idea how she seemed to glow with joy. She'd tied her hair back again, in a braid that reached almost the center of her back. She'd changed into a darker pair of khaki shorts and a button-down short-sleeved matching shirt that displayed the Ohana logo beneath the sharp-edged collar. She faced them when the last of the tour members were on board. "You all ready for an adventure, Cammie?" Daphne asked.

"Uh-huh." Cammie pointed to her white sneakers. "Daddy said I can't wear these, though."

"Don't worry, we've got a solution. Tehani?" Daphne called up the porch steps to the two women standing by the door beneath the overhanging porch. "Can you help Cammie with her boots?"

"Boots?" Cammie's eyes went wide. "I've never had boots before."

"Well, then, let's get you all fitted out." The dark-haired woman who was obviously pregnant walked down to join them. "Aloha, Griff!" She gave him a quick wave. "Not sure if you remember me. I provided you with a list of activities available while you're here in Nalani with your family. I'm Tehani Iokepa."

"As in Mano Iokepa?" Griff returned the greeting, surprised with himself that he didn't catch the detail the first time they spoke.

"He's my brother," she said. "My big brother." She grinned at Cammie. "My annoying big brother."

"I have one of those!" Cammie announced and pointed at Noah.

"Dad," Noah whined. "She's starting again."

Tehani laughed. "I've got some special hiking boots for you inside, Cammie. Come with me."

"Aloha," the other woman said, this one blonde and tanned with a warm expression of curiosity on her face. "Sydney Calvert. Nice to meet you, Griffin."

"Griff, please," he responded. "Appreciate you letting Cammie tag along."

"Our pleasure," Sydney assured him. "How are you enjoying your surfing lessons, Noah?" she asked.

"I love them!" Noah's annoyance with his sister faded upon being addressed. "I could surf every single day of my life."

"Keane wasn't kidding." Sydney laughed and rested a hand on Noah's shoulder. "He said he thought you might be a lifer."

"We're headed back to the beach right now," Griff said. "I was wondering if maybe you all had an extra board

I could borrow. I think Noah could probably give me a few tips."

"You're going to surf?" Daphne's eyes went wide. "Seriously?"

"Why does this surprise everyone?" Griff asked. "I can swim pretty well, you know."

"Oh, I have no doubt," Daphne assured him. "I'm just a bit sad I won't be witness to your early attempts. If you have the chance to take some pictures," she told Noah, "please do."

His son's smile would have brightened the darkest day. "I can do that."

"Noah," Sydney said. "Why don't you come inside with me and we'll find a board for your dad to borrow, yeah?" She pivoted with him and they disappeared inside.

"I know I mentioned this before, but I do hope you know what you're getting into with Cammie," Griff said when he and Daphne were alone.

"I've dealt with plenty of kids on these tours," she said easily. "Don't worry. I've got some extra snacks and fun games at the ready. We always carry disposable rain ponchos with us, along with a first-aid kit. We'll be fine."

"Daddy, look!" Cammie leaped out of the door and landed like a wannabe superhero before she showed off her new, sturdy hiking boots. "Aren't they cool? And look at this!" She spun around to display a collection of blooms tucked into her braid. "I have flowers for my hair!"

"That's very cool," Griff said. "She gets cranky when she gets tired," he told Daphne.

"So does her father," Daphne teased. "Relax, will you? Go have fun with Noah and I'll drop Cammie off when we get back."

"Wait." He caught Daphne's arm before she passed by. "I'd like to have dinner with you. Tonight. Just the two of us." He hoped whispering the offer into her ear would lend a little privacy and up the enticement. The heat that rushed to her cheeks almost touched his face.

"Is that possible?" She angled a look at Cammie, who was jumping up and down around a seemingly delighted Tehani. "What about—"

"The hotel's kids' club is hosting movie night out by the pool. Dinner and snacks and games included. It'll keep them occupied for three, maybe four hours. What do you say?" He lowered his voice and was rewarded with her turning her face. He could feel her breath on his skin, see the temptation in her eyes. "Say yes," he urged.

Her smile was slow, intrigued and flirtatious. "Okay. Yes."

Instead of responding, he kissed her. Quickly, firmly, and found himself wishing they were without an audience. "I'll see you when you drop Cammie off. Oh, there's a sweater in her backpack in case she gets cold. And her sunscreen—"

"Stop." Daphne lifted a hand to his face. "We'll be fine." Noah and Sydney came out behind Tehani, Sydney carrying a bright yellow board under one arm. "Enjoy the afternoon with your son." She hesitated, then kissed him again, chuckled and pointed when his own cheeks went warm. "Now we match. Come on, Cam." Daphne returned to the base of the stairs and held out her hand. "We are off on our adventure. Have you ever played wildflower bingo before?"

"Nu-uh." Cammie shook her head. "What's that?"

"Well, I'll tell you just as soon as we get into the bus. We're off!" she announced as Cammie leaped through the bus door. "See you on the other side."

Griff couldn't decide, for the life of him, whether the knots in his stomach were because he was watching his little girl go off with the woman he loved or because the woman he loved was about to get a good dose of Cammie-reality that no training could prepare her for.

"They'll be okay," Sydney called down from the porch. "Daphne's great with kids."

"She's good with me," Noah confirmed with a sheepish look Griff chose to ignore. The last thing any of them needed was for his kids to get the idea of playing matchmaker. Even though the very thought of his kids approving of Daphne warmed long-forgotten corners of his heart.

"Here's a board for you." Sydney joined Tehani at the base of the stairs and handed it over. "Feel free to keep it for your stay."

Griff accepted it, ran his hand over the initials beautifully painted within a flower design on the nose. "RC." His heart stuttered. "Remy? Was this Remy's board?"

"One of them," Tehani confirmed, some of the light fading from her sparkling dark-eyed gaze. "Daphne told you about him?"

"She did." He paused, tried to find the right words. "He's the reason she came out here." Had a safe place to start over. "He sounds like he was a really great guy."

"He was," Tehani said in a tone that filled in whatever blanks Griff might have had about her relationship with Daphne's friend.

"He'd appreciate you using it," Sydney said. "As far as he was concerned, boards weren't meant to sit in closets and be forgotten. Take good care of it and it'll guide you safely along the waves."

"I will." He accepted the board carefully. He'd expected a throwaway board, one they didn't mind the least bit about losing. But this offering felt like an unexpected gift. "Thank you, ah, *mahalo*."

"Come on, Dad, let's go!"

"Hang on." Sydney called him back. "We're having a bit of a last-minute sunset cruise for the Ohana crew tomorrow evening. You and the kids should come along."

"Really?"

"Yes. Daphne will be there. And the rest of us. It's a small group, laidback since we usually work Saturday nights. It won't be the big song and dance we usually put on for guests, but it'll be relaxing and something different for you all to experience."

"And it'll give you time to put me through the *ohana* inquisition?" he said with a smile.

"That, too," Tehani confirmed.

He could only imagine the questions Daphne's friends— her *ohana*—would have for him once they had him trapped on a boat. But he was certain that Cammie and Noah would love the experience. "Sure. We'd be happy to join you."

"Great. It's the *Nani Nalu*. Six p.m.," Sydney told him. "You can't miss it in the marina. Just look for the Ohana Odyssey logo on the side."

"Okay." Griff glanced over to Noah, who gave an enthusiastic nod. "We'll be there."

"Bingo!"

Daphne smiled to herself as her boots squished in the mud.

Even at the end of their outing, Cammie hadn't quite gotten the handle on the rules of the game. The little girl shouted out bingo every time she spotted any kind of flower, not just the ones pictured on the paper she and the other tour guests had been given.

On the bright side, she'd tested Daphne's knowledge about the surrounding flora much more vigorously than any college exam ever had.

"Keep going on this path for about another quarter

mile." The other people in the group—a family of three that included an eighteen-month-old who had been along for the ride in a state-of-the-art backpack carrier, and a group of five friends on a getaway weekend from Maui, plus, two moms and their preteen sons, went on ahead, chuckling at Cammie's continued exuberance.

They'd been hiking through the bamboo-thick rain-forest for a good hour and aside from one or two bouts of frustration on Cammie's part, Daphne had yet to see any sign of the cranky, ill-tempered little girl Griff warned her about. She had heard more grumbling from some of the others on the excursion, especially when it came to cross-ing the stream that was little more than a trickle of water.

Daphne stopped near where Cammie had and crouched beside her as the little girl held up her marked-up bingo sheet.

"Is this this?" Cammie pointed to the image of *hina-hina*, a small, trumpet-like flower that bloomed in clusters, then to the plant that bore no resemblance at all.

"No." Daphne glanced around, then smiled. "But this is. Here. See? It almost glitters in the sun. That's because there's silver hairs in the petals and it reflects the rays."

"Oooh." Cammie's sweat-and-dirt-covered face bright-ened. "It's so pretty. But we can't pick any flowers. They belong here, not with me."

"It's better for them that way," Daphne said. "One of the things we try to do on the island is to let nature be. We have plenty of flowers available to us, but in the wild, it's important to let things grow as they can."

"Like with the honu turtles," Cammie whispered. "We don't touch them, either. Because they're say-cred."

"That's right. We treat everything around us with re-spect and kindness. And it comes back to us that way.

Come on." Daphne stood up and held out her hand. "The others are going to beat us back to the bus."

"I wish I could stay here for always," Cammie said. "Everything's so pretty and bright." She clutched her bingo sheet against her chest. "Even Taco likes it and he lives in the water!"

"Taco is a very discerning fish," Daphne agreed. "Pretty cool bag he's got to ride in."

"Daddy bought it for me. I don't like to leave Taco alone because he's afraid I won't come back."

"He is?" Daphne didn't need to be a psychologist to understand where that idea came from.

"Uh-huh. He lost his mama and now I'm his mama, so he'll never be lost again." She lifted her arm where the leash to her toy was still wrapped around her wrist.

"That's what that leash is for, huh?"

"Yep." Cammie planted her foot in a particularly muddy puddle. "Uh-oh." She looked down at her shoes. "I'm really dirty."

"That's okay," Daphne said. "So am I. It's part of the fun."

"My feet keep sliding." Cammie giggled as she tried to leap across the rest of the mud.

"Hang on." Daphne crouched down, pointed to her back. "Climb on."

"Really?" Even as she asked, the little girl grabbed hold of Daphne's shoulders and hoisted herself up. "Cool!" She laughed as Daphne stood up and stepped with determination across the sludge. It wasn't the first time she'd had to help people traverse the rather muddy trail, especially after an afternoon rainstorm that had blasted through a little more than an hour ago. But it was the first time she would carry someone out.

Daphne was used to the rain, as were the other island

residents, but everyone else had been scrambling for the ponchos Daphne handed out back on the bus.

"I didn't finish my bingo game," Cammie announced.

"Hmm, how about you come to my house for a few minutes and you can finish it up there." Her backyard would more than complete the game that had no prize attached to it and she needed time to shower and change before her dinner—her solitary dinner—with Griff. "Or I can take you back to the resort and we can try there?"

"I can see where you live?" Cammie squeezed her arms around Daphne's neck as they veered off down the path.

"Sure."

"Do you have any pets?"

"Pets?" Daphne shook her head, reached back and grabbed hold of Cammie's legs to keep her locked in place. "No, I'm afraid not. My neighbor has a cat, though. His name is Tuxedo. Sometimes he stops by for a treat. But I don't have any pets."

"I saw a surfing pig yesterday morning," Cammie said. "Noah didn't really care, but I got to meet her. Her name is Kahlua and she wears funny shirts."

"Kahlua is quite the celebrity around here," Daphne told her. "She's even been interviewed for TV."

"For reals?" Cammie said. "What did she say?"

"Um, her owner did most of the talking." Daphne hadn't realized until now how difficult it was to keep a straight face when conversing with children. "I can send your dad the YouTube link and you can see for yourself."

"How come you don't have any pets?" Cammie asked.

"I don't know." Daphne glanced over her shoulder. "I never really thought about it, I guess. I never had one growing up."

"Never?" Cammie gasped. "Not even a fish? I had a fish. A goldfish. His name was Leon."

"Leon, huh?" Daphne bit back a laugh.

"Yeah, but he died and we had to flush him. Noah and I asked if we could get a dog because we both really want one but that was when Mom left and we stopped asking. Dad has enough on his plate without one."

"Where did you hear that?" The phrasing wasn't close to what a child would come up with on their own.

"We heard him talking with Grandma and Grandpa. They live in a special place for old people and Grandma asked Daddy how he'd take care of a dog when we've got so much going on. I could take care of a dog," Cammie told Daphne. "Do you think you could tell Daddy that? Maybe then he'd be okay with it."

"I'd be happy to let him know you're still thinking about it," Daphne compromised. Her shoulders were beginning to ache, but Cammie seemed perfectly content as a passenger. "Thank you for coming out with me today, Cammie. I hope you had fun."

"I had a lot of fun." Her grip around Daphne's neck tightened again, almost to the point of preventing her from breathing. "You make me feel better about my mama."

"I'm glad."

"I'm sorry about your mama," Cammie said more quietly. "I'm sorry you don't know if she loved you."

"Yeah." Daphne's throat thickened with tears. "Me, too. But you know what?" Time to change the subject.

"What?"

"You are an excellent tour assistant, young lady. You should be very proud of yourself."

"I will be," Cammie announced. "Just as soon as I finish my bingo card!"

Chapter Nine

Guilt was a funny thing. Griff slicked his hair back and took a moment to give himself one serious look in the bathroom mirror. Not to make certain he was presentable enough for dinner. He wanted to see if he could give his soul a good once-over and talking-to.

It wasn't easy, waiting for whatever small openings Daphne gave him in regards to talking about her father. True to her word, she didn't give much more than an inch and he, unfortunately, had to keep reminding himself that he was here in Nalani to convince her to speak to Richard Mercer and not to rekindle the flame that had clearly refused to die out over the years.

He was running out of time to lock in his story; running out of time to solidify his employment situation. And he was running out of time with Daphne. He wanted to deal with this looming obligation once and for all and focus on what was most important.

Trouble was, loving Daphne had, from the time he'd seen her that first evening in the lobby, leaped to the top of that list.

"You need to get it together." He spoke clearly, as if he was worried he might not understand himself. His powers of persuasion hadn't, unfortunately, been adequate enough to knock a hole in that brick wall she'd erected around her heart where her father was concerned. The longer he avoided telling her the truth, the harder it was going to hit when he finally did.

"You should maybe take that as a sign." Maybe he wasn't meant to convince her. Maybe the part of him that knew he shouldn't have taken the deal in the first place was catching up with the rest of his conscience.

Maybe what he should have done was call Richard Mercer's bluff and told him to—

"Dad!" Noah yelled from the sitting room. "Your phone's ringing!"

"Vacations are supposed to be stress free. Reflection time is over." He clicked off the light and retrieved his phone from where it was charging on the kitchen counter. One look at the name on the screen had him debating whether to answer. The debate didn't last long. If he didn't answer, Colin would just call back until he did. Best to just get it over with. "Hey, Col. Hang on a sec, will you?"

Someone—or a couple of someones—knocked on the front door. He walked over, pulled open the door and waved Cammie and Daphne inside. "Sorry." He pointed to his phone. "Work."

Cammie rolled her eyes and nearly dived onto the cream-colored sofa before Griff caught her in one arm and picked her up off the ground.

"I'm not paying to have that thing cleaned," he told his squirming, giggling daughter. "Bath. Now."

"Aww." Cammie pouted, then brightened when she looked up at Daphne.

While his daughter appeared as if she'd been on the losing side of a life-and-death mud battle, Daphne practically sparkled. The blue-and-white-flowered sundress had a bit of a flounce around the knees and on her strappy sandals hung tiny flower charms that matched the charms dangling from her bracelet. Once again, she'd worn her hair loose and long in a way that left Griff's hands itching to dive into its thickness.

"Movie starts in twenty minutes!" Noah yelled.

"I've got her." Daphne chuckled and closed the front door behind her. "I thought about giving her a hose-down at my house but we didn't have any clean clothes. Take your call. We'll be fine."

"I want to wear this to the movie tonight!" Cammie announced as Griff returned to his phone and, at the last second, took the call out on the balcony.

"Sorry, Col. Crazy night. Are we five days out?"

"Close enough," Colin said. "I need details on your story."

Griff shook his head, then remembered his boss couldn't see him. "I can't. Not yet."

"I'm not asking for the full story, just the bare essentials." Colin sounded almost desperate. "Just something I can use with the publisher to prove we're still viable as an investigative source. Give me something, Griff. Otherwise the next call you get from me is going to come with a pink slip."

That nagging, dreadful feeling was back, this time circling like a shark around a surfboard. He had yet to figure out the right tactic to use with Daphne in regards to her father and if he didn't find one soon, his entire deal with Mercer was going to blow up. And take the *Portland Beat* with it.

"This is not for public consumption," Griff said. "And nothing is set in stone, remember."

"Noted."

"I have the opportunity for an exclusive interview." Griff rubbed his fingers hard across his forehead. Even against the inside voices screaming at him to stay quiet, he found himself saying, "With Richard Mercer."

The silence should have boosted his confidence. Instead, Griff felt the weight of what hung on the balance swinging over his head like a cartoon anvil about to drop.

"You're serious," Colin said. "Richard Mercer? An exclusive."

"I am serious. No holds barred. No topic off the table. I'm just..." He glanced over his shoulder into the room. "I'm still working out the details."

"Should I ask what those details entail?"

"No," Griff said. "You shouldn't. But part of the deal I made was that none of this leaks before the interview is done." This was a lie he could definitely live with. "If anyone gets wind of this before I've got it locked in, Mercer will back out." Of that he had no doubt. "Be very selective in who you share this with," he warned.

"I've only got a few cards left to play," Colin said. "You've given me an ace with this, Griff. Whatever you have to do to get this interview, do it."

"The sale's still on, then?" Griff gnashed his back teeth to the point his jaw ached.

"On and moving swiftly from what I'm hearing." Colin sounded less than hopeful. "The publisher's itching to sign. This might stop him. But we'll need more, if only so he doesn't begin to think we're playing games or just plain overpromising."

"What constitutes more?" Griff winced. "I can't publish—"

"I'm not asking for the whole interview. Obviously," Colin said. "Just a summary write-up of what we can expect. Enough to keep the vultures at bay."

Griff could feel the real world outside Nalani begin to push in and doubt was coming in right on its heels. The deeper he got into this deal he'd made with Mercer, the worse he felt about it.

"We're talking a couple of paragraphs," Colin pressed. "I just want a feel for the tone of the article and what you expect to learn."

"The tone is going to be truthful," Griff said. "Details aren't possible considering I haven't had an actual conversation with the man yet." About this at least.

"Good. Good, that'll give authenticity to it being objective and fair. I'll get to work on a contract for exclusivity." Colin swore but his words sounded more upbeat than they had at the beginning of the conversation. "Richard Mercer. In a hundred years I wouldn't have guessed it. How did you get onto it? No, wait, don't tell me. Save it for the article."

That was one tidbit of information he didn't plan on sharing with anyone. Ever. Griff worried. This was getting out of hand. He hadn't wanted to start writing until he got back; until he was far enough away from Daphne that it didn't seem like a complete betrayal of their time together. Now he was having to come to terms with the fact that he wasn't going to be able to hold up his end of the deal with Mercer. Which meant no article, no interview. Ever. "I'll get you something by Sunday." Why did it feel as if he was surrendering his soul?

"Great, Griff. Excellent. Have a good rest of your evening."

"Right," Griff said to the now-dead call. "You, too." He could not, for the life of him, shake the feeling he'd just made a gigantic mistake.

Right now, the only thing bringing him a modicum of joy was the squealing laughter coming from behind the closed bathroom door in the kids' room. So much for not pushing Daphne on her relationship with her father. He didn't have much of a choice now, did he? He needed that exclusive interview with Richard Mercer. Now more than ever.

Noah yanked open the balcony door. "Dad? Everything okay?"

"Everything's fine." It was an automatic response. One he uttered with a forced smile, and he touched a hand to his son's shoulder as he went back inside.

A notification on his laptop began to chime when he passed, and for a moment, he wondered if the universe was somehow conspiring against him. Given the ringtone, however, there was only one person who video-called him on that particular account. "Shoes off the sofa, please." He pointed at his son's feet when Noah flopped back and grabbed his tablet. An entirely different kind of tension tightened his shoulders as he clicked open the video chat. "Hey, Mom."

"Griffin." Maureen Townsend's face filled the entire screen. Her bobbed gray hair looked as neat as a pin as always. The knot of panic that always formed in his chest when she called eased instantly at her smile. As difficult as the last couple of years had been on Griff, caring almost nonstop for his father had left his mother stressed and strained.

"Mom, sit back a little."

"Hi, Grandma!" Noah scrambled off the sofa and wedged himself under Griff's arm. "Hawai'i is awesome! I'm learning to surf!"

"Oh, that's lovely to hear, Noah." Maureen's eyes filled with pride and joy. "You always have loved the water. What's Cammie been doing?" She leaned to the one side, then the other. "Where is she?"

"Getting ready for going to see a movie," Griff said. "They give us dinner, too. Cammie went on a wild flower hike this afternoon." At least he thought that's what it had been. "Is everything okay, Mom?"

"Fine, everything's fine," Maureen said. "I was just missing all of you."

"Dad's okay? You're taking care of yourself?"

"He's the same." She waved off his concern as if it was nothing more than an offensive cobweb. The sadness was there, but she had finally come to terms with accepting the new challenges they were all facing together as a family. "Your aunt Barbara came to visit this week. I stayed a couple of nights in her hotel with her. We had a lovely time."

"That's great, Mom." It was a relief knowing she'd had a break from caretaking, despite being surrounded by a facility of nurses and specialists. His parents—and his mother especially—had taken the in-sickness-and-in-health portion of their marriage vows very seriously. "How is she liking Arizona?"

"She loves it. She told me all about her senior condo community and all the activities they have and she's made a ton of friends. You should see the pictures."

"Next time I see her I'll ask," Griff assured her.

"Noah," Maureen said. "Why don't you get your sister so we can all chat?"

"She's taking a bath," Noah said.

"By herself?" Maureen pinned him with "the look" that even hundreds of miles away still had the desired effect. "Griffin Joel Townsend, what on earth…"

"Hey, Griff, I think you need to call down for some extra towels. Oh." Daphne stopped in the bedroom doorway and held up a hand. "Sorry. I didn't realize you were on a call."

"Daphne Mercer?" Maureen asked. "Is that you? Griff, is that Daphne?"

"Um." Daphne's face went bright red and at Griff's urging, she came closer. "Hi, Mrs. Townsend."

"Oh, my dear girl, look at you, all grown up." His mother was beaming ear to ear.

Instead of feeling good about his mom's reaction, Griff felt like a heel. If she only knew her son's real reason for seeking out Daphne she'd be mortified, not to mention angry.

"Pretty as a picture," Maureen gushed. "Griff, you didn't tell me… Oh, my." Maureen patted a hand to her heart. "Look how beautiful you are. The two of you together again. Reminds me of your senior prom, Griff. What a night that was."

"You haven't changed a bit," Daphne said as she drew close to Griff. "It's good to see you. How are you and Mr. Townsend?"

"Oh, we're just fine. We're fine." Maureen covered her mouth with her hands. "I don't want to interrupt you all. You look so dressed up."

"They're going out to dinner," Noah announced. "Cammie and I are going to the movies at the pool."

"You're having dinner together," Maureen repeated. "Like a date? Oh, are you two dating again? Never mind. None of my business. Don't pay any attention to me. I'm just so…oh, Griff." That smile of joy and approval slid through him all the way to his toes. "This makes me happier than I can even tell you. I can't wait to speak to your father. I bet I get a smile out of him with this news. I'll let you go. Have a good time. Lovely to see you again, Daphne. Just lovely. Call me soon, Griffin, please. I want details. Love you! Hank! Oh, Hank, wait until you hear…" The screen went dark.

"I think that's the first time she's been able to turn off

the call without me telling her how," Griff muttered under his breath.

"She looks great." Daphne rested a hand on his arm. "Is everything okay with your dad?"

"No change, so that's a yes." Griff clicked off his laptop. "That's the happiest I've seen her in a long time." He smiled at her. "Thanks for that."

"I didn't do anything," Daphne insisted.

He took hold of her hand and squeezed. "You were here."

Noah returned to his tablet.

She threaded her fingers through his hair. "I need more towels, please." She gestured down to her damp dress. "Cammie likes to swim in the tub."

"Oh, right. Forgot about that. Hang on." He retrieved a couple of towels from his bathroom and beelined them into Cammie. "I've got it from here. Dry off," he told Daphne.

He needed the distraction of his elated and content little girl to keep him from spinning off his axis. Maybe, if he was lucky, he'd have his thoughts back on track by the time he and Daphne left for dinner.

"You look stressed." Daphne sent Griff a sympathetic look as their server poured them each a glass of chilled white wine. "You're worried about your parents, aren't you?"

Their window table at the Blue Moon Bar and Grill proved the perfect viewing spot for the slow-setting sun. It wasn't the fanciest place to eat in Nalani; Seven Seas at the resort claimed that honor. But dinner service here was an uptick in luxury compared with its breakfast and lunch offerings. Fresh seafood was caught from their own boat every morning and determined the evening's menu, but there was also standard fare—a selection of sushi and sashimi, as well as favorites like fresh catch of the day, steak, burgers and trough salads large enough to feed a table of customers.

Daphne didn't eat here often but when she did she enjoyed the lunar-and-sky-themed decor from the painted ceiling to the midnight blue tablecloths.

"Among other things," he said in a way that made her wonder if he realized he'd spoken out loud.

"It can't be the kids you're worried about," Daphne observed. "I think they're both finally island acclimated."

That got him to smile. "They're the least of my concerns, for a change."

Daphne could understand that. The second they'd brought Noah and a sparkly clean Cammie down to the pool, the two, along with Taco, of course, had dashed out into the crowd of children taking spur-of-the-moment hula classes with one of the island's best luau dancers. Colorful summer lights had been strung across the area and a pair of ukulele players strummed fun, booty-swinging music for all.

"You can talk to me, you know." She reached out when he started to twirl his wineglass with a bit more force than seemed safe. His wine sloshed up and nearly spilled over the rim.

His smile, however, said otherwise and for the first time since they'd become reacquainted, she worried if she was getting ahead of herself where they were concerned. It was one thing to reunite with an old love, but surrendering to the fantasy that this was turning into something more might just be setting herself up for disappointment. Romance aside, it was obvious Griffin needed the one thing she knew she could continue to be: a friend.

"Talk to me, Griff," she urged again.

"It's just hard, thinking about my folks getting older.

It feels." He shook his head, looking a bit dazed and confused. "It feels like I'm running out of time with them. Like the clock of my life is suddenly on fast forward."

She nodded despite her inability to relate. She'd sat at her mother's bedside for two days before Veronica Mercer had passed, lamenting not the time ahead she would lose but all that she'd already lost. Time she'd never be able to get back with her mom. "You'll be relieved to get home."

"In a sense." He didn't sound entirely convinced. "I'm just glad I haven't left anything unsaid where they're concerned. Regrets are a horrible thing to live with, Daphne." His eyes sharpened. "Believe me, I'm still living with a lot of them. I wouldn't wish that on anyone. Especially you."

It took a few moments for the weight of his implication to land. "Why do I have the feeling you're talking about my father again." She sat back, pulled her hands into her lap and clutched her napkin.

"Because I am," he said.

She could have sworn she heard a hint of disgust in his voice. "Why? What does my father matter, Griff? For heaven's sake, he's the reason you broke up with me in the first place. Why do you care—"

"He told you about that? About what he…?" He stopped himself but not soon enough.

"He didn't tell me anything. You just did, though." She shook her head, picked up her menu and stared at the suddenly blurry writing. It hurt. Even after all this time it hurt to think that her father had gotten in the way of one of the few things that had ever made her happy. "I wondered. Once the fog cleared. And I suspected. Did he threaten you? Or did he pay you off?" She hadn't meant the accusation to sound quite so glib.

"There was no payoff," Griff said even as the color drained from his face.

"I'm sorry." Darn it, this was what her father did. He ruined everything, even when he wasn't in the vicinity. "That was out of line." Her appetite was fading faster than an orchid in direct sunlight. "Talking about my father sours my mood so I'm changing the subject." She sent him a glaring look. "All right?"

"Yeah." Resignation rang in his voice now. "But can I just say one more thing?"

"Clearly I can't stop you," she muttered.

"There will come a time when he's not here anymore, Daphne. You must have questions, or at the very least things you want to say to him if only to finally get past everything that's happened."

"I've gotten past everything." It was taking every ounce of energy she had to focus on the menu. "I hadn't given him a second or even a third thought for years. Not until you got here."

"All right, I'll give you that. I guess I just don't want you to have the same regrets you might have about your mother."

Her regrets on that front weren't any of his business, either. "And I don't want our one dinner alone together to turn into some long, messy, unwarranted discussion that will only tick me off," she countered. "I get that you're worried about your parents, Griff. Of course you are, but stop projecting your experiences onto mine. You can't compete, believe me."

"I'm not trying to."

"Good." She flashed a less-than-amused smile. "Then we can move on. What looks good to you?"

"Everything."

The fact that he said it while looking directly at her eased the irritation surging through her system. "How do you do that?"

"Do what?"

"Make me so angry one second then turn on that charm and make me forget why I was upset in the first place." She set her menu down, desperation circling the affection clinging to her heart. "That's not fair."

"No, it's not. But it's my gift." He held out a hand and waited patiently until she took it. "Consider talking to him, Daphne. Even if it's just to say goodbye. Just...don't leave things unsaid. That's all I'll say about it."

For now, she suspected. Feeling his fingers slip though hers, feeling the heat of his grasp through her entire being with something she could only describe as utter and complete acceptance, had her trembling. "We don't have a lot of time before reality returns," she said quietly. "Let's spend what we do have in a positive way." And that way did not include her father.

"Agreed."

She spotted their server on the approach and quickly changed the subject again. "The last time I was here, the ahi poke appetizer was amazing. I highly recommend it."

"Then we'll start with that," he said. "And then you can tell me about your hike with Cammie."

"Fair warning," she told him and grinned at the panic in his eyes. "She wants a dog." And with that pronouncement, normalcy returned.

"If teen me could see us now," Griff said a few hours later as they strolled hand in hand down the beach. The sun continued to lower beyond the horizon, turning the ocean into a radiant display of fire and water. The sight was almost enough to counter the near mess he'd made over dinner. His head was all over the place. With Daphne, with his parents. With Richard Mercer and the paper. The former he could manage relatively fine, but when had the survival of the paper and all its employees landed on his shoulders? Freelance should have meant just that: free. Instead, he was feeling even more trapped than when he'd been working his old job overseas.

He pulled himself back into the present, where families had long ago packed up for the day, leaving only a few locals hanging about the beach, eating dinner by the shore. Taking lazy walks in the damp sand. He did see one woman, dressed in a bright green mumu weaving through the grove of trees lining the beach. Her bare feet kicked up plumes of sand as she stomped around.

"I hear you in there!" the woman called out. "Don't think you can hide from me."

Griff stopped, frowned and tugged Daphne closer. "Should we be worried?"

"No, not at all." She touched his arm and pulled free of his hold. "Haki." Daphne walked over to the older woman who had stark streaks of silver through her black hair. "It's almost sunset, Haki. The *menehunes* are already in bed."

"Ah! Daphne." Haki turned and displayed a suspicious smile. "You were back at the falls today." She reached up and brushed a hand over each of her shoulders. "You didn't bring friends back with you, did you?"

"No, I didn't." Daphne took Haki's hand and held it close to her heart. "I came back alone, I promise. And look." She shook her free wrist, displaying a charm bracelet. "I'm wearing the jewelry you gave me. It protects me from them, remember?"

"You spend a lot of time in their domain," Haki said. "They like you. You're a forest dweller."

"Why don't you head home? In the morning you might have better luck catching them."

"They're tricky," Haki agreed and nodded. "But you're right. I'll get some rest and come back tomorrow. I think they have a new hole in there." She pointed to the palm trees. "I'll let them get comfortable before I seek them out again."

"Okay. I'll let Sheriff Aheona know you're on their trail."

"*Mahalo*, Daphne." Haki squeezed her hand and trudged through the sand up to Pulelehua Road.

"Is she all right?" Griff came up behind Daphne.

"Haki's fine," Daphne said. "She's always been a bit eccentric. She has a house, about two blocks up from the main road. She's been hunting *menehune* since before I lived here."

"*Menehune*?"

"Little island tricksters. They get up to all kinds of mischief and Haki believes it's her purpose in life to protect us from them."

"Has she ever caught one?" Griff asked as he tugged her back to the tide.

"Not that I've ever heard of," Daphne said. "But who knows. Maybe one day." She laughed a little. "Something to look forward to. Lots of island superstitions. Some fun. Some not. It's all part of life here."

"It's going to be hard to go home. Even after so short a visit." For so many reasons. Reasons he couldn't tell her about. "I've thought about you often over the years, Daphne. I'm so sorry about how things ended between us."

"We've gone down that road already so don't start again," she warned. "I mean it, Griff."

"I'm not." And he wasn't. If he made another attempt, he wasn't going to be able to withhold the truth any longer. On the one hand, it might be for the best. On the other? He still had days left with her and he wanted to preserve as much time with her as he could. "I didn't want to break your heart. It's probably my biggest regret."

"Well, you can move beyond that now." She slipped her fingers through his, rested her head on his shoulder as they strolled. "Everything turned out pretty well. I found this place and you have those two beautiful kids of yours. If we'd done anything differently, they wouldn't be here."

"No," he agreed. "They wouldn't be. But there's one thing that hasn't changed for me, Daphne." If he couldn't tell her every truth, he could at least admit to the one that had haunted him for more than a decade. "I still love you. I don't think I ever stopped loving you." He sank his feet into the sand and pulled her to him, brushed his mouth against hers. "It's been you since the first time we laid eyes on each other."

She smiled at him, but it was a controlled expression, one that he suspected hid a myriad of emotions on her end. She lifted a hand to his face, brushed the backs of her fingers across his cheek. "You and I both know there isn't anywhere for this to go. You and the kids go home in a few days. You have a job, a life, your parents, Noah and Cammie have their lives, too. And I'm never leaving Nalani." Her whisper almost broke his heart. Not because he heard sadness or sorrow in her voice, but because he heard loyalty, contentment and commitment. "We can enjoy each other's company for now, though. And maybe one day you'll all come back."

"Noah and Cammie, too?"

"Of course." Tears filled her eyes. "They're great kids, Griff. Very easy to fall in love with." Her voice broke.

"I can't believe you can still say that after spending the afternoon with Cammie on a hike. She really didn't throw you off your game once?"

"How could she?" Daphne whispered. "She's part of you." She rose up on her toes and pressed her mouth to his in a kiss that tasted like every sweet promise he'd ever wanted to hear.

And every goodbye he never wanted to experience.

Chapter Ten

"Hey, Tehani?" Tablet in hand, Daphne called to her friend as she entered Ohana Odyssey. She had to yell over the almost jet-engine roaring of the fans set up around the room. "T?" she called again and clicked a couple of fans off.

Tehani spun around in her chair, eyes wide. "Back so soon?"

"We've been gone three hours." Daphne flipped her tablet around, looked at it and frowned. "I'm pretty sure you forgot to give me the updated list for the tour group." Normally Tehani was so on top of things Daphne never had to double-check the files she received, but not today. She'd had to do some quick updating and replanning before her excursion could begin.

"Oh." Tehani blinked, her dark eyes clouding. "Did I?" She clicked a few keys on her computer and sighed. "Yeah, you're right. Sorry." Outside, the group Daphne had just taken for a tour through the Hilo University horticulture and botanical garden chatted among themselves as they headed down the hill back into town. "Why don't you send me your notes and I'll update it in the system." Her shoulders slumped. "Really sorry. My brain's just foggy, I guess."

Daphne wasn't so sure. She walked around the front

desk that was Tehani's main domain as office manager, tried not to take offense when Tehani quickly clicked her monitor closed and slapped a folder shut.

"Okay, what's going on?" Daphne sat on the edge of the unusually cluttered desk. "You've been acting weird lately and it's not like you to make mistakes like this." She stopped short of mentioning that Wyatt had mentioned it to her, but Daphne had the feeling Tehani wouldn't take that information too well.

"I just sent you the wrong file is all." Tehani seemed inordinately attentive to collecting the loose pens on her desk into a cup. "I'm human, aren't I?"

"Tehani." Daphne reached out and caught her hand. "What's going on?"

Tehani frowned, tucked her hair behind her ear.

"Is it the baby?" Daphne pressed. "Is something wrong?"

"No." Surprise lifted her chin and she shook her head. "No, the baby's fine. My last checkup was great. It's not the baby."

"Then what is it?"

Tehani's expression seemed full of grief. "It's nothing," she whispered. "It's just…" She blew out a long breath and touched two fingers to her heart. "Sometimes it's hard, being here. With Sydney and all of you and not…"

"And not Remy," Daphne finished quietly.

"When is this going to stop?" Tehani asked desperately. "When will I stop seeing him everywhere? There are days I miss him so much I don't know if I can keep going."

"T." Daphne squeezed her hand. "I'm so sorry. I don't know. I don't have that answer. What can we do?"

"Nothing." She shrugged. "That's the problem. There's nothing anyone can do. Some days I just want to run away and start over somewhere else."

Daphne frowned. It was on the tip of her tongue to tell her friend that running away was never the answer, but she couldn't very well utter those words, could she? Not when she'd run herself.

"I just have to push through it to the other side," Tehani said firmly. "I'm just so…" She cut herself off, pressed her lips tight.

"Angry," Daphne whispered.

"Yes," Tehani confirmed, her eyes sparking. "So angry. How can that even be?"

"Because it's natural." Daphne was well acquainted with the stages of grief and certain ones in particular that often left people, herself included, stuck. "You're angry at Remy for not knowing how serious his health issues were." Daphne tried to fill in the blanks. "Angry he's not here for the baby. And you're angry at him for leaving you."

"He abandoned me, Daphne." The desperation in Tehani's voice brought tears to Daphne's eyes. "I know he didn't mean to, but he left me here all alone to do everything without him and I honestly don't know if I can. He's going to miss everything about this little boy's life and that's so unfair."

"It is," Daphne agreed. "But you aren't alone." The emotion in her friend's voice broke Daphne's heart. "I'd think you of all people would realize that. We're all here for you. Me, Sydney, Keane, Mano. And all of Nalani." She couldn't help but add, "And there's Wyatt, of course."

"Wyatt." Tehani laughed and looked to the sky. "Oh, my gosh, Wyatt."

For the life of her, Daphne couldn't decipher what Tehani's tone meant.

"Honestly, I doubt I could have made it even this far without Wyatt," Tehani admitted. "He's just there. Whenever I need…someone. Something. He came over last night to build the crib I ordered. I told him about it like two months ago when the delivery was delayed and he still remembered." She flapped her hands as if trying to hide something. "When he was done all I could do was cry because Remy should have been the one to do it. How do I move on when all I can see is the stuff he's missing?"

"He's not missing it completely," Daphne whispered, hoping, praying she was right. "Remy's still here, T. I can feel him just like I did the other morning on the beach. He's never going to be gone because he's a big part of what has always made Nalani so special."

"Yeah." Tehani nodded, looked down at her belly and tugged her hand free of Daphne's hold. "Yeah, I know. And that might be part of the problem." She straightened the folders and pens and papers, scooting Daphne aside. "Sorry. I get into these moods and can't seem to get out of them very easily and darn it! This kid is such a mover and kicker. I've got to use the restroom. Again." She rolled her eyes and shoved herself to her feet. "I'll go blubber by myself for a bit and I'll be fine. I'll fix the files when I'm back."

"Okay." Daphne stood where she was, eyes scanning the desk for answers to a question she couldn't quite form.

"Hiya, Daphne!" Jordan Adair bounced into the room with her usual enthusiasm. Her long sun-streaked blond hair was knotted on top of her head and her surf suit was unzipped to expose the bright pink bikini she wore underneath. The surfboard under one arm was scarred and battered after having been dragged around the California coast and all across the islands, which explained her tanned skin and taut muscles. The tangle of twine and shell necklaces spoke of her love for all things island related. "Need any help this afternoon? I am a free bird the rest of the day."

"Ah, sure." Daphne caught the scribbled sticky note attached to one of the folders. It was in Tehani's writing and included a phone number and a dollar amount beneath. "No afternoon surf lessons today?"

"Keane's got them covered." She set her board down in the corner and stretched her arms over her head. "Alec and I are coming on the cruise tonight, but that's hours away. What are we doing in the meantime?"

"I've got a preliminary sketch of the new RV campground Mano wants to build on the other side of the resort. I could use your feedback."

"Stellar." Jordan pointed to the nearby locker room. "Give me a few minutes to shower and change and I'll be all yours."

"Hey, Jordan?" Daphne called after her. "Have you heard of Mount Lahani?"

"The new resort in Maui?" Jordan asked. "Yes. I spent a couple of weeks surfing the beaches around there. Pretty snazzy place, high-end. Lots of private beach. It's only been open for a couple of years. Why?"

"No reason." Daphne frowned. "Just curious. I'm going to go clean the tour bus. Give a holler when you're done."

"Will do!"

"Dad, come on! We're going to be late!"

"Yeah, just a second," Griff muttered as his fingers came to a complete halt over the keyboard. He'd finally, after umpteen starts and stops, found his groove in the opening paragraphs of what he hoped would be the first installment of his exclusive interview with Richard Mercer.

It was honest, pithy and filled with as much promise as he felt comfortable conveying. Best of all, it should get the publisher off Colin's back as far as wanting to sell the paper. But even still...

All it took to pull him out of the zone was the noise of a six- and an eight-year-old who had found their second wind after a completely unsuccessful nap time.

Instead they were running on the adrenaline of a non-stop marathon of activities over the past few days that had left him totally exhausted. But happy his kids were having the time of their life.

Griff tried one more time to finish the train of thought he'd been riding, but it was no use. He clicked Save, minimized the window and closed his laptop. What was he thinking trying to write while on vacation?

"You two all ready to go?" His surrender complete, he faced his kids. "What's that?" He pointed to the shell necklace wrapped multiple times around Taco the Fish's neck.

"I made it in craft class this morning," Cammie announced. "They're called puka shells. Oh! I forgot!" She darted back into the bedroom to grab her barely hanging together lei that Daphne had given her. "No, no, no!" She stepped back as a cascade of petals hit the floor. "Daddy! It's dying!" She looked up at him, chin wobbling. "I tried to be so careful!"

"It's okay." Griff hurried over and put his arms around her. "They aren't meant to last forever. Sorry, Cammie. It was pretty."

"But yours and Noah's will last," Cammie sobbed. "And mine's gone and now I won't have one and I want to wear it with my new dress!"

Noah rolled his eyes and flopped back onto the sofa.

"Cammie." Griff hugged her close. "Daphne told you it wouldn't last forever. Yours was so lovely while you had it. I think we can save some of the flowers and do something special with them when we get home."

"But what about tonight?" Cammie hiccupped. "I wanted to wear my princess lei on the boat."

"We'll have to see what else we can come up with," Griff said. "You two get your shoes. It's almost time we go."

"I can't find mine," Cammie grumbled.

"Please try. They must be here somewhere," Griff said.

The last couple of days had been a roller coaster of comings and goings, and emotions. Noah's early morning surfing lessons had left the rest of their days free and they'd stuck with Ohana Odysseys for their plans. They'd gone zip-lining and ATV-ing one day, horseback riding and snorkeling another, and this morning had found them soaring through the air in a helicopter to tour the Big Island with their extraordinary guide Sydney Calvert.

Noah's instant fascination with surfing had paled in comparison with Cammie's awe at having a woman piloting. His daughter's numerous questions had been answered with patience, amusement and, most of all, encouragement.

Poor Sydney probably didn't know the fan she'd earned in his daughter, but Griff saw it as another reason to be grateful. He might have come to Nalani with a less-than-honorable purpose, but the island town had definitely put on a show to remember for him and his children. He'd hoped the afternoon activities and craft class in the children's center after lunch would give him some quiet work time, but alas, he'd found himself wandering around downtown Nalani for the better part of a few hours drinking in the atmosphere that all too soon he would be leaving.

He was as happy with the story proposal as he was going to get. He had until tomorrow afternoon island time to get it done and sent. It would be nice to have it off his plate so he could concentrate on the last few days he and the kids had in Nalani.

By the time he and the kids were headed to the lobby, he'd set the piece aside and was back to being committed to enjoying the evening. One of the last he'd be spending with Daphne. The countdown was on to heading home and returning to the real world that, Griff had to admit, held far less appeal than it had only a few days ago.

They followed the signs to the harbor that housed dozens of moored boats, ranging from simple rowboats to gigantic, wallet-busting yachts bobbing in the water.

"What's the boat's name again?" Noah asked as they walked down the wooden deck.

"Nani Nalu," Griff told him. "Apparently it means 'beautiful wave' in Hawaiian."

"There's Keane!" Noah yelled and pointed ahead to where Keane was loading boxes and crates onto the stern of a catamaran. "That must be it. Come on, Cammie!"

"Be careful!" Griff yelled after them. He could just imagine having to pull both of them out of the water because of a wrong turn.

"Aloha!" Keane greeted them with a wave and a smile.

"Sorry we're early," Griff apologized. "They were anxious to get on board."

"Always a good sign," Keane said.

"Can I give you a hand?" Griff motioned to one of the two handcarts filled with boat provisions.

"Won't say no," Keane said. "Cammie, Noah, shoes off, please. Toss them in the cabinet there by the bench."

"No shoes?" Cammie's eyes went wide when she looked down at her sandals.

"The floors can get a bit slippery," Keane told her. "Better with bare feet. And shoes can scratch up the fiberglass. Thanks. Oh, hey, Wyatt. You know Griffin Townsend and his kids, right?"

"Sure do." Wyatt hopped off the boat to grab a box himself. "Glad you all could join us. Hey, you two. Polunu's just up the stairs there in the main cabin. He's trying out some new drinks for kids we can add to the dinner cruise menu. He'd appreciate a few guinea pigs."

"Can we, Dad?" Noah asked.

"Go ahead." Griff nodded. "Just mind your manners." He could all but see Noah roll his eyes even with his son's back to him.

"Come on, Cammie!" Noah grabbed his sister's hand and led her up the few steps to the second level.

"Nice boat," Griff said as they made quick work of the supplies.

"I spent a lot of time on the *Nani* growing up," Keane said. "The stars aligned for me to buy her and make her my own. Thanks." He hefted the last box out of Griff's arms. "Not all of this is for tonight," Keane informed him. "This is just the restocking for the kitchen and bar we've been expecting." He flashed a smile. "Figured I could put the early birds to work helping me stash it below deck."

"Happy to help." Griff sniffed the air.

He turned and spotted Sydney and Theo headed their way, each carrying a stack of large aluminum foil trays in their arms. Behind them, a curvy brunette he hadn't met before, surfer Jordan Adair, Mano Iokepa and his sister, Tehani, another man Griff didn't recognize and Oliwa, the head bell porter at the resort along with Kiri, one of the assistant water activities supervisors for Ohana Odysseys. "Something smells amazing," Griff said as Sydney and Theo passed.

"Akahi's famous Kahlua pork." Sydney beamed. "We only just pulled it out of her backyard *imu* about an hour ago." She handed over her trays and climbed on board, immediately kicked off her flip-flops. "We are officially off the clock and it is time for some fun!"

The brunette whooped from the middle of the lineup of people coming on board. "You must be Griff." She stopped and nudged Keane with her hip. "I'm Marella Harper. I'm with this one." She giggled a little when Keane kissed her cheek. "I never get tired of saying that."

"And I never get tired of hearing it," Keane countered.

"Ah, the newlyweds," Griff stated. "Congratulations."

"Thanks." Marella's long dark hair cascaded around her shoulders that were covered by the straps of a beautiful coral sundress.

"Akahi sends her regrets," Sydney said as she moved farther onto the boat. "Polunu's wife was hoping to make it, but her new medication's kicking her butt. Nothing interferes with her overseeing the cooking, though," Sydney added. "I told her we'd take pictures." She arched a brow at Griff, then down at his bag. "I hear you're pretty good with a camera."

Griff grinned. "I do okay."

"Understatement of the century," Mano said as he joined the others. "Glad you could make it."

"Thanks," Griff said. "Hi, er, aloha," he greeted the tall, dark-haired man with his arm around Jordan's waist, whom he didn't know. "Sorry. Still getting used to it, I guess."

"No problem. Alec Aheona Malloy. Good to meet you."

"We have the police chief on board," Griff said and couldn't help but smile at the besotted expression on Jordan's face when she looked up at him. "Is it true you two met when you arrested her?"

"He detained me," Jordan countered. "There's a difference."

"Not much of one." Alec chuckled and tightened his arm around the surfer's waist.

"They met the first time he detained her," Theo corrected. "By my count you arrested her three times."

"Only got out the handcuffs once," Alec said easily. "The other times were only warnings really."

"There's a story here, isn't there?"

"Sure is." Jordan laughed. "But it might take a few trips down the coast to get it out of us. Are we all here?" She looked around as people flooded up the steps into the main cabin. "Where's Daphne?"

"Coming!" Daphne hurried down the gangplank, her red hair flying in the evening breeze behind her. She had on a pair of hip-hugging shorts and a top that was the color of red summer lilies. Her legs were bare and the sandals she wore slapped against the wood. "Sorry! Pua dropped off a tray of haupia as I was leaving. Figured this will save me from myself."

"Coconut pudding squares, right?" Griff had been boning up on his island vocabulary. And the local food.

"Got it in one." She stopped in front of him, tilted her chin up and smiled. "Hi."

"Hi." He couldn't help it. He dropped a quick kiss on her upturned lips. "I missed you today."

"Yeah? I missed you, too."

"Daphne!" Cammie yelled from above them. "I made Taco a necklace! And my lei died. It matched my new dress, too." She stepped farther out and did a little twirl to show off the pink-and-purple-flowered frock.

"Whiplash all in one sentence," Daphne murmured and laughed as Griff touched a hand to the small of her back and she stepped onto the boat. "We'll see about getting you another lei," she called up to a bouncing Cammie.

"I think that's it," Keane said as one of the resort workers walked down to reclaim the handcart. "All aboard, everyone. Let's get this party started."

The islands appeared to be in showstopper mode as Keane steered the *Nani Nalu* south around the tip of the Big Island. The sun was taking its time setting in the horizon but meanwhile shined spectacular light to create a show across the water. With the gentle laughter and murmurings of conversation, the evening's cruise was proving to be one of the best things Griff and the kids had done yet.

The hand-crafted, expandable wooden table was large enough to seat the entire party. The rum punch was flowing for the adults while Polunu, the previous owner of the vessel, was entertaining Noah and Cammie with grandfatherly enthusiasm. It occurred to Griff, sitting here, watching Daphne chat and mingle with her friends, the sun's rays catching against the red in her hair, that Ohana was so much more than a business. It was, indeed, a family. One that had welcomed both him and his children without any reservation.

He took the final pull of his beer, released a deep breath and then closed his eyes. Feeling the breeze on his face, he longed to stay right here, in this moment, for as long as he could. The bobbing boat finally started to pass the recent volcanic activity that even now expanded the island's reach.

"Keane's taking things a little slow tonight." Mano Iokepa's voice broke through Griff's thoughts. The hotel manager claimed a seat beside him, set a new bottle of beer in front of him and leaned back. "We should be eating in a few minutes. He likes to find the perfect spot to drop anchor for a little while."

"I'm not in any rush to do anything," Griff admitted. "Is that what Daphne calls island time?"

Mano grinned. "Something like that."

"I almost didn't recognize you," Griff said, indicating Mano's bare but tattooed arms. "I would have bet money you sleep in your suit."

"Not too far off," Mano chuckled. "I'll admit to being a bit of a workaholic." A flash of regret crossed his face before he spoke again. "So. You and Daphne seem to have mended fences."

Suspecting they'd finally arrived at the inquisition portion of the evening, Griff shrugged. "Seems so. That was a long time ago. We're...different people than we were then."

Mano eyed him in a way that reminded Griff of how protective Noah could get when it came to Cammie. "She seems very happy. Happier than I've seen her for ages. Maybe since she got here."

"She makes me happy, too."

"Good to hear." Mano nodded, glanced up as Theo and Alec dropped into chairs around them.

"Is this where the three of you join forces to tell me you'll chuck me over the side of the boat if I do anything to hurt her?"

"Nah." Alec waved off his comment, but his eyes definitely sparked with warning. "No point in doing that. Jordan has a habit of diving in after people around here. She'd have you back on board before you could blink."

"One of the many reasons the police chief here is crazy about her," Theo teased. "He might be here to warn you." He pointed to Mano. "I just wanted to say thanks for agreeing to take pictures tomorrow morning. I know it's an early outing for someone on vacation."

Griff twisted the top off the unopened beer and toasted Theo. "It'll be a nice change, taking pictures of something hopeful and promising. Fair warning, Cammie has announced she's coming, too."

"The more the merrier," Theo said. "It's going to be pretty early, though. Sunrise is usually around five."

"I told her." Griff smiled behind his bottle. "My little girl's a romantic. All those princess movies make her want to witness a real happily-ever-after in person. When she's properly motivated, even a pre-dawn alarm doesn't phase her. Good thing it's tomorrow, though. Not sure she could keep it secret much longer than that."

"She's not the only one." Theo sighed. "In any case, thank you," Theo said again. "I guess now all I have to worry about is whether Sydney will say yes."

Mano and Alec both chuckled as if Theo had made a joke.

"Yeah," Mano said with a roll of his eyes. "I'm surprised she hasn't proposed to you by now."

The engine died down as the boat came around the point and settled in against the waves.

"That means it's time to eat!" Mano slapped his hand on Griff's shoulder. "I'm going to head down and see if they need help setting up."

"He can never stop managing," Theo muttered as the sound of the anchor being dropped rattled against the breeze.

"Daddy!" Cammie, Taco tucked under her arm, raced out of the main cabin and jumped into his lap. "Noah's trying to scare me again."

"Am not," Noah said as he trudged behind her. "I was just telling her about the Night Marchers."

"The what?" Griff asked.

"Huaka'i po," Alec said easily. "They're ghost warriors that walk the earth, usually at night. You'll hear them before you see them, though," he told Cammie. "They'll be banging drums or blowing into conch shells. They're just revisiting the places where they died in battle."

"So, they aren't like zombies who want to eat our brains?" Cammie glared at her brother. "That's what you said they are."

Noah shrugged.

"They are not zombies," Alec said firmly. "We respect them and, if you do come across them, we kneel and bow our heads, and silently thank them for their sacrifice. Zombies on the other hand?" Alec pointed to the ocean. "No need to worry about them here on the islands, Cammie. They hate water."

"They do?" Cammie's eyes went wide even as she grabbed hold of Griff. "You mean they can't get to us out here?"

"That's right," Griff said and aimed a look at his son. "They cannot get to us out here. Really, Noah? Zombies?"

Noah's sheepish grin was offset by Mano's reappearance. "Okay, everyone. Sit up! It's time to eat!"

"Okay, you." Griff shifted Cammie off his lap. "Why don't you—"

"I want to sit next to Daphne!" Cammie raced around the table to where Daphne pulled out a chair beside Alec. "Can I?"

Griff looked into Daphne's suddenly teary eyes. "Of course." She indicated the chair on her other side and got Cammie settled.

"No more zombie stories, Noah," Griff warned his son as Noah nodded and plopped into the chair between Griff and Theo. "Especially at night."

"It was either that or the Kraken."

"Hmm, not sure that would have gone over better." Theo shrugged. "A giant sea monster that gobbles up boats in one gulp." Too late, he realized his voice had carried. Cammie was staring in wide-eyed horror at the group of them.

"He's kidding, Cammie," Daphne said quickly and easily just as Mano and Polunu carried out platters of roasted chicken, roast pork, potato salad and piles of sweet bread rolls. "But don't worry. We have a special anti-Kraken shield on board. Don't we, Keane?" The boat's skipper was making his way around the table, filling water glasses.

"Best one there is." Keane picked up his cue and went

with it. "Anti-Kraken shield is engaged, Cammie. I double-checked."

"Oh." She blinked up at him. "Can I see it later?"

"Absolutely," Keane promised as his wife looked between them with something akin to adoration in her eyes. "I'll even let you turn it off before we head back in."

"Way cool," Cammie whispered before smiling at her brother, who only rolled his eyes harder this time.

Griff watched as Daphne helped Cammie fill her plate, encouraged her to try the flavorful rice, gave her an extra spoonful of the roasted purple potatoes his daughter had developed an affinity for and even got her to sample some poi. The gentle way she had with his children, the natural maternal instincts she put on full display, filled his heart. Even as he struggled with the guilt gnawing inside him.

Once the table was filled and all the chairs occupied, someone clanged their fork against the side of their glass.

At the far end of the table, Keane stood and called for everyone's attention. "Aloha, *ohana*."

As he spoke, the gentle lapping of the water against the hull created a pattern of calm. The sun had finally surrendered, and the sky began to fill with the twinkling stars that made wishes sing in the heart.

When the table quieted, Keane raised his glass. "Thank you to Sydney for suggesting we take this evening for ourselves. There are few things better than spending an evening out on the water with the people you care about the most. Welcome, especially, to Griffin and Cammie and Noah." He looked at each of them. "We are very happy you could join us."

Cammie beamed and turned bright eyes up at Daphne.

Griff's stomach twisted at the abject adoration and joy he saw on his daughter's face. A joy he couldn't help but worry she'd lose when they returned home. Regret knocked gently against the happiness he'd been feeling since arriving in Nalani. The happiness Daphne projected just by walking into the room. Had he made a mistake, bringing his children here? Allowing them to get attached?

No. The kids had already gotten so much out of this trip; Griff, too, of course. He focused instead on Keane's warm and kind words. They all needed to live in the moment. Cammie, Noah and Griff. Even if the moment would eventually come to an end.

Daphne stood at the bow of the catamaran, the nighttime breeze catching her hair as she lifted her face to the darkening sky. She could hear the gentle lapping of the waves against the side of the vessel, hear the muted laughter and conversation of her friends, her *ohana*, drifting from the sky level where they'd eaten dinner under the emerging stars.

The hills of the southern tip of the Big Island rounded like shadows against the horizon and the telltale thin beacon from Cape Kumukahi Light, one of the first lighthouses established in the islands.

Half-filled water glass in hand, Daphne leaned her arms on the railing and stared out into the water that tonight provided the perfect pristine peace she longed for. It hurt a little, to see how well Griff and his children fit in with her life, with her friends, even here during an *ohana* get-together in the middle of the ocean. But it had been nice, to just relax and have fun and not think too deeply about, well, anything.

Not that she'd had much time to think the past few days. Griff's reappearing in her life had moved her into a bit of a fast-forward mode. Only now did she feel his words and suggestions settling over her, unsettling her even as she began to wonder if maybe he was right. Maybe she did owe it to herself to have a conversation with her father. It had been years since they'd spoken, and even during his trial, she'd done everything to avoid both him and her mother. She hadn't wanted to be dragged into his world any more than she already was involved.

The charges Richard Mercer had faced hadn't come as a surprise, but that hadn't meant they didn't break Daphne's heart. To realize her father had been responsible for so many people losing their life savings, their homes. Their futures.

The anger still burned, stoked by her emotions that obviously, contrary to her belief, had yet to settle even after all these years.

Griff's arms slipped around her waist from behind and she stood up as he folded himself around her, rested his chin on her shoulder.

"I was wondering where you disappeared to." His voice was low against her ear and sent her spine to tingling. "We're going to head back in a bit. Early morning for some of us tomorrow. It's proposal day for Theo and Sydney."

Daphne smiled, leaned back against him and covered his hands with one of hers. "We'll be lucky to get a couple of hours sleep before we have to head up to the falls."

"Sleep's overrated," Griff countered. "Aren't you cold out here?"

"No." She wasn't. Even out on the water, where the temperature dipped and the air cooled against her skin, she reveled in it. "Can I ask you something?"

"You can ask me anything."

Her heart clutched and in that instant she pushed aside the thought that he'd be leaving soon. "Do you really think I'll have regrets if I never speak to my father again?"

His entire body stiffened. His arms tightened around her, but when he spoke, there was the familiar gentleness she'd come to expect. "I don't know," he said finally. "Right now, you have a choice, to confront him about the past and your feelings about him. To tell him everything you want to, so he knows the damage he did to you. And your mom." He paused, as if couching his words. "There will come a time when the choice won't be there. And you might wish you'd done something differently."

"Mmm." It made an odd kind of sense. But that the new knowledge came from a man who had every reason to despise her father felt strange and uncertain. "I'm not sure that I'd even know what to say to him."

"Maybe just being there is enough."

"Maybe." She turned, lifted her arms around his neck and nuzzled her lips against the side of his throat. "This is nice. Out here. Just the two of us." She could smell the sunshine still clinging to his skin, taste the salt of the sea against her lips as she pressed her mouth to the pulse at his throat. "I can almost forget there's a routine life for us to get back to."

His hands slipped through her hair, trailed down her back, sloped over the curve of her hips. "For as many pictures as I've taken in my life, I don't think one could be as perfect as this moment is with you. Now it's my turn to ask a question."

"Okay." There wasn't a part of her that wasn't alive beneath his touch. He'd reawakened something within her, something that had fallen into the darkest sleep all those years ago when he'd ended their relationship. "What is it?"

"If things were different, is there a place for me here? Is there a place for us?"

"For the three of you, you mean?" Daphne's heart picked up speed, but this time she refused to get ahead of herself. "Here in Nalani? With me?"

"Maybe." Doubt shimmered in his voice. "Maybe I'm

just thinking out loud. Maybe it's just this island, this moment, but..."

Daphne lifted her head, took a small step back to look up into his eyes that glistened against the moonlight. Her fingers tangled in the silky hair at the base of his neck. "There's more than enough room for the three of you here. With me," she added on a whisper before she drew his face down to hers.

She kissed him with all the love and affection she'd stored up for more than a dozen years. Everything about this instant, about this man, felt so incredibly right and perfect and she didn't want to leave any doubt—in either of their minds—that this was where they were both meant to be. As her mouth moved beneath his, as the boat bobbed gently in the waves and his fingers clenched against the softness of her hips, she surrendered.

"I haven't wanted to say it," she breathed against his mouth. "I couldn't let myself even completely accept it, but I don't want to miss the opportunity before it's gone." She smiled, touching her fingertips to the corner of his mouth. "I love you, Griffin. I can't remember a time when I didn't."

His smile was sad as he rested his forehead against hers. "Maybe there's hope for us, then," he said quietly.

"Sorry to interrupt." Sydney cleared her throat behind Griff and together they turned to her. "We're going to be heading back in a few minutes."

"Kids okay?" Griff asked.

"They're fine. Cammie's conked out but Keane's got her. Just didn't want you two getting surprised and knocked overboard when we turn the boat around." She grinned at them. "As you were."

"I really like your friends," Griff said when they were alone again.

"Me, too," Daphne agreed. "Theo dropped off a bunch of stuff at my house earlier for setting up at the falls. Marella'll be at my house around four thirty. We can swing by and pick you up on our way? We'll be cutting it close with the sunrise, but we should be okay."

"Sounds good. Just text me when you're close to the hotel." He slipped his hand in hers and together they rejoined her friends, her coworkers. Her *ohana*.

Chapter Eleven

"**S**hh!" Marella scampered through the shrubbery to where Daphne and Griff, along with his camera, hid behind the trees near the stone bench at Wailele Point overlooking one of Nalani's waterfalls. "They're coming!"

"Where?" Cammie poked her head out between them, her voice louder than it should have been for someone who had promised to remain silent during the waiting period.

This morning was the first time Daphne had gotten a peek at the grumpy, cranky Cammie that he had warned her about. But Daphne said she couldn't really complain about it since she was a bit cranky herself.

Cammie's excitement about the surprise proposal quickly overtook her sleepiness, though, and had her chatting almost constantly during the ride.

"I wanna see!" Cammie shimmied closer.

"You can in a minute." Daphne rested a hand on his little girl's shoulder. "You were such a big help, Cammie," Daphne went on in a whisper. "We couldn't have spread all those flower petals up the path without you."

Cammie tilted her head up and beamed. The fact that his little girl was far more awake than Griff was evidence of how comfortable she'd become in Nalani. Noah, usually his up-and-at-'em child, had clearly been practically wiped out by last night's nautical adventure. Presently his older offspring was sitting against a nearby tree, sound asleep.

"Do you think Sydney will say yes?" Cammie asked.

"Shh." Daphne crouched beside Cammie and hugged her close. "Yes, but let's be quiet, okay?"

"'Kay." Cammie all but vibrated with excitement. It was only a moment—experience had taught Griff—before she got the giggles. She couldn't keep any kind of secret. Sure enough, she had to cover her mouth with both hands to stop from laughing.

Griff heard Theo's voice drifting up the path. He leaned out, camera aimed and focused on the area that, once the sun was up, was a favorite of locals for its romantic setting and view. The pink and red rose petals strewn across the path lit up like tiny bursts of flame beneath the rising sun's rays, providing a nature-inspired carpet of welcome.

"Oh, look!" Sydney's excited whisper had Griff clicking the first photos as they rounded the corner. "Someone must have lost some flowers." She stifled a yawn. "Did you bring me up here so I'd stop pestering you into taking a sunrise flight with me?" she accused Theo. "I thought we got you over your fear of flying."

Marella dropped down to Daphne and Cammie's level, having, Griff observed, much the same issue as his daughter when it came to containing her laughter. The three of them, together like this, their smiles filled with nothing but joy and happiness, had Griff turning the camera on the trio for a few impulse pictures. Noah, his curiosity overwhelming his desire for sleep, crept up behind to watch the upcoming proposal over Daphne's shoulder.

"Maybe," Theo said as Griff refocused his lens on the couple. A shot of their linked hands, of the gentle, nervous expression on Theo's face. On Sydney's sleepy expression as Theo led her up the small hill to the stone bench and the bright pink-and-orange quilted blanket that covered it.

"Oh!" Sydney reached out, only then seeming to notice the amount of full-bloomed roses and additional island flowers scattered about. "It looks like Daphne's garden exploded," Sydney laughed as Griff shifted to the other side of the tree to keep them in sight. He took a step forward, rotated the camera and continued to shoot.

Sydney dropped down, picking up a handful of the blooms. When she circled around Theo, he glanced in their direction, inclined his head and reached into his pocket.

Griff smiled behind the lens, capturing each second as Theo removed the box from his pocket and turned, dropping down to one knee as Sydney turned toward him, their profiles on full display to the camera.

"I'm gonna cry," Marella whispered and triggered a trio of giggles once more.

"Look at how the sun's catching the waterfall," Daphne whispered as she moved behind him.

"Mmm-hmm," Griff said as he pulled back on the focus to get it, along with the shocked yet joyous expression in the same shot.

"You did all this?" Sydney gasped, looking around at the pretty scene. "Theo, when did you—"

"I asked the *menehunes* for help," Theo told her. "Are you going to answer the question?"

"What question?" Sydney teased as she pushed her long, free-flowing strawberry blonde hair out of her face.

"The only one that matters," Theo said. "Will you marry me?"

Griff kept clicking, making certain not to miss a moment.

"Yes." Sydney's eyes glistened with early morning tears

as the sun arrived behind them and bathed the area in glorious light.

Griff couldn't help but smile as Theo slid the ring on Sydney's finger. Griff waited, his attention on the ring that Daphne had told him about. The ring Theo had had made out of Sydney's late mother's engagement ring.

"Theo." Sydney breathed his name and looked at him with such reverence, such affection, even Griff's semi-jaded heart leaped to attention. "What did you do?"

"I know." Theo winced and a second of uncertainty was captured for posterity. "I hope you're okay with it. I couldn't stop thinking about the fact that you'd locked her ring away in a drawer."

"Okay with it?" Sydney sobbed, covered her mouth, then pulled her hand away and looked down at the ring again. "It's perfect. You're perfect. Perfect for me," she added as he stood up and slipped her arms around him. "I love you, Theo Abacus Fairfax. And yes, yes, yes, to being your wife!" She kissed him.

"Abacus?" Griff asked without pulling his attention away from the lens.

"He's an accountant," Daphne explained. "A nickname. An affectionate one."

"What's an abacus?" Cammie asked.

"We'll google it when we get back," Griff told his daughter. "I'm going to have enough pictures to fill an entire album."

"That's the idea. Oh, this makes my heart so happy," Daphne gushed.

"Are those *menehunes* I hear in the bushes?" Sydney asked from her spot in Theo's arms. "Do I need to sic Haki on all of you?"

"It's us!" Cammie burst out of the bushes first and led the charge. "Were you surprised? Did we surprise you? I helped with the petals." She found herself hauled up into Sydney's arms before being given a big hug.

"They're the best petals I've ever seen," Sydney assured her.

"Great job, Cammie," Theo told her.

"Yay! It's like a princess story," Cammie squealed. "And they live happily ever after!"

"I certainly hope so," Theo said. "Thank you." His expression of relief had Griff capturing yet another shot. "All of you."

"I want to get a couple more shots, from a different angle," Griff told them. "And then we'll leave you alone. Cammie? Come over with Daphne, please."

"Aw, Dad," Cammie huffed much like Noah often did, only now Noah was trudging out of the shrubs like a grumpy bear awakened too early from hibernation.

"Come on, Cam." Daphne held out her hand. "We'll wait over here."

"Great. And how about the happy couple sits here?" Griff pointed to the bench and switched vantage spots with them. "Ring front and center, please." He lifted the camera and captured a moment of perfect happiness for Daphne's friends, just as he hoped this feeling of utter contentment would follow him home.

Leaving the newly engaged couple took more effort than Daphne expected. It was intoxicating, being around such bountiful happiness and optimism. But the winding, sloped walk back to Pulelehua and Nalani proper was filled with gleeful chatter and early debate about wedding plans.

"Daddy, can we come back for the wedding?" Cammie skipped along beside her father as Daphne and Marella led the group back into town.

"That'll depend if we're invited." Griff's quick amused glance in Daphne's direction had Daphne's cheeks warming.

With Marella's arm linked through hers, Daphne reveled in the perfect morning, surrounded by some of her favorite people. The only thing that would make things better was breakfast.

"Who wants *malasadas* for breakfast?" Daphne called out and received a chorus of affirmative squeals.

"I'll have to pass." Marella kicked at a rock in her path. "Keane and I have an appointment with the contractor out at our new place. In fact, I'm going to run on ahead." Marella spun away from Daphne, her long dark hair whipping in the morning breeze. "I'll catch up with you guys later, yeah? Griff? Please don't leave without saying goodbye."

"We won't," he assured her, but only glanced up from his camera for a moment before he returned his attention to the pictures he'd taken.

Daphne slowed down and, when Cammie huffed in frustration at not holding her father's hand, held hers out to the little girl. "Come on. There's a bunch of kanawao hydrangeas up here around the corner. In all kinds of colors."

"Cool!" Cammie skipped beside her.

Griff's daughter was an exuberant sponge when it came to exploring the local flora and it struck Daphne, especially this morning, how much she'd enjoyed her time not only with Griff, but his children, as well. She hadn't really felt much of a pang for a family of her own. She'd all but relegated herself to a solitary existence as honorary aunty to her friends' children, beginning with Tehani. But the three of them together set off a longing inside her. Or maybe it was the first time she let herself admit what it was. Utter and complete love and affection for this trio of souls who had come to her island.

Crouched in front of a bountiful bush of bright blue and white flowers, she dipped her head to breathe in the subtle fragrance. She heard the familiar click of Griff's camera and smiled.

"Whatever you're thinking," Griff said from behind the lens, "keep it up. That's a beautiful shot."

"Am I a beautiful shot, too, Daddy?" Cammie asked.

"Always," Griff assured her. "Noah, why don't you join them?"

"To look at flowers?" Noah scrunched his face up at his father, confusion and dismay shining on his face.

"Just for a second. For a couple of pictures. Memories," he said, looking directly at Daphne.

"Come on, Noah." Daphne held out her arm and tucked him in beside her as Cammie dived over her shoulder. On her back, Taco the fish did a little shimmy out of her backpack and poked one of his ping-pong eyes into the shot. "It would be nice if you came back for the wedding," she murmured and took an extra moment to hug them. "I'm going to need a plus-one."

"Oooh, can we, Daddy?" Cammie asked excitedly.

"Yeah, then I can practice my surfing." Noah raised his arms in the air and danced about.

"We'll see, we'll see," Griff said and returned his attention to the camera. "Did someone mention *malasadas*?"

"Someone did," Daphne replied. "Maru's usually at her cart by now, so let's get there before the morning crowd."

"Is this normal for you?" Daphne crept up behind Griff, who, upon their return to his hotel room after breakfast post-proposal, had been glued to his computer skimming through all the photos he'd taken this morning. "Spending a beautiful day indoors looking at a computer screen when you could be outside enjoying the beach or pool?"

"Yes," Noah said from his spot on the sofa. Cammie's alertness for the proposal excitement had vanished the second they walked back to the room, and she went down for a nap while Noah played games on his tablet.

"Noah, why don't you go put your suit on and grab your board," Daphne suggested and patted Griff's shoulders. "When your sister wakes up, we'll head to the beach."

"Yeah?" Noah brightened immediately and tossed his tablet onto the coffee table. "Way cool."

"That isn't permission to wake Cammie up," Griff called over his shoulder and earned a "yeah, yeah" from his son.

"So you are in there." Daphne knocked a gentle knuckle against the back of his head. "I was beginning to wonder."

"Sorry. I wanted to get these images cleaned up for Theo and Sydney before we leave."

"You still have four days before then." Daphne did her best to ignore the tightening knots that realization triggered in her stomach.

"Exactly. Getting these done will give me more time to play." He reached up and grabbed her hand, pulled it to his lips and pressed a gentle kiss on the back of her fingers. "I'm almost done. Is there any place to get print pictures around here?"

"The Snap Shack. It's just around the corner from Hula Chicken. They've got all kinds of cell phone and camera supplies and they do custom print and framing orders."

"Perfect." He clicked through the rest of the pictures. "What do you think?"

She rested her chin on the top of his head, marveling at the images he'd captured for posterity. "You have an amazing talent for memorializing perfect moments. That color there." She pointed to the arc of the sun hitting the waterfall and reflecting back on an embracing Sydney and Theo. "It's perfection."

"Then that's what I'll go with." He made quick work of saving the files and clicked a few more keys before he stood up. "What time do they open?"

Daphne glanced at her watch. "In about twenty minutes."

"Great. I'm going to head down there and see what's what."

"What about taking the kids to the beach?"

"I'll meet you all there, if that's okay with you?" He pointed to the board leaning against the glass door. "I'll come back and grab that on my way." Griff gave a warm smile. "Won't be long."

"Okay."

She shook her head as he pulled the computer jump drive out of his laptop and slapped it shut. The entire morning had felt so…familial. So natural. It had been all she could do not to suggest he consider moving himself and the kids out here to Nalani, but she knew that was coming from an entirely selfish place. He didn't need the added pressure of that request. He already had his hands full with his parents and his job, and keeping the children where they were stable and happy in school and in life. Asking him—and everyone else around him—to change because she didn't want them to leave wasn't fair to Griff. She didn't want to guilt him into anything. That definitely wouldn't be good for any relationship they might have moving forward.

That he'd asked her if there was room here in Nalani for them had triggered something inside her; a hope she hadn't felt in a very long time. A future she'd long ago bid farewell to as an impossibility in her life. And yet…

Her heart fluttered when he smiled again and waved at her.

The door closed behind him and Daphne found herself standing in the middle of the sitting room, listening to the sound of a not-so-subtle Noah gently prodding his sister awake.

A few seconds later, a sleepy Cammie wandered in from her room, blinking confusedly at Daphne. "Where's Daddy?"

"He's going to get some pictures printed for Theo and Sydney." Daphne found the pink of sleep clinging to Cammie's cheeks endearing. "We're going to meet him down at the beach in a little while."

"Oh." Cammie yawned. "Okay." With Taco tucked under one arm, she looked at her father's laptop. "Can we watch that video of Kahlua the pig you told me about?"

"Oh." Daphne frowned. "I didn't bring my phone with me. You couldn't pull it up on your tablets?"

"We don't have video programs installed." Noah hopped out of the bedroom while trying to shove his sandals on. "Only approved games and apps and they're monitored. You could show us on Dad's laptop."

"We can ask him about it when we get back," Daphne suggested.

Cammie's scowl deepened. "But what if Kahlua is at the beach? I want to be able to tell her and Benji we saw her on TV and I promised last time I'd watch."

Daphne glanced to the desk. "I don't think..." She opened the laptop. The screen blinked on. "Yeah, sorry guys. He has it password protected."

"It's three-five-eight-six-one-one," Noah said without hesitation. "He thinks we don't know."

"358611." Daphne swallowed hard. "That's really it?"

"Yeah. It's his special number," Noah said.

"He uses it for everything," Cammie said and quickly put her hands over her mouth.

"Doesn't sound very safe, does it?" Daphne attempted to laugh, but all she could think was that Griff's special number was Daphne's high school locker combination from back in the day. With a smile curving her lips, she sat down and typed the number in.

The display screen opened, along with the multitude of files he'd left running. "Okay, internet is here." She tapped it open and quickly found the link to Nanali's tourist site, then quickly located the video for Kahlua. "Come on over." She stood up and let them share the chair as she ran the video.

Her heart jumped a bit at their giggles and Daphne found herself hoping that their time in Nalani was something they'd remember with as much fondness as she would. She'd meant it the other day when she'd told Griff his kids had been easy to fall in love with. Granted, she hadn't seen them at their worst. At least she didn't think she had. But Noah and Cammie had both stolen a piece of her heart to the point they'd be impossible to forget.

"That was so good! And so funny!" Cammie spun in the chair. "Wait till I tell all my friends I watched a pig surf in the ocean!"

"I'd rather I was surfing in the ocean," Noah announced. "Can we go already?"

"As soon as Cammie gets her suit on," Daphne assured him. "Cammie?"

"Okay, I'll change. Here." She shoved Taco into Daphne's arms. "Hold him for me, please."

"Forgot sunblock!" Noah raced after his sister as Daphne turned to shut Griff's computer down. She clicked the internet closed, then reached for the power button to put the machine to sleep. She stopped, peered closer.

"Mercer interview," she murmured to herself. "What on earth?" Any trepidation she might have had regarding Griff's privacy vanished when she clicked open the document. Her lungs emptied and her head spun as she scanned the words he'd written.

In the years since Richard Mercer's conviction on more than three dozen federal charges of embezzlement and fraud, the world has heard from dozens of his victims, listened to the testimony of his employees and witnessed the fallout for his family, business acquaintances and friends. But one person has remained silent and never spoken about any of it. Richard Mercer himself.

But he speaks now, in this series of interviews obtained exclusively by Portland Beat *reporter Griffin Townsend. With a no-topic-is-off-limits guarantee, the man responsible for the pain and suffering of so many speaks on the record...*

"Daphne?" Noah called from the doorway. "We're ready to go!"

"What?" Daphne blinked herself out of the spiral she'd fallen into.

"We're ready to go." Noah frowned. "What's wrong?"

"Nothing." Everything. Her ears roared, as if she'd been plunged into an echoing cavern filled with white noise. "Everything's fine." She sounded detached, even to herself. "Sorry. I was just..." She closed the computer and swallowed the racing emotion threatening to take over. "You guys ready?" She grabbed Taco and squeezed the stuffed fish so hard she was afraid his eyes might pop off his body. "Where's your board, Noah?"

"Oh! Right!" He retrieved it from his room as Cammie walked over. She held up her arms for Taco, then lowered them empty. "You look sad, Daphne."

"Do I?" Daphne choked.

"Uh-huh." Cammie nodded and stepped closer. "You can hang on to Taco for a while longer. He always makes me feel better. He'll make you feel better, too."

Daphne wasn't so sure. As she followed the kids out the door, she looked back at the computer. She knew what she'd read. The question was why had Griff written it.

As with most of the shops and businesses in Nalani, Griff found himself pleasantly surprised by The Snap Shack. He'd expected a hole-in-the-wall offering cell phone chargers and a run-of-the-mill photo-developer kiosk, but what he found was a full-service printing business that included custom framing and an array of technology and office-friendly services from brochure printing to document binding.

It hadn't taken him long to convey what he wanted. The extensive frame selections offered a lovely six-image option that would display his favorite eight-by-ten images. It would take a couple of days before they were ready, but he should be able to squeak in delivering it to Theo and Sydney, along with a separate flash drive containing the other pictures, before he and the kids returned to the mainland.

The other order would take a little longer as the perfect frame from the Shack's offerings was currently on back order. The bright floral-accented frame would, from what Cammie had told him about Daphne's house, fit in perfectly with her colorful mash-up of decor. He'd miss seeing her face when she opened it, but maybe that was for the best. He paid for everything up front, arranged for delivery when Daphne's gift was completed and headed to the beach to meet up with her and the kids.

For the best. Griff stood outside the Shack, barely noticing the crowd of people moving up and down the street in what he supposed was typical Sunday fare. The air was filled with the smoky aroma of Hula Chicken's fare spin roasting, and a breeze blew down Pulelehua, bringing with it hints of the ocean and the hibiscus growing all around. He could hear the muted tunes of ukuleles playing along with laughter and cries of happiness that all but permeated the entirety of the town. There hadn't been a minute he hadn't felt welcome here. Everything about this place exemplified what he'd been searching for his entire life, and while Portland was home, it wasn't pulling him back the way Nalani tugged at him to stay.

Stay. He took a deep breath, shook his head. How presumptuous of him. But how hopeful, and hope wasn't something he was familiar with anymore. Or at least he hadn't been until he'd set eyes on Daphne after more than a dozen years.

Every word he'd written in that introduction he had yet to send to his boss had felt...wrong. Strained. Forbidden almost. He shouldn't have been writing it in the first place, but how could he not when he and so many of his colleagues might be out of work if he didn't?

Everything inside him was screaming to walk away from the interview. From his job. From his life in Portland, but that simply wasn't possible. He had responsibilities, his parents, Noah and Cammie, the house...his career.

He had to see this through.

Across the street he caught Alec Aheona Malloy emerging from a narrow doorway, his police chief badge shining against the dull green of his shirt. Alec waved and Griff found himself considering that the universe had once again put someone in his path at just the right time.

"Howzit, Griff?" Alec greeted him as Griff crossed the street at a jog.

"Hey. You got a minute?"

"Sure. Heading to the Vibe for some coffee." He inclined his head for Griff to follow. "This personal or professional?"

"A little of both." Griff knew when he had the other man's attention. The police chief stopped walking and removed his hands from his pockets. "I don't know if this is what I'm supposed to do or not but I'm walking a tight rope and I need someone else around here to know what's going on." It wasn't until this moment that he realized just how much he needed to tell someone the truth, even if it meant earning some ill will among the locals.

"You've got my attention," Alec said.

"What about coffee?"

"Coffee can wait," Alec said. "What's going on? Is this about Daphne?"

"Yes. But it's not what you think."

"You don't know what I'm thinking," Alec said with a narrowing of his eyes. "What should I be thinking?"

Griff let out a long, slow breath. Maybe this was just another mistake he was meant to make. "I don't know where to start." But he did. At the beginning. "I guess I should just dive in. What do you know about Richard Mercer?"

Daphne sat on one of the beach towels, trying to ignore the breaking of her heart while she watched Griff's kids playing and swimming in the ocean. This place always brought her such peace, even in the darkest days she'd experienced. But now? Now nothing was soothing the pain surging inside her.

Less than a week ago, her life had been simple and uncomplicated. Yes, she'd been lonely, and bordering on envious of her friends' romantic entanglements, but now…

Now she was even deeper in love with the only man she'd ever cared for. The man who had taught her what love was. A man who had changed more in fourteen years than she'd been led to believe.

Could Griff really do what she suspected he'd done? Had his trip out here been a complete lie? Had he... She gasped, her gaze landing on Cammie and Noah laughing and splashing in the waves.

Had he used his kids as a way to regain access to her heart?

"Sorry I'm late."

Daphne looked up and over as Griff plunged the end of his board into the sand and dropped down beside her. That charming, disarming smile of his was firmly in place.

"How are they doing?"

"Fine. They're fine." She didn't want to think about how she probably wouldn't look out at the ocean again without imagining Noah riding the water. Or Cammie trying to emulate her big brother. "Pictures all taken care of?"

"Sure are. Among other things." He sounded relieved, as if a weight had been lifted from him. While Daphne felt as if the world had settled on her not-so-broad shoulders. "You okay?" Griff leaned over, stared until he had her attention.

"Actually, no." She had so many questions, so many doubts and suspicions, but none of them seemed to form into any coherent thought. "I'm sorry. I'm going to head home for the day. I've got this...headache." She shoved to her feet, but didn't get a few steps before he caught up with her. "Don't," she whispered, terrified she couldn't keep her voice from cracking. "Please, I have to go."

"What's happened?" Griff demanded. "What's wrong? Did the kids—"

"The kids did nothing," she said. "They're perfect and open and honest and I'm going to miss them so much I ache. But this is where we say goodbye, Griff."

"Why?" he asked. "We don't leave for another few days. I thought we could—"

"You thought wrong." She looked at him hard. "I've got to go."

"This doesn't make sense." When he stepped toward her, she stepped back. "Daphne, talk to me. Just a little while ago everything was fine."

"A little while ago everything was. At least as far as I was concerned." But what did she know? Nothing apparently. "You mentioned something when you first got here. About your job. About not being sure how much longer you'd have it."

"That's right. The paper's in trouble. What paper isn't these days." He tried to laugh it off. "There might be a buyout and that means layoffs. Things could get dicey, you could say, but we might land a big story. One that will show we're still viable and important. What does that have to—"

"Cammie wanted to see the video about Kahlua." She spoke as if from a distance now, as if she were outside her body narrating some horrible dark moment of a romantic movie. "We used your computer. Noah knew the password." She raised her gaze to his, silently challenging him to get there before she had to tell him. "You left some documents open on your laptop."

She knew when he understood. She saw, even with the sun blazing down on them, when realization hit. But she didn't give him the chance to speak before she began reciting, "In these series of interviews obtained exclusively by *Portland Beat* reporter Griffin Townsend. With a no-topic-is-off-limits guarantee, the man responsible for the pain and suffering of so many speaks on the record…"

"Stop." Griff held up both his hands. "Stop, Daphne. It isn't what you think."

"So I'm wrong, then?" Her throat burned with each

word she spoke. "You didn't come here to get information for your article about my father? You didn't come to get some background dirt to add to your story?"

"No." He shook his head. "No, that isn't why I came."

She folded her arms across her chest. "Then illuminate it for me, please."

"I—"

She could see it in an instant. The truth, whatever the truth was, was even worse than she'd imagined.

"Your father's lawyer called me a few weeks ago, asking me to meet with him. I was curious so I went."

"And what did my father want to meet with you about?"

"He offered me a deal, an interview, if I came out here and talked you into meeting with him." He looked out at the ocean, at his kids as if for strength. "It was…" He hesitated. "It was too good to pass up. I don't know what he wants to talk to you about. I only know what he was willing to offer for the chance."

It wasn't what she'd wanted to hear, but it was the truth. She knew that because everything else that had happened since his arrival suddenly made sense. "This is why you pushed me to mend fences with him. To go and see him even though you knew how I felt about it. About him. Our talks didn't have anything to do with me not living with regrets, but as a means to an end so you got your story."

He swallowed hard, winced, and in his eyes she saw the regret he'd been telling her she felt. "It was both."

She huffed out a breath. "Unbelievable. No!" She stepped back when he reached for her. "Don't! I was close. I was this close to doing it. I was considering going back and trying to salvage some kind of… You put that in my head, Griff. You made me think he was worth talking to. You! Of all people! After what happened the first time why—"

"Because I need to keep my job, Daphne. Because I've got my parents and my kids all relying on me to take care of them. I know it sounds horrible and selfish and I'd be lying if I said I didn't give this third or even fourth thoughts."

"Didn't change your mind, though, did it?"

"I gave up everything to come back to Oregon full-time for them, and now I'm barely treading water. That interview with your father could stabilize the paper. But most important of all, it gave me the chance to see you again. To see if there was still something like what we had all those years ago."

"And do you feel it's still there? Now?"

"I hope so. I was..." He dropped his voice and shook his head. "I was trapped. And I... I wanted to see you. Everything I told you about the two of us, everything I admitted to, it was all true."

"Truth hurts," she told him. "You lied to me from the start." It hadn't been coincidence or universal intervention that had brought him back into her life. It had been her manipulative, duplicitous father who had never once thought of putting Daphne—or anyone else—first.

"I tried not to lie," Griff said. "But you shut the door when it came to your father. I had to try something—"

"To get your story. Well, I hope you have a backup plan because I'm not doing it." She took the step forward now and stood in front of him, nose to chin, locked jaw to dazed gaze. "I won't go back. I can't go back. I don't have it in me to face him, Griff."

"Yes," he insisted. "You do. You're the most courageous person I know."

She snorted, rolled her eyes. "Please. I'm a coward. We both know it."

"You made your decision to leave and start over, to

keep your name. You made a life for yourself here, a life neither one of your parents could ever understand the appeal of. That's brave, Daphne. It's only one of the reasons I love you."

"You don't get to say that. Not anymore. Not now." She didn't think she could hurt this much. The pain she'd gone through that first time he'd left her was nothing compared to what she felt now. "You were manipulating me from the start. From the instant I saw you in the lobby of the resort you—" She gasped, finally understanding that truth. "Everything you said and did since you got here was to try to get me to go back." She glared at him. "Shame on you, Griff. Shame on you for filling my heart again only so you could empty it out."

"Dad! Daphne! Did you see? I stayed on for my longest time yet!" Noah raced up the beach and stopped short in front of them. "What's going on?"

"Did they see?" Cammie leaped and jumped beside her brother. "It was so amazing!"

"Hey, guys." Daphne turned her back on Griff and dropped down, touched their faces. "I've had something come up with work and I'm going to have to take off for a few days."

"But." Cammie's eyes instantly filled with concern. "But we don't go home yet. We can't say goodbye now. We want to go on the boat again and look at the flowers and…"

"I'm so sorry, sweetheart." Daphne opened her arms and hugged them both. "I need to do this. I don't want to," she added as she squeezed her eyes shut. "Believe me, I don't want to, but I don't have a choice." She sat back enough to press a kiss to each of their foreheads, then stood up. She forced herself to look back at Griff, who seemed as devastated as she felt, but that couldn't be helped. He'd lied to her and that was the one thing she could never forgive. "Goodbye, Griff."

He nodded, his gaze flat and cool. "Goodbye, Daphne."

She turned and walked away, hugging herself so tight until it was the only thing she felt.

Griff blinked instantly awake. The 3:00 a.m. darkness of his hotel bedroom pressed in on him, his heart ka-thudding heavily. He pressed a hand against his chest, trying desperately to push through the fog of sleep and identify the hollow cavern that had been suddenly carved out of him.

He let out a slow breath, listened to the waves tumbling over one another on the other side of the glass door. The room felt stifling despite the cool air blowing out of the AC unit. An uncertainty, a loneliness of loss washed over him like the tide and threatened to drag him beneath the surface.

Spending the better part of the day attempting to pretend as if he didn't have a broken heart had been exhausting. Consoling his kids and downplaying Daphne's unexpected and sudden exit from their lives had been a lesson in torture. He'd messed up. In so many ways. In every way, if he was honest with himself. And yet... He was desperate for Daphne to change her opinion of him.

He'd betrayed her, lied to her and, yes, even manipulated her. His reasons, excuses and motivations went to the core of everything he held dear, but that couldn't matter now. He'd walked away before when he'd come so close to having everything he'd ever wanted in his life. He couldn't do it again, not fight for it at least one more time. For both their sakes.

His cell rang from its designated charging spot on the

bedside table. The sound cut through the silence as the lit-up screen broke through his reverie.

Like a whale in the middle of the ocean, suddenly breaking the water's surface for one huge gasp of air, he sat up, swung his legs over the edge of the mattress. His hands shook as he reached out, picked up his phone. Even before he tapped the answer button, he knew.

"This is Griffin Townsend."

"Mr. Townsend?" The unfamiliar female voice on the other end's tone was gentle, calm. "This is Gloria Urquat from Tinsley Care Facility."

Griff swallowed hard. "Yes?"

"Mr. Townsend, your mother asked if I would call. I'm so sorry, but your father passed a little while ago. It was very peaceful, in his sleep."

He had no words. He had no air. "Is my mother all right?" he finally managed to ask.

"She's doing very well, considering. Maybe, after all this time, it might come as a bit of a relief for all of you."

Was that what he was feeling? "Would you tell her we'll be home as soon as we can?"

"She said you were on vacation. She asked that you not—"

"We'll be home as soon as we can," Griff repeated.

"Of course," Ms. Urquat said. "I'll let her know. As for the arrangements, I'm not sure if you were aware, but your father had made plans some time ago. We'll be arranging for his cremation in the next day or so."

"I understand." He stared down at the carpet as if it held any answers for him. "Please go ahead with whatever my parents decided." His father hadn't been his father for a while now. He was grateful his dad had prearranged things, but his mind and emotions were racing. He needed to be there. "Please call me if there's anything that's too much for my mom."

"Yes, of course. Safe travels. And our condolences, Mr. Townsend."

"Thank you." He hung up. The cell felt like a ten-ton boulder in his hands.

"Dad?"

Griff turned and found Noah standing in the bedroom doorway. He blinked and held out a hand. The second he felt his son in his arms he felt himself begin to break. "Grandpa's gone, Noah." He held him close and rocked him just as his father used to rock him. "He passed away a little while ago."

"Daddy?" Cammie's voice was quiet as she walked into the room.

"Come here, bug." He sat back as she scrambled onto the bed and Noah, crying softly against his shoulder, clung to him. The three of them, in the middle of paradise, rode out the initial waves of grief together until they were out of tears. "We have to go home," he whispered a while later when they both quieted. "Grandma needs us. And there are things I have to take care of. I'm sorry it's sooner than we planned."

"Okay," Cammie whispered into his bare shoulder. "I don't think I like it here anymore, Daddy. Not without Daphne with us. It's not the same."

No, Griff thought. It wasn't the same at all.

"Cammie's right," Noah agreed. "I want to go home, Dad."

"Then we'll go home," Griff promised. After that? He didn't have the first idea what to do.

Chapter Twelve

All this time Daphne felt certain she understood what being utterly and completely lost felt like. She had, after all, left absolutely everything behind when her mother died and her father went to prison.

She'd started over, with a support system, but it had still taken work to climb out of the despair she'd found herself in.

Now, four going on five days since Griff and the kids had left Nalani, the grief had yet to lessen. It was as if she were a ghost haunting her own life, drifting from work to home to meetings without feeling a thing. Whatever heart she'd had seemed to have abandoned her and left the islands with them.

What was wrong with her? Why couldn't she get through this? She'd done the right thing, hadn't she? He'd lied to her. Deceived her. It had taken her years and a federal conviction to finally find the courage to walk away from her father. She'd sworn she wouldn't ever put herself in the position of being that vulnerable again. Surgical, instant removal from the situation—from the person responsible—was the only solution. She knew better than to make the same mistakes as she had in the past.

But if that was the case, why couldn't she stop dwelling on the paralyzing thought she'd made a horrible mistake?

She'd been trying to convince herself that his motives hadn't mattered. But they did, didn't they? Living the way she did now, where she did, it was easy to forget that life wasn't a bubble of paradise. His life was completely different from hers. His experiences, his goals and dreams, they mattered as much as hers did.

The loneliness she felt without him, without Cammie and Noah, hurt each day with little to no relief. She'd had no true idea what being lonely felt like before now. But nothing could change the fact that he'd been using her. And that, she told herself for the millionth time, wasn't something she could ever forget or get past.

The rap on her door startled her out of her carousel of thoughts. The sunset blazed its way through the windows of the living room, bathing the hardwood floor in streaks of red and orange. Barefoot, she padded to open the door for Sydney, Marella and Tehani.

"We bring wallowing gifts," Sydney said with a sympathetic expression on her face. "You've had five days. It's time to start moving on."

"This isn't necessary," Daphne insisted as her friends paraded in. "I'm doing okay, guys, really. I've put it behind me."

"Sorry, Daph." Marella passed by with an arched brow. "I'm not buying it."

"Broken hearts aren't easy to hide," Tehani whispered before she hugged her. "And they aren't fast to heal." She stepped back, touched a gentle hand to Daphne's face. "I'm so sorry. I really liked him."

"Yeah." Daphne swallowed hard. "Me, too." She did her best to laugh. "Don't really know how else it could have ended." She closed the screen door and joined them in the kitchen. "Can't imagine what I was thinking, letting myself dream about an instant family."

"You were thinking with your heart," Sydney said. "That's never a bad thing, Daphne."

"Not so sure about that," Daphne admitted. "Who brought the chocolate?"

"What chocolate?" Marella blinked in complete innocence.

"I recognize that purple bag." Daphne grabbed for it. "Sully's Island Sweets. Gimme."

"We're calling this the wallowing special." Marella unpacked the delicious assortment of chocolate-covered macadamia nuts, caramels and fudgy brownies. Minutes later they were passing around the sugar while Daphne filled them in on the details. She'd been attempting to keep them to herself by maintaining a distance from her friends. She should have known that wouldn't work.

The sympathy and understanding she was offered provided lots of comfort but didn't do much to take the edge off her grief.

"And I thought the first time he broke my heart hurt," she said at one point. "This pain is ten times worse."

"Question." Marella raised her hand. "And I'm not trying to be obnoxious by taking his side—"

"Tread carefully," Sydney warned. "I don't care how gorgeous those photos are that he gave me and Theo. *She's* our friend."

"What would you have done if he'd told you about the deal he'd made with your father right from the start?" Marella asked Daphne. "Seriously? What would you have done?"

"I don't know." It was a question that had been haunting her at night, in those hours that made your thoughts spin like a cyclone. It was easy enough to ask in hindsight, but answering was an entirely different thing. "We'll never know because he didn't. I thought Griff, of all people, would understand why I can't ever go back."

"And yet you thought about it," Marella pointed out.

"Yes, because he was so persuasive."

"Doesn't mean he was wrong," Sydney commented.

"It's interesting, isn't it?" Marella mused as she nibbled on a chocolate. "That your father reached out to Griff. You said your father hated him back in the day, so why did he—"

"I gave up wondering why my father did anything a long time ago." Even before she'd met Griffin Townsend. "But that answer's easy. He sent Griff because he knew Griff was the only person who had a shot at convincing me to see him." Daphne sighed and stood up, needing to move. "You've been quiet during this intervention of a discussion, Tehani," she observed. "What are you thinking?"

Tehani shook her head. "You don't want to know what I'm thinking."

Daphne stopped, glanced at Marella and Sydney, who seemed equally taken aback. "Sure, I do."

"No," Tehani said firmly and spun her cranberry-juice-filled glass slowly on the table. "You don't. Because then you'd hear me say that I'd give anything to be in your position to have a second chance. You let him go without a fight, Daphne. You let them all go."

"But—"

"He's still here, I mean on this planet, with us," Tehani said almost desperately. "People make mistakes. They make the wrong choices and they mess up. Sometimes for the wrong reasons. Sometimes for the right ones. But Griff is here. We all saw you together on that boat the other night, Daph," Tehani continued. "You were magic together and seeing you with his kids?" She put her hands on her belly. "They love you."

"And I love them," Daphne countered. "That doesn't make—"

"He made a mistake," Tehani argued. "He misjudged the situation because he felt the pressure of everything landing on him. But don't sit here touting that he doesn't care about you or that he did all this to hurt you. If anything he went out of his way not to hurt you. How many times did he try to change your mind about your father?"

"Too many."

"And then he stopped, didn't he? Because he respected your decision," Sydney observed. "I'm betting he's kicking himself pretty hard for how it ended between you two. If he'd told you the truth, if you knew his career and so much else was on the line and dependent on your answer, what would you have done?"

Daphne set her jaw. "I'd have gone back to see my father." She tossed up her hands in frustration. "So why didn't he just tell me?"

"Because he loves you," Marella said. "And he knew how much it would hurt for you to see your father."

"Your father did the manipulating," Sydney said. "Your father did what he's always done best and pulled Griff's strings. That can't have been an easy position for Griff to be put in. And I can't imagine he saw an easy route out."

Another knock sounded at the front of the house and the four friends all turned as Mano and Alec pulled open the screen door and, after kicking off their shoes, walked in.

"I should be charging admission," Daphne muttered. "Come on in to the 'Love Reunited' episode of my life. You guys want something to drink?"

"Your signature tea if you've got it." Mano set his oversize bag on the floor. "I just got back from Oahu a little while ago." He loosened his tie and unbuttoned his top button.

"I'm still on duty, but I ran into him at the resort," Alec told them. "We thought we'd check in on you and see how you're doing."

"Awesome, thanks." Daphne handed each of them a glass of tea. "We were just commiserating over the fact that my father was pulling Griff's strings from the beginning and everyone got tangled up in them."

"Pulling them in more directions than you know," Alec said, then stopped with the glass halfway to his lips. Everyone stared at him. "What?"

"You know something," Sydney asked. "Something we don't."

Alec pursed his lips.

"Alec," Tehani said in a warning tone. "Spill."

Alec winced and took a deep breath. "Griff might have told me what was going on with him and your father, Daphne. Before you confronted him about it."

"Told you what, exactly?" Daphne said carefully.

"Short version? Griff didn't have any intention of taking your father up on his offer. Not at first. But Griff was worried what your father might do if he said no. You know better than anyone how unpredictable he can be when he doesn't get what he wants. Griff was worried whatever backup plan your father might have might hurt you even worse than what he's done so far."

"There it is," Marella announced as she got up to refill her glass. "I knew there had to be another piece to this debacle."

"And here we thought you've been hanging around Ohana so much this week because of Jordan." Marella knocked Alec with her shoulder.

"Why did he tell you and not me?" Daphne challenged.

"I'm guessing because of this." Alec flicked the badge on his chest. "He wanted me to be aware, since he knew you wouldn't go back to the mainland with him, to be on the lookout for anything out of the ordinary or suspicious."

"He was caught, Daph," Sydney said. "If he said no to your dad, he could have put you at risk in some way, and if he agreed, he had to lie to you because he knew you'd shut him down. No-win situation on his end."

"He should have told me all of it," Daphne insisted.

"Yes, well, if everyone did what they should do, then the world would be an entirely better place." Sydney toasted them with her glass. "And I say that as a woman about to marry such a person, if you'll recall our romantic journey. Speaking of my fiancé, does anyone know where Theo is?" She glanced at her watch. "He was supposed to meet me here."

"He's doing some work for me," Mano said. "Syd, you and I should probably talk sometime soon. About Golden Vistas' bid to buy Ohana Odysseys."

"Oh, heavens to Murgatroyd," Sydney muttered and ate the last piece of fudge. "Haven't they gone away yet?"

"We don't think so," Mano said. "Silas called me a few days ago from San Francisco. He's had some feelers out about Golden Vistas since earlier this year, when they made the play to buy Ohana from Sydney."

"You mean what brought Theo out to Nalani in the first place?" Sydney asked. "You talked to Silas about that?"

Daphne understood her dismay. They hadn't heard much from Silas in years, not even when Remy died. This was as much a surprise as Alec's information on Griff's true motivations for coming to see her.

"I did," Mano said slowly. "And he's not liking what he's hearing. He thinks they're coming after Ohana and Hibiscus. But that's for another time." He pinned Daphne with a look that had her shivering.

"What?" Daphne asked. "What's that look?"

"Griff left three days early," Mano said.

"I know." Daphne winced. It didn't make her feel any better to know that Cammie and Noah had missed out on the last days of their vacation. "He didn't achieve his mission objective, so he picked up and ran."

"That's not why he left," Mano said. "I just found out a little while ago. He'd called the bell desk and asked for help expediting changing their flights. His father died, Daphne. From the timeline I was given, it was the night you broke things off with him."

"No," Daphne gasped, touching a hand to her heart. "Oh, no."

"The staff got him and the kids on a plane the next morning," Mano told her. "Word is they were all pretty shaken up."

"They were very close," Daphne whispered, and in that moment, there was nothing she wanted more than to be with him. To be there for Noah and Cammie. She should find out about the funeral. She should send flowers or...

"There's also this." Mano retrieved the bag. "It was left for you in their room. You hadn't been back to the resort so housekeeping left it in my office." He handed it over.

"What is it?" Even as she asked and peered inside, every trace of anger, betrayal and resentment evaporated into useless, forgotten smoke. "Oh." She lifted Taco out of the bag, tears blurring her vision. "Oh, Cammie." She dropped the bag and hugged the fish to her chest.

Marella checked the bag and pulled out a piece of paper. "There's a note." She cleared her throat and read out loud, "Let Taco take care of you so you don't forget us." She flipped the note around. "Cammie and Noah."

"She left me her fish." Tears spilled onto her cheeks. "Oh, man." All the doubts disappeared. "I really screwed this up, didn't I?" She'd let her past betrayals and pain siphon through to the present and hurt not only Griff, but his children, as well.

"I think the two of you did a bang-up job of that together," Sydney said.

"Not to pile on," Alec said, "but I brought something, too."

"Jeez, what now?" Daphne swiped away her tears as Alec returned to the porch, and carried in an oversize wrapped box.

"Jordan called me when The Snap Shack delivered this to Ohana," he said. "She knew I was coming over to talk to you."

"Give me the fish." Tehani reached out as Daphne traded the stuffed fish for the box.

She flipped open the top and reached inside for the brightly painted frame. Displayed was the picture Griff had taken of her and Noah and Cammie in the flower bed after Theo's proposal.

"Looks like a family to me," Marella said.

"That's exactly what it is." Sydney stood up and hugged Daphne from behind. "Now, what are you going to do about it?"

"It was a lovely service."

Griff kept his now-practiced smile in place and nodded like the bobblehead he'd become in the past few days. He had absolutely no idea who the woman was who patted his hand in sympathy before she moved off to stand beside the man she'd come with. He didn't have a clue as to who most of the people were in his house. But it was clear every last one of them had adored his father.

His father's send off was predicably his father in every way. A celebration of his life, not a mourning of his death, held at his favorite pub that he'd frequented, starting during his working years at the factory.

The music and shouts and laughter had been everything Hank Townsend could have asked for and, if Griff had to bet, was something he was enjoying from beyond.

The party had eventually shifted from the pub to Griff's house, large enough to accommodate the dozens of friends who had come to say goodbye. They'd brought food and drink and memories that even now brought a fond smile to his mother's face as she listened.

A legacy of kindness. Griff ducked his head and smiled. A life didn't get much better than that, did it?

"Daddy, can we go out in the backyard and swing?" Cammie grabbed hold of his black suit jacket and tugged. Her new dark navy dress skimmed her knees with an inch of lace hemming the bottom. She looked so far removed from the ebullient, exuberant little girl she'd been last week he almost couldn't recall their days in Nalani. Almost. The truth was, as he'd navigated the initial grief and consoling, memories of Nalani and of Daphne had been close to the only bright spot.

"Did you get something to eat?" he asked, resting a hand on the top of her head as Noah, wearing an identical black suit and white shirt to Griff's, stood behind his sister, keeping his chin up and his eyes clear of tears.

"We're not hungry," Noah said. "We'll eat later."

"Daddy?" Cammie tugged harder on his jacket.

"Sure, go ahead." He nudged them toward the kitchen, where they could go out through the back door. The garden had been a place that brought equal parts pleasure and pain. It was becoming quickly overgrown thanks to his complete ineptitude at gardening. But where there were blooms, struggling buds, and pops of color he imagined a beautiful, kind red-headed woman whose smile had healed his broken and jaded heart.

"Griff." His mother slipped an arm around his waist and gave him a quick squeeze. "How are you doing?"

"I'm fine, Mom." And he was. For the most part. "You?"

Maureen sighed, angled an embarrassed expression in his direction. "He'd have loved every second of this, wouldn't he?"

Griff smiled and even laughed a little. "Yes, he would have." He drew her close. "He's here. I can feel him. I think he wants a beer."

Maureen laughed, patted Griff's chest. "You're a good boy, Griff. You've always taken such good care of us."

"You took care of me," he countered.

"Yes, well, I'm about to do that again." Her smile still carried a hint of sadness and more than a tint of loneliness, but he also saw a familiar determination and spark she'd been missing for the past couple of years. "I talked to your aunt Barbara last night. We agreed it's a good idea for me to move to Arizona to be with her."

"Really?" Griff balked. "You're going to move in together?"

"Heavens no," Maureen scoffed. "We couldn't share a room together growing up and neither of us have grown up enough to try again. No, there's a nice condo for sale in her community. I've already put in an offer. With the money we'll have from selling the house and the money we'll save by me leaving the facility here, it'll be just fine." She caught his chin in her hand and peered into his eyes. "And you can stop supplementing my living expenses."

"I'd do it again in a heartbeat."

"I know you would. But you've got your own life to live, Griff. You need to start doing that without any additional obligations. Maybe fix whatever you broke with Daphne?"

He glanced away, flinching. "What makes you think I broke something?"

"Because she's not here," Maureen said. "Does she even know—"

"Mom, I love you. You know that. But this isn't your business."

"Girl's been my business ever since you brought her into our house that first time," Maureen chided.

"Well, you can put your mind at ease. I'm working on something about Daphne." It hadn't quite come together yet, but it would. Hopefully. "Why don't you go mingle and stop bothering me about my love life?"

She brought his head down and kissed his forehead. "Never. You made him proud, you know," she whispered with the hint of tears in her steely eyes. "So, so proud. Both of us."

"Thanks, Mom."

Because he needed something to do, he headed into the kitchen and eyed the overwhelming collection of pies, cakes, casseroles and charcuterie boards covering the kitchen counter. Nothing appealed, but it was either eat or join his mother in mingling, something he was not willing to do just then.

Plate full, he turned and spotted Colin making his way through the crowd. The look on his editor's face soured whatever appetite he did have and he set the plate on the side counter. "Help yourself," he offered.

Colin waved him off. "Later, maybe. We need to talk."

"Let me guess." Griff cringed. "I'm out of a job."

"Maybe."

Griff shook his head. "I haven't had time to write—"

"He sold the paper," Colin said. "The second I told him about the Mercer article he went back to the buyers and upped the asking price. They agreed. It's a done deal."

"Is it?"

"Too bad I never got you that contract solidifying exclusivity." Colin reached out and snagged a chunk of cheese. "It's your story, Griff. Not *The Beat*'s and not mine. Definitely not the new owner's. I saved that tidbit for our publisher until the last second. You want to write it, you're free to publish it wherever and however you want."

"Hence the maybe being out of a job."

"The entire office is out of one. This one, at least." Colin pursed his lips. "I'm starting up a new online news organization. Everyone who's been let go from *The Beat* is on board. We're going global. I've already reached out to some contacts in other countries about sharing reporters and stories, getting important information where it needs to be, in front of readers. I could use a headline freelancer, if you're interested. You're my first ask. Set your terms."

Temptation tingled once more. "Cammie and Noah come first," he said without hesitation. "I want to work from home and I want flexible hours. And I don't travel for more than a week at a time each month. And I retain all rights to whatever story I might write about Richard Mercer."

"I can live with all that." Colin grabbed a napkin and wiped his hand before holding it out. "We'll work out the legalities and details in a few weeks."

"Thanks, Colin."

"Don't thank me," Colin said. "If you hadn't hit me with the Mercer article, I wouldn't have had the guts to bluff our publisher. He failed and we win in the end. I'll miss *The Beat*, but the future looks bright." He slapped a hand on Griff's shoulder.

Alone again, Griff retrieved his plate. A good part of the anxiety he'd been experiencing lessened and he breathed easier. At least until he reached the living room and saw his ex-wife and her new husband coming in the front door. Lydia, as always, was dressed to perfection with her simple black dress, lethal heels and net-accented fascinator. Her jet black hair was neat, not a strand out of place, and hung in big waves over her shoulders. Raymond, who had equally dark hair and exquisite taste in clothes, looked as if he'd just stepped out of a Fortune 500 boardroom meeting.

"Awesome," Griff muttered before taking a deep breath. "Lydia." He nodded as they approached. "Raymond. Thank you for coming."

"I'm so sorry about your dad," Lydia said in a more compassionate tone than Griff expected. "He was always very nice to me."

"Thanks, Lyd. I'm glad you came."

"Yes, well." Lydia smoothed a hand down the front of her silk dress. "We were family, after all."

"I'll go get us something to drink," Raymond said.

"Actually, if you wouldn't mind waiting a moment." Griff motioned for them to follow him into the corner of the room, away from curious ears. "One reason I wanted you to come, Lydia—"

"You wanted me to see the kids, yes, I know," Lydia said.

"No, I mean yes, but that ball is totally in your court," Griff told her. "You can be as involved in their lives or not as you want to be. It's up to them whether they'll let you."

"Oh." Lydia straightened. "Well, thank you for that."

"We'll keep this out of court," Griff went on. "We'll work it out together. You're their mother, Lydia. I'll leave it to you to decide what that means."

Lydia suddenly looked nervous. "That's lovely to hear."

"Magnanimous of you," Raymond said in a way that caught Griff's attention.

"I'm sorry?" Griff asked.

"Glad to hear you've come around about letting Lydia see her children," Raymond clarified. "It took a lot of work for my assistants to cancel our summer plans with the kids."

"Raymond, I don't think—"

"Hold on." Griff cut her off with a look. "Are you under the impression that I'm the one who prevented Lydia from seeing Noah and Cammie this summer?"

"I did…" Raymond frowned at Lydia, who suddenly was looking anywhere but at the two of them. "Yes. That is the impression I was under."

"Your impression is wrong." It was on the tip of Griff's tongue to educate Raymond on his wife's behavior and dishonesty, but the impulse passed. What good would it do anyone when the truth was out? "This is a conversation the two of you should have in private," Griff said. "Lydia, I'm telling you first. I'm selling the house."

"You're— My house?" Lydia gasped. "You're selling my—"

"That's right," Griff countered. "It's your house. Which is why I'm telling you before anyone else in case you want to make an offer. Market value is fine. I can have my agent send you the information if you're interested."

"I… I…" Lydia stammered. "But where will you go?"

"Me and the children?" Griff echoed. "Someplace smaller," Griff said. "We'll be fine. We might stay in Portland. We might go…elsewhere." Something drew his gaze to the giant window overlooking the yard. A figure moved into sight and even as his mind processed what he was seeing, he watched as Cammie and Noah flung themselves off their swings and darted straight into Daphne's waiting arms. "I'll be sure to let you know where we decide," he said and set his plate down. "Stay as long as you like. You have my cell if you want to make me an offer on the house," he added to a suddenly stern-looking Raymond. "Good luck, man." He slapped his hand on Raymond's arm before he pushed through the crowd to the kitchen.

It took what felt like an eternity, a heart-wrenching eternity, to make it out the back door. It banged behind him as he stepped onto the porch and reveled in the squeals and laughter emanating from his children.

He stood there, unable to move, for a long moment. It looked so completely out of place for her to be wearing black. Her hair was long and razor straight. A simple strand of pearls around her neck.

"Dad!" Noah yelled and ran over. "Dad, look! Daphne's here!"

"She's heeeeeere!" Cammie squealed and hugged Daphne around the neck so tight Daphne coughed. Even as she laughed.

Griff allowed Noah to drag him over. Daphne's smile dimmed a bit when she looked at him.

"I'm so sorry about your dad," she whispered. "I only just found out last night."

"I—" He didn't know what else to say. "Thank you for coming."

"I had something important to return." She bent down and set Cammie on her feet, reached into the oversize bag beside her and pulled out Taco. "Thank you for leaving him with me, Cammie," she said softly. "I think he's ready to be home now."

"Taco!" Cammie grabbed the fish with both arms and squeezed it hard. "Oh, I've missed you so much. But not as much as I missed you." She tried to scramble back into Daphne's arms. Daphne didn't pick her back up, but she did hold her close as Cammie wrapped her arms around Daphne's waist.

"I thought you left Taco on the beach," Griff said to his daughter.

Cammie shrugged. "The hotel room is near the beach."

A six-year-old's semantics. "Are you hungry?" he asked Daphne. "We've got tons of food and my mom—"

"Griff." Daphne reached out and touched his hand. "I'm fine." It was unspoken yet loud enough for him to understand.

"Kids, your mom is inside the house. Why don't you go say hi. And tell Grandma that Daphne's here. But take your time, please."

"I'll go!" Cammie yelled and sprinted for the back door.

"I want to tell her!" Noah started after his sister, then stopped, turned and backtracked to hug Daphne. "What does this mean? Are you staying with us? Are we going back to Nalani with you?"

"Your dad and I need to talk," Daphne said and touched a hand to his head. "But you'll be the first to know the answer to those questions, I promise."

"Really promise?"

"Really promise." She nodded and Noah ran off after his sister.

Griff hadn't felt this nervous since he'd picked her up for their first date. "I think you should know." He took hold of the hand she offered, led her over to the swings Cammie had abandoned. "I didn't plan to leave Nalani without talking to you again. Without…" He dug down for the courage he'd been trying to build. "Without fighting for us. I got it wrong, Daphne. I got it wrong fourteen years ago and I got it wrong even worse this time and I'm so sorry. There's nothing I wouldn't—"

"Stop." She pressed her fingers against his lips. "I should have given you the chance to explain. I had no right to judge you without hearing the truth of the situation. Alec told me you were worried my father might try a different tactic to try to talk to me."

Griff grimaced.

"You had a difficult choice to make, Griff. I don't know that there was a right one in the end. I shouldn't have pushed you away before we tried to figure it all out."

"There was only one thing that mattered to me." He moved closer, pulled her in. That she leaned in boosted his confidence. And his hope. "Seeing you again. When all is said and done, your father's offer gave me the chance to do the one thing I'd wanted to do for years." He bent his head, rested his forehead against hers. "Whatever else went down, that was all I cared about. Not one bit has changed since that night on the boat, Daphne. I love you. I can't imagine not loving you and if it takes me the rest of my life—"

She lifted her head and kissed him. Kissed him so gently at first he worried it was another goodbye. But then she clasped the back of his neck, held him firmly and deepened it.

"Third time's a charm, isn't that what they say?" she murmured against his lips. "I felt empty without you and the kids in Nalani, Griff. I don't ever want to feel like that again."

"We were coming back," he said as his heart lightened. "The kids and I agreed you were worth fighting for. However long it took."

"And what about now?"

"We're coming back," he whispered. "To Nalani. To you and Ohana and the Hibiscus Bay and all the magic that place holds for me and the kids."

"What about your work?"

"Taken care of." He kissed the tip of her nose. "I'll fill you in later."

"And your mom?"

"Moving to Arizona to live with her sister."

"And their mom?"

"That'll be up to her," Griff said.

"I guess that takes care of everything I was worried about." She smiled at him. "I do have a couple of questions for you."

"Okay." He braced himself, convinced his dreams couldn't possibly be coming true.

"I want to go see my father."

He frowned. "You do?"

"I do." She nodded. "Whatever else I thought or felt, you were right. I owe it to myself to close that door forever. So I can be happy." She touched his cheek. "Will you go with me?"

"To see your father? Yes, of course. You want me to make the arrangements?"

"Since you already know how to do that." Her smile lit up her eyes. "Please. That just leaves one more thing. Because I'm sure Cammie and Noah will want to know what's going on between us."

"They aren't the only one," Griff joked.

She kissed him again, then stepped back. "Graduation night, when you broke things off with me, were you going to propose?"

He didn't hesitate. "Yes."

"Then we've wasted enough time already. Griffin Townsend, will you marry me?"

He laughed, nodded and picked her up, swinging her around until they were both dizzy. She clung to him, arms locked around his neck. "In the words of Sydney Calvert, yes, yes, yes, I will marry you!" He kissed her quick and hard. "And the sooner the better."

* * *

"Why did I expect this to be like the movies?" Daphne scooted her metal chair closer to Griff as the echoes of clanging doors and muted conversation echoed in into the main visitor's room. A half-dozen other inmates were visiting with family and friends. Security guards stood by the two doors while others walked around the room like silent sentries.

"Depends on the movie," Griff said. "You okay?"

"Other than the fact that I'm doing something I promised myself I would never, ever do?" She threaded her fingers through his and lifted his hand to her mouth, kissed the back of his knuckles. "I'm fine." She couldn't imagine not ever being fine again now that Griff was in her life, permanently.

Was it wrong for her to feel so free and excited when only yesterday Griff and his mother had officially said goodbye to their father and husband? She hoped not. Telling Cammie and Noah about her and Griff's plan to not only marry, but that they would all be living in Nalani, was a moment she didn't think she'd ever forget. Griff's only regret, he'd said, was that he hadn't taken a solitary picture of their announcement. She'd been instantly welcomed by his children, and his mother, who had been thrilled at the prospect of having an excuse to come out to the islands.

"Did Lydia make an offer on the house when she called you earlier?" Daphne asked.

"She did not," Griff said. "I got the impression that she and Raymond have hit a bit of a rough patch."

"Because she was telling her new husband you were the reason she wasn't spending time with her kids?"

"Everyone needs a wake-up call," Griff said. "This might have been hers. She wants to make a complete break of things with me and make a fresh start with Raymond."

He hesitated. "Might mean Noah and Cammie spend more time with her. If it's what they want."

"They'll want," Daphne said gently. "No one can replace their mother."

"Oh, I don't think that's true," Griff teased.

Daphne stiffened at the sight of the older man being led through the far door. "Okay," she whispered more to herself than to Griff. "Here we go." She straightened in her chair, locked her knees together even as her hold tightened on Griff's hand.

Her father looked old. Far older than she remembered. Older and diminished. It was obvious the last few years had not been easy on him, but there was an odd, unfamiliar light in his eyes that had her resisting the urge to squirm in her seat.

There were no cuffs. No leg shackles or any of the restraints she expected to see. The clothes he wore certainly weren't designer, but they were far from the fluorescent orange jumpsuits that a stereotype might have dictated.

Knees trembling, she stood up, smoothed a hand down the front of the pink-and-white flower-print dress she wore. She'd wanted something from her new life, her good life, to come with her to this place where, hopefully, she'd finally have some closure.

"Daphne." Her father's voice sounded thick, unfamiliar.

She blinked, looking for the stoic, cold, distant man she'd known all her life. "Hi, Dad." Her smile was quick, almost fleeting. Her fingers flexed around Griff's hand, drawing her father's gaze down before he lifted it back to hers.

"I knew I hadn't underestimated your powers of persuasion," Richard Mercer said. "Sit, please," he urged Daphne as he lowered himself into the chair across from them. "Thank you for coming."

"Griff said you wanted to talk to me." Her mind raced, unable to land on a coherent thought. She'd lived in a kind of fear of this man. The kind of fear that only came from being ignored or used depending on his mood.

"What I want to talk to you about is between you and me," Richard said.

"Then it's too bad this was a wasted trip because he's not leaving." Daphne tightened her hold when she felt Griff pull away. "We have a flight to catch this afternoon," she added. "Time's ticking."

Richard's lips twitched. "You remind me of your mother with that tone."

"Do I?" Daphne refused to flinch. "You broke her heart."

"I know." There was none of the expected pride she'd assumed she'd hear. "Prison is a unique experience, Daphne. It's given me a lot of time to think. Especially about the mistakes I've made. I'll apologize to your mother, when I see her one day."

It wasn't wholly a surprise to hear a comment like that. "Is that why you wanted to see me?" Daphne asked. "Are you sick? Are you dying?"

"Aren't we all in one way or another?" Richard folded his hands on top of the table. "But no. I'm as healthy as a man my age can expect to be. I can't apologize for what I did to your mother to anyone other than her. What I can do is tell you, Daphne…" He shifted his gaze to Griff. "And to you, Griffin, that I'm sorry. I'm sorry I didn't see what you had as something that was special and to be protected. I'm sorry that I interfered and broke the two of you up. It's hard to admit when you've broken someone's heart, but that's what I'm doing. I figured it was time I come clean about that."

"There's no need to rehash it all," Griff said. "We've moved past it."

"Have you?" Richard's expression shifted to one of near self-satisfaction. "Details, please. Are you dating again?"

"No," Daphne said. "We're engaged." She tucked her hair behind her ears. "It'll be short, though. We're getting married next week. In Nalani. On the beach."

"I see." Richard nodded. "Moving fast this time, then."

"We've lost enough time," Daphne said.

Richard looked at Griff and frowned. "You didn't tell her, did you?"

"Tell me what?" Daphne demanded.

"I told you we don't have to rehash—" Griff began.

"And we agreed there would be no more secrets between us," Daphne reminded him. "What's this all about?" She looked from one to the other. "What don't I know?"

"She has enough to resent you for, Richard," Griff said. "Don't add to it."

"Maybe that's meant to be my penance," Richard said. "Maybe we can't move forward until we know what we're leaving behind. Last chance, Griffin."

Griff shook his head. "It doesn't matter now."

"I threatened him," Richard told Daphne. "The night he graduated high school, he was going to propose. He came to me, ring in his pocket, to ask permission."

"And you said no." Daphne's voice went flat.

"If only that's all I'd said," Richard lamented. "I saw the effect he had on you. The awakening. Before him, you never once blinked when you were told what to do, where to go, what we expected of you, but after—"

"He helped me discover myself." Daphne squeezed Griff's hand.

"I don't like to lose, Daphne. And I didn't do well with the idea of losing you, so I gave him a choice. He could propose to you, marry you and take you into whatever life the two of you wanted, or I'd call in some favors and have his father fired from the factory. Griff could have you, or his father could have his job, his retirement, their home."

It took Daphne a moment to form a response. When she did speak, her voice cracked beneath the emotion. "I knew."

"You did?" Griff asked.

She shook her head. "Not the exact details, but I knew something had to have happened for you to leave me behind. And Dad was too…smug after you went away." She looked to her father. "He made the right choice. A choice I would never have and will never question or argue with. Because in the end we won. I have an amazing future now, not only with him, but two wonderful kids."

"Yes," Richard said with a slow nod. "You are." His smile was a sad one. "And now it's time for me to finish coming clean. There was only one person I wanted to find you in Nalani. That was Griff. I have made countless, disastrous mistakes in my life, but keeping you two apart was my biggest one. Your mother made me see that the last time I saw her. The last time I spoke with her. She never forgave me, you see, for ruining your chance of happiness. And she wanted you to be happy, Daphne. Because she never was." He sat back in his chair, looked at Griff. "You're together now. As you always should have been."

"So the whole interview offer was a bluff," Griff said. "You never had any intention—"

"I'm doing my best to make better choices," Richard said. "That includes keeping the promises I've made. I'll see the interview through, Griff. If that's what you want, whatever format you want," Richard said. "Whenever you're ready to start, I'll be here."

Griff shook his head. "I don't think I quite believe—"

"Whatever format? What does that mean?" Daphne asked, but even as the words left her lips, she knew. "Oh." She sat back, blinked. "That's not a bad idea... You'd be willing to do that?" She looked to her father.

"Do what?" Griff asked.

"I'm buying into the partnership with Ohana and taking the landscape designer job with Mano," Daphne told him. "As far as income, we'll be fine. You have options, Griff. You're not locked into a series of articles any longer. The door is open for you to do whatever you want to with the interview. What about a book?"

Her father inclined his head. "Always were the sharpest pencil in the box. It's something you might want to consider, Griff. With your reputation and contacts, I think an authorized biography might bring you more in the long run than a series of articles."

"Maybe." Griff glanced at Daphne. "The idea holds some appeal."

"Is that a yes?" Daphne asked.

"I have a condition," Griff said. "All of the profits go into a dedicated account to be dispersed to the victims of your fraud," he told her father. "That's it. That's the only way I do this."

Richard shook his head. "You just can't help but be noble, can you?"

"You shouldn't profit off your crimes," Griff stated. "Neither should anyone else. I've got a new job lined up. I don't need the money. Other people do. You'll sign off on that?"

"Yes, but with a caveat," Richard said. "I want to see you again, Daphne. When you're available. And I'd like pictures of the wedding. Of your family."

"That's all?" she asked, daring to hope. Was it possible, after all this time and everything they'd been through, that the father she'd always wanted had finally emerged?

"That's more than enough." Richard held out his hand. "Is it a deal?" he asked Griff.

Griff looked at her, the question in his eye. She nodded as he clasped her father's hand, then she reached out and covered them both with hers.

"It's a deal," she whispered.

Epilogue

The bride went barefoot. As did her groom. For practical purposes rather than fashion. Sand and heels simply didn't mix.

With Noah standing up as best man, Tehani as maid of honor and Cammie as both flower girl and ring bearer, Griff and Daphne exchanged vows at sunset on the private section of beach at the Hibiscus Bay Resort. The plan for a small, intimate wedding was overruled by Nalani, as the whole town spilled out around the wedding party, filling the beach to the point of overflowing.

The evening breeze kicked up and made the tablecloths lining the long picnic tables flutter. Homemade delicacies awaited the presentation of the Kahlua pig from the imu smoking not far in the distance.

The sound of drums and ukuleles and guitars filled the air, with hula dancers performing traditional numbers along the outer rim of the crowd.

Griff, with a little help from his new friends, stole a few moments with his bride, who wore a simple but classic knee-length white dress with exquisitely embroidered colorful flowers trailing up from the hemline. She laughed as they walked arm in arm back down the makeshift aisle. Their ears rang with the cheers and shouts of celebration and joy.

She gasped as he spun her behind the grove of trees that allowed for a lengthier kiss filled with promise and passion.

"Happy?" he asked as they swayed to the music that grew in volume.

Daphne's eyes glistened with tears as she looked out to see Cammie and Noah, along with Griff's mother, joining in with the hula dancers. Sydney and Theo embraced and twirled toward the shore, where they splashed, barefoot, into the tide.

Marella and Keane helped steer everyone to the buffet, not that anyone in Nalani ever needed help in finding the food. The wedding cake, which they'd ordered at the last minute from Little Owl Bakery, sat perfectly arranged on a side table decorated with flowers that matched the rainbow dotting Daphne's dress.

"I don't think I could be happier," Daphne said and sighed softly.

Tehani stood off to the side, hands wrapped protectively across her stomach, her dark hair catching in the evening breeze. There was no mistaking the sadness she saw on her friend's face, or the concern she saw on Wyatt's as he watched Tehani from afar.

Daphne's curiosity had gotten the better of her. She'd looked into the Mount Lahani resort and discovered they'd recently announced an expansion to their tour and excursions packages for guests. It was a job perfectly suited to Tehani and her organizational and people skills. But moving to Maui? Daphne hadn't quite found a way to broach that subject with anyone just yet. Not Sydney, not Marella, not even Griff.

More shouts of congratulations snapped her out of her worry. Today wasn't the day.

"Happy?" Griff asked as he pressed his lips to her temple.

"Hmm." She smiled. "Did you see the card Cammie and Noah made for me?" Daphne asked Griff.

"No. And not for lack of trying," he said. "They refused to let me check it out."

"Well, it must be okay to show you now." She reached into her pocket—her wedding dress had pockets!—and pulled out the folded piece of paper.

Griff let go of her long enough to open it. "Happy Wedding Day, Mom." The words were in a border of tiny hearts and flowers, and two big smiles had been drawn below.

She smiled now at the tears in his eyes and slipped her arms around him. "You were worth the wait." Her hushed voice cracked with emotion. "You all were."

He kissed her, drew her close and clasped the card between them. "So were you."

* * * * *

A Little Bit Of Love

Synithia Williams

MILLS & BOON

Synithia Williams has published over twenty-five novels since 2012. Her novel *A Malibu Kind of Romance* was a 2017 RITA® Award finalist, and she is a 2018 and 2019 African American Literary Awards Show nominee in Romance. Her books have been listed as Amazon Editors' "Best Book of the Month" in Romance. Reviews of Synithia's books can be found in *Publishers Weekly*, *Library Journal*, *Woman's World*, *Kirkus Reviews* and *Entertainment Weekly*. Synithia lives in Columbia, South Carolina, with her husband and two kids.

For additional books by Synithia Williams, visit her website, synithiawilliams.com.

Dear Reader,

I knew I wanted to write Sheri "Li'l Bit" Thomas's story from the moment I thought up the character in *Summoning Up Love*. Maybe it's because I'm messy. Maybe it's because I love Jazmine Sullivan's "Bust Your Windows" and Carrie Underwood's "Before He Cheats." Either way, I wanted to write a story about a woman who'd been at her lowest in romance but didn't give up her dream of finding love. I also knew from the start that I wanted her to find love where she least expected it—with the man who arrested her after she busted a window. Many of us have experienced heartbreak, and sometimes when it hurts, it's hard to imagine being in love again. This story is about rebuilding, finding peace with life and learning to be honest about what you want in a relationship. I hope you enjoy Li'l Bit and Deandre's road to happily-ever-after. And listen to the songs I mentioned, but don't bust any windows!

Happy reading,

Synithia

DEDICATION

To the ladies looking for love. It's out there.
You deserve it.

Chapter One

Sheri "Lil Bit" Thomas squinted at the back door of her restaurant. She couldn't be seeing what she thought she was seeing. The dim lights in the back parking area and the waning 4:00 a.m. moonlight had to be playing tricks with her eyes. She shuffled around in the canvas bag she carried instead of a purse, pushing aside her wallet, multiple lipsticks, old receipts and other random items until her hand finally settled around her cell phone. Pulling it out, she turned on the flashlight and beamed the bright light on the back door.

"Well, damn," she muttered to herself.

Her eyes weren't playing tricks on her. There were scratches around the lock. Scratches and a dent in the metal door as if someone had taken a crowbar to it and tried to pry their way in. Sheri glanced up and down the alley that separated the back doors of the row of businesses on the south end of the strip in Sunshine Beach and the chain-link fence of a parking lot behind another row of buildings. No one and nothing was there. Whoever had tried to break into her restaurant was long gone.

Cursing to herself, she cut off the flashlight and dialed her mom's number. She balanced the phone between her ear and shoulder, while she reached into her bag and felt around for the keys to the building.

"Lil Bit, what's wrong?" Dorothy Jean's voice was scratchy, as if she'd just woken up, and filled with concern.

"Why does something have to be wrong?"

"Because you only call me this early when there's a problem. What's wrong?"

Her mom was right. Sheri didn't call this early unless something was going on. Her mom helped in the restaurant, but she didn't come in until right before they opened at seven. Sheri knew her mom was not about to get out of bed before 5:00 a.m. so she tried to reserve her calls for help at the restaurant before opening for when she was desperate.

"I think someone tried to break into the restaurant."

A heartbeat passed as if the words had to sink in before her mom shrieked, "What? Are you sure? Are they still there?"

Sheri shook her head even though her mom couldn't see. "I don't think they got inside. Scratches on the door. That's why I'm calling. Did you see scratches yesterday?"

"Scratches? There weren't any scratches. Did you call the police?"

"Not yet. Like I said, I don't think they got past the dead bolt, but still."

"Girl, if you don't get your narrow behind off this phone with me and call the police, I'm getting dressed and coming." Her mom's voice was breathless and a little muffled. She'd probably jumped out of bed and was scrambling around her room. "Is JD there?" JD was their main line cook.

"Not yet, but he should be here soon," Sheri answered. "He's usually right after me." She looked down the alley again as if he might magically materialize.

"Goodness, you're there alone. Call the cops. Now. I'm on my way."

"Yes, ma'am." Sheri hung up and then dialed 911.

JD arrived right before the cops did. Tall and stout with golden brown skin, JD had an ever-present scowl on his face, unless he was listening to old-school jams. Then he grinned and crooned out the hits with a surprisingly mellow voice.

When Sheri left her job waiting tables at the Waffle House to open her own restaurant, JD was the first person she'd thought of asking to help her. He'd been the best line cook at Waffle House. She hadn't wasted any time calling and begging JD to come work for her when she'd received a grant from the town of Sunshine Beach for small business owners willing to open in south end—an area the town was desperate to revitalize. To her surprise and excitement, he'd immediately said yes.

"What happened to the door?" he asked. His yellow T-shirt had The Breakfast Nook, the restaurant's name, across the front and he'd matched it with a pair of gray sweats and a pair of white New Balance sneakers.

Sheri was in the kitchen waiting for the cops to arrive. She'd already pulled out the ingredients needed for the buttermilk biscuits and pancake mix and slipped a red apron over her own yellow The Breakfast Nook T-shirt and jeans. The person hadn't succeeded in breaking in, so she'd had no good reason to at least get started pulling together what they'd need to start breakfast.

"I think someone tried to break in," she said.

JD's scowl deepened. He crossed his arms and looked around the room as if wishing the would-be robber would pop out so he could jump them. "When?"

Sheri shrugged. "Last night. I didn't notice scratches on the door when I left yesterday. Did you?"

He shook his head. "I would have noticed scratches. Who would break in here?"

"I don't know, but I don't like it," she muttered.

The reflection of blue lights flashing in the dining area caught her attention. "The cops are here."

JD recoiled. "You called the cops?"

"That is what you do when someone tries to break into your place of business."

JD waved a hand. "You don't need a cop to tell you what happened."

"What happened?" Sheri headed to the front door.

He wagged a finger toward the front of the restaurant toward the street. "Probably one of those kids hanging around on the corner. They see you doing well and think there's money up in here."

"It might not be the kids," Sheri replied, but JD only grunted.

Sheri didn't want to immediately blame the teens who hung out along the strip. She used to be one of those kids. The south end of the beach was where most teenagers hung out. When she was younger, the south end was the area with the record and video game stores, an arcade and restaurants with the kind of cheap, delicious foods a teenager could afford on a budget. Many of those same hangout spots had closed over the past fifteen or so years, but the few remaining places were enough to still make the south end a popular hangout spot.

The town wanted to revitalize not just because of empty storefronts bringing down the property value at the beach but also because of the number of young people who loitered in the area. Sheri, who'd grown up loving that part of the beach, had jumped at the chance to open her breakfast and brunch spot in the area where she'd spent so much time in her youth. She wanted the area to get back to the thriving center it had once been but wasn't convinced revitalization had to come at the cost of kicking out all the teens. Sunshine Beach wasn't as lively as Myrtle Beach and didn't lean into the Southern charm like Charleston. The town was trying to find a way to get more tourists to visit.

"Probably one of those kids hanging out on the corner," Officer Duncan said after looking at her back door and checking to make sure nothing else was damaged or taken. "We've had a string of break-ins and vandalism. Most coming from a young group that's calling themselves a gang."

JD snorted. "Gangs, in Sunshine Beach? What are they representing? Whose subdivision is harder than the other?"

Officer Duncan gave a half smile. "You'd think we wouldn't have that problem here, but unfortunately, we do. Even for a small town we've got young people who think being in a gang is cool."

Sheri crossed her arms. "Well, what is the town doing to give these kids other alternatives? Most of the places that kept them busy on this end of the beach are shut down. The town cut the budget for the after-school programs at the community center. They have nowhere to turn to."

Officer Duncan tore a sheet of paper from his notebook and held it out toward her. "Talk about the town's budget is above my pay grade," he said. "This is a copy of the report I'm going to file. I recommend you keep that dead bolt on the back door, but also put in some cameras in the back just in case they come back. We'll increase patrols over the next few days."

"Increased patrols won't make the kids hanging out feel more comfortable." If anything, increased patrols might cause anxiety for the kids.

Officer Duncan winked. "Exactly."

Sheri pulled back and frowned. "Look, I don't want my business broken into or anything, but I don't think scaring the kids is the answer. There has to be something else we can do."

He looked exasperated with her plea but thankfully, no signs of frustration came through in his voice. "Look, if you want to get involved, the man who owns the burger shop asked us to start a neighborhood watch after his place was broken into the other week."

"There's a neighborhood watch?" That was the first she'd heard, and she'd been open for just over a year.

Officer Duncan nodded while adjusting the belt around his hips. "The next meeting is in the old Kings Clothing store building on Wednesday evening. Maybe come and learn more about the problems these kids are causing before you start worrying about police presence making them uncomfortable."

Sheri lifted her chin. "I will."

Her mom rushed in just as Officer Duncan was leaving. Like a hurricane, Dorothy Jean Thomas flew through the back door and surveyed everything. Seeing her mom move with such efficiency through the building was something Sheri wouldn't have thought she'd see when she'd come home years ago to help her recover from a stroke. Seeing her mom up and thriving, something she couldn't have imagined even three years ago, made giving up the job in Charlotte and starting over worth it.

"Oh my word, what happened?" Dorothy Jean said, examining Sheri from head to toe. She'd put her short, pixie-cut-style wig on crooked and her yellow The Breakfast Nook T-shirt was on backward. "Are you okay? Did they take anything? Who broke in here? I'm going take a switch to their behind."

JD waved off her mom's words. "Just some kids, Dorothy Jean. They didn't even get in here."

Her mom pressed a hand to her ample chest. Sheri and

her mom had the same shape, top-heavy with not much to brag about in the hip and thighs department. "Thank goodness. You sure nothing is taken?"

Sheri reached out and straightened her mom's wig. "Nothing was taken. They didn't even get in the back door."

Her mom raised a hand. "Praise Jesus." She slapped Sheri's hand away. "Are you okay?"

Satisfied that her mom's wig was correct, she stepped back to avoid being swatted at again. She'd deal with the backward shirt later. "Other than being annoyed that the police want to scare the teenagers away and being aggravated that we didn't get the chance to start on the biscuits yet, I'm good."

"You don't worry about those kids. Especially if they're trying to break in. If they are trying to break in it's only because they've got nothing to do. An idle mind is the devil's playground." She pointed at Sheri. "As for the biscuits, I can help you and JD get them started."

JD grunted and nodded in agreement with her mom. He turned away from them and started grabbing the ingredients needed for the biscuits.

"I can't help but care about the kids in the area," Sheri said. "I used to hang out down here. Every kid who's down here isn't a juvenile delinquent. There just isn't much to do in Sunshine Beach for teenagers."

"That's not your problem to solve." Dorothy Jean glanced at the clock on the wall and threw up her hands. "Goodness, look at the time. JD, when do your helpers get here? We got to get the biscuits made and someone needs to start getting the chicken battered and ready for the fryer for the chicken and waffles."

"They'll be here in a second," JD grumbled. Typically, he'd already be complaining about the kitchen crew not being there by now, but as much as he complained he also was protective of the people he worked with. Because her mom asked, he wasn't going to throw them under the bus.

"I'll start the chicken if you help with the biscuits," Sheri said.

They split up and began preparations for their breakfast offerings. The rest of the kitchen staff arrived a few minutes later. Despite being busy with the prep work, Sheri couldn't get her mind off the way JD, her mom and Officer Duncan were so eager to accuse the teens in the area of the break-in. Just another reason to push the kids off the strip like they'd tried to do when she was younger. A curfew and increased police patrols had resulted in what they wanted. Sheri and her friends found other places to hang out and the south end of the beach had lost a lot of business. By the time they'd lifted the curfew and put the police in other areas, the south end businesses had declined. Now, they wanted revitalization without considering every part of the population who used the area.

Not if she had anything to do with it. She was going to the neighborhood watch meeting and instead of complaining, she was going to demand that the Sunshine Beach Police Department do something to help the teenagers in the area instead of just trying to scare them off.

Chapter Two

Sheri stood outside the old storefront that used to be a popular clothing store. Now the vacant building was being used as the location for the neighborhood watch meeting, the place where she would make her case that the new businesses and the teens who hung out in the area could find a way to coincide. She'd never really gotten involved with community issues, but that didn't mean she couldn't start now. Everyone had to start somewhere. She took a fortifying breath and nodded firmly.

A folding table stood inside the door. Multiple papers and flyers covered the tabletop. A young white woman Sheri didn't recognize sat behind the table and greeted Sheri just as she entered. She wore a dark blue shirt with the Sunshine Beach PD seal on the chest.

"Hi, I'm Rebecca. I'm a community liaison with the Sunshine Beach Police Department," she said cheerfully. "Sign in here, please."

Sheri returned Rebecca's smile before scribbling her name, business and contact information on the sign in sheet. "I own The Breakfast Nook. This is my first meeting."

"That's great and welcome!" Rebecca said shaking Sheri's hand. "The neighborhood watch only recently started as part of the department's efforts to become more involved in the community. This is just the second time we've pulled the group together. Thank you for coming by tonight." Rebecca handed Sheri a few sheets of paper. "Here's your agenda and information on the latest crime report."

"The latest crime report? Why do I need that?" Sheri quickly scanned the paper and saw the attempted break-in at her restaurant listed near the top.

"We go over what's been happening in the neighborhood. This keeps everyone in the loop so they know what to be on the lookout for."

Sheri nodded, even though seeing the list of recent crimes in the area made her stomach twist. Sheri folded the paper in half as she went farther into the building. Metal chairs were set up in neat rows facing the back wall. A podium with a microphone attached to it stood in front of the chairs. Several people already mingled around the refreshment table set up in the left corner or sat in the chairs reviewing the same information Sheri had been given.

She recognized a few of the other shop owners. When she'd been setting up her restaurant, she'd made a point to go by and introduce herself to the other owners on the block. There was Ivy, who owned the tattoo and piercing parlor. She was curvy, with honey gold skin, a wide afro of reddish-brown curls and beautiful tattoos of flowers and the African goddess Oshun on her right arm. Then she saw Jared, the owner of the CDB oil shop. She remembered the tall, lanky white guy with curly brown hair from high school. He'd been cool back when they were in school and he'd been just as laid-back and welcoming when she'd reintroduced herself after opening her restaurant. She also recognized Mr. Lee and his wife, a sweet Korean couple who'd run the souvenir shop for as long as Sheri could remember.

Some of the newer owners who'd taken advantage of the grants from the town were also in attendance. She'd met Kelly, a mahogany-skinned self-proclaimed geek taking her chance on her love of comics by opening her own comic book shop, at the orientation meeting for people interested in the revitalization grants. Her eyes met with Belinda, someone else Sheri remembered from high school, though they'd run in opposite groups. While Sheri hung out in the south end of Sunshine Beach, Belinda had attended ballet lessons and cotillions. Sheri hadn't believed her eyes when she'd visited the new yoga studio and discovered Belinda was the owner. In high school Belinda belittled the kids hanging out at the south end of the beach.

Sheri tried not to hold Belinda's attitude in high school against her. People could change. Lord knew she'd gone through a rough patch that some people still judged her for. One that she couldn't even blame on youth. She'd vandalized the car of her ex, Tyrone Livingston, thanks to too much tequila, her cousin's bad influence and a bruised ego. So, she would not judge Belinda because the woman had come across as stuck-up when they were teens.

Sheri went around and spoke to everyone she knew and introduced herself to a few people she didn't. Surprisingly, many of the residents in the surrounding neighborhoods were also in attendance. She'd assumed the meeting was focused on the commercial area, but the crime watch zone extended into the residential district.

A few minutes after she'd made her way around the room and gotten a plate of cookies and a cup of lemonade, the door opened and the officer who'd responded to her attempted break-in entered, followed by another man. Sheri's brows rose as she took in the tall, handsome Black man behind Officer Duncan. He wasn't in uniform like Officer Duncan, but his commanding presence and quick, efficient scan of the room gave her a "he's in law enforcement" vibe. He looked familiar, but she couldn't place where she knew him from. His chin was free of a beard, and his dark hair was cut in a neat fade. His broad shoulders filled the dark blue T-shirt he wore, and his tan slacks fitted just enough to show off strong legs.

Sheri quickly made her way to one of the seats near the front of the room next to Ivy. She leaned over and asked, "Who's the guy with Officer Duncan?"

Ivy glanced over her shoulder. Her curly red hair made a halo around her face and a nose ring stud was the only visible piercing outside of the three in both ears.

"Oh, that's Lieutenant King. He's the head of the community outreach team at the Sunshine Beach Police Department and the one who started up the crime watch for our neighborhood."

The cookie in Sheri's hand dropped into her lap and her heart slapped against her rib cage. "Lieutenant King?"

Ivy raised a brow and nodded. "Yeah, why?"

Sheri closed her eyes and cursed. Recognition slammed into her hard and fast. He was the same officer who'd arrested her when she'd decided to channel Jasmine Sullivan and bust the windows out of Tyrone Livingston's car.

Lieutenant King and Officer Duncan moved from speaking to Rebecca to join the rest of the group. He seemed to know everyone there and asked about their business. When his eyes scanned the front row, they skimmed over her before jerking back. Sheri stopped chewing the cookie. She waited for recognition to brighten his eyes. For a frown to cross his handsome face before he lectured her again on how *"a guy isn't worth catching a charge"* as he'd done the night Tyrone's neighbors called the cops.

He didn't do either. A heart-stopping second after his eyes met hers, he gave a brief nod of acknowledgment before glancing away and continuing his conversation with Mr. Lee. Sheri let out a sigh of relief. Then she frowned. Did he recognize her, or was he pretending he didn't to be polite? Not like he had a reason to be polite and act like he didn't remember. Unlike her family, who loved to remind her of her moment of stupidity.

His conversation with Mr. Lee wound down and then Lieutenant King's deep, rumbling voice called out to get everyone's attention before he started the meeting. He was quick and efficient as he went over the crime report: three break-ins, five attempted break-ins, two reports of stolen items from unlocked vehicles, numerous calls of loitering and one public drunkenness.

Even though she had a copy of the crime report, hearing the listing of all the activity in the area was surprising. She knew that end of Sunshine Beach had its challenges, but she'd considered them limited to the lack of investment in the shops over the years and the need for renovations. She had not considered that crime was truly a problem.

"With the increase in activity lately, the Sunshine Beach Community Outreach Unit would like to host an outreach event in the area," Lieutenant King said after completing the report. "This will also give us an opportunity to learn more about what's happening in the area and help you come up with solutions to improve the situation."

"Please do," Belinda said in an exasperated voice one row behind Sheri. "These kids in the neighborhood and their antics are scaring away my clients. No one wants to finish a yoga class only to go out and find a bunch of delinquents hanging out around their car." The slightly fake, welcoming tone Belinda had used when Sheri had greeted her was gone, replaced with one of disdain and irritation. So much for not judging too early.

Sheri spun around in her seat and scowled at Belinda. "They aren't delinquents."

Belinda raised a brow. "Then what do you call them? I didn't want to go so far as to say *thugs*, but if the shoe fits…" Belinda waved a hand.

Sheri stood up and placed a hand on her hip. "They aren't thugs, either. They're just kids."

"Kids who like to break into cars and take whatever they see," Belinda continued. A few other people in the room made sounds of agreement. "As far as I'm concerned, if the city really wants to revitalize this part of town they'd do something about these delinquents."

Sheri opened her mouth to shoot back, but Lieutenant King spoke before she could go off. "The city *is* doing something. It's engaging with you all who are invested in the community like we're doing tonight and finding ways to reduce crime while also not displacing the kids who just want to come out and enjoy the beach."

Sheri spun toward him, pleasantly surprised he hadn't immediately agreed with Belinda. "Thank you. Just because some kids are making trouble doesn't mean they all need to be treated like criminals."

"I agree," he said evenly.

"I used to be one of those kids," Sheri said. "I loved hanging out on the south end because this was the end that had stuff for teenagers to do. I chose to open a restaurant at this end because of those memories. I want to achieve my dream here but also keep some of the things that made the south end special."

Lieutenant King nodded and smiled. "I couldn't agree with you more."

His smile was like sunshine on a cold day, warming Sheri's insides in a way that she wasn't quite prepared for. Her cheeks prickled with embarrassment from her reaction, and she nodded. "Thank you." She looked away quickly before he noticed she wanted to grin back at him and gave Belinda a triumphant look.

"Which is why I think you'll make the perfect head of our neighborhood outreach committee."

Sheri blinked and she looked back at him. "Say what now?"

Lieutenant King placed his hands on his hips and stared at her with confidence and authority. "Congratulations on being appointed as the head of the South End Community Outreach Committee."

Chapter Three

Deandre King stared at the front door of The Breakfast Nook. The words were painted in a gold script across the door and a sign emblazoned with the same words hung above the door. He remembered when the restaurant opened. Once he'd taken over as the head of the department's Community Outreach Division he'd kept up with the people using the grants given out by the city to support new businesses along the south end of the beach. In the year since The Breakfast Nook opened there'd been a steady stream of people coming in and out, but this was his first visit. Breakfast might be the most important meal of the day, but Deandre didn't make breakfast a priority. He wasn't a big fan of what was considered breakfast food, so he hadn't thought of visiting a restaurant focused on breakfast and brunch.

Maybe that's why he hadn't realized that the Sheri Thomas who opened the place was the same woman he'd arrested when he'd first moved to Sunshine Beach and taken the job with the police department. He'd forgotten all about her after she'd been bailed out and the charges dropped. Well, mostly forgotten. The guy she'd been so angry with that she'd thought taking a bat to his car was worth it had gone on to get a television show investigating ghosts with his brothers and was engaged to someone else now. Deandre had thought about Sheri when he heard that bit of news. He'd wondered what happened to her and if she'd moved on.

Now he knew. She had moved on. Started a business. And, apparently, was going to be working with him to plan a community outreach event in the area. A community event he'd championed to have so he could prove the area could be restored without the heavy hand of law enforcement. The way she'd championed for the area the night before had made him quickly pick her to help, but was she really the right person to help him, or had he been blinded by her enthusiasm and made a knee-jerk decision?

"One way to find out," he muttered before opening the door.

The smell of food and coffee greeted him. Despite forcing himself to eat a banana that morning with his coffee to get something in his stomach and avoid not eating anything until lunch, his stomach rumbled, and his mouth watered. He might not be a fan of breakfast, but whatever they were cooking sure as hell smelled good.

A young girl at the front greeted him. She looked to be in her early twenties, had dark brown skin and long braids that fell past her waist. "Welcome to The Breakfast Nook. Did you place a carryout order?"

He shook his head. "No, I'd like to speak with Sheri Thomas if she's available."

The girl frowned. "Sheri is in the back and helping wait tables. I can sit you in her section if you'd like."

"That's fine."

She nodded, grabbed a set of silverware rolled up in a napkin and took him to one of the empty seats near the back of the restaurant. Once he sat down, she pointed to a QR code on the table. "You can scan that for the menu."

"I'll just have some coffee," he said.

She raised a brow. "You sure? We have great chicken and waffles. Plus, our pancakes are delicious."

He shook his head. "Just coffee. Pancakes aren't my thing."

"That's because you haven't had my pancakes," a woman's husky voice came from his side.

He turned away from the hostess and met Sheri's big, brown eyes. She was attractive; he'd noticed that the night he'd arrested her. Slim, but curvy enough to make his eyes want to linger on her full breasts and pert ass. He'd wondered why a woman as good-looking as her would even bother with vandalizing some guy's car. She could easily find someone else who'd appreciate her...unless she made busting taillights a habit.

She sashayed over to stand next to the hostess. *Sashay* was the only word that came to his mind watching her walk. "Go back to the front, D'asa, I've got him."

D'asa walked away and Sheri focused back on him. The lights in the restaurant glowed off her dark brown skin, and she'd pulled her thick, black hair into a ponytail that stopped just past her shoulders. All hers or a weave? he wondered. Didn't matter. Either way she looked good.

The wariness that had been on Sheri's face when she'd first seen him at the neighborhood watch meeting was gone. At first, he'd chalked up her hesitancy to unease from meeting a cop. He understood caution and mistrust was some people's initial reaction. Later, when she'd stood up and confronted Belinda from the yoga studio, he'd recognized her voice and realized who she was. Her hesitancy made even more sense then.

"You sure you don't want any pancakes with the coffee?" She leaned a hip against the chair across from him.

"I don't like pancakes."

Her eyes widened as if he'd declared that he hated sunshine. "Who doesn't like pancakes?"

He lifted a shoulder. "A person who prefers waffles when he does decide to eat breakfast."

She chuckled, and her laugh was like her voice, husky, throaty, and both brushed over him like an unexpected caress. Heat flared in his midsection along with a spark of arousal. He shifted in his seat. It had taken two years after losing his wife to accept that his heart might be broken but his body still had sexual urges. He'd needed another year to be open to the idea of possibly dating again. But this was the first time in the six years since she'd passed that he'd had a strong reaction to someone. He frowned, not liking the idea of Sheri causing the reaction. He'd arrested her before, for goodness' sake.

Sheri cocked her head to the side. "No need to get upset. I can make waffles if you want. Though, after working at the Waffle House for years I'm kind of tired of them."

He relaxed his features, not wanting to explain that his frown was caused by his body's reaction to her and not because of his aversion to pancakes over waffles. "Coffee is fine. I actually came by to talk to you about the community outreach event."

"I figured as much." She glanced around the room as if judging the level of activity before looking back at him. "I can talk for a few minutes. I'll get you some coffee and be right back."

A few minutes later, she came back and set a cup of coffee in front of him along with a plate with a biscuit on it and a selection of jams and honey.

He raised a brow as he watched her settle across from him. "I didn't need a biscuit."

"You look like you need something in your stomach. Go ahead, try it."

"This wasn't necessary."

She slid the plate closer to him. "I know, but I can't help it. My mom likes to feed people and I do, too."

"I guess that's why you opened a restaurant." He sliced the biscuit in half and reached for the grape jelly. Not because he wanted it, but because it would be rude to continue to reject her offering.

"One of the reasons. I worked at an expensive steak house when I lived in Charlotte after graduating from the University of South Carolina with a degree in hospitality. I was the business manager there but came back home when my mom got sick. I took the first job I could find, which was at the Waffle House."

"That's a lot different than a steak house." The biscuit smelled delicious and when he took a bite, it nearly melted in his mouth. "Damn, this is good."

Her full lips spread in a triumphant smile. "I knew you'd like it. And, yeah, Waffle House is a lot different, but they pay decent, the tips are good and I needed the flexibility to work early in the morning or late at night so I could take Mom to her appointments during the day. That taught me how to be quick on the go. When Mom got better, and I heard about the city wanting to revitalize what used to be my favorite hangout in town, I decided to give opening my own place a try."

He looked around the restaurant and back at her. "Looks like you're doing pretty good."

She shrugged. "I'm doing okay. I survived my first year, so that's worth celebrating. My customers are mostly locals, but I'm trying to get those people visiting the bougie north end of the beach to come on down to the south side and give my place a try."

"But you don't want to kick out the teenagers like some of the other shop owners."

She shook her head, the smile on her face disappearing. "I don't. I used to be one of those kids. I loved hanging out down here. We don't have to displace the people who live in Sunshine Beach just to draw in the visitors looking for a quaint beach experience. We can make it work."

"How?"

Her bright eyes widened, and she threw up her hands in a "Who knows?" fashion. "I don't know, but that's what we're figuring out together, right?"

He took another bite of the biscuit and nodded slowly while he considered her words. After he washed it down with the coffee, he studied her. "You don't have a problem working with me?"

She hesitated a second before shaking her head. Her eyes narrowed slightly as she asked hesitantly, "Why would I? Because you're a cop?"

He chuckled softly. She was willing to play dumb if he was. But playing dumb wasn't his style. "Because I'm the cop that arrested you a few years back."

She flinched, closed her eyes and let out a heavy breath. "Damn, I thought you didn't recognize me."

"I didn't at first."

She opened her eyes. "What gave me away?"

"I thought you'd take a baseball bat to Belinda's head like you did that car." He softened his words with a smile.

She laughed and waved a hand. "My baseball bat days are over. Belinda is bougie as hell, but not worth catching a charge over."

"Neither was Tyrone Livingston."

She sighed and crossed her arms on the table. She sat forward and met his eye. "Neither was he, but that's over and done with now. No, I don't mind working with you. If you don't mind working with me."

He wanted to know more about why she'd done what

she did. Had she and Tyrone been serious? Was she still interested in Tyrone? He cut those thoughts short. Her baseball bat days may be over, but her fiery personality was still there. He needed her fire to bring the community together, but not in any other way. He'd always told his son to stay away from women with drama. Sheri was drama.

He lifted his coffee mug and saluted her. "I don't mind working with you at all."

She uncrossed her arms and slapped her hand on the table. "Good. Glad that's out of the way. So what do we do next?"

He looked up as another person entered. "How about we meet up tomorrow afternoon, when you're not working, and talk about some things."

"Works for me. Your place or mine?" She cocked a brow.

Deandre choked on his coffee. Sheri's eyes widened and she handed him a napkin. He took it and wiped his mouth. Did she have to sound so sexy saying that? "Excuse me?"

"Where do you want to meet and plan?" She spoke slowly as if he were having a hard time comprehending.

Considering where his mind had gone, he was having a hard time. Too much time had passed since he'd had sex. Now his brain was finding innuendos where there were none. "My bad. I can come back here after you close. Or we can use the Kings store again. It's become the spot for the Community Outreach Division's work on the south end. The city is thinking of setting it up as a visitor center later."

She sat up straight. "I like that idea. Yes, let's meet at Kings. We close at two and it takes some time to clean up. How about three? That work for you?"

He thought about his day. DJ, his son, had wrestling practice until six. He'd still have time to get home and get dinner together before he got home. "That works."

Sheri beamed. "Good. Enjoy your biscuit. It's on the house, partner." She winked and he sucked in a breath. "It's about time for the late morning rush. Let me finish helping out but stay as long as you need."

Just like that she got up and walked away, oblivious to the way he'd reacted to her. He watched her greet the guy who'd sat down at the table next to him. Deandre tried not to focus on Sheri as he finished his biscuit and coffee. His efforts were in vain. He was aware of her movements. Her husky laugh with customers, the friendly greeting she gave them all, the way her hand touched the shoulders of some regulars when she chatted them up. He quickly downed his coffee, dropped a ten-dollar bill on the table despite her saying not to pay and got out of there before he became even more rattled than he already was.

Chapter Four

Sheri went out the front of the restaurant to bring in the sign with the specials handwritten in chalk from the walkway. It had been a busy day. Her shoulders ached and her feet were tired, but she wouldn't trade the feeling for anything else. She loved that the restaurant was doing well. She'd worried so much and prayed so hard that stepping away from a steady paycheck to open her own place would be worth the fear and uncertainty. So far, it had been. So, she would accept every ache, pain and fatigue that came after a busy day.

The sound of a catcall whistle from her left caught her attention. She looked up and sighed after spotting the group of boys standing a few doors down from her restaurant. She'd seen the boys before. Teenagers, who roamed up and down the strip after school and on weekends. She'd never witnessed them doing anything wrong, but she knew their hanging around outside the businesses was part of the reason some other shop owners wanted something done to keep the kids out of the area.

One of the boys stood in the middle. His mouth spread in a wide grin as he eyed her from head to toe. He rubbed his hands together and tried, she assumed, to look interesting.

"Hey lady, can I get your number?"

Sheri couldn't help herself, she laughed. Did this little boy really think she was about to give him her number? "Young man, you don't want my number. I've got shoes older than you."

He lifted a thin shoulder. "I like my women seasoned."

"Seasoned? Lord, child, get out of here with that nonsense. Go try that mess with a girl your own age."

His friends laughed. Sheri shook her head and picked up her sign. She headed back inside. But she heard him grumble, "I didn't like her old ass anyway," before the door closed.

Sheri scowled. "Old?" she mumbled to herself. She was older than him, but she wasn't old. She locked the door with a flip of her wrist before heading to the back of the restaurant.

The "old ass" comment irritated her all the way from the restaurant to her mom's house. It was the first time she'd been referred to as *old*, within earshot at least. She knew the kid was just trying to save face after she'd shot him down, but the words had hit a mark. Sheri was, indeed, getting older. She would be forty in a couple of years. While her life was good, she still wasn't where she'd thought she'd be at this age. She'd expected to still be living in Charlotte, or maybe to have moved to Atlanta or even New York. She'd be working for a high-end restaurant, married to, or at least dating, the perfect man and on the road to having the two beautiful kids she'd always wanted. She never would have imagined she'd be back home in Sunshine Beach, living in a house next to her mom's, still single with no prospects.

She pulled into her mom's driveway and let out a sigh. Even though she wasn't where she thought she would be, she wasn't in a bad place, either. She constantly focused on that. She owned her own business, and her restaurant was successful. She'd inherited her grandmother's home next to her mom's, so she didn't have to worry about a mortgage, and she'd finally shaken off the stigma of taking a baseball bat to her former lover's car. All in all, her life could be worse. She wouldn't let a kid calling her an "old ass" make her start to doubt herself.

Internal pep talk complete, she went inside to check on her mom. It was part of her daily routine. Leave the restaurant, check in at her mom's house to make sure she was still feeling good, taking her meds, and maybe grab a meal if her mom had cooked. She knocked on the screen door before opening.

"Ma, it's me," she called out.

"In the kitchen," her mom called back.

Sure enough, the house smelled divine. The familiar smell of her mom's fried chicken filled the air. Sheri's stomach grumbled. She'd been so busy today she barely had time to eat. She wondered if Lieutenant Deandre King had eaten later in the day. The thought made her frown. She did not need to worry about whether or not he ate. The man was grown and could find his own meals. She blamed her mom. Her mom couldn't stand to see people not eating when there was plenty of food around. It was why Sheri had brought him the biscuit with his coffee. She'd caught the way his eyes had lingered on some of the plates on the tables. She hadn't been able to help herself. Her need to feed people kicked in, and she'd brought him food.

Her mom stood in front of the fridge, and pulled out two cans of Pepsi in her hands as she headed toward the door that led to the back patio. "I'm sitting out back with your aunt."

"Aunt Gwen's here?"

"Yeah, she stopped by after she got off work. Come on out back."

Sheri quickly moved to the back door and opened it for her mom. Her mom's sister Gwen sat under the umbrella connected to her mom's patio table. It was a warm and humid afternoon, so an oscillating fan was plugged up to speed along the intermittent breeze. Despite the heat, her mom and aunt loved sitting on the back porch.

"Hey, Auntie." Sheri went over and gave her aunt a hug.

"Hey, Sheri, your mom said you would be here in a little bit." She was still in the dark blue uniform she wore as part of the custodial crew for the city of Sunshine Beach. She wore wire-framed glasses and her salt-and-pepper hair was pulled back into a ponytail.

Sheri pulled out a chair and sat around the round, glass patio table. "Did you need to see me?"

Her aunt took the Pepsi from her sister with one hand and pointed at Sheri with the other. "Why didn't you tell me someone tried to break into the restaurant?"

Sheri gave her mom a look. But her mom just shrugged. "What? You thought I wasn't going to tell her?"

"It wasn't that big of a deal. They didn't get in. I went to the neighborhood watch meeting, and they're already working on plans to try and help the south end."

Her aunt nodded. "They need to do something. The south end of the strip used to be a nice, safe place to go. Now, it's full of kids doing God knows what."

Sheri shifted her chair to try and get in the direct aim of the fan when it turned her way. "The kids are doing the same thing I did as a kid. Hanging out and looking for something to do."

"Well, I don't like it," Gwen said with a frown.

Her mom nodded. "Me, either. I'm glad the city is trying to make the south end better, but I need them to do something about the crime. How can your business stay successful if they're breaking in all the time?"

Sheri held up a finger. "First of all, it was one attempted break-in." She lifted another finger. "Second, we're looking at solutions."

Her mom's eyes narrowed. "That's why you were talking to that cop earlier today."

Sheri didn't bother to ask how her mom knew even though she hadn't come in this morning. JD probably called and told her mom the second Sheri had sat down at the table.

"Yes, that's why he was there. He's in charge of the new community outreach division. They want to create a better relationship between the department and the citizens. He wants to get my ideas."

Her aunt grunted and shook her head. "I don't trust cops."

Her mom nodded. "Me, either."

Sheri understood where they were coming from. She remembered the way her family and neighbors hadn't trusted law enforcement in and around Sunshine Beach when she was a kid. The delayed response to calls, the lack of engagement in their community, the harassment by the less-than-stellar cops. The mistrust ran deep and over generations.

"I get it," Sheri said. "And I'm not saying I'm going to marry him, I'm saying he wants to help the community, so I'll work with him and see if he's for real."

Gwen leaned forward with a skeptical look in her dark eyes. "What if he's not?"

Sheri shrugged. "Then, I'll find another way to help the community. I want the south end to be like it used to be. Working with the police is just one way to get there, but not the only way."

Her mom nodded. "Well, I hope he turns out to be okay. I would hate for a man that fine to be dirty."

Gwen sat up straight. "How do you know he's fine?"

"D'asa told me," her mom said. She looked at Sheri with a raised brow. "Is he?"

Fine wasn't enough to describe that man. Intense, good-looking, sexy, commanding. All of that and she still didn't think she'd accurately captured everything appealing about Deandre King.

Sheri waved a hand. "I mean, he's alright. I don't care about that. I'm just trying to help the neighborhood."

Her aunt waved a finger at Sheri. "Well, don't think about that. Even if he is fine. It's hard enough to trust a man, but if he's a cop." She sucked her teeth and shook her head. "No telling what he'll do."

"What's he gonna do, Gwen?" her mom asked laughing.

"I don't know, but I don't trust men and I don't trust cops, so obviously, you can't trust a man cop."

If Sheri were honest, she didn't trust herself more than she didn't trust men in general. Her judgment and track record when it came to guys wasn't great. She didn't have a hard time finding a guy. It was just that the type of guys she was typically attracted to turned out to be the worst kind of guy for her. Men like Deandre wouldn't usually cross her radar. Sure, he was good-looking, but he was a "nice" guy. Sheri had to admit she always went for a hint of bad boy with her good looks.

But bad boys, playboys and wanna-be thugs had given her nothing but a world of disappointment and embarrassment. Maybe she needed a nice guy like Deandre in her life. It wasn't as if he would give her a chance. He'd arrested her when she was at her worst. Nope, no need to focus on how sexy Deandre King was. That ship wasn't sailing.

Sheri sighed and patted her aunt's hand. "Don't worry.

I'm not trying to do anything with Lieutenant King but help the community. No matter how cute he may be."

Deandre did everything he could to leave work on time. He rushed to the grocery store to pick up ground beef, hamburger buns, frozen fries and sloppy joe sauce for his son DJ's favorite meal. DJ's birthday was that weekend. Deandre had to work, but he'd set a personal objective to try and make every other day of the week special for his kid.

They'd moved to Sunshine Beach right after DJ's mom, Jamila, passed away suddenly. The aneurysm took her from them quickly when no one was at home to deliver first aid or call the hospital in enough time to possibly save her. As much as it had pained him to find his wife like that, he was thankful that he'd gotten home before DJ. She'd passed away a few days before his son's birthday, which was why Deandre tried his best to make DJ's birthday special.

He made it home in enough time to get the sloppy joes created and was just taking the first batch of fries out of the fryer when the back door opened. He turned off the deep fryer and spun toward his son.

"Hey! You're just in time. I've got dinner ready," Deandre said cheerfully.

DJ gave him a look that said the cheerfulness wasn't needed or very much appreciated. Not surprising. DJ was a good kid, but he was filled with teenage attitude. Deandre spent a lot of time trying to figure out when he'd gone from being his son's best friend to the person he wanted to spend the least amount of time with. They'd been close before his wife passed and had grown closer in the years after they'd lost her. But, sometime in the past year and a half, his relationship with DJ had shifted. His son's answers were short, his eye contact brief to nonexistent, and the time they'd spend hanging out together only happened when Deandre forced it.

"Yeah, I'm here," DJ said in a flat tone.

DJ reminded him a lot of his mother, with the same wide-set brown eyes, flat nose and dimpled chin. His height, broad shoulders and growing muscles all came from Deandre. His son wore a pair of dark blue joggers and a white hoodie. He'd let his hair grow out. The curls at the top were thick and wild enough to make Deandre want to cut them, but he was trying to let his son express himself. That's what Jamila would have wanted.

"I made dinner." Deandre pointed toward the plate of hot fries and the pan with the sloppy joe mixture on the stove.

DJ glanced at the food and shrugged. "I'm not hungry." He turned to leave the kitchen.

"Hold up," Deandre called.

DJ didn't sigh out loud. He wasn't outright disrespectful, just mildly disdainful with receiving attention from his dad. Still, Deandre *felt* the sigh and eye roll as he watched his son's shoulders lift and lower.

DJ turned around. "Yeah?"

Deandre raised a brow. "Yeah?"

"Yes, sir?" DJ replied in the same flat tone of voice he'd used before.

Deandre wrestled back his growing annoyance with considerable effort. "You've been in school all day and then you had wrestling practice afterward. I don't believe you're not hungry."

"I already ate."

"Ate? When and where?"

"My boy Jay wanted to get some pizza so we stopped by the place down on the strip and got something to eat."

Deandre looked at his watch. DJ wouldn't have had time to eat if he was coming home straight from wrestling practice. "When did you have time to do that?"

"After school."

"What about wrestling practice?"

DJ shifted his stance. He glanced away quickly before meeting Deandre's eyes and lifting his chin. "Oh, I quit."

"You quit?" Deandre asked, narrowing his eyes. He braced his hands on his hips and stared at his son. DJ had loved wrestling. He'd won a medal the year before. "Why would you quit?"

DJ shrugged. "The coach started changing stuff up. I didn't like it, so I quit."

"Change things up how? And, why didn't you tell me?"

"Just new rules and stuff. This is why I didn't tell you. I knew you'd have a bunch of questions."

"I'm going to ask questions because you liked wrestling. If the coach was acting weird, then you tell me and I can talk to him."

DJ waved a hand. "See, that's why I didn't tell you. I knew you'd go all *cop* on me and want to make it a big deal. I was just tired of wrestling. It took up too much time and I want to hang with my boys. So, I quit when he started changing the rules. That's all."

Deandre's argument deflated. He didn't want to *go all cop* on his son. Deandre set rules and insisted on order in his house, but he never wanted his son to feel like he was being treated as a suspect. It was one of the things he'd promised Jamila when they'd gotten married. She'd said if they were going to build a family they had to treat each other like family. Meaning Deandre couldn't come in setting law and order as if they were the people he arrested every day.

Deandre dialed back the steel in his voice and tried to

sound more like a father and less like a cop. "I still think you should have talked to me about it."

"I'm talking to you about it now."

Deandre took a deep breath. He would not get frustrated with his son and let this spiral into an argument. "Before you make big decisions like that I need to know."

"Okay," DJ said in a flat tone.

"Okay what?"

"I'll tell you before I make big decisions."

The quick agreement wasn't a win. It was a deflection tactic. Something DJ had also started in the last year. Instead of talking about anything Deandre tried to discuss, he said "okay" or agreed to whatever Deandre said. It had taken Deandre a few weeks to catch on that his son was using the quick agreement to end the conversation faster.

"And you need to call me if you're going somewhere after school. Anything could happen and I wouldn't know where you were."

"Okay."

Deandre waited for more, but the wait was a waste of time. DJ wanted the conversation to end and, honestly, he wanted to move on and try to salvage the rest of the night. "Let's eat and we can talk some more."

DJ rubbed his stomach. "I'm full from pizza and I've got homework."

He tried a different approach. "Did you want to do anything for your birthday?"

"You're working, so no. I'll just hang with my boys."

There wasn't any accusation in his son's voice, but the reminder still sent a knife through Deandre's heart. He'd tried to find a way out of working, but the police chief was scheduled to speak at a community event with several politicians on Saturday, and she wanted him, as the new head of the Community Outreach Division, to also be there.

"But we could still do something. I'll be done by three or four."

DJ lifted a shoulder. "Okay. You just tell me where you want me to be."

"I want you to tell me what you'd like to do. We could go to dinner with your grandparents. Or check out a movie."

"Grandma and Grandpa said they'd take me to breakfast. I'm going to a movie with my friends. I'm good."

The guilt wrapped around Deandre's heart tightened its grip. DJ already had plans for his birthday. Plans that didn't include or require him. "Squeeze in some time for me. Let's grab something to eat before you go to dinner with your friends. That work?"

"Okay. Now, can I go do my homework?" DJ asked.

Deandre bit back suggesting DJ to do his homework downstairs so they could talk while he ate. He already knew what the answer would be. Instead, he nodded. "That's fine."

DJ turned and walked out without another word. Deandre watched his son go, then looked at the sloppy joes and French fries he'd made. He didn't know how they'd gotten to this point, and what scared him even more was that he didn't know how to change things, either.

Chapter Five

Sheri went inside the Kings store, now the home of the south end's neighborhood watch, for her meeting with Deandre. She'd spent most of the day making sure everything was settled at the restaurant so she could leave in enough time to meet him that afternoon. She didn't like to leave the rest of the workers by themselves at closing time. Not because she didn't think they could close up without her, but because she didn't want to give the impression that she wasn't just as willing to work late and hard with them. After the attempted break-in, they were all more than willing for her to leave early and meet with Deandre. They'd practically pushed her out of the door.

Inside was dark compared with the bright sunshine outside the building. Only half of the overhead fluorescent lights were on. Deandre sat at a desk in the back corner of the open space. He'd been looking at his phone when she'd walked in but gave her his full attention when the doors opened. He put his phone down and stood.

"Come on in." He pointed to a seat in front of his desk, one of the folding chairs they'd set up in rows for the neighborhood watch meeting. "Have a seat."

"Is this your office?" she asked, raising a brow. She looked around the wide, empty space as she crossed over to him. During the neighborhood meeting, she'd been so caught up in what was happening that she hadn't paid attention to what the inside of the building looked like.

Without all the people inside, it was dark and dreary. There wasn't anything in the space except for the desk in the corner. She supposed the tables and chairs put out for the meeting were stored away behind one of the doors along the back wall.

Deandre shook his head. "No, I have an office down at headquarters. But since I started working in the Community Outreach Division, I try to meet people in their neighborhoods. When I'm in the south end, this is where I meet people. Coming down to the police station isn't always comfortable for everyone."

Sheri hung her purse on the back of the folding chair before sitting down. "Can you blame them for not being comfortable?"

He shrugged and his broad shoulders stretched the material of the dark blue polo shirt he wore. "Not really. I understand why they would feel leery about being down there. Our conference rooms look a lot like interrogation rooms. I'm trying to build bridges, not intimidate."

"That's good to hear."

"Why is that?"

"Some cops like to intimidate people."

She waited for him to deny it. Or get defensive. Instead, he nodded. "Some do. I don't."

She watched him, impressed and surprised by his answer. She lifted a brow and studied his shoulders. "Come on, a big strong man like you. You've never intimidated anyone?"

The corner of his mouth quirked. "I learned long before I became a cop that my size and voice intimidates some people. Just my presence can heighten the tension in a situation. Instead of leaning into that, I chose to figure out the best way to diffuse the situation versus making it worse."

Dang, she was even more impressed. He was self-aware. She thought back to when he had arrested her. She could tell he'd been irritated with the situation, but he hadn't tried to tower over her, talk over her or try to make her feel afraid. She'd been pissed off, angry and afraid of what would happen that night, but she hadn't been afraid when he was around.

"I think I'm going to be okay working with you." She stretched her legs out in front of her.

Deandre leaned forward and rested his forearms on the desk. They were muscled and toned, just like the rest of him. "You didn't think you'd be able to work with me before?"

Sheri jerked her eyes away from his arms and back to meet his direct gaze. "I wasn't sure. You're the cop who arrested me. But the more I talk to you, the more I think you're okay."

This time the lip twitch turned into a half smile. "I appreciate that."

He continued to hold her gaze as he smiled. The air electrified. Sheri's pulse increased and sparks shot across her skin. The man was handsome but when he smiled, he was devastating.

His cell phone chimed. He looked away, breaking the spell and allowing Sheri to breathe. She rubbed the back of her neck. She had to get a hold of herself. Yeah, it had been a while since she'd had sex, but she wasn't so hard up that she would risk embarrassment by trying to hook up with the cop that arrested her. Besides, he was cool with her and everything, but he did not seem like the type of cop who also tried to slide his phone number on the traffic ticket he wrote you. She'd bet money he was not interested in her in any kind of way outside of helping him reach out to the south end community.

"Dammit, DJ," he muttered. His fingers tapped against the screen as he frowned down.

"Anything wrong?" she asked.

He looked up and then looked embarrassed. "I'm sorry. I didn't mean to curse."

Sheri chuckled. "*Dammit* is far from being one of the worst words I've ever heard. Any trouble?"

He shook his head. "No, it's my son. He was supposed to be going back to wrestling practice but instead he's gone home."

"You have a son?" Which meant there was a mother. Which meant he might be married or in a relationship. Further proof why she did not need to be salivating over the man in this meeting.

He nodded. "Yeah, he's sixteen. A sophomore in high school. He suddenly decided to quit wrestling but won't give me a good reason."

"Oh. Well, I'm sure he has a good one."

"I wish he'd tell me." He gave her a curious look. "Do you have kids?"

She shook her head. "No. Wanted one or two one day, but just haven't met the right person to impregnate me."

He blinked. "Oh."

Sheri laughed at his stunned expression. "You don't have to look so… I don't know, surprised. Having a kid is a big deal. I can't be having one with just anybody."

His shoulders relaxed and he held up a hand. "I'm sorry. I just never heard it phrased that way. But I understand what you mean."

"What about your son's mom? Is she your wife?"

He nodded. "She was. She died, six years ago."

Sheri put a hand to her chest. "I'm so sorry. I didn't mean…"

"I know. It's a little easier to say it now. That's why we moved to Sunshine Beach. Her family lives here. I wanted my son to grow up with family around. My family is… not as reliable."

"In what way?" she asked, then flinched. "Sorry, I'm being nosy."

He shrugged. "And I'm dumping personal stuff on you. My bad."

She kind of liked that he was talking to her. It made him seem a little less off-limits. Not that she was going to cross those limits. But seeing a personal side of him took away some of the space she'd expected to be between them.

"It's okay. I've been told I'm easy to talk to. You'd be surprised the personal things my customers say to me when I bring them their food. I guess I've got that kind of face."

"It is a nice face," he said.

Heat flooded Sheri's cheeks. She pressed a hand to one. "Oh, well, thank you."

He glanced away and then shifted in his chair. "I mean, you seem trustworthy. I get a sense about people. You're a good person."

"I try to be." She got a vision of the disappointment in his face when he'd taken the baseball bat from her the night of her arrest. Her cheeks burned even more. "At least, I've been trying harder to be a better person."

He cleared his throat. "So, about the community outreach."

She snapped her finger. "Yes, about that. I was thinking a fair or something. We invite people over to talk about what's happening in the area and what we'd like to see."

"People like who?"

"I don't know. Like folks who work for Sunshine Beach. We haven't heard from council members. Or the ones making plans for the area. Then there are the people in law enforcement."

"People don't just come out for a panel discussion from politicians and bureaucrats." His words held a hint of humor that surprised Sheri. He could also tease. She liked that.

Sheri slid forward in the chair. "Then let's make it more than that. Let's make it fun. Draw them in and then teach them something while they're here."

"That could work."

"I know it can. We can bring it up at the next neighborhood watch meeting. Get some ideas and form a committee to help plan."

"You came with all the ideas already, huh?"

She grinned. "I mean, it is why you asked me to help. You could tell I'm a good person and that I can get things done."

"That is true. Okay, Sheri, let's plan a fair."

Chapter Six

Deandre sat at his desk in headquarters working on paperwork when there was a knock on the door. Looking up, he spotted LaTisha Fuller. They'd worked together when he was on patrol, and he'd become friends with her and her husband, Omar. Their son was about the same age as his and he'd quickly latched on to other people he could connect with and give his son a community when he'd moved to Sunshine Beach.

"What's up, Tisha?"

LaTisha pointed over her shoulder. "Chief wants to see you. What did you do now?"

Deandre thought about everything he'd worked on this past week and couldn't think of anything. Not that he made a habit of messing up and being called to meet with the chief. He played by the book and followed the rules. "Nothing that I know of."

LaTisha laughed. She was a little under six feet tall, with golden brown skin and a halo of curly hair she wore slicked back in a tight ponytail. When he'd left patrol and accepted the offer to head up the Community Outreach Division, he'd hoped she would've accepted the role of heading up the section with him. But she hadn't wanted to be strapped to a desk. He couldn't blame her, and, thankfully, their friendship remained intact.

"Well, she's itching to see you, so you've probably done something."

Deandre scooped up a notepad and pen and headed out the door. "If I did something, then I'll deal with it."

Latisha shook her head. "You're always acting like stuff doesn't bother you."

"It bothers me, but I put things in perspective. I realize what's worth the effort and what isn't. Chief wanting to see me, that's not worth any anxiety until I get there and find out why. No need to borrow trouble. She may have something good to say."

Latisha shrugged. "I hope so. Lunch later?"

He checked his watch. "Nah, I'll be taking a late lunch. Maybe tomorrow."

"Sounds good." She held out her fist.

He bumped his fist with hers before turning the corner to head to the chief's office. The police chief was still considered new, since the previous chief had worked for the department for twenty years. She'd been hired to take over the Sunshine Beach Police Department six months after he'd moved to the town and taken a job with the force. Higher-ups had brought her in because the previous chief had been caught up in one too many scandals with his subordinates. The final affair was with a married woman in Dispatch. Her husband had blown the whistle, sending text messages, pictures and emails to the local news. Once his bad deeds could no longer be hidden, the department went under scrutiny and everything wrong about the way he ran things came to light. The previous chief had created a lack of trust in the community, a high turnover rate of officers and a toxic environment that didn't offer any benefit for doing the right thing. Chief Montgomery had been hired and given the task of fixing all of that. And she'd taken her job seriously.

Suddenly, people were held accountable for their actions. Transparency and integrity were valued over sweeping things under the rug and an unwritten policy of talking through smoke and mirrors. She'd slowly made changes and they were finally starting to see the benefit of her efforts.

He knocked on the door and entered after hearing a terse "come in." Chief Montgomery gave him a quick glance before looking back at her computer. Her fingers flew furiously over the keyboard as she typed.

"Lieutenant King, come on in and have a seat."

Deandre entered and sat down in the chair across from her desk. "I heard you wanted to see me."

"I do. Let me finish my thoughts on this." She was short but had enough confidence and attitude to make up for her stature. She wore her brown hair in a short style. Her cheeks were slightly flushed beneath her pale skin and her eyes narrowed as she typed. Whoever was on the other side of her email had obviously pissed her off.

"Go right ahead."

Her chin lifted and lowered before her brows knitted and she went back to typing. Chief Montgomery had spent the past fifteen years in law enforcement after an eight-year stint in the army. She was straightforward, no nonsense and one of the few people he knew who truly believed in always doing the right thing. She was a stickler for following the rules but was also empathetic enough to try and understand why decisions were made. He liked that about her and believed that was the reason why she'd been able to make the department better.

She finished with a few hard taps on the keyboard before her lips moved as she read over the email. Then she hit the enter key hard. "There, that's done."

"Who's getting eviscerated now?" Deandre teased.

She looked at him and raised a brow. "The town manager. I swear that guy likes to push my buttons."

"What's the problem now?" On the one hand, the town manager respected the way Chief Montgomery had improved the police department. On the other hand, the popularity she received for doing so and the love of the community meant her power with the elected officials and the public was higher than his. The battle of egos commenced whenever the two were together.

"That's why I want to see you," she said. "What's happening in the south end?"

"I met the with community liaison. We're looking at dates to have an outreach event in the neighborhood. Why?"

Chief Montgomery pointed at her computer and frowned. "He's once again griping about crime in the area. Mostly because business owners are griping to him. He doesn't want to hear about the community outreach team. Instead, he wants to hear about the number of arrests we've had."

Deandre scoffed. "Why, so he can turn around and blame us for ruining the town's reputation with the residents?"

"The Community Outreach Division wasn't his idea, and he doesn't like it. The man hired me to make things better, but he fights me on everything I'm trying to do."

"Your work proves him wrong all the time. That's what matters." Deandre had seen that for himself several times over the past six years. The chief and town manager would argue about one of her ideas, but things would turn out great and her approval ratings in the community went up several more points.

"Yeah, well this time he's got at least two council members on his side. They want to see arrests for the break-ins, and they want more patrols to handle the hoodlums in the area." She held up a hand. "Their words, not mine."

Deandre nodded but his shoulders tensed. "There aren't any hoodlums. Just teenagers with nothing to do."

"Well, I need to give them something. Maybe your outreach event will work out. I can ask them to come and speak. Elected officials love a chance to speak."

"If they're willing to come, we'll have them. We were even thinking about asking the public defender and solicitor's office to show up. We'll take a few council members."

She nodded. "Good. Let me know when you finalize a date and I'll get it on their calendar. This has to work out. I don't need him to give me any more crap about the community outreach division. If we can show that having a presence in the neighborhoods that's positive and not just to scare people but still get results, then I can shut him up."

"I'll get on it. I'm meeting with Sheri later today to go over possible dates and locations."

Chief Montgomery stopped in the middle of turning back to her computer to give him a sharp glance. "Who's Sheri?"

"She's the community liaison. She agreed to help after the last neighborhood watch meeting. She wants the area to get better, but not at the expense of kicking out the kids who rely on the area as a place to hang out."

The line between Chief Montgomery's eyes lifted before she nodded. "Good. Let me know what you'll need. I'll see if I can get it for you."

"I will." He stood and turned toward the door.

"And Lieutenant,"

Deandre faced her. "Yes, ma'am."

She clasped her hands on her desk and met his eyes with an intense stare. "We've got to make this good. I don't know if he means it, but he threw out dissolving the

Community Outreach Division to focus more on a tactical team that focuses on crime. I can't let that happen."

Deandre understood exactly what that would mean. An increased police presence and a heavier hand from law enforcement. A stronger push to not only remove the teenagers from the area, but revitalization efforts that also pushed out the current businesses for ones that were higher-end like the north side of the beach. Gentrification in the name of community improvements.

The Community Outreach Division had been Chief Montgomery's idea—an idea Deandre had supported and been more than willing to support after seeing how well the similar division had worked back in his hometown. He'd accepted the offer to head the division because he'd wanted to be part of the solution to rebuild trust in the police force. He'd become a cop because he wanted to make a difference, not because he wanted to be in control or scare people. The Community Outreach Division could make a difference not just by reducing crime in the area, but also by building a much-needed bridge between the force and citizens that hadn't trusted in the town's willingness to meet their needs.

He gave her a thumbs-up. "We won't let that happen."

Sheri held her breath and leaned forward as she watched and waited for Deandre to take a bite of the fried chicken she'd brought him. They'd agreed to meet up at the neighborhood center to talk about plans for the "Connecting the Community" outreach event—a name she'd come up with that morning while making biscuits. Her kitchen was good at making sure they didn't have too much leftover food by the time they closed, but today she'd asked them to try and have a few extra pieces of chicken available. She'd also packed some of the biscuits he'd liked and a side of her special collard greens. He'd already mentioned not eating breakfast, and when she'd visited him the other day to discuss plans, she'd seen the protein bar and sandwich that looked like it had come from a gas station on his desk.

She didn't need to feed the man. He wasn't her responsibility, but there she was. Arriving with a basket packed and insisting that he eat.

"Mmm." Deandre's eyes closed. He licked his full lips and nodded. "This is good."

Sheri's lips parted as she sucked in a shallow breath. She wasn't sure if it was the compliment or the way her eyes followed the movement of his tongue on his lips, but either way she clapped her hands. "I'm glad you like it."

His eyes opened and he raised a brow. "You *knew* I would like it."

She shrugged and tried not to look too smug. From the way he'd enjoyed the biscuit the other morning, she'd been confident he would love her fried chicken. Her chicken and waffles was the most popular item on the menu. "I assumed you would, but it's always good to get confirmation."

"You didn't have to bring food."

Sheri reached down in the bag she brought and pulled out a bottle of water. "I had some left over. We're meeting and I figured we needed to eat. It should be enough for you to take home." She twisted off the top and set the bottle on his desk.

"How much do I owe you for this?" He took a sip of water from the bottle.

"You don't owe me anything. Consider it a bonus for working with me to put together the community event."

"You don't have to feed me because of that. I'd help regardless."

"Yeah, but hopefully the food will really put your heart into it." She winked.

He chuckled and quickly looked down at the food. "Believe me, my heart is already into this. I want to make this event just as successful as you do."

"Oh really? Why?" She sat back and crossed her legs. She was still in her jeans and The Breakfast Nook T-shirt, which was stained after a busy day. Whereas he looked neat and put together in his wrinkle-free police station collared shirt and khakis. She wished she'd thought to bring a change of clothes before they'd met.

"The Community Outreach Division is still new. Although our chief wants it to be successful, some of the higher-ups aren't convinced that this is the fastest way to clean up the South End."

Sheri sat up straight and pointed a finger at the sky. "The south end doesn't need to be cleaned up. We're not dirty."

Deandre held up a hand as if to surrender. "I didn't mean it like that."

"I know what you're trying to say, but words matter. Saying the area needs to be cleaned up makes it sound like something is wrong with the south end. We just need more help for the businesses, investment from the town and meaningful things for the kids in the area to do. That's not cleaning up, that's just providing support."

"I hear what you're saying. I won't use those words anymore."

Sheri studied his features and didn't see any signs that he was just agreeing to make her be quiet or move along. His gaze remained steady and his voice was sincere.

She nodded and returned to leaning back in the chair. "Thank you. You're the officer most of the people in the area will deal with. Think about what you're saying so that you don't push them away."

"Point taken." His voice remained even. He didn't seem upset or irritated by her correction.

"What kind of support do the higher-ups think the area needs?"

"Not the community outreach kind. The town manager wants to create a tactical team to focus on crime. There are concerns about gangs and the access to opioids in the community."

"That doesn't sound like support." In fact, it sounded like a scare tactic.

"For the people that are complaining about the break-ins and drug trafficking, it sounds like the perfect answer."

Sheri let out an annoyed breath and shook her head. "I remember what it was like dealing with the police in Sunshine Beach when I was a teenager."

His head tilted to the side. "What was it like?"

She considered trying to find a nice way to say what was on her mind. But the interest in his eyes made her want to speak the truth. If they were going to work together on bringing the community together, then he would need to know how some people still felt about the police department.

"Don't trust them. Don't call them. Don't say anything because they're always looking for trouble. I was terrified when I found out one of Tyrone's neighbors called the cops on me."

"You didn't think someone would call the cops when you went over with a baseball bat?" A spark of amusement lit his eye.

Sheri shrugged and looked to the ceiling. "I was listening to my cousin and blasting angry, love-gone-wrong songs. I wasn't thinking clearly." She focused back on him and patted her chest. "But when the blue lights pulled up, it hit me just how bad things could go."

"I didn't want to terrify you."

"I'm glad it was you and not someone else. I was surprised by how...calm you were." She thought back to that night and the way he'd quickly diffused the situation. He'd been direct and to the point and taken charge without throwing his ego around. "I could tell you were disappointed maybe, but you weren't belittling, and you didn't treat me like I was nobody. I don't ever want to get arrested again, but if I have to, then I'd prefer it be like that."

"Going in guns blazing only makes a situation worse. I'm not that kind of person or cop. Our chief is the same. She spent her first year or two weeding out the bad apples in the bunch. We're not perfect, but we're on the right path."

"That's good to hear. Honestly, my family warned me about working with you."

"Because of our past connection?"

She shook her head. "Nooo! I did not tell them you were the cop who arrested me. I try not to bring up that part of my life with my family."

"Then why didn't they want you to work with me?"

"Just because you're a cop. They remember the old days even more than I do. They're worried you'll take the hammer approach to helping out the neighborhood."

"The hammer isn't my first approach."

She narrowed her eyes and grinned "But you will use it?"

The corner of his mouth quirked before he lifted one broad shoulder. "Only when necessary. My late wife talked about how she used to love hanging out on the beaches when she grew up here. She loved this place and always talked about us moving back here one day."

"She was from here? I know you said you moved after she passed because your in-laws were close, but we have a lot of people who move to Sunshine Beach later in life."

"She was. Grew up here and then moved to Greensboro after graduating from North Carolina A&T."

"Hold up? Was your wife Jamila Davis?"

Deandre blinked and froze for a second before nodding. "You knew her?"

"I mean, I knew who she was. She was what…two years behind me in high school. Her family goes to my aunt's church, so I'd see her around. I heard she went to A&T and that she passed away a few years back."

Sadness filled his eyes and a bittersweet smile hovered around his lips. "Yeah, that was her."

The sorrow in his eyes made her want to get up and give him a hug. Which was completely inappropriate, so she asked a question that would hopefully remove some of the pain. "How did you two hook up?"

The sadness left his eyes and he let out a soft laugh. "We met at a protest."

"Wait, what? Don't tell me you arrested her?"

He grinned and shook his head. "I didn't arrest her. It was a peaceful protest. I was there to protest, too. Against a new ordinance the city was passing. We caught each other's eye in the crowd. She came up and said hi and… That was it."

The way he spoke the words, as if some magic spell had come over him that granted him everything he ever wanted, made her want to believe fairy tales existed. She leaned forward and rested her elbow on his desk. "How long were you married?"

"Eleven years," he said slowly. His eyes still focused on the past.

She nodded but didn't know what to say. That was a

long time to be with one person only to lose them so permanently. She didn't have the right words and instead of saying something wrong she decided to stay quiet.

"It was a good eleven. I wouldn't trade them. Even if I knew how they'd end."

"Sounds like you really loved her."

"I did. Maybe one day…" He looked at her and their gazes connected.

He didn't have to finish his words; the wistful look in his gaze told her the rest. Maybe one day he'd fall in love again. What would it be like to be loved by this man? To be loved so much that even knowing the ending would be tragic, he still wouldn't walk away?

Sheri's breath caught in her throat. She was fantasizing about falling in love with him while he talked about his late wife. To make matters worse, she'd leaned on his desk and was right in his face. He looked away quickly and she pushed back to sit fully in her chair.

"I hope that one day, if you're ready, that you can find someone who makes you happy."

He glanced back at her. She couldn't read his expression or what he was thinking. That didn't stop her heart from racing faster or for the air to feel thin and hot around her.

The door opened. And a voice called out. "Hey, Dad, you here?"

Deandre blinked and stood. "Yeah, I'm here. Meeting with Ms. Thomas to talk about the community event. Come and say hi." His words were rushed, almost guilty.

Or maybe Sheri was projecting. Thank goodness for the interruption. His heart had been given away a long time ago and wasn't going to be given away anytime soon, much less to her. Plus, he had a teenage son. She was far from ready to be anyone's stepmom. Her attraction to Deandre wasn't going to go away, but she would have the decency to be professional while they worked together and keep all fantasies to herself.

She stood as well and turned to meet his son. When she spotted the kid, she had to blink twice. His son froze in place, his eyes wide.

"It's you," Sheri said.

Deandre frowned. He looked from Sheri to his son. "You've met."

"The other day," Sheri said. "He offered to help me with my sign." Right before trying to hit on her and calling her an "old ass."

Deandre's frown cleared up and he smiled. "Oh, good. I'm glad to see that DJ was being helpful."

"Yeah, real helpful," Sheri said dryly.

"You know me, Dad. I'm always trying to help my elders." DJ looked at Sheri and gave an innocent smile.

Sheri's eyes narrowed. Was he was calling her old? Again! Sheri pulled back the attraction she felt for Deandre and shoved it to the darkest corner of her mind, slammed the imaginary door with a kick and locked it. Being interested in a man who had no interest in her was one thing. Being interested in a man with a sly teenager who liked to play games was 100 percent out of the question.

Chapter Seven

Sheri was flipping through the rack of shirts in TJ Maxx with her cousin Cora by her side talking endlessly about the last date she'd gone on, when the sound of a familiar voice caught her attention. She stopped searching and lifted her head. Sure enough, walking across the store to the men's section was Deandre, a cell phone pressed to his ear.

"Deandre!" she called before she could think.

He stopped walking and glanced around. Her cousin stopped flipping through the clothes and followed Sheri's gaze toward him. Deandre caught her eye, lifted a hand and smiled.

Cora leaned over and whispered. "Lil Bit, who is that?"

"The cop I'm planning the community event with."

"Oh? Then why are you calling him like he's your man?" Cora cocked her head to the side and narrowed her eyes.

Sheri elbowed her cousin. "Shut up. I'm not calling him like he's my man."

"Mmm-hmm," was Cora's unconvinced reply.

Deandre spoke into the phone before pulling it away and sliding it in his back pocket. He walked over to talk to her from the other side of the aisle. He was dressed in regular clothes, a basic black T-shirt that fitted his muscled arms and broad shoulders perfectly and a pair of blue basketball shorts that stopped right above the knee.

"Everything good?" His gaze scanned the area before gliding across her face as if checking to make sure everything was okay around her. Or, maybe she was projecting. The guy probably always scanned the perimeter.

"Yeah, everything is good. I recognized your voice when you were walking by. You didn't have to get off the phone. I just wanted to say hey."

He nodded. "I was looking for a reason to end that call. My friend LaTisha can sometimes get on a roll."

Sheri's heart dimmed. Based on the name, she assumed his friend was a woman. Did he mean friend as in, they were cool, or friend as in *girlfriend*? Why did she care? She'd already decided she was not going to do anything about the attraction she felt for Deandre.

"This is my cousin." She pointed to Cora watching intently next to her.

Cora shoved her hand over the rack. "Nice to meet you." She leaned forward, nearly spilling her cleavage out of the tank top she wore, and poked her tongue out of the corner of her mouth. Sheri rolled her eyes at her cousin's familiar flirty move.

Deandre shook her hand. "Deandre. Nice to meet you, as well." When he tried to pull back, she didn't let go.

Cora tilted her head to the side and eyed him. "You look familiar. Have we met before?"

Deandre shrugged. "I'm not sure. I'm around town a lot. You might have seen me. I'm in the Community Outreach Division of the Sunshine Beach Police Department."

Cora finally let go of his hand. "Maybe that's it."

Sheri was glad Cora didn't immediately recognize him. She'd been with Sheri the night Deandre arrested them for acting like some broken-hearted vigilantes. No telling what Cora would say when she put two and two together.

"Well, it was good seeing you," Sheri said quickly. "I'll see you Wednesday at the neighborhood watch meeting, right?"

"You will. I hope the rest of the neighborhood is as excited about your idea for the event as I am."

"I hope so, too."

Cora tapped her chin. "I swear we've met before."

Time for them to go. She looked at Cora. "We better check out if we want to get to the grocery store and pick up the stuff your mom needs for the potato salad."

Cora's attention immediately snapped back to that. "Girl, you're right. We've been in here way too long. Nice meeting you." She waved and headed to the register.

"Same here." Deandre looked back to Sheri. "See you on Wednesday."

"If you need anything before then just give me a call." She should be following her cousin instead of prolonging the conversation, but she didn't always make the best choices when she talked with a guy she was feeling.

"I think we're good. Even though I have been thinking about the chicken you dropped off the other day."

Pride ballooned in her chest. He'd been thinking about her. Well, her chicken, but she'd take that. Maybe he'd told someone about her food who would check out the restaurant. "If you've been thinking about it, then I'll have to bring some over."

"No need to do that."

"I don't mind feeding you." Honestly, she'd like to do a lot more than feed him, but she kept that thought to herself.

Her thoughts must have shown on her face because his smile faltered and he glanced away. Her mom always said everything she thought came through on her face.

Deandre pointed to the men's section. "I'd better go. I was looking for some shirts for my son."

Yes, the son who called her old. A good reminder of why she needed to keep her thoughts in her head instead of showing up in her expressions or words. "I'll let you go. See you around."

Sheri turned away and followed her cousin to the checkout. They'd put their purchases in the back of the car and were driving to the grocery store when Cora slapped the steering wheel.

She pointed at Sheri. "He's the cop that arrested us!"

Sheri closed her eyes and groaned. "Damn. I'd hoped you wouldn't remember."

"I remember everything. Why didn't you tell me?"

"Because I didn't want to make a big deal out of it."

"Does he know who you are?"

"He does. He remembered me almost immediately."

"And he doesn't mind working with you?"

"No, and I don't mind working with him. We talked about it, and for the sake of supporting the businesses in the south end, we agreed to work together."

Cora glanced at Sheri from the corner of her eye. "But you like him."

Heat spread across Sheri's face. She focused extra hard on keeping her expression neutral. Cora could always read her like a book. "Yeah, he's nice."

Cora pursed her lip. "Don't play with me. I mean you want to sleep with him."

Sheri scoffed and looked out the window. "No I don't."

"Girl, if you don't quit lying to me. I've known you all my life and I can tell when you like a guy. You get that horny look in your eye."

Sheri spun back toward Cora. "I don't have a horny look."

"Yes you do, it's like this." Her cousin batted her eyes, pursed her lips and lifted her shoulders with exaggerated breathing.

Sheri crossed her arms. "You ought to stop! I am not that bad."

Cora laughed and fixed her face. "You're bad enough. So, are you going to sleep with him?"

"Hell no! We're working together."

Cora sucked her teeth. "You're working together on a community event. That's not the same. And my man is sexy." Cora's voice dipped with the last sentence, and she licked her lips.

"He's a widower with a teenage son who called me an old ass the other day."

"Wait, what?"

Sheri recounted the story and running into him later. "I didn't want to tell Deandre what happened."

"Why not? He should know if his kid is acting up."

"It's not my place." Sheri didn't have kids and therefore tried not to get into the business of parents. She didn't know his parenting style or how he'd handle her saying anything negative about his son.

"We knew that everything we did as a kid in Sunshine Beach would get back to our moms. That's why we didn't act the fool too much. These kids don't think we will say anything. Besides, if he's hanging with the kids who the other business owners are saying are the problem, it'll get back to him sooner or later. You might as well give him a heads-up."

Cora had a point. Deandre's eyes lit up when he talked about his son. He'd be embarrassed if he found out his son was causing problems. "You really think I should tell him?"

"Yep. And then, you can sleep with him."

Sheri laughed. "I'm not sleeping with anyone. I'm not signing up to be a stepmom."

"Who said anything about being a stepmom to his kid? I said sleep with him." Cora shook her head. "There you go being all romantic and delusional again. Girl, just get yours and move on."

The words put Sheri on the defensive. Cora loved pointing out that Sheri was too quick to get caught up in a fairy tale when dealing with guys. Cora was only about getting what she could and moving on when the guy no longer served a purpose. Sheri had tried to be detached with her hookups and that had gotten her arrested. Proof that she could not separate feelings from sex.

"I'm not set up to just sleep with someone. Call me old-fashioned if you want to, but I'm ready to settle down. I don't want to get caught up in a guy who is only looking to have a good time."

"I told you not to get attached just because the sex is banging," Cora said in a lecturing tone.

"You did and I thought I could be okay. Well, I wasn't. Every time I try, I catch feelings. Let's face it. I'm not built for the hookup lifestyle."

Something Sheri had finally accepted about herself. Since high school she'd tried to be like Cora. When Cora said she needed to date multiple people, Sheri had done that. When Cora said never like a guy more than he liked you, she'd pretended as if she wasn't waiting by the phone for a guy to call. She'd spent so much time trying to be the independent, *I don't need a man*, love-and-leave-'em type that her friends and the single women in her family said she should be because she'd been too afraid to admit that she wanted what her mom and aunt hadn't had—a long-term committed relationship with a man. Marriage, a house and kids. All that jazz. But she was almost forty with no prospects in front of her and a police record because she spent too much time lying about what she really wanted in a relationship. No more.

Her cousin sighed and patted her shoulder. "You know what. You're right. I've accepted that."

Sheri brushed off Cora's hand. "I'm not about to sleep with Deandre only to find out I don't like his kid and he's not looking to settle with a woman he once put in handcuffs. Not in the good way. We'll just be friends."

"What if I sleep with him?"

Sheri cut her eyes at her cousin. "Don't even go there."

Cora sighed as if Sheri was asking for her right ovary. "Fine. Gotta ask. I won't go there."

"Thank you."

After the Tyrone situation, she and Cora had a "Come to Jesus" talk. Her cousin had been interested in Tyrone and admitted she was jealous when Sheri started seeing him. That's why she encouraged her to damage his car and started rumors online about his dating habits to try and sabotage his career. Sheri didn't agree with what her cousin had done, but she was family, and Sheri's mom always instilled in her that she couldn't turn her back on family. They'd made a truce with a strict rule. If one liked a guy, even a little bit, the other didn't mess with him. They didn't need any more messy situations.

She glanced at Sheri again as she started singing along to the song on the radio. She just hoped her cousin would stick to her side of the bargain.

"I don't see how this is going to help us," Belinda spoke up in the middle of Sheri's presentation.

Sheri stopped talking midsentence and raised a brow. *Oh, we're interrupting people now?* Sheri thought to herself. She'd barely started talking about why they wanted to have the Connecting the Community event and how it would benefit the area when Belinda started shifting in her seat. Sheri could feel the heat of her hard stare. Now she wasn't even going to let Sheri finish making her case?

"I see you're eager to jump in," Sheri said. "Since you won't let me finish my presentation, why don't you give us your thoughts."

Belinda had the decency to look halfway chastised. "I'm just saying, I don't see how a community event is going to stop the crime or the kids hanging out in the area."

"First of all, the goal isn't to stop the kids from hanging out. This is their town, too, and they deserve to have access to the beach just as much as your yoga clients. So, let's get that clear. The goal of the community event is to give residents and business owners information about what's happening in the area, give them a chance to hear from more than just the police department, and bring people together."

Belinda crossed her arms and raised her nose in the air. "Well, it sounds like more of a warm-and-fuzzy approach to our problem."

"Are you saying you want a cold-and-hard approach? For the police to come through and treat the teens and residents like criminals and not form any type of connection with the community?"

Belinda glanced at Deandre before looking back at Sheri. "That's not what I'm saying."

Sheri put a hand on her hip. "Then what are you saying?"

Belinda sputtered, "You're trying to make me sound horrible."

"You're doing a good job yourself."

Mumbles went through the group. Belinda's eyes narrowed. Sheri raised a brow and dared her to clap back.

Deandre stepped forward. "No one is trying to make anyone look bad." He spoke in an even, "everybody calm down" tone of voice. "We know that there are a lot of challenges in the south end. We hope this event will allow us to reach the people in the area who may not be coming to the neighborhood watch meeting. Not all business owners are here or all residents, but they have concerns. We don't want to leave them out of this conversation. We also don't want to increase the police presence just to scare the people who live and work in the south end. If we increase patrols, we want people to know we're here as a community partner as well as to keep them safe. Not to hurt anyone or make them feel unwelcome." He smiled at the end, the dimple in his cheek peeking out.

The fight in Belinda's eyes melted and she grinned back, her head tilted to the side. "I think that's a great idea."

Sheri blinked. "Seriously?" Belinda wouldn't let Sheri get through her presentation, but Deandre flashes a dimple and she's cheesing and agreeing with the event?

"Thank you, Belinda," Deandre said. "I hope this means you'll help us plan for the event."

Belinda nodded so fast she looked like a bobblehead doll. "I'd love to help."

"That's great." He looked at Sheri and nodded.

Sheri rolled her eyes. "I guess so."

Deandre gave her a look. Sheri shrugged. She could read the "play nice" in his eyes. She didn't want to play nice. She wanted to call out Belinda for being a hypocrite, but now wasn't the time. They were trying to convince people to be excited about this event. If Deandre's dimples made Belinda shut up and go along with her idea, then that would have to work.

The rest of the meeting was spent going over ideas

for the community event. They even agreed on keeping Connecting the Community as a name after Belinda said it wasn't "the most clever" name she'd ever heard. Sheri stuck around after the meeting to talk with some of the other business owners and residents. Despite Belinda's original negativity, most of the others were excited about trying to do something that wasn't going to scare people away from the area.

"I mean, I moved over here because I want to see the area revitalized," Kelly, the owner of the comic book shop, said after the meeting. She wore a superhero T-shirt and jeans. "I'm glad that the city is willing to invest in this area and not just write us off as a bad part of town."

Sheri was vindicated hearing other people didn't feel the same way as Belinda. "It's on us to remind them that we're just as relevant as the north end of the beach."

Kelly's eyes lit up and she snapped her fingers. "Exactly. Hey, I'm having a drop-in at my comic book store this weekend. If you're not busy, you should come on through."

Sheri lifted a brow. "Really?"

"Yeah. I invited some other business owners, too. It's another way for us to get to know each other. And, with me being fairly new in town, it's a good way to meet up with new people."

She wasn't a big comic book fan, but she liked Kelly. She only hung out with family members, and if she was going to be staying in Sunshine Beach and wanted to make new friends, she'd need to make an effort to get out of her comfort zone. "Sounds like fun. I'll come through."

Kelley grinned and gave her a thumbs-up. "Great!" She looked over Sheri's shoulder.

"What about you, Lieutenant King? Will you be able to come by?"

Sheri turned as Deandre walked up beside her. "If I'm invited. Is it okay if my son comes with me?"

"Sure, the more the merrier," Kelley said with enthusiasm.

"Then I'll try to come through," Deandre said.

"Awesome! I'll see you both later." Kelly smiled and waved before leaving.

Sheri turned to look up at Deandre. He didn't try to tower over her, but when he stood close she was reminded of how tall he was. Tall, strong and tempting. Heat flooded her midsection and spread through her body. Sheri took a step back before her thoughts started playing out on her face again. "The meeting went okay."

He nodded. "It did. I'm hoping that means we'll have a good turnout."

"I think we will. If every business promotes it and the residents tell their neighbors, then we'll have a lot of people show up."

"I'll borrow some of your enthusiasm," he said with a half smile.

Sheri's stomach flipped. She understood why Belinda had changed her mind so quickly just because he smiled. The man was good-looking and seemed to be a decent human being. Basically, he was perfect.

"Belinda seems to like you," she blurted out.

He frowned. "I knew you were going to say that."

Sheri grinned and pointed. "So you know she likes you."

He waved a hand and shook his head. "I don't know that. I said I knew you were going to say that."

"Why, because she looked like she wanted to throw her panties when you popped that dimple on her?"

Deandre laughed. "Like she wanted to do what?"

Sheri waved her finger toward his face. "That dimple. You have to know the effect it has on women."

He rubbed his cheek. "It has an effect, huh? Well, then, I'll make sure I use my power for good instead of evil."

Sheri rolled her eyes and grinned. Good-looking, decent and has a sense of humor. He was everything she wanted. *If* there was a chance they could be anything more than temporary lovers.

"Be sure you do that." She looked around the now empty space. "Where are all the helpers who stayed behind last time to help you lock up?"

"I only have one or two, and they had to leave early. I'm good. It doesn't take much to clean up. I'll leave the tables and chairs out until tomorrow and get my son to help."

"Why doesn't he come to these meetings?"

Deandre walked toward the front of the room and she followed. "Even though I enjoy working in the community, these meetings are technically work. I don't bring him to work with me." He stopped at the front door.

"You seem to be out in the community a lot. He isn't interested in getting involved?"

"I'd love for him to take an interest, but he's at the age where dad being a cop isn't as cool as it was. When he was younger, I could show up in my car and turn on the lights and he'd think I was the best dad in the world."

Sheri smiled, imagining a younger version of his son being excited to see the lights on his dad's car. Then she thought about the way he'd called her "old ass" and couldn't imagine him being thrilled about blue lights. "Teens are like that."

He crossed his arms and leaned against the wall. Sheri was glad to see that he didn't seem to be in a hurry to leave, but instead appeared to be enjoying talking to her. "I know, but it's still taking me some getting used to. We were close before his mom passed and got closer after. It's hard watching him pull away. I wish I knew what was going on with him, but I don't."

She opened her mouth, ready to tell him about running into his son that day, but then closed it back. Now wasn't the best time. Not when he was already feeling bad about his kid growing further away from him.

Deandre's brows drew together. "What?"

She shook her head. "Nothing."

He straightened and gave her a no-nonsense stare. "No, it's something. What did you want to say?"

"It's not that big of a deal."

"Obviously it is, or you wouldn't hesitate to tell me. Is something wrong?"

"Not exactly." When he continued to watch her with concern, she decided to take Cora's advice and be honest with him. "I just… Well, I ran into your son. Before you introduced me to him."

"When?"

"Outside of my restaurant when I was closing up. He was with a group of teens. Some of the same kids that the other business owners have complained about. He was kind of rude."

Deandre's stance shifted and his gaze sharpened. "Rude how?"

Sheri held up a hand and shook her head. "Damn, see, I wasn't trying to get him in trouble."

He reached over and wrapped his hand around hers. He gently lowered her arm before letting her go. The touch was firm, but surprisingly gentle, and way too brief. "If he's acting out in the community, I need to know. What happened?"

Sheri forced herself not to rub her wrist. Not because he'd hurt her, but because she still felt the heat of his quick touch and she wanted to savor the feeling. To rub it in so she could melt in it later.

She told him the entire story. "It was just kids being kids," she said. "I wasn't hurt or anything, but I just thought you should know since you're trying to connect with the people in this area."

He frowned and ran a hand over his face. "I'm sorry, Sheri."

"For what? You didn't do anything. Please, if you talk to him, don't be too hard on him. It really wasn't that bad."

He raised a brow. "I'll talk with him and get him to apologize."

Sheri closed her eyes and groaned. "Now he really is going to think I'm a mean old woman."

"He'll know that if he acts up in this area that it'll get back to me and that actions have consequences."

She opened her eyes and met his gaze. He seemed concerned, but not upset with her for telling him about what happened. She'd been right in her assumption that he wouldn't go off on her for pointing out flaws in his kid.

"Fair enough," she said. "But I still feel like a snitch. And you know snitches get stitches."

His lips quirked and he laughed again. "No one in my family will be giving you stitches. Seriously, thank you for being honest with me. It's good to know. I want my son to grow up into a responsible person. If he's being rude to adults in the area, then I need to know."

"Hopefully, this won't come up again. And we can only talk about fun stuff when we're together."

"Fun stuff?"

He pushed away from the door. He didn't come closer, but with him standing straight and giving her his complete attention, it made her mind think of all the fun but inappropriate stuff they could do. Like the two of them wrapped in each other's arms. His body between her legs.

She blinked and pushed that thought out of her head. "You know, like the community event, the chicken I bring you, stuff like that."

"In between the fun stuff, can you let me know a little bit more about you?"

She pressed a hand to her chest. Her heart beat frantically beneath her rib cage. "Me?" Thank goodness her voice didn't tremble like her insides.

He nodded. "Yes. I'd like to know more about my partner."

"Your partner?" Her cheeks heated. Damn, she liked the sound of that.

"Yeah, my partner on planning. Plus, I'll be in the area a lot. We can be friends."

Friends. He wanted to be...friends.

Sheri's stomach plummeted. Even if she were able to be a hit-it-and-quit-it girl, she still didn't have a chance with him. She was holding back from salivating over him, while he'd, very easily, put her in the friend zone.

She grinned but the movement felt stiff. Embarrassment churned her stomach, but thankfully, he didn't seem to have any idea about the fantasies going through her mind. She would be a professional and work with him on this project without making a fool of herself.

She took a step forward and opened the door. "We sure can. Friends it is."

Chapter Eight

Deandre drove home with the weight of what Sheri told him pressing down on him, urging him to speed the few miles to their house, but the reminder from his late wife that he should always get the full story before going into "cop mode" with the family held him to the speed limit. He would get to the bottom of things and find out if what Sheri said was the truth. And if it were, why would DJ do that?

Deandré knew his son wasn't perfect, but he'd always believed he was a good kid. Good kids didn't go around trying to hit on women old enough to be their mother or call them names when they were rejected. As much as he didn't want to believe what Sheri said, he'd also dealt with enough delusional parents in his career to hesitate before saying "my kid would never do that."

His in-laws' car was in the driveway when he pulled up. He'd forgotten they'd mentioned coming over to check on DJ while Deandre worked late at the neighborhood watch meeting. They often stepped in to spend time with DJ when Deandre had to work. Their support for him and DJ after Jamila's death was invaluable. His parents currently lived in a rental house in Denver. Since retirement, his parents embraced the "live it up" lifestyle and spent most of their time traveling to places they'd always wanted to visit. He didn't blame them; they'd raised him and his three brothers and wanted to enjoy their life. A part of him wished they'd spend more time with DJ, but he was forever thankful for Jamila's parents for providing a level of consistency even Deandre couldn't handle on his own.

He went inside and found Cliff and Rose sitting on the couch with DJ. The three of them watched a sitcom on television. His in-laws laughed at something on screen while DJ looked unamused. Which was his typical look lately. At least he didn't have his phone in his hand. Rose and Cliff had a strict rule that DJ couldn't scroll when he was with them. A rule DJ followed with minimal complaint.

Rose spotted him first. "Hey, Deandre, how was work?" He'd liked Rose from the start.

She'd treated him like family from the moment Jamila had introduced him to her. They got along well, and, with his own mother so far away, he'd easily accepted and absorbed the love she'd given him when he'd married her daughter.

"It was pretty good. The area seems excited about the event. So that's a good thing. I didn't think you would still be here."

Cliff pointed to the television. "We were going to go, but then I remembered my show was coming on. DJ was okay with watching it with us."

He glanced at DJ. "Well, that was nice of him."

DJ shrugged. "I'm a nice kid."

"When you want to be," Deandre countered.

Rose reached over and patted DJ's shoulder. "He always is."

Deandre sat in the chair next to the couch. "I want to believe the same thing, but I've been hearing some things."

"Things like what?" DJ asked.

"Things like you're going around saying inappropriate things to some of the shop owners on the south end."

Deandre didn't mind having the conversation in front of Cliff and Rose. If anything, DJ would be more likely to tell the truth in front of them. The glacier-cold wall DJ had built in the past year didn't extend to the relationship with his grandparents. He was more patient and accepting of their questions and prodding into his life. Deandre wished he'd get the same treatment, but, thankfully, Cliff and Rose and Deandre were a team in parenting DJ. If he came to them with any problems, they wouldn't hesitate to bring the situation to Deandre for them to work together on a solution.

DJ rolled his eyes. "She's lying. I didn't say anything to her."

Rose turned to DJ. "Her who?"

Deandre leaned forward. Disappointment tightened into a knot in his stomach. "Yes, DJ, her who, because I didn't say anything about where I heard it."

"I don't have to guess," DJ said with an irritated sigh. "I already know. I was just joking with her. That's all."

Deandre cocked his head to the side. "Joking? Do you joke with me or your grandparents like that?"

DJ huffed but shook his head. "No, sir."

"Then what makes you think it's okay to joke around with any other adults that way? Come on, DJ, what's going on with you? You quit wrestling and now you're hanging around, insulting adults you don't know."

Cliff sat up straighter. "You quit wrestling?" He sounded just as shocked at Deandre had.

DJ shrugged. "It's no big deal. Nothing is going on. I just didn't want to wrestle anymore, and I really was just joking. I'm not going through something."

Deandre pointed at his son. "You're going with me on Saturday to apologize."

DJ threw up his hands. "Come on, Dad."

"You're coming. You understand me? I'm working hard to build trust with the people in that area and I can't have you going behind my back undermining the trust and proving to them that the kids in the area are part of the problem. There are some business owners who think you and your friends are the reason for the break-ins and increased crime. They want us to come through arresting you all and scaring you away. If you're running round with a group of kids who think it's funny to hit on older women and call them *old ass* when they tell you no, then you're not helping. You understand?"

Rose pressed a hand to her chest. "Old what? DJ, did you say that?"

DJ closed his eyes and let out a heavy breath. He hesitated a beat before opening them back and nodding. "Okay. I get it. Don't embarrass you."

"It's not about embarrassing me. It's about also protecting you. Look at me, DJ."

His son slowly turned and met his eye.

"There are people who want to take my job and weaponize it against you and your friends. Don't give them a reason to do that. That's what this is about. Do you understand that?"

Some of the defiance left DJ's eyes. "I get it."

"Good."

"Can I go to my room now?"

Rose reached over and patted his leg. "You want to leave us now that we know what you did? Don't do something if you'll be embarrassed for us to find out about it later."

"Yes, ma'am. I've got homework," DJ said in that same, unconvincing voice that irritated Deandre.

Rose sighed but nodded. "We'll see you another day."

"Okay, Love you." DJ hugged her and then Cliff before disappearing down the hall to his room.

"Teenagers," Cliff said shaking his head.

"Tell me about it," Deandre replied. "He's still a good kid, but he's pushing boundaries."

"They'll do that. I remember when Jamila would fight us on everything," Rose said.

"Hold up," Cliff cut in. "She fought you on everything? She never argued with me."

Rose rolled her eyes and grinned. "That's because she was a daddy's girl through and through."

Deandre lifted his lips in a wistful smile. "DJ's personality is so much like hers. I wonder if he'd still be doing this if she were around."

"He would," Cliff said matter-of-factly. "Teenagers like to spread their wings and see how far they can go."

"Maybe, but boys are different with their mommas," Rose said. "He'd still be butting heads with you, Deandre, but he'd have a softer side in the house to calm him down."

Deandre leaned back in his chair. "I'll work on developing my softer side."

"Or, you can find a nice woman to settle down with," she said with wide, hopeful eyes.

Deandre closed his eyes and smiled. In the past year, Rose had gotten it into her head that Deandre needed a wife. At first, he'd been surprised. Not because he expected his in-laws to want him to remain alone for the rest of his life after losing Jamila, but he just hadn't expected them to actively try and push him into the arms of another woman, either. But they both were strongly on the side of him getting back in the dating pool.

"If I find the right person I'll consider that. But not because DJ needs a new mom. We're doing okay."

"Have you been looking for the right person?" Cliff asked curiously.

A vision of Sheri drifted into his mind. Her bright eyes,

wide smile and sexy figure. She wasn't as dramatic as he'd assumed she would be, but she did have a fiery spark to her personality. One she'd wanted to let out on Belinda today.

He sat up straight and his eyes popped back open. What was that? Yeah, he found her attractive, and yes, she'd awakened his sex drive, but why would he think of her when he thought of a potential future wife? She wasn't even in the running.

"Hmm." Rose narrowed her eyes on him. "I think there may be someone."

Deandre shook his head. "Nah, there isn't. It's not like that."

Rose and Cliff shared a look and grinned. "What's not like that? Who is she?"

Deandre held up a hand. "There is no she and there is no situation to update you on. Right now, I'm focused on keeping DJ out of trouble and making sure the town sticks behind their promise to support the revitalization of the south side of the beach."

"There's always time for a little romance," Cliff said with a wink.

"He's right," Rose agreed. "We want to see you happy, too, Deandre. And, you know Jamila would have wanted you to be happy, as well."

Deandre nodded. "I know. I'm not trying to rush into anything. But I hear you and I appreciate that you want good things for me."

They exchanged another look, communicating silently in a way that Deandre had once hoped he and Jamila would get to. But they never would get to that point, and while the pain of her loss would never go away, he was no longer too gutted to poke at the scar.

He did have a quick moment with Sheri earlier. When their eyes met, and she'd wanted to keep arguing with Belinda but he'd pleaded with her to be nice. She'd understood him. He'd imagined her voice saying *"Fine, this time for you,"* before she'd let the conversation drop. Maybe that's why he was imagining her as more than just a partner in this project. But deep down, he knew it could be more if he let it. The instant attraction, the connection, the way he just *liked* her. He hadn't felt that since…

"Anyone want something to drink? I'm going to get some tea." He cut off his own thoughts before they could take hold.

"I'll take some. We'll leave after the show is over," Cliff said.

Deandre nodded and looked at Rose, who shook her head and said she was good. He went to the kitchen and prepared the drinks. He'd deal with getting through today, helping his son and the community event. That's it. He wasn't quite ready to deal with the weird message his libido, or maybe his heart, was trying to deliver to his brain.

Chapter Nine

DJ sighed for what had to be the hundredth time since Deandre told him to get in the car so they could go to the gathering at Kelly's comic book store. Deandre hadn't expected DJ to jump up and down with excitement to apologize to Sheri, but he had hoped his son wouldn't act as if he were being dragged to the guillotine. Comic books were one of the few things DJ still enjoyed reading.

"Come on, DJ, what's the sigh for?"

DJ looked at him as if he should know exactly what the sigh was about. "I didn't have to come here tonight."

"You're here to apologize."

"I can do that anytime. Why tonight in front of everyone?"

"I won't make you apologize in front of the group. You like comic books. I thought you'd enjoy coming to the store."

"Manga."

Deandre frowned. "Say what?"

DJ rubbed a hand over his face and gave Deandre a "you're clueless" expression. "I read mangas. Not comics."

"Aren't they the same thing?"

DJ closed his eyes and shook his head. "Bruh..." he sighed. "They are completely different things."

"Well, *bruh*, maybe there are mangas in here."

"There aren't."

"How do you know?"

"I've been in that shop before. It's all comics, maybe a few mangas, but not what I'm reading."

"Well, check out the comic books anyway. Maybe you'll find something you like."

"Yeah, maybe," he said just a tad shy of sarcastically.

Deandre accepted that he wasn't going to get anything more positive out of his son, and parallel parked the car in a spot a few storefronts down from the comic book store. They got out of the car and went inside. Several other business owners and some residents mingled inside the store. Deandre's eyes searched the crowd until they landed on Sheri standing in the back talking with Kelly. Sheri threw her head back and laughed at something Kelly said and Deandre's breath hitched in his throat. Damn, she was fine.

"Can I go after I apologize?" DJ's voice cut into Deandre's thoughts.

He blinked and looked over at his son. "I may not be ready to leave."

"My boy Julian is at the pizza place. He said he'll pick me up."

Deandre shook his head. "You came with me, and you'll leave with me. End of discussion."

"Oh, man," DJ muttered.

"Come on. Let's go say hello."

"And get this over with," DJ mumbled.

They were stopped by several people who recognized him as they made their way across the room. Even though DJ didn't want to be there and was more than happy to show his irritation to Deandre, the kid had enough home training to not act out or say anything rude while they spoke with the people in the store. DJ was all yes ma'am and no sir with eye contact and a pleasant expression when he spoke. Pride swelled in his chest. DJ was "pushing boundaries" as Cliff said, but he was still a good kid.

They got to Kelly and Sheri just as soon as it looked like Sheri was about to walk away. She caught his eye and smiled. It was so bright, he wondered if she'd been waiting for him to arrive. No, he was reading too much into that. She always smiled like that.

"Lieutenant, how are you?" Kelly asked.

"I'm good, Kelly. How are you?"

"I'm great. Is this your son?" Kelly asked, grinning at DJ.

"It is. This is Deande Jr., or DJ for short."

DJ nodded to them both. "It's nice meeting you."

"Likewise. Do you read comics?" Kelly asked.

DJ shook his head. "Not really. Mostly mangas."

Kelly pointed to a section across the room. "Ah, I've got a few but not many. I hope to expand the section one day. Maybe you can tell me some of the series you're reading, and I can get them in stock."

DJ's brows lifted. "You'd do that?"

"Of course. I like mangas, but comics are my true love. But I would like to bring in all types of customers. Just let me know." She nodded at someone who called her name from across the room. "Let me check on this. Thanks for coming, Lieutenant. Nice to meet you, DJ." She left the three of them.

"I'm going to check out the mangas," DJ said, turning away.

Deandre cleared his throat and placed a hand on his son's shoulder. DJ sighed and turned back. "Yes, sir."

"Aren't you forgetting something?" Deandre tilted his head toward Sheri.

DJ looked like he wanted to roll his eyes, but his son was also a smart kid and knew better. He turned to Sheri.

"I'm sorry for what I said the other day. It was rude and it won't happen again."

Sheri's eyes widened. She looked at Deandre, then back at DJ. "Oh, well, thank you for apologizing. It's accepted."

DJ nodded then looked at Deandre. "Now can I check out the mangas?"

"Fine, go ahead." DJ quickly ran off.

Sheri chuckled. "How much did it hurt him to have to apologize to me?"

"Enough to warrant about fifty million sighs on the car ride over and a request to leave immediately afterward."

Sheri crinkled her nose. "That much, huh? You didn't have to get him to do that, but I do appreciate it."

She wasn't dressed in her usual The Breakfast Nook T-shirt and jeans. Instead, she wore a sleeveless tan-colored shirt that fitted her breasts perfectly and a pair of distressed jeans that hugged her curves. A gold chain with her nickname, Lil Bit, hung just above the swell of her breast. He forced himself to keep eye contact and not let his gaze wander over the smooth brown skin of her neck, chest and shoulders.

"I did have to get him apologize. I let him know that kind of behavior is what's making some people want him and his friends banned from the south end of the beach. I think he understood."

"Well, for what it's worth, that was the only thing I've seen happen with him and his group of friends. They don't really cause any trouble as far as I know. I don't think he's running around with a really bad crowd."

"That's good to know. He doesn't know how much I worry about him. I get it, he's sixteen and able to be out in the world on his own to an extent, but it's still hard for me to not want to protect him like he's still six years old."

Sheri placed a hand on his arm. "I think I get what

you're saying, but don't let him hear that. I don't know any sixteen-year-old who wants to still be viewed like they're six." Her eyes sparkled with humor.

She gently squeezed his bicep before her hand fell away. He didn't know if the movement was meant to be reassuring, or a way for her to feel the muscle, but either way, his arm seemed to sizzle from where she'd touched it.

"I'll try and remember that," he said.

She glanced away and nodded as she caught someone else's eye. Was she about to walk away? He wasn't ready for their conversation to end. "How long have you been here?" he asked quickly.

She looked back at him. "Not too long. It's a nice thing to get to mingle with the other shop owners and learn more about Kelly's store. I think I may host something at the restaurant later for everyone."

"That would be a good idea."

"Yeah, keep the vibe going and help us all get to know each other as we build up the area." Her eyes darted to the side again. Whoever she'd noticed before must have gotten her attention.

Deandre shifted his stance a little to the left. Sheri's dark brown eyes lifted back up to meet his. "I hope I get an invite."

Sheri's tongue darted out and touched the edge of her mouth. "You'd come?"

He would, but the hope in her voice and the way her lips lifted in the sexiest of smiles triggered something in his brain. He'd rearrange his entire schedule to make it to anything she ever put on. "For you? Of course I'd come."

Her hand lifted to toy with the chain around her neck. His eyes followed the movement of her slim fingers above her breasts and there was a stirring in his groin. He quickly lifted his eyes back to hers.

Sheri sucked in a breath, then pointed to his left. "I'm going to go say hello to Ivy and see if she wants to host something at her tattoo parlor. I'll talk with you later."

Deandre wanted to find another reason to keep her talking to him, but he was also blurring the line between their working together and flirting. Sheri solved his problem by dashing across the room before he could think of something else to say. Which was probably for the best. What was wrong with him? A few weeks ago he wasn't even entertaining the idea of doing anything about his attraction to her. Now he was searching for ways to keep her nearby? He'd better get this under control because she was obviously not interested in him that way. He wanted this project to succeed and hitting on his project partner was a surefire way of ruining everything.

Sheri spent most of the night trying to avoid being alone with Lieutenant King again. Not because she didn't enjoy his company. That was the problem. She enjoyed his company *too* much. The man was handsome, thoughtful, kind and funny. He was all the checkboxes she made for herself after realizing that one-night stands and friends-with-benefits type situations weren't going to work for her anymore. Which meant her attraction for him was about to have her make a dumb decision. A potentially embarrassing decision when he rejected her if she hit on him.

Sure, there had been that one time when he'd checked out her cleavage. She had to admit, her cleavage was amazing in her shirt. She'd worn it partially because she'd wanted him to see her. But, like a gentleman, he'd lifted his eyes quickly and looked apologetic. The man was a man, but he obviously was not a man coming to her for anything other than the community event.

Despite her growing attraction for Deandre and her efforts to avoid him, Sheri had a good time at the comic book shop. It was the first time she'd had a chance to mingle with some of the other business owners and not focus on crime in the area or ways to get support from the city. Outside of her cousin Cora, Sheri didn't have a lot of friends. When she'd moved home, family was her support system. They were whom she spent time with when she wasn't working. The friends she'd had while she'd grown up had either moved away or were married with their own kids and things to deal with. So hanging out with Kelly and Ivy from the tattoo parlor made her want to branch out and expand her social circle.

"Let's do this again," Sheri said when she was saying goodbye to Kelly later that evening.

"Have a get-together at the comic book store? Sure."

Sheri shook her head. "No, I mean let's hang out sometime. I'm just going to be straight up. I mostly hang out with my cousin, and even though I love her, I wouldn't mind expanding my social circle. If you're cool with it, let's hang out sometime."

Kelly grinned and nodded. "I'm cool with it. I need to get out more." She looked to Ivy. "What about you?"

"I work late hours at the shop, but if you give me enough heads-up, then I can make it work. I'm down."

"Cool. I'll send out some dates and we'll see what works." Sheri kept her voice calm and collected even though she wanted to bounce with excitement.

She was finally making some new friends. She wanted new friends. Not because she didn't like hanging out with Cora, but she also needed different viewpoints. Cora was cool and all, but she didn't always encourage Sheri to make the best decisions.

Speaking of her cousin. Sheri pulled out her cell phone and texted her. She'd let Cora borrow her car while her car was in the shop, and she'd dropped Sheri off and promised to be here by nine to pick her up. Sheri had texted her to make sure she was still coming, but the return texts had stopped.

R U on the way?

Can u catch a ride?

Sheri cursed and looked up at Ivy and Kelly. "My bad. I need to make a call. We'll catch up soon."

They waved as she walked outside. She was going to have to curse out her cousin and she didn't want to do that in front of everyone in the room.

Once outside, she dialed her cousin's number. Cora answered on the fourth ring. "What do you mean *catch a ride*?" Sheri said immediately.

"Look, I thought I'd be done, but Tim needed a ride." Cora didn't sound the least bit apologetic for leaving Sheri stranded while she gave someone else a ride.

"Who the hell is Tim?" Sheri put a hand on her hip.

"You know, the guy I've been trying to hook up with?"

"You said you needed my car to run an errand while yours was in the shop. Not because you were taking some guy for a ride."

"He's not just some guy. Do you ever listen?" Cora had the nerve to sound exasperated with Sheri.

"I'm listening now while you tell me you're giving someone a ride in my car."

"I said it was an errand. I didn't say what kind."

Sheri pinched the bridge of her nose. She took a deep breath before asking. "When will you come and get me?"

"See, what had happened was—"

"Cora!" Nothing good ever started with those words.

Cora plowed ahead. "I told Tim I would take him to pick up some money from his boy's house."

"I don't give a damn about his boy."

"But he owes me the money," her cousin said as if that were explanation enough. "So, I said I'd take him to get the money."

Sheri tapped her foot. She wanted to shake Cora. "Still not my problem."

"Well, his boy lives in Myrtle Beach."

"Myrtle Beach! You're an hour away."

"And his friend is having this party, so, can you catch a ride? I promise I'll be back as soon as I can."

"You're gone with my damn car! How am I supposed to get home?"

"Uber? Lyft? Call your momma?" Again, Cora didn't sound apologetic. She had the nerve to sound as if Sheri should already have the answer for how to get home.

"I'm not calling my mom. You said you'd be here to get me by nine."

"My bad. Look, I'll pay for the Uber."

"You know what. Forget you and Tim. You owe me and when I see you, I'm going to cuss your—"

"I know you will. Send me the cost for the Uber and I'll send you the money. Bye!" She ended the call.

Sheri stomped her feet and cursed again. "I don't want to call a damn Uber!"

"I'll give you a ride home." Deandre's voice came from behind her.

Sheri spun around. Deandre watched her with a concerned expression. His son watched her as if she were as pitiful as she felt. Stranded at the beach while her cousin ran off with her car.

Sheri shook her head. Her cheeks burned with embarrassment. "You don't have to do that."

"I couldn't help but hear some of your conversation. I wouldn't want you waiting out here for some stranger to take you home. Let me give you a ride."

"But…" She glanced at his son. "I live kind of far out."

"I'll drop off DJ and then take you. I live about five minutes from here."

She could order an Uber and go back inside to wait. She was sure she'd have fun talking to Ivy and Kelly some more. But it was embarrassing enough to be stranded. And he was there, and he was offering to give her a ride. And, even though she'd tried to stay away from him most of the night, the reckless side of her brain couldn't resist a man who was willing to step in and help when the opportunity presented itself.

"If you don't mind, then sure," she said before she could second-guess or remind herself how this was not going to help her get over her attraction to him.

Deandre looked as if he'd been hoping that would be her answer. "Good, let's go."

Deandre was parked a few cars down from the store. DJ got in the back seat and Sheri took the passenger side. When they were in the car, Sheri tried to think of something cool or interesting to say but her mind drew a blank. Not that it mattered. Other than showing mild irritation when his dad offered to give her a ride home, DJ had shown more interest in his phone than he had in Sheri, or his dad, for that matter.

"Thanks for this," she finally said once they'd dropped DJ off and were heading to her place. She'd given him the address and he'd known the area.

"You don't have to keep thanking me. It really is no problem."

"I know, but you could be doing anything other than

dragging me out to my house. I swear I'm never letting my cousin borrow my car again."

"Does she usually leave you hanging like this?"

"It depends. I don't usually have to go so far as to let her use my car. Hers is in the shop, and she swore this would just be a quick trip. But when it comes to Cora and a man, then, yes, she will drop me like a balled-up receipt."

Deandre shook his head, then chuckled. "Damn, not like that."

"Exactly like that. She's my cousin, and I love her, but she doesn't always make the best choices. Or support me making the best choices."

"Is she the friend that encourages bad behavior?" His voice was light, not judging.

She nodded. "Most definitely. To be honest, she's part of the reason you got called out to arrest me that night."

He turned to look at her quickly before glancing back at the road. They were farther away from the town now. The streetlights were now nonexistent, and the sliver of a moon barely lit up the road. "How?"

"I don't throw all the blame on her. I mean, it was me holding the bat. But she did encourage me to use it." Sheri shook her head and groaned. "I still can't believe I did that. It took me way too long to live that down."

He was silent for a second before asking hesitantly, "Were you and he…very serious?"

"We weren't. I knew it, but when you get caught up in something, reason doesn't always make sense. So, when my feelings got hurt, and Cora and I were watching *Waiting to Exhale*, that's how we ended up there. It wasn't until later that I realized Cora also liked Tyrone. That may have played into her encouragement."

"For real?"

"For real."

He was quiet again. Sheri looked out the window, wondering what he was thinking but also hesitant to ask. She didn't like to play the mind-reading game, but she couldn't help but worry that he was thinking she was immature and overly dramatic.

"The event tonight was cool," she blurted out. Anything to keep him from thinking about her bashing the car of a guy she was no longer interested in.

"It was," he said evenly.

"We're thinking of having more. It'll be a good way to bring the community together."

"I like that idea. I don't get out much, so it'll give me a reason to socialize."

"Why don't you go out much?"

Did that mean he wasn't dating? They'd been planning the event for a few weeks, and he hadn't mentioned a girlfriend. Not that she'd asked. There also hadn't been phone calls, texts or anything that gave the appearance of him having someone in his life.

"Between the job and raising DJ, I didn't worry about a social life. Now that he's getting older, it's time for me to try to figure out how to interact with people again."

"I think you interact pretty well."

He nodded. "Most of my interactions aren't in a social setting. My former partner and friend LaTisha, along with my in-laws, keep asking me to get out there and start living my life again. In fact, if they don't drag me out of the house, I don't do much of anything."

"I love going out and doing stuff. I had a side job as event staff at the convention center in Myrtle Beach. It was a great way to get out, meet people and see interesting events. But once I opened the restaurant, I gave it up. Now, I'm kind of like you. Looking for excuses to get out and do stuff."

"Do you hang with your cousin a lot?"

"We hang a little, but we haven't as much since I opened the restaurant. She's got her thing and I've got mine. We catch up when we can, but lately it's been a lot of her dropping me for other interests."

"Hmm."

She raised her brow and looked at him. "Hmm, what?"

"Nothing, just looks like we're in the same boat. Need a reason to go out and socialize."

"Well, if you ever see something you're interested in and want a partner, let me know. I'll go with you."

Damn, why had she said that? Did it sound like she was asking him on a date? Because she wasn't. Not really. She said the words before she could think about them and talk herself out of making the suggestion.

"We're friends, you know," she said quickly. "Friends hang out."

He nodded slowly. "They do."

That wasn't much of a reply. Her cheeks burned and she wanted to get out of the car and walk the rest of the way home. What in the world was wrong with her? She was Sheri "Lil Bit" Thomas. She wasn't afraid to talk to anyone or try something new. She knew her own mind and was confident in herself and her abilities. So why did conversations with this man make her wonder if she was somehow lacking? Sure, he'd seen her at her worst, but that wasn't all of her. She had to get herself together. They were friends and working together on this project. That was it. She was not going to act like a schoolgirl with a crush on the popular boy that was so hard she couldn't even speak to him.

"So it's settled, then, friend," she said. "We'll hang out if we see something interesting." She infused her voice with confidence, and an "I will not be hurt if you say no" string of steel. The string was micrometers thick and could be bent, but it was still steel.

He glanced at her again. "Settled."

They were silent for the next few minutes. The radio played soul music thanks to the local station's *Saturday Night Juke Joint* playlist. She sang along to some of the songs and was pleasantly surprised when Deandre did the same. She glanced his way and their eyes caught. They both grinned and continued to sing along with the lyrics. The rest of the trip went by fast but was the most fun she'd had all night.

She wished it would last longer, this impromptu singalong with Deandre that didn't make her feel immature or overly flustered.

"Thanks for dropping me off."

He put the car in Park. "I'll walk you to the door."

"You don't—"

"I know I don't have to," he cut in. "But blame it on my upbringing and being a cop. Your house is dark, you live away from town and I'd feel better walking you to the door."

She pointed to the house next door. Her family owned most of the property on the road. Two years ago, before her grandmother passed, she'd split two acres so her daughter could build a home and given the quarter acre where she'd built her home to Sheri.

"My mom's light is on, so I'm sure she's watching from behind her curtains."

"Even more reason for me to walk you to the door. I don't want her to think I don't have any manners."

Sheri couldn't help but laugh as she opened the door. "You're worried about what my mom thinks?"

"You never know when I'll need to make a good impression."

Her heart rate tripled. She shook her head as she got out of the car. He was just being nice. He walked her the short distance from the gravel drive to her front door. She hadn't left the porch light on, and with the limited moonlight, the only illumination came from the tall light on a pole along the border of her property and her mom's they'd installed to light up the side yard where they had cookouts long into the night with family.

She unlocked her door, then turned back toward Deandre. "Thanks again, for the ride and bringing me home."

"You're welcome." He shifted his weight.

Sheri got the impression he had something to say. "Anything wrong?"

"That guy... Tyrone. Do you still have feelings for him?"

The question was so out of the blue that she took a step back. "What? No. Why would you ask?"

"If we're going to hang out, I just wanted to know if there was someone you had feelings for."

"Definitely not him. You know he's getting married, right? We made our peace with each other, and I wish him well."

He slowly lifted and lowered his head as if letting her words settle in. "No other guys in the picture?"

"Not right now." She cocked her head to the side. Her pulse pounded as a wild thought entered her mind. "Are you asking for a reason?"

"Just curious."

"No, you don't ask that kind of stuff just because you're curious. Is there a reason?" She had to know. Otherwise she'd be up all night wondering why he asked and what he meant. She wasn't about to put herself through that kind of torture.

He straightened his shoulders, and even in the darkness of the porch she could feel the intensity of his gaze. "Because I want to know for personal reasons. If you're available."

Her breathing hitched. Okay, so maybe he was interested. "I'm available," she said quickly.

He nodded, a short, succinct movement of his head. "That's good to know."

"Why?" She shifted closer.

"I'd like to get to know you. Not just for the community event and not just as a friend."

Sheri's knees felt like Jell-O. She wanted to jump up and down and twerk, but instead, she held in her excitement and nodded. "Oh…well… I like that idea."

God how she wished there was more light for her to see. She could swear his body stilled, but she couldn't see his face. The humid night air felt electric and ten times hotter, thicker. Was that just her? Did he feel it, too?

"Good. Then it's official."

She blinked. "What's official?"

"You and me. We're…officially getting to know each other."

She smiled, loving his direct manner. "We are."

"I'll call you tomorrow, then."

"I like that."

He nodded and took a step backward. Sheri was excited, but she wasn't ready to let him go. Not just yet. "But you can kiss me tonight."

There was just enough light for her to see the way heat flared in his gaze. He glanced at her mom's house. Then back at her. Time seemed to slow down before he stepped forward and pulled her into his embrace. The kiss was soft, and sweet. He explored her mouth with the same direct confidence he'd used to confirm that they would officially get to know each other. She wanted him to kiss her deeper, harder. If she were honest, she wanted him to back her against the wall, and kiss every part of her body. She pressed forward, but he pulled back.

"I'll call you tomorrow," he said in a deep, rumbling voice.

"But…"

He silenced her with another kiss. When he pulled away, he smiled. "Tomorrow."

Chapter Ten

Sundays were the busiest day in the restaurant, and Sheri typically didn't have time to have any thoughts in her head other than prepping food, serving customers and making sure everything was happening on schedule. But this Sunday, she had an extra bounce in her step and nothing but personal thoughts filled her head.

He'd said they were officially "getting to know each other," so did that mean she was officially dating Lieutenant Deandre King? Did that mean she could refer to him as her man, or was "getting to know each other" not an automatic step into official relationship status? Was she being silly for overthinking this? Shouldn't she just go with the flow and let whatever happened happen? No. Going with the flow meant not knowing where she stood and misunderstandings. Clarity was important.

"Lil Bit, if you don't quit daydreaming and get your food off the counter, then I'm going to throw an egg at you." JD's gruff voice broke into her thoughts.

Sheri blinked and shook her head. "I'm not daydreaming." She was preoccupied. There was a difference.

Cora came up to her side. Her cousin sometimes helped on the weekends. She hadn't agreed to come in today, but Sheri assumed she'd shown up in an attempt to make up for ditching Sheri the night before.

"Yes, you are," Cora said. "This got anything to do with whatever man dropped you off last night?"

Sheri's head whipped to the side so she could eye her cousin. "Who said a man dropped me off?"

Her mom sidled up next to JD in the kitchen and peered at Sheri with a hand propped on her hip. "I said it because I saw it. It was dark last night, but I recognize a man's shoulders."

JD slapped his spatula on the griddle. "I don't care who dropped her off. I made those waffles and eggs and they're gonna get cold if y'all keep clucking like chickens. Take the food and worry about the man later."

Sighing, Sheri grabbed the plates off the serving station and hurried from the kitchen before she could be further questioned. She wasn't ashamed to tell her family about her and Deandre, but she wasn't ready to get their input, either. A part of her was dying to talk to someone, but she could guess her mom's and Cora's opinions. Her mom would warn her not to trust or date a cop and Cora would find something negative about Deandre to put a damper on Sheri's excitement. She wanted to enjoy this moment, before she let family come in and cast their shadows of doubt.

She took the food to the table for her customers. "Here you go. Can I get you anything else?"

The two women glanced over their food, eyes brightening the way she liked to see. "No, I think we're good for now."

"Extra napkins, please," the other lady said at the same time.

"I've got you." Sheri got the napkins and then went to serve the next table that had just been seated.

They were busy, as usual. They even had a waitlist started. She glanced at the people lined up outside through the window and nearly stumbled. Was that? She squinted and leaned forward. Her heart jumped. Yes, that was Deandre standing outside. He was with a woman she didn't recognize, another man and had DJ with him. He'd said he'd call her today, but she hadn't expected him to show up.

"What are you smiling at?" Cora scooted up next to Sheri. She looked out the window, too. "Isn't that the cop you saw at TJ Maxx the other day?"

Sheri turned and hurried away to fill the drink order for the table she'd just visited. She hoped Cora would move on to her own tables, but no, her cousin just followed her to the back where they prepared the drinks.

"Is he the one who dropped you off?" Cora's voice dripped with judgment. For what reason, Sheri didn't know. Cora tended to go straight to judging Sheri's relationship decisions from the start.

"Why are you worrying about who dropped me off?" Sheri grabbed the sparkling wine out of the cooler to make mimosas. "No one would have had to drop me off if you hadn't left me hanging."

Cora held up a hand. "Didn't I say I'm sorry? Besides, I'm here now helping out."

"You're not helping. You're over here bothering me. You know we're busy. We can talk about it later."

"He did drop you off, didn't he?" Cora's eyes lit up with the excitement of new gossip. "Girl, wait till I tell your mom."

Sheri reached out and grabbed Cora's shirt before she could head in the direction of where her mom worked with JD making the food.

"What, are you a snitch now? Why are you going to tell her?"

"Because she was worried about you. I'm just looking out." Cora tried, and failed, to look and sound innocent.

Sheri didn't believe that for a second. Cora was eager to

tell Sheri's mom to start drama in the middle of the busiest shift. "No, you're being messy. I don't want messy right now. Not with him, okay."

Cora raised her brow. "What's that supposed to mean?"

"It means what I just said. He's a nice guy. He wants us to get to know each other. So that's what we're doing."

Cora scrunched up her nose. "Get to know each other? Sounds like a simple way to say he just wants to sleep with you."

"He's not trying to sleep with me. He's taking it slow."

"For what? You're both grown. Girl, something is probably wrong with him."

Sheri rolled her eyes and groaned. Why had she even bothered to give an explanation? Cora didn't believe in taking things slow. She got hers and moved on and dealt with guys who wanted the same. "Nothing is wrong with him. He's just a nice guy. Can I be with a nice guy for once?"

Cora threw up her arms. "If you say so. Let me go help at the front." She turned and walked out of the kitchen.

Sheri closed her eyes and groaned. Damn, Cora, and her negative attitude. She would immediately jump to saying something was wrong with Deandre instead of seeing what he'd done as something decent.

Sheri left the kitchen to deliver the mimosas. Cora was at the front talking to the hostess, their younger cousin D'asa. D'asa looked outside, grinned, then nodded. Sheri had to take her customer's order, so she couldn't run up and find out what Cora had said. The next few minutes were harried as she put in the order, delivered more food and greeted another set of customers. When she was able to check on Deandre's progress again, he and his party were seated, but they were across the room. Not in her section but in Cora's.

Double damn! So that's what Cora was up to. And her

cousin wasted no time rushing up to Deandre's table to take their order. Sheri took a step in that direction to intervene. She did not need Cora's messiness this early in whatever kind of relationship she was starting with Deandre.

"Excuse me, Sheri, can I get a refill?" the customer at the table next to her asked.

As much as she wanted to curse for being interrupted, she remembered customer service was something she prided herself in and overcame her need to snatch Cora by her ponytail and pull her away from the table with her man. She turned and smiled.

"Sure, I've got you." She took the cup and went back to refill it and prayed Cora wasn't going to do something to sabotage this relationship before it started.

Deandre hoped he would be seated in Sheri's section but felt he did a decent job hiding his disappointment when the hostess put them across the room from where she worked. He hadn't intended to come here for breakfast, but when LaTisha and her husband, Rob, called to see if he was up so they could drop off the chain saw they'd borrowed before going to breakfast, and then mentioned they were checking out Sheri's place, he'd found himself inviting him and DJ along before the thought could finish forming in his mind.

"Now I know why you wanted to come eat here," DJ said with a smirk.

LaTisha raised a brow and gave DJ a curious look. "Why?"

His son looked across the room at Sheri talking to a couple at another table. "For her."

LaTisha and Rob both turned in that direction. "The waitress?"

"She owns the place," Deandre said quickly.

DJ sat forward in his chair, a frown on his face. "Is this why you made me apologize? Because you like her?"

"Wait? You like her?" LaTisha asked with a big smile as she pointed over her shoulder.

Rob chuckled and shook his head. He was shorter than Deandre, with a bald head, golden brown skin and well-defined muscles gained from hours in the gym. He was a paramedic who'd met LaTisha when they'd both responded to an emergency. Twelve years later, they were still together. "I knew you had a reason for coming," Rob said.

Deandre focused on DJ instead of the teasing looks in his friends' eyes. "I had you apologize because it was the right thing to do. Not just because I like her."

DJ shook his head and glared down at the menu. Deandre didn't get a chance to respond to his son's mumbled "whatever" because LaTisha was tapping his arm.

"Hold on. You like her for real?" LaTisha's voice rose in pitch with her excitement.

"Can you not announce it to the entire restaurant?" Deandre said, looking around at the other tables. Who, thankfully, seemed to be preoccupied with their own conversations.

LaTisha lowered her voice, but her enthusiasm was still visible in her eyes. "When did this happen? How did you meet her?"

"She's helping me with the community event."

The waitress walked up to their table, immediately blocking Deandre's view of Sheri across the room. He looked up and recognized her as Sheri's cousin Cora. Cora studied him through squinted eyes. She was sizing him up. For what he didn't know. Had Sheri already told her about what happened the night before?

"Well, hello, Officer." Cora's voice was syrupy sweet. "It's good to see you again."

"Good seeing you, too."

She looked at LaTisha. "This your girlfriend?"

Deandre coughed. "What? Nah?"

LaTisha returned Cora's smile with a fake one of her own before slipping her arm through Rob's. "I'm with him. And I'd like coffee and orange juice, please."

"Water and coffee for me," Rob replied.

"I'll take an apple juice," DJ ordered.

"Coffee and water," Deandre finished with a nod.

Cora looked at the four of them. He could see the irritation in her eyes. He'd bet she wanted to linger and get more information out of him, but thankfully LaTisha peeped her game as well and cut it short.

"I'll be right back with those drinks." She turned and walked away.

"What's up with her?" LaTisha asked as soon as Cora was out of earshot.

Rob shrugged and picked up his menu. "It's not the first time someone asked if you were with Deandre."

"Yeah, but she said that with intention." LaTisha cut her eyes in the direction Cora had gone.

LaTisha had been his partner and they hung out after work, so people had assumed they were together before. Nothing ever happened between them, and Rob was just as much his friend as hers. Most of the time the assumption wasn't made was when the three of them were together.

"That's Sheri's cousin Cora," Deandre said. "I think she's a bit of a troublemaker."

DJ lowered his menu. "Didn't you warn me to stay away from girls with drama?" he said. "I'd think you'd do the same."

"Cora is not Sheri, and we're just…getting to know each other."

DJ rolled his eyes. "Sure."

"Leave your dad alone." LaTisha waved her hand at DJ. "It's good that you're testing the waters."

"And Sheri is not her cousin."

Cora returned with their drinks. "Have you been here before?"

LaTisha answered, "It's our first time."

"I can tell you the specials."

"No need," LaTisha said with an unwavering smile. "I want the chicken and waffles."

Rob ordered, then DJ and finally Deandre. Which didn't leave Cora much time to chat. She hurried away. Sheri came out of the back as Cora was heading into the kitchen. Sheri stopped her cousin, who said something that made Sheri cringe and glance their way. Cora continued to the kitchen and Sheri made a beeline their way.

"Is everything good over here?" she asked.

Deandre shifted forward and smiled. A sheen of sweat beaded her brow, her ponytail was tousled and what looked like syrup stained her yellow The Breakfast Nook T-shirt, but she still managed to look sexy as all get-out. She was obviously busy, with many more things to focus on besides him and his friends. He shouldn't have come to distract her, but when he'd been faced with the chance to see her, he hadn't been able to stop himself from coming.

"We're great. Busy morning?"

She nodded. "Yes, Sunday is our busiest day." She looked to LaTisha and Rob and held out her hand. "Hey, I'm Sheri Thomas."

Latisha took Sheri's hand. "LaTisha and Rob Fuller. I've been wanting to try this place for a long time."

"Well, I'm glad you decided to give us a try." She looked at DJ. "Good to see you again, DJ."

DJ barely glanced up from his phone. "Yeah, same."

Sheri's smile stiffened at the edges. Deandre nudged

his son's foot under the table. DJ gave him a "What's the matter?" look before sitting up and giving Sheri a plastic smile. "Good seeing you, too, ma'am."

Deandre placed a hand on her forearm. "We dragged him out early."

"It's no problem. I'm just glad to see you." Her eyes met his and he knew that despite the rush of people, her nosy cousin and his rude kid, she meant the words.

"Likewise."

"You all enjoy your meal. Give me a call later, okay?" She squeezed his shoulder before going back to her tables across the room.

LaTisha and Rob both beamed at him. "She likes you, too."

"I'd hope so," he said, trying not to let it show how much those words made his morning.

DJ sucked his teeth but kept looking at his phone. Deandre decided to let it go for now. No need to make a scene in the restaurant and ruin breakfast. DJ was more than likely still upset about having to apologize. He'd eventually come around.

The conversation drifted to the neighborhood and the latest renovations to LaTisha and Rob's house. The food came and Cora realized they didn't want to chat with her and went on about her business. At the end of the meal, she came back and gave him a smug look with her hand on her hip.

"Looks like your food was comped today," she said.

"What?" Deandre looked around the room. Sheri met his eyes and winked. "No, I can't let her do that."

"She's the owner and can do what she wants. You better not hurt her, that's all I've got to say."

Deandre frowned. "I don't plan to hurt anyone."

Cora snorted. "That's what they all say. Have a good rest of your day." She turned and sauntered off.

"Ignore her," LaTisha said. "Your girl really likes you."

"Free food is cool," DJ agreed.

"I really shouldn't," Deandre said.

"Dad, why you arguing? She's *your girl* now, right? Just take the W and move on. I'll meet y'all at the car." He got up and walked out.

He looked at Rob and LaTisha. "It's too much."

"It's her restaurant, don't make a scene. Just make it up to her later in a nice way," LaTisha said.

"How?"

Rob winked at him. "You'll think of a way." They got up and headed to the door.

Deandre stood as well, but instead of going to the door he crossed the room to where Sheri was turning away from a table. She grinned at him, and he had a funny sensation in his chest that he hadn't felt in years. Something that told him that if he wasn't careful, he could fall hard for Sheri. It was part of the reason why he wanted to take things slow. He'd tried quick hookups and casual flings after his wife passed, but that life wasn't for him. He was open to a long-term relationship, maybe even getting married again one day. He wasn't sure if Sheri was the person he'd do that with, but he didn't want to rush into sex with her and create an awkward situation.

"Did you enjoy the food?"

She had the same hopeful look in her eye that she always had when she brought him food. She looked so cute he couldn't help himself. He placed his hand on her hip, pulled her forward and kissed her quickly.

"I enjoyed seeing you more. I owe you."

She leaned into him. The light press of her breasts against his chest caused a stirring in his midsection that made him want to pull her closer and kiss her deeper. He definitely needed to take things slow with Sheri or else he'd lose himself.

"You don't owe me anything."

"I do." He'd figure out something nice to do for her. "Call me when you're done. Okay?"

She bit the corner of her lip and nodded. "Okay."

He needed to pull away but couldn't help himself. He kissed her again before letting her go and walking out. He could feel the eyes of the entire restaurant on him as he left. He didn't care. Sheri had agreed to be with him, and with the way he was feeling, he didn't care if the entire world knew.

Chapter Eleven

Sheri jumped in the shower and changed clothes as soon as she got home from work. As promised, she'd called Deandre when she was leaving work. He'd asked her to go out on their first official date. Bonus point, he'd already planned what they were doing that evening. They were going to the movie at the park downtown, and he was bringing a picnic basket of treats. She'd nearly swooned when he'd told her the plans. He'd put some thought into their first date. She couldn't remember the last guy who'd taken the time to plan a date. Most of the guys she'd dated asked her out and then put all the effort of planning on her shoulders. Deandre was a take-charge kind of person and she liked that.

The thoughts that bothered her at the start of the day no longer took up as much room in her brain. When he'd kissed her, no matter how quick and sweet the kiss was, it had been a definite show of them being together. At least, that's how she was taking it. She would still tell him what she wanted out of a relationship. She was too old to play games or be dishonest with herself. If they were dating, she wanted it to be exclusive and she'd tell him she was looking for something that could be serious. If that scared him away, then she'd be better off in the long run. Having her feelings bruised now was better than being heart-broken later.

She'd agreed to meet him at the park, even though he'd offered to pick her up. She did not want her family to see him coming by. If they knew she had a date with him, they'd immediately find a reason to come to her house just so they could see and talk to him. She'd barely been able to get out of the restaurant on time after he'd kissed her. Her mom hadn't seen, but Cora had, and she'd made a point to make sure everyone in the kitchen knew what happened.

She'd seen the look her mom had given her, but they'd been too busy for her to pull Sheri to the side and talk. That, and JD had already said he wasn't in the mood to have his kitchen slowed down by gossip. So, her mom had let things slide. She'd had to leave before closing to run an errand with her aunt Gwen, and Sheri had thanked her lucky stars when she didn't see her mom's car in the yard when she'd pulled up.

She wasn't meeting Deandre for another hour, but she was going to get out of the house before her mom had time to come and question her. She was showered, dressed and heading to her front door in no time. She'd opted for a light blue jumpsuit with spaghetti straps. The soft material was thin enough to keep her cool and her shoulders and décolletage looked amazing when she wore it. She'd taken her hair out of its usual ponytail so it hung thick and loose around her shoulders. She slid her "Lil Bit" necklace around her neck and paired it with large, silver hoop earrings. She hoped she looked casual but sexy at the same time.

She opened the front door and froze immediately. Her mom and Aunt Gwen both stood on the front porch. Her mom's finger hovered just above the doorbell.

"Where you going?" her mom asked.

Sheri barely stopped herself from stomping her foot with frustration. She tried not to show her irritation on her face, but something must have crept through because her mom crossed her arms and gave her *the look*.

Sheri fixed her face and smiled. "Just got to run some errands. I may hang with Cora later."

Her aunt Gwen shook her head. "I know you're not going out with Cora because she's running behind that man in Myrtle Beach tonight. So what man are you running behind?"

Sheri sighed and walked out onto the porch. If she let them in the house, she was trapped for at least an hour. "I'm not running behind anyone. Just going out real quick."

"It's that cop, ain't it?" her mom asked. "Cora told me he kissed you today."

No need lying to her mom about what happened with Deandre. "He did."

"Why's he kissing you all in the middle of your job?" Aunt Gwen asked, sounding affronted.

"Because we're dating."

That was met with silence as the sisters exchanged looks. Sheri couldn't decipher the look, but she could imagine the things in their head. *There Sheri goes again. What's going to happen with this guy? Is she going to embarrass the family one more time?*

Ever since the Tyrone fiasco, her mom had questioned Sheri's dating decisions. She was afraid Sheri would get caught up with another guy who would have her acting out and doing foolish things like damaging a car. Her mom was a firm believer in not playing the fool for any man. Something she'd preached to Sheri, which meant when Sheri had done just that over Tyrone Livingston, a known playboy at that time, she'd been so disappointed to have her daughter acting "desperate and dumb" over a man. Sheri swore her mom viewed her actions as a personal failure on her mothering abilities.

"Dating, huh?" her mom said.

"Yes. Dating. He asked me and I said yes. Anything wrong with that?" She would not feel bad about wanting to be with a guy instead of pretending as if she were good with keeping things casual or claim she didn't need or want a man. Sheri didn't need one to provide for her, but she did enjoy having a guy in her life.

Her mom threw up a hand. "Nah, nothing wrong. I'm just saying…"

"That you're happy for me and hope things work out," Sheri insisted.

Her mom's eyes narrowed. "You know he's got a kid. You ready to play step momma?"

Sheri wasn't sure if she was ready to play stepmom. She wasn't even sure what was going to happen with this. She doubted DJ liked her, but she wanted to at least see what it was like to date a nice guy. She'd only focus on her relationship with Deandre and worry about how things would play out with her and his son if things progressed that far.

"I'm ready to see what happens. No one is playing step momma."

"You be careful," Aunt Gwen said. "I'm not hating or anything. I just don't want you to get hurt."

Her mom grunted and studied her nails. "Or act out like you did last time."

Sheri was used to them bringing up her past dating mistakes, but her defenses rose. She'd messed up, but she'd learned from her mess-ups. No matter how much she tried to prove that, she was getting tired of her family's inability to focus on anything else.

"I'm not going to act out. That was a one-time thing. Can we not bring it up again?"

Her mom stared longer but nodded. "I guess you're not letting us in so you can run and meet him?"

"I just have stuff to do before I catch up with him later."

"Bring him to the house so we can meet him," her mom said.

"Why? You don't need to meet him yet."

Gwen nodded. "Dorothy Jean is right. We need to make sure he's good people. I think I know his in-laws."

"He's not married."

"Well, his late wife was from around here and I know Cliff and Rose. They go to your cousin's church, and they are really involved with their son-in-law. So, he may not be married but he has in-laws."

"And a kid," her mom chimed in. "Think about that while you out having fun with him tonight."

Sheri hadn't considered the rest of his family despite his mentioning he'd moved to Sunshine Beach because his late wife's family was from here. Sheri had known who his late wife was, but she didn't know her parents like that. If her aunt knew them, then she could get all the information she wanted on Deandre, DJ and his family. Which also meant his family could get any information they wanted on her, too. So many people in town knew she'd been arrested after damaging Tyrone's car. The gossip had died down until the brothers got the television deal and then it came back up thanks to internet trolls. Trolls stirred up thanks to her cousin Cora's digging into his past. Would his in-laws be okay with him dating her? Did he listen to them?

She shook the thought out of her head. She wanted to learn about him from him. Not from what people thought of him. Deandre seemed like the type of guy who would feel the same. The good thing was, he already knew her shady relationship past better than anyone and they'd talked it out. She wouldn't worry about his in-laws unless they became serious.

"I've really got to go."

"Go on, have a good time. But be careful, Lil Bit." Her mom's voice was serious in the end.

She and her mom had different views when it came to relationships, but she knew her mom cared about her. She'd been hurt by Sheri's dad when he'd left her and she shielded her heart. She didn't want Sheri to have the same heartbreak.

She gave her mom a hug. "Ma, don't worry. I know what I'm doing this time."

The date was even better than Sheri hoped it would be. Deandre had ordered sandwiches along with a meat, fruit and cheese tray from a local restaurant that he already had spread out on a blanket. He'd paired it with a blackberry lemonade that was delicious. When she'd asked about wine, he let her know that he didn't drink due to the job. When he was a patrol deputy, he'd stopped drinking alcohol and the habit stuck even when he was no longer on patrol.

The movie was *Grease*, and he hadn't believed her when she said she'd never seen the entire movie before.

"I'm not really a musical person, plus, I didn't even know what it was about."

"I was in chorus in high school, and they made us watch it because we sang all the songs from the movie for our end-of-year performance," he'd told her as they sipped lemonade and waited for the movie to start.

Sheri's eyes widened. "You were in chorus?" That explained the impromptu sing-along in his car when he'd driven her home. He liked singing.

"I was."

"Did you play any sports?"

"I played football and ran track. I sang in the choir at my grandmother's church growing up, so I liked music. I wasn't really interested in the band, but chorus was fun. Plus, they had the best field trips. What about you? What activities did you do in high school?"

"I was a cheerleader, but that was about it. I wasn't in any other clubs or anything else. I couldn't wait to graduate and get out of Sunshine Beach."

"What brought you back?"

"My mom got sick. I thought I'd stay in Charlotte working at that steak house until I got a job at another high-end restaurant. But I moved back to help take care of my mom after her stroke. My aunts and cousins were around, but I didn't want to leave her in their care."

"She seems to be doing a lot better now."

"She is. Sometimes I can't believe she recovered. Thankfully, my aunt had just watched something on the news about recognizing the signs of a stroke. She saw my mom was dizzy and numb so she called 911. She got to the hospital in time, but she still had to go through rehabilitation. When she started physical therapy, she asked if I planned to move back to Charlotte, but by then I knew I couldn't leave her. I started working at Waffle House for the flexible hours and decent pay and then got the wild idea to open my own restaurant."

"Are you happy here in Sunshine Beach?"

She thought about it, then nodded. "I am. Growing up I just wanted to experience a new place. But when I came back I realized how much I love this town. I might have been able to open a restaurant in Charlotte, but opening my restaurant here was so much better. I had people I could call on and help me like Aunt Gwen, my cousin D'asa and even Cora. Then there's JD. He left Waffle House to come and work with me. My family is here and can help me fill in while I work to build up my staffing levels. Then there are the people who knew me growing up and want me to succeed. It's just a different sense of community that I didn't have in Charlotte."

"Did you have friends up there?"

"Yeah, some work friends and a few from college. We keep in touch. When I get a chance, I go up and visit every once in a while. What about you? Do you still keep up with friends and family back in Florida?"

He shook his head. "Not so much. DJ was ten when my wife died. We moved to Sunshine Beach a year after. At first it was too hard to keep in touch with the people and the life I left behind. It was easier to start over here."

"I'm surprised you moved closer to your in-laws instead of your own parents."

"Her parents are the ones who stepped in and helped me with DJ when I needed them. I love my parents, but they're off living their own life. They felt bad for me when I lost Jamila, but they'd already moved to Destin. Just last year they moved to Denver. They're enjoying their retirement, and I can't blame them. They come down and visit us, but they weren't ready to move closer and help me raise DJ. When Rose asked me to move to Sunshine Beach so they could help with DJ, I didn't hesitate. I turned in my resignation, packed our stuff and moved."

"It's good that you're close with your in-laws. Even after…"

"I love them just as much as I love my parents. I'm forever grateful for them and the way they helped out."

"My aunt Gwen says they go to my cousin's church."

"Mount Olive AME?" he asked.

She nodded. "That's the one. My cousin Faith and her husband, Gary, go there."

"I'll ask them if they know them."

She shook her head. "No need. My cousin Faith is cool, but she's messy. They probably know all my business and the trouble I've gotten into. They may tell you to stay away from me if they know who she is."

She tried to keep her voice light, but a part of her worried that was the case. Even before Tyrone, back when she was a teenager, she would sometimes get into trouble. She wasn't ashamed of her past or the mistakes she'd made, but she was tired of defending herself. She liked Deandre, but she didn't want to have to defend herself to him or his family.

Deandre leaned forward and met her eyes. "They can tell me, but it doesn't mean I'll listen."

A flutter when through her chest. "Why not?"

"Because what they think about you, or your cousin, doesn't matter to me. All I care about is how *I* feel about you."

The words settled over her and wrapped her in a comforting embrace. She eased closer to him and warmth spread through her chest. "How do you feel about me?"

"I'm still figuring it out, but so far, I'm feeling pretty good about you."

"Pretty good, huh? What does *pretty good* mean?"

He reached for her hand and threaded his fingers with hers. "It means that I want to get to know you. I don't want to see anyone else while I do that. That I'd like for us to take our time to see where this goes. Is that cool with you?"

More than cool. In fact, it was perfect. Sheri squeezed his hand. "Cool with me."

They didn't talk as much during the show. She watched as many people sang along to the songs in the movie. Deandre didn't sing along with as much enthusiasm, but he did hum and nod his head a few times like a true chorus kid. After the movie, they packed up their items and he'd walked her to her car before suggesting they walk to the ice cream place downtown.

"I've got ice cream at home," she said.

He frowned. "Oh, are you ready to get back?"

She lifted a brow. "That's my not-so-subtle way of inviting you back to my place."

His eyes darkened. She'd parked on a side street about a block away from the park. The streetlights kept the roadway well lit, and there were several other people who'd watched the movie who'd also parked in the area, but the look in his eye made her feel as if they were the only two people on the street.

"I don't know if that's a good idea."

She poked out her lip. Not the least bit embarrassed to show her disappointment. "Why not? It's just ice cream."

Deandre raised a brow. "It's more than ice cream. Or, at least, I'm going to be thinking about more than ice cream."

"No rush or no other expectations. I just don't want the date to end just yet." Which was true, but she wouldn't pretend as if she didn't want to kiss him again. The brief kisses he'd given her before only made her crave more.

"Neither do I."

She stepped forward until their bodies almost touched and lowered her voice. "Then come by. Just for ice cream. Nothing else. We'll both be good." Though the way he looked at her, with so much heat and longing she felt like her skin would catch fire, made her want to be anything but good. She wanted to be naughty.

The question flashed in his eyes for another second

before he nodded. "Just for a few minutes. I need to get home and check on DJ."

She grinned. "A few minutes works for me."

Chapter Twelve

Deandre watched Sheri get into her car before walking around the corner. His stomach churned as if he were about to go on the most important job interview of his life while his heart pounded as if he'd just won an Olympic gold medal. He was just going to her place for ice cream. He wasn't trying to push for anything more. This was their first date, and he'd never been the type of guy who expected something on the first date. But that didn't stop his imagination from going to all kinds of places. Places where he had Sheri in his arms again. Felt her lips on his and got to spend endless amounts of time kissing and caressing her skin.

"Deandre? I thought that was you."

The sound of Chief Montgomery's voice stopped him in his tracks. He turned, caught her eye and smiled. "Chief, how are you doing?"

Deandre kept his voice pleasant, even though he wanted to just wave and hurry to his car. Most days he wouldn't mind stopping to talk to the chief, but the memory of how Sheri looked at him before she'd gotten in the car, as if she was thinking the same thoughts as him, had Deandre ready to be rude and on his way.

"I was here for the movie in the park. The family just went to the car." She pointed over her shoulder where her husband and two daughters were chatting next to her large SUV.

Deandre waved at her husband before focusing back on her. "Tell everyone I said hello. I was just about to leave."

"I know, I saw you here earlier." She took a few steps forward. "With Lil Bit Thomas."

Deandre blinked, surprised to hear the chief use Sheri's nickname. "You know Sheri?"

She crossed her arms and watched Deandre with an assessing gaze. "Not very well. I know who she is. She's the one you arrested back when you were on patrol." The words weren't a question.

Deandre's defenses went up. "She was."

"And now you're dating her?" That was a question, and the chief's tone said she hoped the answer was no.

"She's also working with me on the community event for the south end of the beach."

"Are you telling me that you're just working together?"

Deandre respected Chief Montgomery, but he didn't like the questioning or the judgment in her eye. "Can I know why you're asking?"

Chief Montgomery stepped closer. "Look, I don't like to step in and make comments on my employees' personal lives. But I want you to also know that the work we're doing in the south end is important. They already think I'm going too soft on the crime in the area. If the higher-ups find out that the officer I put in charge of the area is also, I'll just be frank, sleeping around with one of the business owners down there, it won't look good."

"I'm not sleeping around with anyone. And even if I were, it doesn't matter."

"Look, I'm not telling you this to be mean. I'm telling you this because I need you to understand the situation we're in. Everything we do is going to be scrutinized."

"Look, I understand what you're trying to say, but I don't plan to stop seeing her because the higher-ups are going to scrutinize my motives. She cares about the neighborhood as much as the rest of the community and she's the one who stepped up to help. If they have a problem with me seeing her, then they can come tell me to my face."

"I'm just trying to look out for you."

Deandre held up a hand. "I appreciate the thought, but I don't need you to look out for me when it comes to my personal life."

She looked like she wanted to say something else, but instead she pressed her lips together and nodded. "Fine. I'll stay out of it."

"Thank you." He turned to walk toward his car.

"But…"

Sighing, Deandre faced her again and raised a brow.

"If this becomes a problem, then you deal with the fall-out. Understand?"

"I understand, but there won't be any fallout."

His irritation at the intrusion grew with each step he took toward his car. He wished he could ignore her worries and warning as foolishness, but he'd worked in the department long enough to know that if Montgomery thought it was necessary to say something to him, then her concerns had some validity. People may look at any relationship he formed with Sheri and their past together and try to use that to undermine any work he did in the area. It was messed up and unfair but knowing Chief Montgomery had pressure on her to use a stick approach versus a carrot to reduce crime in the area meant that those in favor of the stick weren't afraid to pull out their own.

The thoughts bothered him on the ride to Sheri's place. He arrived at her home several minutes later and tried to push them to the back of his mind. He didn't want to ruin the night with talks about what Chief Montgomery had said.

Sheri greeted him at the door with a smile and a bowl of ice cream. "What took you so long?"

He took the bowl of ice cream and grinned. "Ran into the chief on the way to my car."

"Oh really?" She took his free hand and pulled him farther into the house. "Is everything okay?"

"Yeah, she was there with her family. She stopped me to talk about something."

Sheri's house was cute and decorated with comfortable-looking furniture. Pictures of her family lined the walls. They stopped in her living area that was separated from the kitchen by a small island.

"Nothing too bad, I hope." She grabbed another bowl of ice cream off the counter.

"Nothing bad, but she was…concerned." When Sheri raised a brow, he decided to be honest. Otherwise, she'd notice he was distracted and that would ruin the night. "About us."

He recounted what she said and his response for her to stay out of his personal business. By the time he finished, Sheri had put down her bowl of ice cream and paced in front of her couch.

"Are you serious? No one will ever let me live down one mistake."

He put his ice cream on the coffee table and placed his hands on her shoulders. "This isn't about your past mistake. This is squarely on me."

"Yeah, but if I was Belinda or some other Goody Two-shoes in the town they wouldn't care so much. They'd probably applaud you."

"Did you hear what I said? I told her to stay out of my personal business. I don't care what they think. I mean it,

Sheri. I haven't been this interested in someone in a very long time. I'm not going to stop getting to know you because of something like this."

The corner of her mouth lifted. "You're so straightforward and honest."

"Is that a bad thing?"

"No." She raised her arms and wrapped them around his neck. "It's actually very, very sexy."

Fire flooded his veins and stirred in his groin. If she kept looking at him like that, he was going to be hard as a rock. "You know I only came for ice cream?"

"I know, but that doesn't mean you can't have a little sugar." She lifted on her toes and kissed him.

Thoughts of ice cream fled as her tongue glided across his lower lip. Deandre opened his mouth and let her deepen the kiss. She was just as straightforward with her kiss as she'd said he was with his words, and he loved it. She tasted like strawberry ice cream and he loved strawberries.

His cell phone rang. He wanted to ignore it, but not many people called his cell. "Sorry." He pulled back and reached to get his phone out. To his surprise, his son was calling. "It's DJ."

She stepped back and pushed her hair behind her ear. "Handle that. It could be important."

She licked her full lips and he bit back a groan. He had to clear his throat before he answered. "DJ, what's up?"

"You still at the movie?"

Sheri played with the Lil Bit necklace around her neck, drawing his eyes to the swell of her breasts just below the neckline of her jumpsuit. "Huh…ah, nah, it just ended."

"I've got a problem."

Deandre's focus immediately went to his son. "Problem, what's wrong?'

"I'm kind of embarrassed to say, but I locked myself out

of the house. Can you come home and let me in? I didn't want to call because I thought you were still on your date."

Guilt twisted his insides. He never wanted his son to feel as if he couldn't call him. If he'd gone straight home like he'd planned, DJ wouldn't be locked out. "Nah, don't ever feel like you can't call. I'll be home in a few minutes."

"Cool, thanks, Dad." The relief in DJ's voice made Deandre feel like his son's superhero. He hadn't felt like his son's hero in a long time.

"I'm on my way." He ended the call and looked at Sheri. "DJ's got a problem. I need to check on him."

"I get it. Please, go check on him." Even though he could see the disappointment in her eyes, her voice was understanding. He could relate to the disappointment. Now that he knew DJ wasn't in any immediate danger, the passion he'd felt in her arms came rushing back.

He took her hand and pulled her closer to him. "Rain check on dessert?"

She grinned before lifting up to kiss him again. "Rain check." Her lips pressed his once more before she lightly bit his lower lip.

He thought his erection would burst out of his pants. He wanted to linger over the kiss. To trail his lips across her chin to her chest just in the spot where her necklace sat. But the sound of DJ's voice pulled him back. His son was locked out of the house. Sure, he could call Rose and Cliff, but DJ had called and asked him for help. He wouldn't pawn him off on someone else. He'd have time to kiss Sheri later. "I'll call you tomorrow," he said before leaving.

Chapter Thirteen

Sheri entered the storefront that was starting to feel like a second home to her. They were a few days away from the Connecting the Community event. Which meant this was the last planning meeting before the big day. Most of the business owners and residents were excited. Everyone had come together to think of ways to encourage people from outside the South End to attend. Ivy had created a social media campaign to drum up interest. Deandre and the police chief had encouraged the city to promote the event on its social media pages. The city of Sunshine Beach even sent out a press release to local media, which Sheri had also forwarded to her childhood friend Vanessa Steele-Livingston. Vanessa lived in Charlotte, but she was a news anchor and had roots in Sunshine Beach. She'd reached out to her connections at the local affiliate to get them interested in following the story.

The event started as a forum for community members to learn about what the city was doing to address crime in the town and ways the community could participate. As interest grew, they'd expanded the day to include several vendors from the area who didn't have a storefront but lived nearby selling their goods along the sidewalk. All the shops would be open during the event and Sheri had extended her hours so that the restaurant wouldn't close until two hours after the event ended.

The team of people they'd pulled together to help were all at the last planning session. Sheri's eyes narrowed when she spotted Belinda giggling next to Deandre. She and Deandre hadn't hidden their relationship from the group, but they also hadn't made a big deal about it. Most had guessed there was something going on, because he offered to take her home or they talked openly about getting together later in the week. But Belinda still flirted as if Deandre were single.

Sheri was mostly amused by Belinda's attempts. Deandre was clearly not interested and hadn't followed up on of her blatant hints about them getting together to discuss "the neighborhood." But, when Belinda put her hand on Deandre's shoulder, Sheri's eyes narrowed. She barely got to touch him the way she wanted. She wasn't about to stand by and watch Belinda grope him.

"Hey, everyone, sorry I'm late," Sheri announced herself a little too loudly.

Deandre looked her way and the light in his eyes when he saw her that hadn't been there when he looked at Belinda cleared away the storm clouds of jealousy swirling over Sheri's head. "We were just getting started."

He left Belinda behind and met Sheri halfway across the room. Sheri rose up on her toes and pressed her lips against his. The kiss wasn't long enough. Not for her, but it was good enough for her to make her point. Deandre was spoken for.

Deandre's eyes widened. "What was that for?"

"Just because," she said loud enough for anyone listening to hear. She lowered her voice. "And because we didn't get to finish what we started last night."

The light in his eyes quickly flared into a fire. They'd

made a point to try and see each other whenever they had time. But every time they went on a date, DJ seemed to have some type of crisis. Locking himself out of the door was just the first of many times. Since that night three weeks prior he'd run out of gas, lost something he needed help finding, or needed his dad to help him get something last minute for school. All of the calls were legitimate, but Sheri was starting to suspect DJ was interrupting them on purpose. She just didn't know how to say that to Deandre without sounding paranoid.

"I do plan to finish what I started," he said in just as low a tone.

"When? I'm growing anxious." She tried to keep her voice light, but some of her frustration crept in. She appreciated that he liked taking things slow, but she was tired of having to handle her own needs when she was dating a deliciously sexy man.

Some of the heat left his gaze and was replaced with an apology. "Soon."

His eyes were filled with the same frustration, making her want to jump him in a crowded room. He wasn't just teasing her or playing hard to get. Deandre felt some, if not all, of what she felt, which made her not want to make him feel guilty for having to cut things short because he was being a good parent.

She patted his chest. "It's no problem. I was just teasing."

"You sure?"

She nodded. "I'm sure."

"Good, because DJ is hanging with his grandparents tonight, and I was thinking that maybe…"

"You can come over for ice cream?" She grinned so hard her cheeks hurt.

"Most definitely."

She did a hip shimmy to celebrate, then looked back to Belinda. She didn't bother to hide her smug "he's mine" smirk. She'd been patient enough with Belinda. Now it was time to clearly put up her boundaries.

Deandre lightly tapped her hip. "Let's get started." He called the meeting to order. Sheri grabbed a seat next to Kelly.

Kelly leaned over and lightly elbowed Sheri. "Finally giving Belinda the hint to back off, huh?"

Sheri smirked and winked. "She's lucky I didn't snatch her hand off him."

Kelly held out her hand palm up and Sheri rubbed her palm over hers. They both giggled; the modified high five was something they'd started when they'd hung out after the first neighborhood get-together. Sheri didn't want to jinx anything, but she was pretty sure she and Kelly were on the way to becoming good friends.

The door to the center opened. DJ walked in followed by two older adults who looked familiar. A second later, everything clicked. They were Jamila's parents. Deandre's in-laws.

Deandre gave them a puzzled look. "What are you doing here?"

Rose led the three of them farther into the room. "Well, DJ was telling us about all the work you put into planning the community event, and we decided to come and see if we can help in any way."

Deandre seemed surprised, but pleased. "Sure, I'd love for you to help out. Everyone, this is Rose and Cliff, DJ's grandparents."

Several excited exclamations came around the room as everyone welcomed them. Sheri joined in the welcomes and watched as Belinda quickly ushered them over to the empty seats next to her. Sheri tried, and failed, not to feel some type of way about that. Instead of acting jealous, she focused on what she was there for. Rallying the community to support revitalizing the south end.

The meeting went by quickly. Everyone knew their assigned tasks and was ready to see everything come together that weekend. After things wrapped up, Sheri chatted with Kelly and some of the others before approaching Deandre. He was talking with his in-laws, DJ and Belinda. She wasn't sure if Cliff and Rose knew about her, and she didn't want to make a bad impression. She took a reassuring breath. All that mattered was how Deandre felt.

"Deandre, we were taking DJ to get some tacos. You should come eat with us," Rose was saying as Sheri walked up.

Deandre glanced Sheri's way. "Uh… I already—"

"We're going to the place you like," DJ cut in. "Come on, let's all have dinner together."

Deandre caught Sheri's eye. "I was going out with Sheri."

Sheri stepped next to Deandre. "Hi, nice to meet you all."

Rose's brows rose and she looked at Sheri with interest. "Oh, so you're Sheri."

Cliff snapped his fingers. "You're Dorothy Jean's daughter." He spoke as if he'd just figured out the answer to a riddle.

"I am. I think one of my cousins goes to your church."

"They sure do," he said. "How's your aunt Gwen doing? Me and her were close back in high school."

"She's doing good."

Rose's eyes narrowed on her husband. "You still asking about her? All these years later." Rose sounded more exasperated than upset.

Cliff shrugged. "It was just a question."

Sheri looked from them to Deandre. Deandre raised his brows and looked just as confused as she felt.

Rose looked back at Sheri. "Your aunt Gwen was his high school sweetheart."

"Oh… Well, I didn't know that." She wasn't sure what she was supposed to do with that information.

"Dad," DJ cut in. "Come with us to get tacos. I'm thinking of joining wrestling again."

"I thought it was too late?" Deandre asked.

DJ shook his head. "Coach said I could still join. But I'm not sure. I wanted to talk to you about that."

Deandre glanced from DJ to Sheri and back. She wasn't a detective, but she could deduce what was going on. He wanted to be with her, but also wanted to find out about DJ rejoining the wrestling team. He'd mentioned his frustration with DJ quitting suddenly. As much as she wanted them to finish what they'd started numerous times, she wouldn't pull him away from his kid.

She shrugged. "Go on with them. We'll catch up later."

"Sheri you can come with us," Cliff offered.

Sheri quickly shook her head. Rose didn't seem seriously upset about him asking after her Aunt Gwen, but Sheri was not about to potentially put herself in a situation where she'd have to answer questions about his high school sweetheart all night. "Nah, you all got it. I've got stuff to do. I just wanted to say hi and meet you."

"Maybe next time. A friend of Deandre is a friend of ours," Rose said, sounding friendly enough.

"She's more than—"

"Good, let's go," DJ cut Deandre off. "I'm hungry."

"Me, too," Rose agreed. "Nice to meet you, Sheri. Let's go."

Sheri walked out with them. She caught DJ's gaze as Deandre locked the door. The smug satisfaction as he looked at her proved she wasn't being paranoid. Deandre's son was purposely trying to keep them apart.

"You ready to tell me what you're doing?" Deandre asked DJ when they walked into the house after dinner. DJ had decided that he no longer wanted to spend the night with his grandparents and was going home since Deandre was done with work and was also going home.

DJ looked up from his phone. "Checking my phone."

Deandre shook his head. "That's not what I'm talking about. You wanted me to come to dinner so we could talk about you joining wrestling again, but you never brought it up."

DJ shrugged. "We talked about other stuff."

"And you came to the meeting tonight."

"*You* said I need to be more involved so that people won't treat me like I'm some thug. I thought you'd be happy I showed up."

Deandre took a long breath and gathered his thoughts. "You know what I mean."

"I don't know what you're talking about." DJ turned to go toward his room.

"You're always calling when I'm with Sheri."

DJ faced him again with a raised brow. "I can't call you when you're with her?"

"That's not what I'm saying. But I've noticed the pattern. You went from barely wanting to spend time with me to suddenly needing my help whenever I'm with her."

"I can't help it that things mess up when you're around her. If you don't want me to bother you when you're with her I won't." DJ tried to sound pitiful, but Deandre didn't miss the dare in his son's eye. He hadn't wanted to believe that DJ was intentionally trying to keep him away from

Sheri, but tonight proved something he'd tried to pretend wasn't happening.

"Don't twist my words."

"I'm not twisting your words. I'm just saying what you're telling me."

"What's your problem with her? Is it because I made you apologize?"

"I don't have a problem with her. I don't see why you're interested in her in the first place, but I don't have a problem."

"You don't have to see why I'm interested in her. You just have to understand that she and I are together right now."

DJ looked away and shook his head as if he couldn't believe what he was hearing. "Did you arrest her?"

Deandre's head snapped back. How in the world did DJ know about that? He didn't come home and talk about the stuff he'd see when on patrol. He also hadn't talked about Sheri's past with him.

"Who told you that?"

He shrugged. "I overheard it somewhere. That she was acting all ghetto and you had to arrest her. You always told me to avoid girls with drama, but you're with someone like that."

The judgment in DJ's voice made Deandre's neck tighten. He took a second to take a breath and count to five before responding. If he reacted negatively, DJ would lash back and they'd get nowhere. "First of all, what you heard and what happened are not the same. Second, Sheri isn't dramatic or ghetto. So, mind what you say."

DJ threw up a hand. "Fine. Are we done now?"

"No, we aren't done."

"You want me to like her, fine, I can like her. But she

better not come in here trying to act like she's my momma, 'cause she ain't."

Deandre shook his head, confused by how the conversation had just gone left. He and Sheri had just started dating. DJ had known he'd gone on dates before. He'd even joined in with Rose and Cliff when they'd started pushing him to date again. So, why was DJ suddenly against it? Or was it just he was against Sheri?

"She wouldn't do that." DJ snorted and Deandre narrowed his eyes. "Listen, you're going to be nice to her and you're going to stop playing these games when I'm with her. I'm always here to help you. Don't doubt that, but I know what you're doing. I don't know why, but I don't like it. So, if you've got something to say, now's the time to say it."

"I don't have anything to say." DJ closed his mouth and stared at the ceiling as if suddenly bored with the entire conversation.

Deandre wanted to shake him. DJ was shutting down again. He didn't know what to do or how to make his son open up to him. He wanted to make DJ sit down and not move until he told Deandre what was going on in his brain. Deandre couldn't ever remember struggling with his own dad like this, but then again, he also hadn't spent a lot of time having heart-to-heart conversations with his dad. To this day, other than the weekly call to check in on his parents, he didn't talk to his dad much. He wanted more than that for him and DJ. In a few years he'd be going to college and become even more distant. But he didn't know how to bridge this gap.

"Fine, DJ, but when you're ready to talk, I'm ready to listen."

DJ nodded and turned. "Uh-huh," he said before going down the hall to his room.

Chapter Fourteen

Sheri took a deep breath and then glanced at the crowd. The committee agreed that holding the question-and-answer session with town leaders at the Connecting the Community event outside instead of crowding everyone inside the store used for the neighborhood watch meetings was the best way to get more participation. The town agreed to set up a stage in the vacant lot between the old record store and the pizza parlor. They'd also supplied the chairs for people to sit, and a microphone.

The amount of people who were picking their seat for the question-and-answer session surprised Sheri. The entire turnout for the event had surprised her. Sure, she'd hoped they would have a lot of people come through, but Sheri was a realist. She hadn't had much hope that a huge crowd would show up for what was essentially a public meeting. But they had. The amount of participation in the event had blown everyone away. The shops along the strip had several new visitors. The vendors stayed busy, and the weather was perfect enough for the beachgoers who'd come just to enjoy the water to also wander up to see what was happening.

Someone stepped to Sheri's right. Sheri turned and met the eyes of the police chief. She liked Chief Montgomery well enough. The woman seemed to be interested in turning around the police department and doing what was right for the town and the residents. But, after what Deandre said about the chief's concerns with their relationship, she wasn't sure if the woman liked her.

"You ready?" Chief Montgomery asked, nodding toward the crowd.

Sheri shrugged. "Ready as I'm going to be."

"How did you get picked to moderate the panel discussion?"

"Since I'm the de facto chair of the planning committee, I was *encouraged* to do it."

She kept her voice light, but her stomach was a jumble of nerves. Sheri could talk to almost anyone, but public speaking wasn't her thing. She'd wanted to help from the background, but when the rest of the group had urged her to serve as moderator for this panel, she'd agreed. The discussion had been her idea. She'd been up half the night practicing what she was going to say so she wouldn't screw anything up.

Montgomery stared at her quietly for a second before nodding as if the answer were acceptable. Sheri just stopped herself from rolling her eyes. She didn't like being assessed by the police chief.

"I'm not here because Lieutenant King wants to show off his new girlfriend," Sheri said. "You don't have to worry about that."

Montgomery's shoulders stiffened before her eyes narrowed. "I wasn't worried about that. Lieutenant King knows how important this event is. For all of us."

"I do, too. I care about this area because I'm from Sunshine Beach and I hung out here as a kid. I don't want to see the town turn it into a carbon copy of the bougie, touristy north end, and I don't want them to ignore us and treat it like a crime-riddled problem. We're on the same side."

Again, Chief Montgomery stared at Sheri for a long moment before lifting and lowering her head. "He said you cared."

Sheri lifted a brow. "Believe him now?"

"I do."

She wouldn't dare show it, but relief rushed through her. Instead, she gave Chief Montgomery the same stiff nod that she'd given Sheri. She believed Deandre when he said he didn't care what people thought about their relationship. That didn't mean she wanted his boss to think she was somehow going to ruin his career or reputation.

"The rest of the group is here. Let's get started."

Chief Montgomery took her seat. They'd pulled together an impressive panel—the town manager, solicitor, county sheriff, mayor and district attorney. Sheri hoped everyone's participation was a good thing and meant they took reinvestment in the south end seriously.

Sheri looked back at the crowd. Deandre stood at the back with several other officers. He gave her a smile and thumbs-up. She lifted her hand in a quick wave, before bringing the microphone to her face.

"We'll get started now. Thank you all for coming out to the south end neighborhood's Connecting the Community event. The growth and success of the south end equals growth and success for all of Sunshine Beach. Which is why we have many of the leaders from the town and the county here today to talk about their plans to continue to reinvest and keep the south end safe for everyone."

There was a round of applause and cheers from Kelly and Ivy. Sheri grinned and relaxed. Having the rest of the business owners here helped calm some of her nerves. She wanted this event to go off perfectly, so everyone would see the great things the south end had to offer.

"Administrator, I'll start with you. The town has invested heavily in retrofitting the vacant buildings here and partnering with small businesses like mine as part of their revitalization efforts. Can you tell us what led to that decision?"

The panel discussion went smoothly. As a business owner, Sheri was glad to hear from everyone on the panel about the ways they wanted to see the community continue to thrive—from more investment by the town to help businesses grow, to the connection of law enforcement to connect people to mental health and substance abuse assistance as a way to help address crime. By the time they opened the discussion to questions from the audience, Sheri was leaning back in the chair relaxed and happy about how great things had turned out.

Kelly gave the sign that there were five minutes left. Sheri sat forward and spoke in the mic. "We've got time for one last question." She looked at the woman standing at the microphone they'd set up in the crowd for questions. "Go ahead."

"This question is for you," she said with a raised brow and pursed lips.

Sheri sat up straight and returned the woman's direct stare. She looked kinda familiar, but Sheri couldn't immediately place her. "Okay, what's your question?"

"I think it's great that you pulled this together, considering you also have a criminal record. Was that part of the reason why you chose to have this event?"

Sheri sucked in a breath. Had she misheard? She must have misheard, because that question had nothing to do with the event and was a shot aimed right for Sheri.

She focused on her again and realized she was someone from her aunt's church. One of the people who always had something negative to say. Sheri didn't want to sit here and accept being disrespected. She also couldn't curse the woman out like she wanted to with so many law enforcement officers on the stage. No, Sheri had to be the bigger person. She had to prove she wasn't the same hotheaded person this woman was trying to prove her to be.

"Ma'am, I have no criminal record." Mostly true. She was never convicted for the damage to Tyrone's car. "I'm a business owner who cares about the community. I also know the importance of second chances. I don't shy away from any mistake I may have made. I got the chance to be a part of the city's program to bring life back to a part of town I care about. I want to do my part. I don't participate in idle gossip or spend energy trying to tear other people down. I suggest that anyone who wants to see things get better do the same."

There was applause from the crowd. Kelly was already next to the woman and took the microphone before she could answer. The lady glared at Sheri. Sheri stared back with a fake smile on her face. She was not going to give this woman the benefit of getting a rise out of her.

Sheri stood, and the rest of the panel thanked her for doing a great job. She smiled and nodded patiently, but she wanted to get off that stage, find the woman and ask just what the hell did she think she was doing. But that would only embarrass Sheri and make a scene.

Despite the negative last question, several people came up to Sheri when she left the stage and thanked her for doing a great job pulling everything together. By the time she escaped them, the crowd had dispersed, she didn't see her hater anywhere and the only ones around were family and friends.

Her mom and Cora came over. "You did a great job!" her mom said, pride in her eyes.

"Don't worry about that woman," Cora said. "We'll deal with her later."

A hand rested on Sheri's shoulder. Deandre. "No need to deal with anyone. Sheri already dealt with her."

Sheri grinned at him. "Did I?"

"She ran out of here with her tail tucked between her legs." He squeezed her shoulder. "Great job."

That was true. Sheri had long moved on from the mistakes of her past. The life and relationships she had now was more important than having it out with someone whose opinion didn't really matter.

"Everything did turn out pretty good, didn't it?" she said. "Hopefully it'll help. And we'll get more people to join the neighborhood watch." She looked at her mom. "How's the restaurant?"

Her mom had managed things for Sheri earlier in the day, but said she would leave to see the panel. "Good. Don't worry. We know how to close things out. I told the family to come to my house later this evening to celebrate you showing the town who's boss."

"I didn't do all that," Sheri said, grinning.

"Girl, you know your mom don't need much of a reason to have a cookout," Cora said.

"True." She looked at Deandre. "Want to come eat with us tonight?"

"You won't be tired after all this?" Concern filled his dark eyes and he squeezed her shoulder again.

The last of Sheri's irritation melted away. She was tired, but she'd drink ten cups of coffee if she needed to stay up and spend more time with him. "I'll be good. Besides, it's just a small family thing. Bring DJ with you."

Maybe if his son was with him, he wouldn't have a good reason to pull Deandre away.

"You sure?"

She nodded. "I am." She had a feeling DJ didn't like her, but she was going to at least try.

"Cool. We'll swing through."

Chapter Fifteen

Deandre had a different definition of "a small thing" compared with Sheri. That's what he thought as Sheri introduced him and DJ to her aunts, uncles and several cousins. He was pretty good at remembering names, but he doubted every name would stick. There were at least three Willies and four Ericas.

DJ had not been excited about coming. Not that he'd said anything, but his lack of words and excess sighs expressed his lack of interest more than if he'd complained. Thankfully, some of Sheri's younger cousins knew DJ from school and pulled him in with the group of other teenagers.

Sheri took him over to a table with her uncles and a few male cousins. "Sit tight while I fix you a plate."

Deandre shook his head. "I can fix my own plate."

She grinned and patted his shoulder. "I know. It's my rule. First time you're here, I'll fix your plate. After that, you're on your own."

Her uncle, the first Willie if he remembered correctly, chimed in. "You better let her go on and fix you a plate." The other guys at the table agreed.

"You all be nice to Deandre until I get back." Sheri pointed at each of the men at the table.

Willie waved her away. "We got him. And make sure you bring him the big piece of chicken."

Sheri rolled her eyes before walking away. Deandre sat in one of the black plastic chairs set around the fold out table.

"Lil Bit must really like you," Willie said, grinning. "I ain't never seen her fix any man a plate."

The guy next to him, her cousin Kenny, he thought, nodded. "She sure doesn't. Not even before that mess with Tyrone."

Willie elbowed Kenny. "Don't be telling all of Lil Bit's business."

Kenny pointed to Deandre. "Hell, he knows. He's the one who arrested her."

Willie's eyes widened before narrowing. "You a cop?"

Deandre nodded. "I am. Hope you don't hold it against me."

"Depends. You a good one or a bad one?"

"I try real hard to be a good one. And I don't put up with the bad ones."

That seemed to satisfy her uncle because he nodded. "Well, if Lil Bit likes you, then you might be alright. But, for real, you arrested her?"

He wasn't about to dig up that situation today. "So, Willie, I heard that red sixty-seven Chevy out front is yours," Deandre said. "You remodeled that yourself?"

Willie laughed and wagged a finger at Deandre. "I see what you're doing. Cool, cool. You must like Lil Bit, too. Good. She's a good woman. Treat her right."

"That's my plan."

"That is my Chevy out front. Man, I had to drive all the way to New Jersey to get that engine."

Willie spent the next thirty minutes talking about the work he'd done to remodel the truck. He followed that up by taking Deandre to look under the hood and then for a test drive to see how well it ran. Deandre took it all in stride. He had a feeling Willie was partially checking him out. He found out through their conversation that he was Sheri's mother's brother. He'd been the father figure in her house after, per Willie, Sheri's dad hadn't bothered to live up to his responsibilities.

Sheri rushed up to him as soon as he and her uncle pulled back onto the side of the road. The driveway and front yard were filled with cars.

"Uncle Willie, where did you take him?"

"Just for a ride. What? Your man can't spend some time with your uncle?"

"He's here to spend some time with me," she said with a sly grin.

Deandre walked over and wrapped his arm around her shoulder. "I had fun with your uncle. The truck runs like a dream."

"Told you it would," Willie said as if Deandre shouldn't have expected anything less. "You two go on and get your time in. I'm going to get me a piece of pound cake."

"You better hurry," Sheri said. "They cut it ten minutes ago. I made it, so you know it's going to go fast."

"Damn, let me hurry up. Come around again, Deandre." Willie threw up a hand before power walking toward the backyard where the food was set up.

Sheri laughed and turned to him. Deandre kept his hands on her hips. "Sorry about that. Uncle Willie loves that truck, and if you show a hint of interest, he'll take up all your time."

She'd changed into a loose, dark blue sundress that skimmed over her curves and constantly drew his eyes to the sway of her hips. The Lil Bit necklace sparkled in the late afternoon sunlight just above her cleavage.

Deandre tried to pull his mind away from how good her hips felt beneath his hands. And how much he wanted to pull her closer kiss the spot above her necklace. "I really didn't mind. He's a cool guy. Loves you, a lot."

"I know. He's like a dad. He helped mom a lot when I was growing up. I think he still tries to look out for me. He likes you if he told you to come around again."

"That's a good thing. I'd like to come around some more." He glanced toward the backyard. "How's DJ?"

"Good, actually. He's still hanging out with my cousins. They were playing Uno a little while ago."

Deandre pulled out his phone with one hand and texted. You okay? To DJ. He quickly texted back. I'm good.

Deandre smiled and slid his phone back into his pocket. "I'm glad he's having fun."

"I was going to my place to grab the other pound cake I made. I didn't lie when I said the first one was going to go fast. I always keep an extra hidden so that I can have a slice. Want a piece before everyone else gets it?"

"You had the energy to make a pound cake after the event today?"

She gave a sly wink. "Me and my momma made them yesterday. She planned this cookout weeks ago to celebrate me becoming a community activist."

She walked toward her house, and he followed from behind. He put his hands on her bared shoulders and gently massaged. He couldn't help but touch her. "You know you're amazing, right?"

She grinned over her shoulder. "I know."

The quiet inside her house was welcome after the noise of the music and conversation from everyone outside. Even though Uncle Willie was cool, he'd talked nonstop for the past hour. The few minutes inside her place were the first moments they'd had the chance to be alone for a long time.

Deandre took Sheri's hand to stop her from picking up the cake. She faced him and raised her brow. "What's up?"

"Nothing. I'm finally alone with you. I can't help but want to do this." He pulled her into his arms. She came willingly. Her arms wrapped around his neck, and she lifted on her toes to kiss him.

He felt like he hadn't kissed her in years. Had it only been a few days since he held her in his arms? Why did a few days without her feel like he'd gone nearly a lifetime? Why did every moment he spent with her still not feel like enough time? He knew why, but he wasn't ready to say it out loud. But damn, if holding her like this didn't make his feelings impossible to ignore.

She pulled back and smiled at him. Emotion tightened around his heart. He was so close to losing himself when it came to this woman.

"If you keep kissing me like this I'm going to forget about that cake and take advantage of us having a few minutes alone." The devilish spark in her eye combined with the huskiness of her tone made him instantly hard.

He knew exactly how he wanted her to take advantage of their time alone. "Will anyone come looking for you?"

The teasing light left her eye and desire flashed instead. "No. What about..."

"He's good and distracted."

They stared at each other, contemplating how long they had before they'd be missed or people would start wondering what was taking so long. He wanted their first time together to be special. Drawn out. Where he had the chance to savor every part of her body. But the look in her eye and the way her hips pressed forward against him said there would be enough time for drawn out and savor later. He hadn't been spontaneous or felt this rush of excitement in years. The responsible cop and parent in him knew they should get the cake and go back to the cookout. The man who'd had the time with her in his arms interrupted too much said take everything he could get now.

Sheri saw the moment he made the decision and she wanted to jump for joy. There was no time for jumping. Not when they only had a few minutes together. She lifted on her toes, wrapped her arms around his neck and kissed him with all the restrained desire pulsing through her body. The second he'd gotten out of his car wearing a beige T-shirt that clung to his chest and shoulders and those shorts that showed off his strong legs she'd wanted to climb him like a tree.

Deandre's kiss was just as hot and urgent as hers. Did he feel the same way she did? As if she would explode into a thousand pieces if she didn't get the chance to touch him? To feel his body against hers? The way his hands gripped her breasts and behind said he had to. She wished they had more time, but that would wait until another day. The weeks of interruptions and broken dates were the longest foreplay she'd ever had.

They moved frantically, knowing each second could be interrupted like so many precious seconds before. She slid her fingers beneath his shirt, marveled at the warm softness of his skin over the hard muscles beneath. Deandre moaned, low and deep, before his large hand palmed her breast through the thin material of her dress. His fingers rubbed over, then toyed with the hardened tip until she whimpered and pushed forward for more.

He wrapped an arm around her waist and lifted her up. Sheri grinned and wrapped her legs around his waist. Yes, he most definitely felt the way she felt.

Deandre moved and set her on the kitchen table. The table wobbled, nearly toppling Sheri to the floor.

"In the chair," she said laughing. "If this ends because you drop me I'm going to strangle you."

Deandre grinned as he kicked out the chair and sat with her straddling his waist. "I'll strangle my damn self."

She rolled her hips to push his erection against the juncture of her thighs. Pleasure exploded through her body. She reached down and pulled at the button of his shorts. Deandre stopped her movement by tugging on the straps of her sundress and bra. Pinning her arms against her side, she wiggled and he tugged until her arms were free and she reached around to unhook the bra until her breasts spilled out.

Deandre moaned. "You don't know how much I think about your breasts."

The raw desire in his voice nearly pushed her over the edge. "How much?"

"Every damn time you wear this necklace." He leaned forward and kissed her chest right above her Lil Bit necklace. "You play with it and usually when you're wearing a low-cut shirt. Then all I can think about is your chest, your breasts and what I want to do to them."

Sheri's breathing hitched and she arched her back. "Show me what you want to do."

"Yes, ma'am." His warm hands cupped her breasts, lifting them before he sucked the hard tips between his lips. Sheri twisted her hips. Her hands grasped the sides of his head. Wanting more and never wanting this moment to end.

She reached for his waistband again. Deandre dropped one hand to quickly unfasten the button while his other hand and mouth remained on her breast. They shifted and shoved until his pants and underwear were out of the way and he sprang free.

"Do you have a condom?" she asked.

"My wallet." He reached down into the back pocket of his shorts and pulled out the wallet and then the condom.

"You're always this ready?"

"Since we started dating? Hell yes."

Sheri grinned, loving the need and urgency in his voice. He quickly opened the foil package and covered himself. Then he placed his hand on her back and pulled her forward. "Come back here."

"Yes, sir," she said, her voice thick with need.

She took his solid length in her hand. He was thick and hard and felt so damn wonderful as she slid down on him. They both groaned with pleasure before their lips came together in a hard kiss. She rocked back and forth. Taking him deeper. Moaning with each movement because every touch and slide was better than the one before.

Deandre's hands gripped her waist. His strong arms guided her up and down first in slow, deep strokes that grew fast, more frantic and urgent. She gripped his shoulders, her head thrown back as her world constricted to nothing else but the feel of him inside her, his strong hand on her hip, his lips on her breasts and the pleasure rushing through her body. He pulled the tip of her breast deep into his mouth and she was lost. She shattered into a million stars as her body squeezed around him. He cried out with his own release, his fingers digging hard into her hip as his body jerked.

Sheri collapsed against his chest. Their breathing was choppy as they both came down. She lifted her head. He watched her through slitted lids, contentment and another emotion she couldn't quite name on his face. Because she believed in fairy tales and perfect endings, she wanted to believe that was love on his face. But it was too soon for that, right?

Deandre cupped the back of her head and pulled her

forward to kiss her slowly. As if they had all the time in the world and didn't need to rush back before people came looking for them. Her heart fluttered. Maybe it was too soon, but it was too late for Sheri. She was falling hard and fast in love again.

Chapter Sixteen

"Another good day," Sheri said to her mom and Cora as she put the bank deposit for the next morning in the safe.

"Sure was," her mom said. She leaned against the door-frame of the office. "I think more people came out after seeing you at the event on Saturday."

"Well, I'll take it." Sheri closed the safe and double-checked the lock. "We were doing good already, but I'll never turn down more business."

Cora pointed at Sheri and grinned. "Ain't that right."

Sheri and her mom both laughed. Sheri's phone chimed. She picked it up and checked the text message.

I've got an hour alone.

Sheri grinned as she quickly replied. Where?

My place? DJ just left to see his grandparents.

OMW!

"Sheri!" Cora's voice snapped. "Girl, why are you grinning at your phone like that?"

Sheri shrugged and stood. "I've got to go."

Her mom shook her head. "It's Deandre. That man has her acting brand-new."

Sheri let out an incredulous laugh. "No he doesn't."

"Yes he does. Normally, I'd tell you to be careful, but I like Deandre. Even if he is a cop. Willie said he's a nice guy."

And that's all it had taken for her mom to warm up to Deandre. She didn't trust most men, but if her brother gave a guy the stamp of approval, then she was willing to give him a chance. Sheri didn't care if her uncle's cosign was what it took for her mom to be okay with her dating Deandre. She was just glad that their relationship wouldn't be a problem.

"That's because he *is* a nice guy," Sheri said. "I guess it's true that there are a few of them left out there."

Cora smirked. "Are you sure he's nice or are you just blinded by the sex?"

"What?"

"You heard me. We all know it don't take that long to get a cake from your house."

Sheri's cheeks burned. Really? Cora had to call her out right now in front of her mom. Her mom knew she wasn't a virgin, but that didn't mean she wanted to be called out for getting a quickie at a family cookout.

"Mind your business, Cora," Sheri warned. "Let's get out of here." She left the office and went toward the back door.

"I'm just saying," Cora said, following her.

"No, you're just doing too much."

Her mom spoke from behind them. "It's okay, Lil Bit. He is a nice guy. Don't be embarrassed for enjoying each other."

"Thanks, Ma." Sheri wanted the entire conversation to end.

Cora, unfortunately, wasn't ready to let it end. "You don't have to be embarrassed, but you do need to be careful."

"Careful for what? Deandre is cool. He's respectful and isn't about playing games. It's all good."

They went out the back door and Sheri pulled out the key to lock it behind them.

"Yeah, well, you better watch that son of his."

Sheri frowned. "DJ? Why?"

"Emory said that he was bragging about being in a gang," Cora said, referring to one of their younger, teenage cousins.

Sheri nearly dropped her keys. "What? He's not in a gang."

"Well, that's what he said," Cora spoke as if she were repeating the God's honest truth. "He said him and his boys control this end of the beach and that everyone knows not to go messing with their group."

"Emory must have misheard. DJ wouldn't be in a gang. His dad is a cop."

"Yeah," her mom agreed. "Let's be honest. I love Emory, but the girl likes to exaggerate. Besides, there aren't any gangs in Sunshine Beach."

Not exactly true, but DJ and his friends hardly qualified as a gang. "I've seen DJ with his friends, and they don't look like a gang. They look like regular teenagers who hang around the area."

Cora waved off Sheri's words. She gave Sheri a look that was both pitying and disbelieving. "You're just being delusional because you're all into Deandre."

Sheri stopped walking and faced her cousin. "I'm not being delusional. I'm also not going to start spreading rumors about gangs in the south end. Especially rumors that Deandre's son is part of one."

Cora put a hand on her hip. "It's not a rumor when the boy said it himself."

"Did you hear him say that?"

Cora glanced away before lifting her chin defiantly. "I'm telling you what Emory said."

"We all love Emory, but Mom is right. She can exaggerate. I think you just want to try and find something wrong with Deandre."

Cora's jaw dropped. "Ain't nobody trying to find something wrong with Deandre."

"Really, Cora? Don't even play like that. It's what you do. You always hate on whatever guy I'm dating. I'm not following you down the yellow brick road this time." Sheri turned to stalk away from her cousin.

"I don't know what you're talking about. I don't lead you down any roads."

Sheri spun back. "Yes you do. You always try to find something wrong and push me into doing something dumb."

"You make your own decisions. Don't blame me because you pick the wrong guys."

"No, Cora, you pick the wrong guys. And then you want to find something wrong with every guy that I try to spend time with. It's not going to work this time. I'm not going to let you bad-mouth Deandre or his son."

Her mom stepped between them. "Both of ya'll stop right now. You are not about to fall out in this parking lot over a man. You're family. You understand me?"

Her mom's intervention did nothing to calm Sheri's irritation. "I understand, Ma, but it has to be said. Cora is going too far."

Cora rolled her eyes. "You know what, I don't know why I'm even talking to you. When you figure out that his son is some wanna-be thug, then I'll be the first to tell you I told you so." Cora turned and stomped off.

"You won't be telling me anything," Sheri called after her.

Her mom put her hand on Sheri's arm. "Lil Bit, stop. Why are you being like that with your cousin?"

"Because, Ma, you know how she is. She makes everything worse and always looks for the negative."

"But she doesn't mean you any harm."

"Yes she does. She did it before and she'll do it again."

Her mom pointed. "Don't go blaming Cora for the decisions you made. Did she egg you on? Yes, but at the end of the day you took the bat to that man's car."

"Ma." Sheri wanted to argue. Her mom was supposed to take her side. Dorothy Jean didn't give her a chance to continue.

"Don't 'Ma' me. It's the truth. Cora isn't perfect, and she was wrong for encouraging you, but you can't go putting all your activities on account of her."

"But she made things worse." Not just that night, but by spreading rumors when she was jealous. Not to mention the way she constantly ditched Sheri whenever some new guy came around. Cora was family, but she didn't always act like a good friend.

"Then be mad at her for the things *she* did. Not for the things you did. And I don't know if Emory is right or not, but where there's smoke there's usually fire."

"You think DJ is in a gang? Seriously?"

"I don't know enough about the boy to say anything about him. But if Deandre really is your man, then how about you tell him what was said at the party. Let him figure it out before you get lost in love. Because if he is in a gang, then honey, you're signing up for a lot more than what you bargained for."

* * *

Deandre bit the corner of his lip as he watched Sheri stretch as she sat on the edge of his bed. She raised her arms high over her head with her back arched and her breasts pushed forward. Even though they'd just made love, he wanted to pull her back into the bed and get lost in her body all over again.

"I needed that." Sheri grinned at him over her shoulder.

"Did you?" He shifted on the bed until his legs straddled her and his feet rested next to hers on the floor. He wrapped his arms around her waist and brought her back to his chest.

She nodded and leaned into him. "I did. It was a busy day at the restaurant."

Deandre kissed her shoulder and breathed in the sweet scent of her skin. "There are a lot more people on the south end of the beach since the event. Which is a good thing."

"Do you think things will get better?"

"I think it showed the town leaders that the people in the area are serious about making things even better. Montgomery also told me they heard loud and clear that the business owners and residents don't want us coming through with a heavy hand. I think they finally understand and are good with us becoming a part of the community."

Her eyes widened and she squeezed his arms still around her waist. "That's great. I'm telling you things aren't that bad."

"I know they aren't."

She moved to get up, but he held on to her. "You sure you don't want to stick around for dinner? DJ will be home soon and can join us."

Her body stiffened. Deandre let her go. She didn't pull away but she shifted so that she could look at him. "I don't know. I'm trying not to come on too strong around him. I think we need to ease into the time together."

"I know what he's been doing."

She glanced away. "What do you mean?"

"You know what I mean. We both know he's been trying to keep us separated. I talked to him about it."

Her body relaxed and relief filled her gaze. "What did he say?"

"He said he wasn't trying to do that. Then made me feel guilty for saying that he was calling just to interrupt us."

She cringed. "Dang."

"Yeah. I don't want him to think I don't want him around or calling when we're together. That's why I asked you to stay. I'm thinking you and I are going to be together for a while. I want him to get used to you being a part of our life."

"You want me to be a part of your life?"

The hopeful smile on her face made his lips turn up. "Yeah. I told you I'm not about sleeping around. I like you. We're good together. I'd like to see where this goes."

The seconds she took to study him while chewing on the corner of her lip were the longest, sexiest seconds in his life. "So would I."

"I'm not asking you to step in and be DJ's mom or anything. But I would like for the two of you to start getting along."

"I would like to get along with him."

"So will you stay?" She glanced away again. Deandre frowned. "What's wrong?"

She shifted until she could face him better, her hand resting on his thigh. "I need to tell you something. It's part of the reason I was so wound up when I got here."

Dread tightened his shoulders. Things were going so

well, he hoped she wasn't having any concerns about their relationship. "What is it?"

"Something my cousin Cora said. Which, I don't believe because she's always stirring up trouble."

"What did she say?"

She sighed and looked like she didn't want to say it. He gently squeezed her hand. She met his eyes. "She says that at the cookout the other day, DJ was bragging about being in a gang."

Deandre jerked back. "A what?"

"I know. It's the dumbest thing. There's no way he would be in a gang when his dad is a cop. Then she started talking about how I shouldn't get involved with you because of DJ and that you weren't as great as I thought. That's why I don't believe her. I think she's just trying to start problems."

Deandre swung his leg from around her and sat on the edge of the bed. He shook his head. "He couldn't."

"I don't believe it."

Deandre thought about the last few months. The withdrawal from the things DJ usually liked. The new set of friends that he didn't want to bring around. The way he was cagey with his answers about whom he'd been with and what they were doing. "He wouldn't."

Sheri placed a hand on his knee. "I know. Cora is just being messy."

"But if he's saying things like that, then I need to talk to him about it."

"I'm not trying to get him into trouble."

"I know you're not, but I'm glad you told me." All kinds of thoughts and concerns spiraled through his brain. Had he missed something so big with DJ?

"Look, I can't prove he really said that. It's what I got

from Cora, who said our younger cousin Emory heard him say this. This is literally hearsay."

"Even if it's hearsay, I still need to let him know. If he said it, then I need to know why. If he didn't say it, then I need to find out what he said that could have made them think that."

Maybe it was just a mix-up. Confusion over a turn of phrase. He could make sure DJ was aware that words held power and could cause big problems if he wasn't clear.

"Wait, do you think there's something to this?"

The concern in her eyes mirrored his own. He was glad that she cared. Glad that she'd told him and was still willing to stick with him in this relationship after hearing something so negative about his kid. Something he prayed was not true.

"I don't know. But he has changed in the last few months. I don't know what's going on with him. I'd rather rule this out than pretend as if he never would get involved with the wrong crowd and be wrong."

Chapter Seventeen

Deandre sat up on the couch when the sound of the key in the front door's lock echoed through the quiet. Sheri had left two hours ago when it was obvious that DJ wasn't coming home anytime soon. When he'd called his in-laws to see if they were still with DJ, he'd been shocked to learn that DJ had never made it to their place.

Deandre had been disappointed and confused. DJ's lie wasn't one that he would be able to get away with. Which meant he didn't care about being caught. Deandre wasn't sure what was going on with his son, but he was going to get to the bottom of everything tonight. He'd tried to respect DJ's space and give him the room he needed to go through whatever teenage transition he was having. But lying to him was something he was not going to accept.

The front door opened, and Deandre waited. There was no need to rush forward. DJ would see him as soon as he crossed the threshold. His son walked in slowly, his brow furled and shoulders slumped. He quietly closed the door and locked it behind him. When he turned and entered the living area, his gaze collided with Deandre's. He paused for a second, eyes wide as if for a split second he was surprised to find his dad there. Maybe a part of him had hoped he wouldn't get caught. But the second of surprise quickly faded, and DJ straightened his shoulders and lifted his chin.

Deandre clenched his hands into fists. This was what they were doing? His son was really going to flex on him? After he'd done wrong? The level of audacity made Deandre's stomach churn and his blood boil. He took a long breath and calmed himself. They were going to have a showdown, but he was the adult. This wasn't going to go anywhere if he let anger rule him.

"Where have you been?" Deandre asked.

DJ glanced away and rubbed his chin before looking back. "With some friends."

"You were supposed to be going to your grandparents' house."

DJ lifted a shoulder. "My plans changed."

"You didn't think to tell me about your change of plans?"

"I didn't think you'd care."

Deandre frowned so hard his forehead hurt. He slowly stood and crossed his arms. "Why wouldn't I care? When I called your grandparents, and they said you never came by, they were worried. They thought something happened to you."

Guilt flashed in DJ's dark eyes before he blinked it away and lifted his chin again. "I didn't tell them I was coming. There wasn't any reason for them to worry."

"But you told me that. I expected you to be with them. They weren't the only ones worrying. I worried."

"Well, I'm fine now." DJ patted the front of his hoodie and joggers as if to support the statement.

"Fine now?" Deandre paused, breathed, then continued. "Boy, have you lost your damn mind? You don't change your plans and tell me you're going one place and then go somewhere else. That's not how this works. You're supposed to call me."

"You told me not to call when you're with *Sheri*." DJ rolled his eyes and said Sheri's name as if it were some kind of disease.

Deandre uncrossed his arms and planted his hands on his hips. "You know good and damn well that isn't what I said or what I meant. Now, if you have a problem with Sheri, then you tell me that straight up. What you won't do is try to use that as a reason to lie to me. Now give me your phone."

DJ scowled. "For what?"

"You know what for. You're on punishment. You aren't allowed to leave this house except to go to school, to be with me or with your grandparents. You can't use your phone, laptop or any other electronic device in this house for anything other than homework. I'm disabling the internet on everything in here."

DJ scoffed. "Whatever." He pulled out his cell phone.

Deandre crossed the room and snatched it from his son. Then he froze. He sniffed the air and leaned in closer. His eyes narrowed as he realized what he smelled. "Were you smoking weed?"

DJ's eyes widened. "What? Nah! I swear!"

"You've already lied to me once. Don't lie to me again. I know what weed smells like and I smell it on you. Is it true? Are you in a gang?"

"Dad, I wasn't smoking weed. Some guy I knew had it—"

"Some guy you knew? Are these the so-called friends you're hanging with? No, we're not doing that. I didn't want to believe Sheri but—"

"Sheri? So, she's snitching on me again?" Disbelief filled DJ's voice.

"She's not snitching. If there's something going on with my son, then I need to know. Gangs and drugs? DJ, how could you?"

"I'm not—"

"You're getting tested."

"What?" DJ's eyes bugged with disbelief. He threw up his hands.

"Right now." He grabbed his son's arm and pulled him down the hall to Deandre's room. Deandre went into the bathroom and pulled out the at-home drug test he kept. Something he never thought he'd have to use.

"Do this. Right now."

"Dad, you're really going to drug-test me?"

Deandre tossed the box and DJ caught it. He crossed his arms and glared. "Yes. I really am."

Sheri didn't see Deandre again until later in the week. He'd given her an update via text and phone calls of what DJ had been up to. She was glad that he'd made his way home safely, while also hating the fact that Deandre had worried about him. She'd even called her mom to apologize for some of the antics she'd done as a kid.

"I didn't realize how much kids could make their parents worry," she'd said as she'd sat on the porch with her mom and aunt the night before.

"You never stop worrying. You and Cora would get into some things, but thankfully you were never too bad. At least I didn't have to worry about you being in a gang or anything."

Sheri had nothing to say to that. Deandre hadn't confirmed the rumor about DJ being in a gang. But that hadn't stopped Cora from making sure everyone in the family knew. Sheri was so done with her cousin and her antics. But she'd deal with that later.

When Deandre texted her at work and asked if he could come by after she got off, she'd quickly agreed. She missed him. And even though DJ wasn't her son, she wanted him to be okay. She worried that she was the reason for his acting out. She was falling hard for Deandre, but she didn't want to be the reason he and his son grew further apart.

Deandre looked tired when he got to her place. She cut him a huge slice of the lemon pound cake she'd baked and set it in front of him at the table. Despite the weariness in his eyes, his face lit up at the sight of the cake.

"When did you have time to bake this?"

"Don't worry about all that." She'd baked the cake during the day at work. "Just eat. You probably skipped lunch again today."

"I ate lunch. It just wasn't as good as your fried chicken."

"You should have come by the restaurant."

He shook his head. "Busy day. We're looking into the suspected gang activity in the south end."

She sat next to him. "There really is a gang problem?"

"Some kids are grouping up. It started with two separate groups fighting during the football season and the problem's escalating. We're figuring out a plan with the school district to see if we can curb it before things turn violent."

"Is DJ...?"

He sighed and shrugged. "I can't prove anything. I drug-tested him. It came back negative. Thankfully. But he's hanging with some kids that I do think are a part of the problem."

"What can we do?"

He looked up from the cake and raised a brow. "We?"

"If I can help in any way, I want to. I know I'm not family, but I care about you. Which means I care about DJ."

He took her hand in his. "You don't know how much I appreciate that. I wish DJ would give you a chance."

The words iced her heart. She pulled on her hand. "He doesn't like me."

Deandre didn't let her go. "He doesn't know you."

"But he doesn't want to try and know me. If I'm the problem..."

"You're not." He squeezed her hand.

"I'm part of the problem. Or you dating me is making it worse. Do you think we should—"

"No," he said firmly. "Let's give it some time."

"We've given it time. I don't want to end things, but maybe we do need to take a step back. Let you focus on DJ and whatever is going on with the kids he's hanging around. I know it's not ideal, but it's probably the right thing for now."

He sat up straight. "You want to break up?"

She shook her head and her hands. "No, hell no! We're just chilling for a while. If you're not available or have family and work stuff, I understand. Right now, DJ is your priority and I respect that."

Deandre put down the fork. He placed his hand on the back of her head and pulled her forward for a kiss. It was quick and hard and made Sheri want to climb on his lap and take him deep. When he pulled back, she was breathless.

"Thank you for being great," he said.

Sheri's cheeks tingled as she grinned. "You just like my pound cake."

"No. I like you. And hopefully, we'll get through this."

Chapter Eighteen

Sheri walked into the alley behind her restaurant and froze. The space was darker than usual. The overhead lights that illuminated the back doors of the businesses were out. It wasn't unusual for one or two to go out. They weren't the LED lights that lasted forever, but for them all to be out wasn't normal. She'd decided to go into the restaurant early to work on the schedule for the following week before everyone else came in and things got busy. She hadn't seen Deandre in two weeks, and when he'd texted her last night asking if they could meet up when she got off, she'd immediately said yes.

She missed him. Way more than she'd thought she would. So, getting up earlier than usual so she could get out of there as soon as possible after closing was an easy decision. They hadn't had problems with break-ins since the Connecting the Community event, so she also hadn't worried that whoever had tried to rob the place weeks ago would be back.

What little light came from the streetlights and waning glow from the moon glinted off broken glass on the ground behind the building. The lights weren't out because the bulbs were old. They were out because someone had vandalized the building.

She pulled out her cell phone and turned on the flashlight. The light from her phone seemed bright as the sun when she used it at home, but in the dark alley it felt inadequate. She studied the area but there weren't any signs that anyone was still there. She just needed to unlock the door, get in and then she'd call the police. The business owners had gone in together to purchase cameras to monitor the alley as part of the recommendations to have better surveillance in the area. The police could pull the footage and they'd quickly find out who'd done it. Probably just some bored kids, and no one who meant any real harm.

She pulled her keys out of her purse and then quickly walked to the back door. The hairs on the back of her neck stood up as soon as she put the key into the lock and turned. A second later, the sound of footsteps hurrying down the alley echoed off the building.

Sheri turned to see two figures approaching her fast. She didn't wait to find out what was going on. She opened the door and rushed inside, her heart pounding. She tried to turn and slam the door, but the people behind her were already there. One of them slammed into the door. The impact was so sudden and unexpected that Sheri stumbled back.

The person came inside, followed by another figure. They wore masks over their faces and were dressed in all black. She guessed based on their size that they were male, but from what she could see of the first one, she immediately assumed teenager or young adult.

"What do you want?" She tried not to sound intimidated despite her racing heart and the cold sweat breaking out over her body.

"The money in the safe. All of it," the guy said. Definitely a teenager.

Sheri frowned. "I don't have money in a safe."

"You've got money in here. I know you do. Now get it."

Sheri held up her hand and shook her head. "Look, I don't keep cash in here like that. I'm not a bank or a convenience store. If you're looking for money, you came to the wrong place."

She did have money in the safe in the office, but there was no way she'd let on that there was anything there. She needed them to leave as soon as possible. And preferably without damage to her or the restaurant.

"That's a lie. Now give me the money." He reached into his pocket and pulled out a gun.

Sheri's heart dropped to her stomach. The room spun and she took a step back, arms raised. "I swear I don't have anything."

The other kid stepped forward. "Hey, J, you said you were just going to scare her."

The first one looked at the second. "And if she doesn't give us the money, I'm really going to scare her."

Sheri blinked. She had to be hearing this wrong. "DJ?"

The second kid's eyes swung to her. Her stomach twisted into a tight knot. She shook her head. No, not DJ. Why in the world would he be robbing her?

The first kid, J, stepped into her line of sight. Gun still pointed straight at Sheri. "To hell with that. I'm not playing. Give me the money or I'm going to shoot your ass."

"Yo, J, hold up," DJ said, his voice panicked and tight. "That's not what we talked about."

"I don't care what we talked about. This place is always busy. I know there's money up in here."

"Nah, I'm not down for this," DJ said, taking a step back.

"You want to be a part of us, then you have to be down." J looked back at Sheri. "And if she knows who you are, then she'll snitch." He focused on DJ. "So we can't leave her to tell."

"What? Nah, man! No." DJ moved back toward the door.

J turned his back to Sheri. That was all she needed. She grabbed a bowl off the counter and tossed it straight for J's head. She missed and hit his hand instead. The gun went off. The sound of the shot was like a crack of thunder in the small space.

J cursed as the gun fell from his hand. Sheri grabbed a rolling pin and ran toward J. Kid or not, she was going to clock him. He was going to shoot her! Which meant she felt no guilt about trying to defend herself. She swung, but he was fast. He ducked out of the way. Then his hand shot out as he punched the side of her face. Pain exploded through her head. Sheri stumbled and fell to the floor.

"The cops!" DJ yelled.

"Shit!" J ran toward the back door, shoving DJ out of the way as he hurried out.

Sheri placed a hand to the side of her head. Pain throbbed with every heartbeat and her vision was blurry. She'd never been punched in the face. The experience was new—and horrible. DJ rushed over. Sheri flinched when he reached for her.

"Sheri, damn, I'm sorry. It wasn't supposed to go down like this. I was just trying to…"

She scowled. "Scare me! Well, it worked!"

"Lil Bit!" JD's voice echoed as he burst in the back door. His frantic eyes searched the room, landed on DJ standing above her and fury filled his face. "You little punk." He rushed forward and grabbed DJ by the back of the neck.

Sheri jumped up, the room spun and she shook her head to clear the fog. Not a good idea. That just made everything hurt worse. "Hold up. It wasn't him."

DJ struggled against JD's hold, but he didn't let go. "Then why's he struggling? I'm holding his behind right there until the cops come."

Sheri stared at DJ. He didn't struggle against JD's grip. If anything, the fear in his eyes said he knew he'd messed up. Sheri wished she didn't have to make the call, but what he'd done? What his friend had done? It couldn't be ignored. She nodded slowly to not make the pain in her head worse.

"You call the cops, and I'll call his dad."

"I told you to stay away from him."

Sheri sighed before dropping the ice pack pressed to the side of her face. She glared at Cora standing at the base of the stairs leading up to the porch. Sheri had wanted to spend a few minutes alone to process everything that happened that day. The day felt like a blur. The police coming. DJ getting arrested. Her mom insisting Sheri go to the hospital to get checked out, and Sheri compromising with a trip to urgent care instead. Followed by going to the police station to give a statement.

In all of that she'd only seen Deandre in passing. He'd been dealing with the fallout with DJ. Their eyes met as they crossed paths in the station. He'd taken one look at her face, scowled and stalked away. She wasn't sure if she should call him or leave well enough alone.

She had enough to deal with and wasn't in the mood to deal with Cora's smug attitude. She narrowed her eyes at Cora. "Did you come here to gloat?"

Cora held up her hands in surrender before coming up the stairs. "I came to check on you."

"And to say I told you so."

Cora leaned against the porch rail. She sucked her teeth and shook her head. "Your eye is swollen."

"I already knew that. If you came to point out the obvious, you can go." Sheri picked up the ice pack and put it back on her face.

Cora sighed and crossed her arms. They sat there in silence for several minutes. Sheri refused to break the silence. She was mad. Mad that DJ would go so far to scare her. Mad that Deandre could barely look at her. Mad that she'd had to shut the restaurant down for the day because of this foolishness. And, especially mad that Cora had been right about DJ all along.

"Look," Cora finally said. "I didn't come to say I told you so. I was worried about you."

"I'm fine. You've checked on me. Now you can go."

"Lil Bit, don't be like that. I didn't want things to turn out like this. Deandre *is* a nice guy."

She looked at her cousin. "You're ready to finally admit that."

Cora huffed out a breath before flicking her bang out of her face. "I never said he wasn't. I just knew his son was a problem, and you got all mad at me."

"I got all mad because you seemed to love telling me how things weren't going to work out with him. You know how hard it's been for me to move on since that mess with Tyrone. Why couldn't you at least be supportive?"

"Because I was jealous."

Sheri blinked. "What?" That was not what she expected.

Cora rolled her eyes. "Don't act like you didn't know. Why do you always end up with the good ones and I get the bustas?"

"Good ones?" Sheri dropped the ice pack to point at her chest. "Since when do I get the good ones?"

"You do okay. The nice guys like you and the sorry ones come my way. So, yes, I was jealous. But I wouldn't try to intentionally hurt you. Not after you got in trouble back then."

"Did you intentionally try to hurt me then?"

Cora met her gaze. "No."

Sheri believed her. Plus, her mom was right. Cora had egged her on, but ultimately, the decision to take her revenge on Tyrone for hurting her was her own. "Were you glad to see my heart broken?"

Cora's shoulders straightened. "No! I knew he was going to hurt you. That's why I was down when you wanted to mess up his car after he did. Not because I was happy about how it went down. Just like I'm not happy about what happened today. You really think I want to see you robbed and beat?"

Sheri slumped back in her chair. "No. And I didn't get beat. I got hit once." Despite everything, she knew Cora wouldn't wish bad on her. Her cousin was messy, and gossipy, and an instigator, but when push came to shove, she'd always been there for Sheri. Even when she was doing dumb things or making foolish decisions.

"I told you about DJ because you thought Deandre was perfect. Well, girl, he's not. When I heard his son might be in a gang, then I knew that was going to be trouble. I was just trying to give you a heads-up. That's all."

Sheri closed her eyes and dropped her head back. "I wanted this to work out."

"I don't see how it can. Not when this happened. DJ doesn't like you and I'm not going to be cool with watching him try to hurt you."

"I know. But…" She looked at her cousin. "Cora, I really like Deandre. Like, I think I love him."

Cora's eyes widened. She quickly moved and sat in the chair next to Sheri. "Lil Bit? You serious?"

She nodded, tears welling in her eyes as the anger from the day turned into pain. "I do. But if his son hates me enough to do this…"

"Then how can you make it work?"

"I don't know. Even if I want to try, Deandre might not. He barely looked at me today."

"Because his son tried to rob you and you almost got shot. If he did look you in the eye without a problem, then I'd say that's a problem. Don't you take on any responsibility for this one. This is on Deandre and his son. Not you."

"I know." Sheri sat up and swiped at her eyes. "I just really hate that when I finally find a guy that I can love, it has to end like this."

Cora sighed. "You know what?"

Sheri put the ice pack back on her face. "What?"

She waited for Cora to tell her to move on. That she didn't need to waste tears for a man. That she was better off without him.

"Maybe things will work out."

Sheri swung her head toward Cora so fast that her headache throbbed. "Come again?"

Cora shrugged. "I'm just saying. You've been through a lot. Deandre is a good guy. Maybe, and that's a big *maybe*, he feels the same and ya'll can make this work."

Sheri grinned before reaching over to lightly push her cousin's shoulder. "That's the nicest thing you've ever said to me."

Cora rolled her eyes and pushed Sheri's hand away. "I've been around you too long. Got me hoping in fairy tales. But who knows. Maybe the little bit of love you're feeling for him will work out."

Sheri grinned even though in her heart she wasn't sure how they would make it all work. She looked at the sky and sent up a silent prayer. "Maybe so."

Chapter Nineteen

DJ knocked on Deandre's door after midnight. Deandre stared at his closed bedroom door. He was angry, frustrated and disappointed. But mostly, he was tired. It had taken calling in every favor he had and pulling his position with the police department to keep DJ from spending the night in jail. At first his plan was to let his son spend the night in jail. Maybe two. If he wanted to be a damn thug, then he'd see what life was like for one. But Rose had cried and Cliff had begged, so Deandre had pleaded with the judge and the chief and pulled money out of his savings account to get his son out on bail.

He hated that he had to do that. Hated that he was using an advantage that so many other people didn't have in this situation. Hated that DJ had put him in this situation in the first place. That he'd *missed* it. That missing this had damn near cost Sheri everything.

DJ knocked again. "Dad, you up?"

Deandre wanted to ignore him. Wanted to turn off his light, pull the covers over his head and forget this horrible day. But he couldn't. When he signed up for parenthood it hadn't been just for birthdays, holidays and special occasions at school.

"Come on in, DJ," he called back.

A second passed, then another before his son opened

the bedroom door. He'd showered and changed into pajamas, a pair of basketball shorts and a T-shirt. His shoulders were slumped, and he looked wary as he entered Deandre's bedroom.

"I just want to say I'm sorry. About today."

Deandre narrowed his eyes. "You're sorry? Do you even realize how much of a privilege it is for you to even be here, in my room, saying you're sorry? You should still be in jail right now with your friend J. But I had to pull strings to get you here to even tell me you're sorry."

DJ flinched and crossed his arms in front of his chest. For the first time in months, he looked like a kid. No defiance and frustration in his eyes. Just sadness and fear.

"I know. I messed up. Things got out of hand. It wasn't supposed to go down like that."

"Then how was it supposed to go down? What did you want to happen?"

"Just to scare her a little," he said in a small voice.

"For what? Do you hate her that much? Is the idea of me dating her so bad that you want to scare her off? Scare her so bad that you get a kid who's trying to recruit you into his gang to come at her with a gun? You hate her enough to risk this armed robbery charge?"

That part had come out in the aftermath. DJ wasn't officially in J's gang, but he'd started hanging with them and showing interest. Deandre had been shocked, hurt, but mostly he'd been disappointed in himself. He hadn't been there for his son. He hadn't noticed what was going on. He should have pushed for more information. He should have made DJ tell him what was going on. Instead, he'd gotten lost in work and missed all the signs.

"No, I mean…" DJ paused, then sighed and held out his

hands helplessly. "I don't know. I just… She was getting all your attention."

"What?"

"You've been busy. With the switch in your job and you're always worried about fixing the south end of the beach. You're never around. And then, all of a sudden, she was there. You already weren't paying attention to me and then you had her. It was like you didn't care about me anymore."

Deandre frowned. He got up from the bed and crossed the room. "DJ, I will always care about you. You're my son. I love you. No matter what's going on."

"I didn't mean to join them. It was just hanging around. I was losing on the wrestling team and the other guys started teasing me. But when I started hanging with J, they left me alone. It got out of hand. I didn't know how to get out." His voice cracked. "They wouldn't let me out."

Deandre put his hands on his son's shoulders. "That's when you come to me." He moved his face until DJ finally met his eyes. "There is always a way out, understand? I'll fight this entire damn world to help you. No one is going to take advantage of my son. You hear me?"

DJ nodded. He hastily wiped his face and looked away. Deandre's own eyes burned. "But, DJ, even if you felt that way, you should have told me. I asked you over and over to talk to me. Why didn't you?"

"I thought you'd be upset."

"Yeah, I would have been, but I would have helped you figure a way out."

"Then she told you what I said that day when I was with J."

"She told me because she cared about you. She didn't want you to get in trouble."

He used *cared* because he wasn't sure how Sheri felt now. He hadn't had the chance to talk to her. He didn't even know what he would say. How could he approach her after what DJ had done? He couldn't blame her if she never wanted to see either of them again.

"I know, but... You told me that you'd always love Mom."

The softly spoken words tore a hole in Deandre's heart. He squeezed DJ's shoulder. "I will always love your mom. The way I feel about Sheri is different. It won't replace that love or make me forget your mom."

"I don't want you to forget her."

"I won't. Just like I won't stop trying to be there for you. If you need me to be around more, or to be more available, I will. We'll start over. We'll get through this and figure out the best way forward. Even if it means without Sheri in my life."

The last words burned like acid as he spoke them. He didn't want to give her up, but this crisis showed him one thing. His son needed him, and he'd missed the signs. He wouldn't blame it on his relationship with Sheri. DJ had started acting differently before they'd come together. But he wouldn't put her in harm's way again.

"For real?" DJ asked.

Deandre nodded slowly. "If that's what it takes to make things right with us, then I will."

DJ looked at the floor. "I didn't think you'd do that for me."

Deandre gently shook DJ's shoulder until he looked back up. "Son, I love you. You're the most important thing in my life. You're in a world of trouble for this. But that doesn't take away that I want to help you."

DJ's eyes glistened. He quickly wiped them and Deandre pulled him into his arms. For the first time in months, DJ hugged him back.

"I love you, too, Dad."

one pulled him back like gates I've the officer's hand on this
Deandre is his home.
"I love you, boy." Thnk

Chapter Twenty

Sheri was in the back going over the sales receipts for the day when her mom came into the office.

"Lil Bit, that boy is out there to see you."

Sheri looked up from her calculator and frowned at her mom. "What boy?"

Her mom crossed her arms and twisted her lips. "Deandre's son."

Sheri's jaw dropped. She never expected DJ to come see her. "What for? I said everything I needed to say in court earlier."

Sheri had gone to his bond hearing and told the judge she was not pressing charges against DJ. His friend J, on the other hand, was not getting his charges dropped. Though she hadn't forgiven DJ for agreeing to go along with this, he at least hadn't come with the intention of trying to shoot her. He also didn't have to stick around and help her even though he was going to be arrested. J hadn't bothered to show any signs of remorse, where DJ had apologized to her. Something she was sure Deandre had a hand in, but knowing he wasn't a bad kid, she'd given him a second chance just like she'd been given.

"He says he wants to say something to you. You want me to kick him out?" her mom asked a little too eagerly.

"Is his dad with him?"

"Nope. Just him."

Intrigued, Sheri stood. She wasn't afraid that he'd hurt her. Not after what happened and not with the workers in the restaurant still there. "I'll go see what he wants."

She left the office and went out into the dining area. The restaurant had closed an hour earlier and most of the waitstaff had finished up cleaning their areas and were finalizing end-of-the-day prep in the kitchen. DJ stood by the hostess's stand, his head bent as he kicked at the floor. He was still dressed in the suit and tie he'd worn for court earlier that day, but now the tie was loose.

"You wanted to see me?"

DJ's head jerked up. He glanced around nervously, as if he wasn't sure why he'd come, before finally meeting her eye. "Um…yeah. I mean, yes, ma'am."

Sheri pointed to one of the tables. "Want something to eat?" She couldn't help it, food always made difficult talks a little easier.

He shook his head. "Nah, I'm good." He pulled out a chair and sat.

Sheri sat opposite him. He scratched at the table for several seconds before Sheri asked, "What's up?"

"Why did you drop the charges?" he blurted out.

Sheri took a long breath before crossing her arms and sitting back in her chair. "Because you stuck around to help me."

His brows drew together. "That's it?"

"That, and you're not a bad kid. Everyone deserves a second chance. I got one."

"When you messed up that guy's car?" he asked.

She let out a dry chuckle before shaking her head. She would never live that down. "No, before that. When I was your age. Hanging out down here on the south end of the beach. Me and my friends thought it would be cool to steal key chains from the gift shop. We would try to see who could get the most. Well, one day I had the most and I was the one the security guard caught."

DJ sat forward in his chair. "You were stealing key chains? Why?" he asked as if that were the most asinine thing he'd ever heard.

She shook her head and laughed. Looking back, it was an asinine decision. "No good reason other than the key chains had dirty phrases and we wanted them."

He nodded as if that made sense, then leaned forward and asked, "What happened?"

"The security guard called the police, but the store owner, Mr. Lee, got there at the same time. He told the cops he'd given me permission to take them. Later, he told me that I was a good kid and didn't need to mess up my life trying to steal his key chains. He gave me a second chance when he didn't have to. All because he saw potential in me even when I wanted to be dumb with my friends. I don't know why you decided to run with J and his crew, or why you decided that scaring me was what you needed to do, but I've seen you with your dad, your grandparents and around other adults. You're not bad. So, this is my second chance for you. What you do with it is up to you."

DJ chewed on his lower lip. His eyes studied the table for several seconds before he sat up and met her eye. "I didn't want you with my dad."

Sheri shrugged. "I figured that much."

"I thought you'd be drama. That you'd get mad at him and mess up his car. That's what I heard anyway."

"Rumors aren't always the truth. But I will give you that. I made some bad decisions before."

"And you and my dad, y'all broke up…because of me?"

"He wants to focus on being there for you because he loves you. I want to make sure your dad is okay because I care about him. And, believe it or not, I care about you, too."

DJ nodded slowly. "I meant what I said earlier today. About being sorry. My dad didn't make me say that. I just wanted to play a prank. I didn't think J would…" He trailed off and drummed his fingers on the table.

Sheri reached over and placed her hand over his. "Thankfully, nothing bad happened. But, DJ, if this happens again, things may not turn out okay. For your dad's sake, try not to run with that crowd."

She pulled her hand back. DJ looked down at his hand before focusing on her again. "If I said I never wanted you with my dad, would you walk away?"

She sucked in a breath. Stepping back from Deandre had already been difficult to do. She loved him and missed him. The realization that she loved him made her chest ache. She wanted to see him smile, bring him lunch so she knew he would eat on a busy day, and listen to him talk. But she knew how much he loved his son. If being with her would damage his relationship with DJ, then, yes, he might still choose to be with her, but at what cost? She didn't want to put him in that situation and find out.

"I don't want to come between you and your dad," she said honestly.

"I don't want to come between you and my dad," DJ said. "Not anymore."

Sheri sat up straight, surprised by his words. "What?"

"Look, I don't know how this works. My dad didn't really date like that after Mom passed. I don't want him alone forever, I just didn't want him with…excuse me for what I'm about to say, someone I thought was kind of rachet."

Sheri blinked, then laughed. She wasn't offended. It wasn't the first time someone had tried to label her, and it wouldn't be the last time. "I don't think your dad would be into me if I was."

He smiled. It was the first time he'd smiled at her. "True."

She raised a brow. "So… You're good with me and him together?"

He nodded. "Yeah. If you'll give him a second chance. And, if you're cool with me."

Sheri's mom came from the back into the dining area. "Sheri, his dad is here to see you."

Sheri and DJ swung toward her mom. "Deandre's here?"

Her mom nodded. "He came to the back door and knocked. He's lucky JD didn't hit him with a rolling pin. He scared us knocking on the door like the damn police. You want to see him?"

Sheri and DJ exchanged a look. Deandre was, in fact, the police. But they wouldn't point that out.

"Yes, send him in here." Her mom went back toward the kitchen and Sheri turned to DJ. "Does he know you're here?"

DJ shook his head. "Nah. He left me at home while he went out. I came here on my own."

"Are you going to get in trouble for being here?"

DJ shrugged. "I don't know. Maybe."

Sheri rolled her eyes and sighed. Teenagers. She and Deandre would have a time with him.

Deandre came from the back. He looked at Sheri, then DJ and back at her. Her heart ached with the need to cross the room and wrap her arms around him. She missed being with him so much.

His focus finally settled on his son. "DJ, what are you doing here?"

DJ stood. "I came to thank Ms. Thomas for not pressing charges."

Deandre's worried expression morphed to one of surprise. He clearly hadn't expected that answer. "Oh."

"And, to tell her that I'm good with you two being together." He walked to his dad. "I'll let ya'll talk." DJ placed a hand on his dad's shoulder. He looked back at Sheri, smiled, then went toward the kitchen.

Deandre watched with a slack jaw as his son disappeared into the kitchen. He swung back to Sheri several seconds after DJ disappeared "What did I miss?"

Sheri stood. "I don't think he thought I would give him a second chance. He wanted to know why."

"And when you told him why?"

"Then he understood that I wasn't doing it just because I love you, but because I was given a second chance. I didn't expect him to give us his blessing."

Deandre held up a finger. "Hold up, go back. What did you say?"

"I said I was given a second chance."

He shook his head. "Nah, before that. That you weren't doing it because why?"

Sheri's heart jumped and her palms turned slick. She'd said she loved him. Just blurted it out as if they'd been saying it to each other for years. When she may have jumped the gun. She could brush over it. Take the words back or pretend as if she hadn't said them. But she wasn't the type of person to back down from what she said or lie.

"I said, I didn't just do it because I love you."

Deandre was across the room with his arms around her in two steps. His mouth covered hers and he kissed her as if he'd learned the secret to everlasting happiness and that secret was in her arms. Sheri didn't hesitate. Her arms wrapped around his neck, and she lifted to her toes, pressing her body against his as she kissed him just as desperately. When he broke off the kiss, their breathing was ragged.

"I love you so much," he said in a tight voice. "I missed you. I thought you wouldn't want to be with me after what happened. That's why I came here."

She pulled back and frowned. "You came here to break up with me?"

"No. I came here to convince you that somehow, we'll make this work. That I believed DJ had learned his lesson and, if you were willing, we could start over."

"How did you know DJ would be good with us?"

"He was floored when you dropped the charges. His grandparents got on him about how wrong he'd been when you'd been nothing but nice to him. He admitted he messed up. I didn't know he would come here."

"I'm glad he came. We needed to talk and air things out. I want to start over with you, too, but I gotta admit, knowing that DJ is okay makes this even better."

"Does that mean you agree? That we'll give this another shot? Even though I once arrested you and my son made a horrible decision that nearly ruined your life?"

Sheri considered everything. What she was agreeing to. To try and heal the rift between her and DJ. To try and make a relationship work with Deandre. To, maybe not be a stepmom right away, but be there for both Deandre and DJ as they figured everything out. All things she never thought she'd want to do. Things she wouldn't have considered if she hadn't met and fallen for the last guy on earth she ever thought she'd be with.

She met his eyes and said with her entire heart, "Yes.

Let's give this a shot and see if we've got enough love to make this work."

Deandre grinned and placed his forehead on her. "Lil Bit, we've got more than enough."

* * * * *

Special EDITION

Believe in love. Overcome obstacles. Find happiness.

Available Next Month

Dog Days Of Summer Teri Wilson
A Small Town Fourth Of July Janice Carter

....

One Suite Deal Michele Dunaway
Rules Of Engagement Nancy Robards Thompson

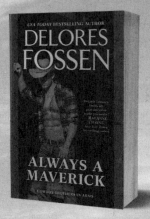

Subscribe and fall in love with a Mills & Boon series today!

You'll be among the first to read stories delivered to your door monthly and enjoy great savings.

WE SIMPLY LOVE ROMANCE

MILLS & BOON SUBSCRIPTIONS

HOW TO JOIN

1

Visit our website
millsandboon.
com.au/pages/
print-subscriptions

2

Select your favourite series
Choose how many books. We offer monthly as well as pre-paid payment options.

3

Sit back and relax
Your books will be delivered directly to your door.